THAT MOMENT WOULD CHANGE
THE REST OF THEIR LIVES. . . .

There was a long timeless moment of looking, and her world turned upside down as she discovered that it wasn't friendship she felt, not friendship at all. She now knew why her heart beat so fast at the thought of him and her knees knocked at the sound of his voice. She, Coffee Katie, had fallen for an outsider, an *Englisher!* So this was how it felt to be struck with love?

"What on earth are you doing in that outfit?" J.D. thundered.

"If I'm your Amish consultant, I thought I should dress Amish."

"Your line of reasoning eludes me." He walked all around her, shaking his head.

Even in the throes of her newly discovered passion, Katie was capable of a spurt of anger against the beloved object of it.

"We Amish don't believe worldly appearance is of any significance," she proclaimed.

"In that case," said J.D. dryly, "you're a lot more Amish than you led me to believe because, take it from me, your worldly appearance at the moment would have no significance for anyone."

Katie felt a momentary stab of pain, then she couldn't help being struck by the humor of it. Her laughter rang out warm and free.

J.D. then surprised himself as much as he surprised Katie. He hadn't intended to kiss her, but her lusciously full red mouth was right there, laughing up at him. He was only human, after all, and even the Amish were allowed to be human. Katie, still clutching her milk pail, lifted her face and he kissed her, gently, lovingly, thoroughly. She was still straining towards him when he removed his mouth from hers. With a grieved little murmur of disappointment, she let go of the pail and milk spilled all over his expensive leather shoes and French lisle socks.

. . . . AND IT WAS ONLY THE BEGINNING!

* * *

"Jacqueline Marten has written one of the year's best romance novels!"

—Harriet Klausner, *Affaire de Coeur*

JUST A KISS AWAY

JACQUELINE MARTEN

PINNACLE BOOKS
KENSINGTON PUBLISHING CORP.

PINNACLE BOOKS are published by

Kensington Publishing Corp.
850 Third Avenue
New York, NY 10022

Pinnacle and the P logo Reg. U.S. Pat. & TM Off.

First Printing: August, 1995

Printed in the United States of America

For my dear, my favorite, and my only brother
Elliot Joel Stern
and his namesake, Eliahu Yitzhak
Lucas Vail Marten
born October 12, 1993

Acknowledgments

To Sara Freed, who shared both rare rapport and her memories of growing up Mennonite in Pennsylvania during a four-hour Japanese dinner in New York City.

To Nancy Grant of Dr. Carl Nelson & Associates of Virginia Beach, who contributed her experiences as a hospital supervisor working with conscientious objectors.

To Lisa Dawson, Kate Duffy, and Eileen Bertelli for both help and morale. To you, too, Denise!

Author's Note

Strawberry Schrank and Maiden Falls, Pennsylvania, and Basking Reade, Maryland, are fictional towns. Strasburg, Bird-In-Hand, and Intercourse exist. There are no Copper Hill and Pine Tree Roads (that I know of). Route 340 is painfully real.

The Sugarcreek Budget is a weekly newspaper that serves the Amish-Mennonite communities throughout the Americas. A correspondent from each one of their many small communities (eg: Orville, Alabama; New Holland, Pennsylvania; Gladwin, Michigan; Haley, Oregon; Bancroft, Ontario, Canada) sends in a column of casual chatty personalized news of his or her own community or religious fellowship, dealing with births, deaths, crops, and accidents ranging from carriage crashes to a cut finger; also friends' and neighbors' visits . . . thus keeping the Amish and Mennonites in touch with their own all over the continent.

The *Budget* features poems, obituaries, and in memoriams. It also announces showers for neighbors in need of help. The help requested may be money for hospital bills or a plea for greeting cards and visits.

GLOSSARY

Since parts of the story are set in Pennsylvania-Dutch Amish country, some characters use idiomatic phrases and expressions which are still commonly used in Amish and Mennonite communities today. The following is a glossary of such expressions, listed in the order of their appearance.

mutter—mother
fodder—father
will komm—welcome
grossfodder—grandfather
mein kindt—my child
als—always
fer schtay?—do you understand?
druwwel—problem
Englisher—non-Amish
I give you the right—I agree with you
ain't?—frequently used at the end of a sentence, e.g. You're finished with that job, ain't?
yet—often used the same way as *ain't,* e.g. You're feeling well, yet?
oy, anyhow—oy!
grossdawdy haus/grossdaadi haus—separate dwelling on the same farm, or attached to the farm, which is for grandparents when they retire, so they can remain an active part of the family circle and yet have privacy and dignity

brootz—fret
grossmutter—grandmother
ja—yes
Ich wutt—I wish
es dode—death
koom—come
kapp—cap
stroovlich—untidy, messy
unser Satt Leit—our sort of people
anner Satt Leit—the other sort of people
denk schond—think shame
sindhoftich—sinfulness
letz—wrong
donk Gott—thank God
all—over, finished, or done, e.g. Is the pie all?
it wonders me—it's a big surprise to me
wonderful—(adj.) very, exceedingly, e.g. This yard is wonderful dirty
meidung—ban, excommunication
Gott in Himmel—God in Heaven
spritz—rain
made down—came down
kopp—head
Ordnung—Amish Rules of Order
gude—good
soohn—son
doomb—dumb
layg's uff der dish—lay on the table
dee schnide opp ge numma—take the edge off
hausfrau—housewife
schtrap—strap
glutz kopp—dumbbell
recht opp—right off
Swartz-cousins—first cousins
drowel—worry
gude mon—good man

rumspringa—courting
schtarn wedder base—darned mad
bolla—testicles
mawd—maid
mutze—Sunday dress coat for men
halsduch—cape or breast cloth over a woman's dress
schwetz uff—speak up
un so?—and so?
sind—sin
make your dirt away—clean up
fer doom'd—damned
doom kopp—dummy
danke—thank
minoot—minute
say die wilder howwer—sow your wild oats
Gott willich—God willing
leebgronk—lovesick
mitt kindt—pregnant
bubbel—baby
nay—no
recht—right
tzu foll in leeb—to fall in love
narrish—crazy
doppel—awkward one
brilla inwer ferschittie militch—don't cry over spilt milk
unner's ew erscht—upside down
schoff frau—working woman
arawid—work
denk—think
schoff mon—working man
wee gayt's?—how do you do?
's bescht—it's best
dogs drawma—castles in the air
leeblich—adorable

Prologue

On an unseasonably cold morning in early April, when New Yorkers were sleeping the sleep of the tired, the just, and the hung over, a mobile television van sped down Park Avenue toward the Murray Hill section of the city and came to a slow halt in front of the Macedonian Tea Room. A crew promptly erupted from the back of the van and began disgorging miles of wire and a half-ton of camera equipment onto the sidewalk.

At the same time, almost as though on signal, the double doors of the restaurant burst open for four Macedonian waiters outfitted in an American costumer's notion of Greek peasant ceremonial dress—red velveteen knickers, white stockings, and patent leather pumps. Their cream linen shirts had balloon sleeves ending at the wrist in three inches of gold embroidery; maroon velvet caps with shoulder-length gold tassels sat jauntily on four heads of curly black hair.

The shivering waiters commenced rolling out two rows of globe-topped brass stands, which they placed at intervals all the way to the gutter. Having looped thick braided red ropes between the standards to form an aisle, they added the finishing touch of a plush red carpet.

Long before early breakfasters began ducking under the braided ropes to enter the restaurant, walking from their nearby high-rises and brownstones or dashing out of taxis, a friendly, vocal, curious crowd had begun to form.

First there was just a smattering of passers-by, most with hefty copies of the Sunday *Times* bundled in their arms like babies. Then, much in the manner of cells multiplying themselves, two people became four and four became eight, and soon they were standing three deep on each side of the red-carpeted aisle, talking, gesticulating, speculating . . . a bag lady brushing elbows with a millionaire, a pickpocket edging toward the tempting bulge of a wallet in the back pants pocket of a young stockbroker.

"It must be a wedding!" said a girl with her face made up to look like a white clay mask. She appealed to one of the two tired-looking policemen who had just emerged from their patrol car to add a further touch of excitement to the scene. "It's a wedding, isn't it?"

"No, miss," he denied politely, "it's a TV show."

"It's a TV show," the girl proclaimed to her neighbor on either side, and soon the stirring message was winging its way throughout the crowd, reaching both sides of the aisle. *It's a TV show!*

The outdoor audience grew. More police arrived in the wake of a smaller television van, and behind the two was a limousine the size and color of a funeral car, out of which stepped a handsome, husky, middle-aged man with receding blond hair. He turned to smile and wave, apparently unbothered by the biting wind that lifted the sides of his navy blue blazer and whipped his paisley tie in the frosted air.

He continued to woo the crowd while a uniformed chauffeur tenderly assisted the second occupant of the car onto the red carpet. She was almost as tall as her companion, and so wrapped from head to toe in silver mink that only a hank of elegant red hair was visible till she lowered her high furry collar to reveal the smooth pink English complexion, the two rows of perfect white American-capped teeth, and the God-given violet eyes, for all of which she was famous.

A murmur of recognition rippled through the crowd and became a swelling wave. "It's Chuck and Dodie Mitchell."

Chuck Mitchell, the great ex-halfback, known in his football days as Chinatown Chuck because of his passion for Chinese food, and his equally famous wife, Dodie, the toast of Liverpool in her long-past teenage days as a singing star, were now the host and hostess of a popular syndicated talk show.

A middle-aged woman in high-heeled orange suede boots, who usually saved such enthusiasm for bargain-hunting at Macy's, addressed those around her with an almost religious fervor. "Chuck and Dodie must be filming 'Celebrity Brunch in the Big Apple'!"

The matron next to her, dressed from the skin out exclusively by Bloomingdale's, was unexpectedly stirred to an equal pitch of enthusiasm. " 'Celebrity Brunch'!" she gasped. "Do you really think so?"

"Well, it's Sunday, isn't it? And it's them, right?" said the lady from Macy's.

The lady from Bloomingdale's nodded judiciously. "You must be right."

The rumor spread as fact, and the crowd agreed.

It's "Celebrity Brunch in the Big Apple"!

Neither confirming nor denying, the police went before and behind Chuck and Dodie up to the double doors of the Macedonian, which were flung open to admit them and then quickly closed again.

"Ahhh!" sighed the crowd in mixed ecstasy and disappointment. The young stockbroker decided on a bold move. He would call that girl he had met at the Dennings' party on Friday night—that Julie girl, who was small and sweet and shy. Her appearance was misleading in one respect. As soon as they had started talking, she was actually quite interesting and seemed to have a mind of her own. Unfortunately, he was just as shy. He had cursed himself all of yesterday for not arranging a specific date with her.

It wasn't too late, he decided suddenly. He could phone her this morning—even this very moment—to ask her to have breakfast with him at the Macedonian Tea Room. It would be a good conversation opener to be able to say that "Celebrity Brunch" was being televised there.

If she was human, she would be interested in *that*. He reached for his wallet at the same second chosen by the pickpocket for his theft. Their two hands met in the stock-broker's pants pocket, and with a yelp of fright, the pick-pocket let go of the wallet and made off through the crowd.

The stockbroker, grinning at what he regarded as a lucky omen and another ice-breaker with which to regale the Julie-girl, opened his wallet and found the slip of paper on which he had written her telephone number. Boldly, confidently, he pushed aside one of the brass stands and walked along the red carpet, disappearing inside the Macedonian just as the arrival of a baby-blue Rolls Royce diverted the attention of the crowd from this defection in their ranks.

Only someone who had never owned a TV would have failed to recognize the flashing, toothy smile of the man who emerged from the Rolls Royce. The few in doubt had only to glimpse the fur-lined velvet cloak he flung back over his shoulders with fur-gloved hands, so that all could see the dazzling display of his silver brocade jacket with its jewel-studded lapels.

"It's Gregorio Grieg!" piped a boy in the front row.

Gregorio tossed his cloak once more, flashed his brilliant smile again, and strode with unexpected vigor along the aisle.

As he reached the end of the carpet a second-year student from Cardozo Law School leaned impulsively across the braided rope, holding out her *Times*. "Mr. Grieg, would you sign my paper, please?"

He stopped and asked kindly, "Do you have a pen?"

"Oh, gosh!" She shifted the *Times* under one arm and started hunting frantically in her pockets.

"Never mind. It's too chilly for autographing, anyhow. Have these instead."

The beautiful fur gloves were pulled off his hands and deposited on top of her newspaper so speedily that the world-famous pianist had plunged through the double doors before the stupefied student could even thank him.

The crowd broke into wild applause.

The next three guests were something of an anti-climax. A U.N. delegate was considered no big deal. Then, voicing general opinion, the Macy's lady pointed out that the famous clothing designer's own suit looked rather drab. An elderly, face-lifted princess who owned a famous cosmetics firm was another sad disappointment.

Flagging interest revived somewhat, even among the camera crew, when a taxi u-turned in front of the police car and skidded to a stop adjacent to the TV van. The man who got out of it was of medium height, compact build, and ordinary good looks. He had a bronzed, lined face, dark, curly hair, and wore dark wool trousers, a fisherman's knit sweater, and an army-style khaki windbreaker. He waved to one of the cameramen, who waved back enthusiastically.

"Hey there, J.D.!" shouted another cameraman.

J.D. looked back over his shoulder and squinted up toward the roof of the van. "I thought you were shooting in Spain, Bill?" he shouted in turn.

"Company went broke," said Bill laconically.

J.D. raised both hands in silent sympathy. "Call me," he said. "I may have something for you."

"Will do."

"That's J.D. Shale," someone in the crowd announced importantly.

"Who's J.D. Shale?"

"He's a hot-shot producer."

The cameras followed J.D.'s entrance into the Tea Room. "That's all, folks," bawled one of the policemen. "And they won't be coming out for hours. Want to break it up?"

One of the crew consulted a slip of paper, then mega-phoned through cupped hands, "No, there's one more."

As he spoke, another taxi came screeching along the street. It barely avoided sideswiping a Cadillac, and came to a bucking stop. Seeing no passenger on the back seat, a policeman opened the rear door and peered inside. The rider was down on her knees on the floor.

"Praying?" the patrolman asked with the friendly familiarity of New York's Finest. "I don't blame you."

"It's an idea," said a voice that appeared to be torn between tears and laughter, "but this just happens to be where I was thrown when the spaceship landed."

He held out his hand, and she took firm hold and found herself lifted by wrist and waist onto the red carpet.

"Thank you."

She leaned across to hand a bill to the driver "No change, cowboy. It was quite an adventure riding with you. Did you happen to notice this is the east side, not the west?"

The policeman grinned, the nearest spectators roared their appreciation, and the cab driver, without deigning to answer or express thanks, crashed into gear and zoomed off in search of fresh prey.

The young woman brushed off her London Fog raincoat. "Thank you again." She beamed at the policeman as she pulled off a six-foot wool scarf wrapped around her head and throat, unloosening a thick fluffy halo of pale gold curls accented by two narrow streaks of white hair pointing outward like arrows just above a pronounced widow's peak. Her skin coloring was a pale gold, too, healthy and glowing; her eyes were a brilliant Mediterranean blue.

"She looks like an advertisement for face cream and shampoo," the Bloomingdale's lady muttered enviously.

A girl in front of her turned around. "She should!" she announced with proprietorial pride. "That's Katryn Kauffman Coffee!"

Katryn Kauffman Coffee!

The name was carried through the crowd as the famous feminist writer entered the Macedonian.

Katryn handed her coat, scarf, and cashmere gloves in at the check room and turned to find Dimitri, manager of the Tea Room, hovering at her elbow.

"Ms. Coffee, such a pleasure to see you again."

"Entirely *my* pleasure, believe me, Dimitri. I hope I have room for all of your specials."

"I would be bereft if you did not eat as joyously as usual. Never, never—God be praised—have I heard you utter the word *diet* in my restaurant. Diet!" he shuddered. "The curse of the modern world. No, no, not there, turn to the right here," he interrupted himself. "All the other guests have been introduced."

"Oh, dear, I hope I'm not too late. I was a last-minute fill-in—then I had trouble getting a cab."

"Not at all. It's conducted very informally. I believe the Mitchells prefer the gradual arrivals. Such a charming couple. Have you met them?"

"No, I never—oh, my gracious!"

The Aegean Room had been redecorated since her last visit to resemble the garden courtyard of an ancient Greek villa, complete with statuary, shrubbery, a small pool and waterfall, and a wall mural representing one side of the house.

"How unusual—and—and charming," murmured Katie.

Cameras followed the Mitchells as they came forward to welcome Katryn to "Celebrity Brunch." Their greeting of her, for the benefit of a coast-to-coast audience, was both long-winded and laudatory. She cringed inwardly, although her face remained immobile throughout her hosts' hymns of praise.

"Our next guest," Chuck began the formal presentation, "Katryn Kauffman Coffee, needs no introduction. She is a world-renowned writer and lecturer, a former model, and a prominent editor of the influential magazine *Love And Marriage.*"

He turned toward Dodie, who chimed in graciously, "In spite of all her private accomplishments, Katryn considers herself first and foremost an advocate of women's interests."

She turned and smiled at the guest, allowing a glimpse of her own enchanting profile.

"I believe you were only twenty-two, were you not, Katryn, when you had your first best seller?"

"Twenty-three," Katie corrected scrupulously. *"Bundle In The Trundle, a History of Quaint Courting Customs;* it came out the week of my birthday."

"A great title," Dodie continued. "But then, your books and articles always have witty titles." She consulted a slip of paper she'd whisked out of her purse. *"In Bed Unwed, From Maid To Laid,* and *Bawdy Bedroom Laughter,"* she recited.

"The titles help sell my books, but the books are meant to be taken seriously. *Kissed To Death* is about lives destroyed by AIDS. Believe me, there is no lighter side to that!" Katryn pointed out quickly.

Trying to divert her attention from serious topics, Chuck ignored Katie's answer and boomed, "I believe your most sensational best seller is still considered to be *Once A Virgin, Twice A Virgin,* is it not?"

The Princess Elena had joined their group in time to hear the last question.

"I always keep copies of *Once A Virgin* on hand in my salons," she addressed directly to the cameramen. "My customers steal it regularly," she added languidly.

Uncertain whether to express delight at her book's popularity or distress at its theft, Katie refrained from

either alternative and accepted the Princess' be-ringed fingers for a surprisingly strong handshake.

Princess Elena appeared equally surprised. "Ah, you do
not need my exercise classes. You are no hothouse flower."

"I grew up on a farm. I own one, too. Growing up, the
chores were part of my daily work. Now, for recreation, I
milk and garden and help with the harvest."

The film crew shifted to another group, and Katryn was
introduced, without benefit of the camera's all-seeing eye,
to Belasco, the clothes designer. As they talked, she uttered a sudden exclamation of joy, hastily excused herself,
and sped across the Aegean Room to fling herself enthusiastically at Gregorio Grieg.

He received and returned her embrace with equal fervor,
then held her off to peer down at the radiant face.

"You look well, Katie, my little one," he told her.

"Never mind the small talk. How long have you been
back from your Australian tour? Why haven't you called
me?"

"I telephoned your office twice."

Katie smote her forehead. "You must be the mysterious
Mr. Gregory. I have a new secretary," she explained. "But
you might have called me at home."

"I did. Three times. You are never at home, dear girl,"
he complained.

"I never got a message!"

"I left no message. Me, I do not talk to machines," he
informed her haughtily.

She linked her arm through his. "Never mind. What
does it matter when fate was kind enough to arrange this
meeting for us?"

"Fate," said Gregorio, "had nothing to do with it. When
I learned from Mrs. Mitchell that the dancer Hansi Fuller
could not appear today, I suggested you in her place."

"So that's how it happened . . . not that it matters.
Greg, I'm taking three months' leave from the magazine,

starting in mid-June, to work on a screen treatment. I'll stay at the farm, of course . . . with no guests except late August when Crystal and Arnold are coming with my godson. I'm not counting you, of course. *You"*—she hugged his arm tight to her side—"are family. If you can make it any time . . ."

"I think I can manage a few days, perhaps a week late in June before I go to Europe."

He returned the pressure of her arm, and J.D. Shale, studying the two from the shelter of a huge fake marble column purporting to be a Grecian pillar, brought his shaggy eyebrows together in so intimidating a scowl, the hovering waitress prepared to offer him a plate of rice and meatballs wrapped in grape leaves backed away hurriedly.

A very intimate, cozy twosome they seemed to be, reflected J.D.; there was genuine affection in their touch, their glances, their total absorption that ignored the cameras . . . but it had to be contrived . . . it must be. Regardless of what the gullible public believed, the tight-knit circle of show business, the small insular world of the jet-setters and deal-makers, was tolerantly aware that if Gregorio Grieg had any interests outside his career, a woman was not likely to be one of them.

There was a sudden hush in the room and the bell-like clink of crystal glasses. Gregorio Grieg glanced over his own shoulder, then touched Katryn's lightly. "Champagne is being served. I think our hostess wishes us to gather together."

Katryn made a moue of distaste. "I wish we could leave this three-ring circus and slip out to Oscar's for an omelette and some privacy."

"I, too, Katie, but we have a part to play, both of us," he reminded her gently. "Your magazine wants more subscriptions and advertisers, your publisher wants book sales, and your organization wants increased membership."

"And no one cares what Katie wants!" she said with unexpected fierceness.

"Katie," he said wisely, "wants the same things as everyone else. If not, she would live year-round at her farm in Pennsylvania instead of in her New York apartment on Fifth Avenue. One usually cannot go back, my sweet. You are fortunate that *you* can do it part-time to suit your needs."

"You're right, blast you!" Katie admitted as they linked arms again and moved in the direction of the champagne table. "Only sometimes, Greg . . . sometimes . . ."

"Do you think, Katie, that I, too, do not know about the *sometimes?*"

"Oh, what a selfish beast I am!" She clung to him remorsefully. "As though it were my grief alone. You do know, don't you, that not a day goes by without my thinking of him?"

Gregorio pressed her arm affectionately.

J.D. Shale, following a discreet six steps behind them, was unable to hear, but well able to see. His brows drew together in another ferocious frown.

He arrived at the champagne table in time to hear the manufactured version of Katryn Kauffman Coffee, bright and artificial, saying to Dimitri, "Thank you, I would adore a glass of champagne."

As she accepted the brimming glass, a wool-clad arm snaked around from behind her and strong brown fingers clamped the slender stem. "There's a bowl of strawberries on the hors d'oeuvres table. Allow me to throw a few into your glass."

At the sound of his voice, all the color drained from Katryn's face, leaving it milk-white. Luckily, J.D. had firm hold of the glass or it would have been dashed to the floor. She uttered a choked little cry of protest, which came too late; he was already halfway to the hors d'oeuvres table.

"Steady," said Gregorio quietly as he changed his position to give her a few seconds of privacy. "Smile, Katie. The cameras are turning this way."

Katie smiled through chattering teeth. "Did you know he would be here?"

"His name was not on the original guest list Mrs. Mitchell mentioned to me," Gregorio replied in an undertone.

J.D. Shale returned and held out Katryn's champagne glass, in which two plump strawberries now nestled just above the stem. "I had to sip from the top so it wouldn't overflow," he said casually. "I hope you don't mind."

"Not at all," said Katryn, willing her hand not to shake. "It was k-kind of you to remember that I like strawberries in my champagne."

"Kind?" the quirked eyebrows and mouth denoted enormous skepticism. "Since when do you think I am kind, K-K-Katie?"

"Katryn, if you please. I'm all grown up now. And I *don't* think it, but there are social niceties one must observe, so—"

"So there are," interrupted Gregorio. "Smile prettily for the cameras, my children. How do you do, Mr. Shale?" He held out a strong, beautifully kept hand. "A pleasure to meet you. I have heard so much about you."

They exchanged a hearty grip and smiled for the benefit of the hovering cameras.

"You find it a pleasure to meet me after having heard about me from Katie—pardon me, Katryn?"

There was a touch of pain beneath the self-mockery in his voice, thought Gregorio. Katryn, gulping down her champagne, heard only the jibe.

"There is pleasure, if not in the meeting, in having one's private opinions proved correct," answered Gregorio suavely.

J.D. laughed.

"Touché! I can imagine what those private opinions are," he said good-naturedly.

"I doubt that, Mr. Shale. I doubt that very much."

"So do I," said Katryn belligerently. She had finished the champagne and was plucking out the strawberries with her fingers. "I think," she said, popping the second one into her mouth, "I would like some more champagne."

"Take it easy, Katie," said J.D. "As I recall, you had very little tolerance for that stuff."

"Katryn, my name is Katryn. Dimitri, may I have another glass of champagne?"

As Dimitri rushed to furnish it, J.D. Shale shrugged and went off to get her a small dish of strawberries.

"Ladies and gentlemen," Dodie Mitchell's sweet, penetrating voice rang out, "the buffet is ready. Please fill your plates and come to the table."

Katryn found herself separated from Gregorio as she moved along the buffet. Princess Elena was on one side of her and the U.N. delegate, Lars Gunderson, on the other.

"Do you know what is this, Miss Coffee?" asked Mr. Gunderson, poking his fork gingerly into a chafing dish.

"Souvlakia. Chunks of lamb and vegetables."

He helped himself to a small portion. "And this?"

"Mussels."

He dropped the serving fork back into the dish and moved on. "These?"

"Mixed rice and chopped beef. Delicious."

"I will take your word." He served himself another very small portion.

"Don't worry," Katryn soothed him as she helped herself liberally and looked down the table "There are smoked salmon, bagels and cream cheese, scrambled eggs, ham, roast beef, and plenty of salads at the other end."

A smile of pleasure illuminated his face at this information. In his eagerness, he rushed ahead of her. Katryn was grateful to find Gregorio again at her elbow.

"Make sure you sit next to me," she hissed.

"My dear Katryn, whatever do you think he can do to you in a public place?"

"I don't know." She helped herself to some olives. "But if there's any disagreeable possibility," she predicted darkly, "believe me, he'll come up with it."

"I think you worry needlessly, but I shall sit next to you. Take care"—laughter trembled in the voice he was trying to make sound serious—"you are spilling your champagne onto the scrambled eggs."

"Oh Lord, I had better get rid of it." This she did by pouring the drink into her mouth, strawberries and all.

Oh Lord, echoed Gregorio inwardly.

Katryn smiled in relief as she slipped into the place directly on the right of Chuck Mitchell and Gregorio promptly sat down next to her. She rejoiced too soon. The left-hand seat near Chinatown Chuck was vacant, and the first person to get to it was J.D. Shale.

He sat right opposite her, which was almost worse, she realized belatedly, than being alongside him. She would be under the constant scrutiny of those mocking dark eyes.

Damn him. Damn him. *Take it easy, Katie.* How dare he talk to her in that unhurried, unworried way, as though they were casual friends who might have partied together only the week before?

The Princess, trailing her chiffon scarves into a plate of Greek salad, took the seat next to J.D. Shale, and Mr. Gunderson sat beside her and to the right of their hostess. As soon as the clothing designer, Jay Belasco, took occupancy of the only remaining seat on Dodie's left, Mr. Gunderson tucked an oversized damask napkin into the neck of his shirt and began the serious business of eating. He did not so much swallow his food as absorb it, with the single-minded rapaciousness of a piranha.

Having tried several subjects and been unable to get the man to open his mouth for anything except to eat, Dodie turned in desperation to Belasco.

"I was interested in your remark about the average shopper's instinctively knowing the style that suits her best," she chattered brightly. "Isn't that a rather self-defeating attitude for a designer who wants the ladies to chuck out their wardrobes each year to buy *his* new styles?"

"Perhaps," said Mr. Belasco tranquilly, "if they believed me." The TV camera honed in on him, and he gave a pleasant little chuckle. "Fortunately for me, dear lady, they do not."

"Can you give me an example of what you mean, Mr. Belasco?"

"Well, the first one that comes to mind is right at this table. Mr. Grieg here." He fingered the jeweled lapel of his neighbor's jacket. "A beautiful piece of brocade, fit for a queen's bridal. Ordinarily, an utterly absurd fabric for a man's garment and yet somehow uniquely right for Gregorio Grieg. On the other hand, if someone else"—he smiled down the length of the table—"let us say, Mr. Shale . . . If *he* were to don such a jacket—forgive me, Mr. Shale—he would look like a court jester."

"In short," called J.D. from his end of the table, "an utter ass. I couldn't agree with you more, Mr. Belasco."

The Princess nodded her bewigged head and Mr. Gunderson ate on, while Gregorio flashed his famous toothy smile at one and all.

"Ah," he said genially, "but you are all assuming I dress as I do to express my own unique personality, and in this you are wrong. My dear friend Katie here has many times over the years scolded me for playing what you so aptly call the buffoon. She would like to see me dressed in a formal funereal tuxedo playing a shining black Steinway at Lincoln Center. It was once my own wish, too."

He shrugged elaborately. "Unfortunately, although I was

an exceptionally good pianist, I was *not* one of the immortals. Exceptionally good pianists abound in this country, but they seldom prosper. So, at last, I took the advice of another good friend, who reminded me that even the finest pianist is still in show business and must act accordingly. On the day I became a U.S. citizen, I held a press conference at which I wore my first spangled jacket, and I replaced my trench coat with a fur-lined cloak rented from a theatrical costumer. I announced in a fervor of patriotism that as of then, any concert hall I played in must have my piano painted red, white and blue. Would you believe—I scarcely could myself—that on the strength of that one interview, concert halls all over the country . . . all over the world . . . hastened to comply and offer me the rich contracts and tours that my most serious attitude had never secured me?"

"Do you have any regrets, Mr. Grieg, about how you—er—might—appear to people?" asked Chuck Mitchell.

"After every concert, Mr. Mitchell," said Gregorio Grieg gently, "I fall asleep at night to the remembered sound of applause. The next day I read the reviews that deprecate my playing and depress my pretensions, and I cry all the way to my stockbroker's."

"Ms. Coffee," Chuck asked her, when the laughter had died away, "do you now think Mr. Grieg was right and you were wrong?"

"There was never any right or wrong about it," Katryn said. "Just a difference of opinion on technique."

Dodie leaned across the table, willing to spark a little controversy in the interests of adding excitement to the show.

"But do you still disapprove of Gregorio Grieg's jackets?" she persisted.

Under the table, Gregorio's fingers pinched Katryn's leg in warning. She winced and kept hold of her temper. "About as much as he disapproves of my skirts," she said lightly. "He thinks *I* dress much too conservatively."

"Is that true, Gregorio?" Princess Elena challenged obligingly.

"Of course," said Gregorio smoothly. He turned a little toward the designer. "Did you notice her clothing, Mr. Belasco?"

"Certainly," said Belasco promptly. He looked up at the ceiling and recited with closed eyes: "An ankle-length wool skirt, Scotch plaid but not one of the clan tartans, pinks and purples predominating. A ribbed cotton turtleneck in a pale pink and a wool cardigan vest in a plum color. There is a gold nugget on a linked chain around her neck." He opened his eyes. "Am I correct?"

The Princess and Gregorio applauded; Mr. Gunderson reached across the table for a basket of pita bread.

"Do you approve of Ms. Coffee's outfit, sir?" Gregorio asked Belasco.

"It suits her," said the designer after a few seconds' hesitation.

"But could you dress her to look like a much more beautiful woman?"

"Ah, that is another question. Of course I could."

Unexpectedly, J.D. Shale entered the debate. "Why should he?" he asked pugnaciously. "She looks fine to me."

Mr. Belasco appeared ready to drop the argument; Gregorio Grieg seemed bent on mischief.

"But Mr. Shale," he pointed out mournfully, "it is such a waste. She has legs of extraordinary beauty. Most women would shorten their skirts to show what today, on national TV, she takes pains to cover up entirely. That loose wool waistcoat—vest—whatever it is called—conceals a ripe, appealing figure. As for—"

"I suggest you all keep in mind," Katryn interrupted firmly, "that, in my dress—as in everything else I do—I am concerned only to please myself."

"Since when is that news?" J.D. asked her tartly. "From

coast to coast—hell, the whole world over—we know you are only concerned with pleasing yourself. One has only to read your books."

"Have you read Ms. Coffee's books?" Dodie asked him eagerly. "Somehow, Mr. Shale, one doesn't quite connect . . ." She hesitated, then made another false start. "You seem so . . ."

"Overly masculine?" he retorted maliciously, "like her typical male character? Hell, yes, I've read all her books. I can't knock the opposition, can I, without genuine ammunition?"

"And would you knock *all* her books?" Mr. Belasco asked unexpectedly.

J.D.'s glittering black eyes met the electric-blue glare of Katie's head-on. "Hell, yes!" he said again. "Except for *Kissed To Death.*"

The Princess sipped daintily at her seventh glass of champagne. "I keep *Once A Virgin, Twice A Virgin* in all my beauty salons," she hiccuped confidingly to stations from Maine to California. "My customers steal it regularly."

A surprising voice spoke up. *"Once A Virgin, Twice A Virgin*—that is one funny book," said Mr. Gunderson with a mournful look at his empty plate. "My wife she reads to me pieces—no, that is wrong—passages she reads to me aloud when we are in bed. Very funny. I like best the—the—you know"—he appealed to Dodie—"the underneath title."

"Subtitle."

"Yes, the subtitle. I forget, but it is very funny. Ha ha."

"You mean, *A Maidenhead Does Not a Maiden Make?"* said Dodie with a provocative glance at Katryn, who once more felt the pressure of Gregorio's warning fingers on her thigh.

J.D.'s glittering eyes swiveled once more toward Katryn.

"Taken, no doubt, from your own experience?" he said nastily.

Katryn Kauffman Coffee gave him the look that had quelled many a heckler in a hostile audience. "Who else's experience would I use?" she asked quite sweetly.

"Mr. Belasco." Chuck spoke up in some haste. "What can you tell us about the new fall lines?"

"Nothing," said Mr. Belasco gently. "They are still secret."

There were five seconds of frozen silence before the perfect hostess came up with a plastic smile and a pleasant question. "What are your plans for the coming summer, Mr. Grieg?"

"I am fixed in New York for a while," Gregorio told her kindly, "to make ready for my TV special, which airs in September. Then I have a small—that is to say, a short—mid-west tour. In the summer months I have a Scandinavian concert series and family visits in Greece and Italy. But first, in June, I will take a little time for myself to visit Katie at her farm."

"You own a farm, Ms. Coffee? How . . . how quaint."

"Not quaint at all. It is a complete working farm, though I confess to doing very little of the work myself since I am here in New York most of the time."

"And your farm is in—?"

"Pennsylvania." She added quickly, "Forgive me, but I prefer not to be more specific since I value my privacy when I go there."

"And do you milk cows and feed chickens and—and mow hay, or whatever it is"—Dodie wriggled her lovely shoulders—"that one does with hay?"

"I *can* do all those things," said Katryn impassively. "I have in the past; I will in the future."

"Somehow it doesn't quite fit in with the strong feminist image of Katryn Kauffman Coffee."

"Then perhaps the image is wrong."

"In fact, you're quite the little milkmaid, swinging your little milk pail in"—Katie looked up, alarmed—"in Pennsylvania," finished J.D. "Is that what we're supposed to believe?"

Her face, which had suddenly heated to red when he mentioned the milk pail, had gone quite pale again. "I don't give a damn what you believe," said Katie quietly.

The Princess held out her champagne glass for a waiter to refill. "I keep *Once A Virgin, Twice A Virgin* in all my salons," she slurred to him as he poured. "My customers steal it regularly."

"Gregorio," prompted Dodie quite vivaciously, "you and Ms. Coffee seem to be long-time friends?"

"We met in Europe on her first modeling assignment," he answered obligingly.

"You never talk very much about your modeling career, do you, Ms. Coffee?"

Katryn laughed quite naturally. "Only because it wasn't much of a career," she acknowledged. "I was neither tall nor slender nor beautiful enough to be in demand for anything except"—she glared defiantly at J.D.—"a healthy milkmaid type. Once I started writing, I was very glad to give it up."

"I wonder if you would mind telling us about your current projects," Chuck appealed to her.

"Not at all." Katryn appeared anxious to smooth over any past displays of temperament. "Right now I'm working on a two-part series for the first fall issues of *Love And Marriage;* it's called 'Then Come Kiss Me.' "

" 'Then Come Kiss Me'!" Dodie gave a girlish trill of laughter.

"Another of your provocative titles," Belasco said unexpectedly.

Katryn leaned across Gregorio to smile warmly at the designer. "I'm afraid the credit for the title must go to Mr. Shakespeare. It's from *Twelfth Night.* She looked over at J.D. Shale with a sudden peculiar smile, then quoted softly,

> *"Then come kiss me, sweet and twenty*
> *Youth's a stuff will not endure."*

Entirely brisk and business-like, she continued, "My articles deal with the American obsession with youth, particularly with the absurd notion that love and sex and joy are the exclusive prerogatives of the young."

Belasco nodded courteously. "With a premise so true, and written in your usual astringent but sympathetic style, I am sure it will be an excellent series," he assured her.

"Thank you very much, Mr. Belasco." Katie turned back to Chuck. "My other project is a bit more unusual and exciting," she told him. "After a tour across the country to speak on behalf of battered women, I'm taking a leave of absence from the magazine to work on my first screenplay, a science fiction fantasy, *If the Men Were All Transported.* Yes, Mr. Belasco. It is—I hope—another of my provocative titles and it, too, is not original, although the source is unknown."

She quoted again, laughingly,

> *"Reuben, I have long been thinking*
> *What a good world this would be*
> *If the men were all transported*
> *On this side the Northern Sea."*

My script deals with a twenty-first century civilization in which men and women are living on opposite sides of the world, both sexes completely segregated and separated after the age of ten except for a once-a-year mating season."

J.D. snorted aloud in disdain.

"Now that one sounds more like you," he said. "From title to content, it contains your usual anti-male bias."

"I happen to be pro-woman, not anti-male," said Katryn quietly.

"Bullsh—" With difficulty he swallowed the last syllable, and Gregorio and Belasco turned away from the cameras to hide their smiles. "Everything you say or do or sponsor or join has an anti-male bias. It's been that way for years. You may have changed your name, Katie, but you damned well haven't changed your attitude."

Dodie's ears perked up like those of a well-trained hunting dog who has just flushed a pheasant. "Oh," she said brightly. "Did you change your name for your career?"

"No," answered Katryn.

J.D. snorted again, addressing himself only to her.

"Merely fancied it up a bit in a way your own people would consider much too 'high-toned.' How come such an ardent truth-seeker is ashamed of her own background?"

"I am *not* ashamed of my background, J.D." Katryn stood up, put both hands on the table, and leaned across to him. "If you would take the trouble to recall your own research, you should know that my background, which," she flung at the table at large, "happens to be both Mennonite and Amish, would be more likely to be ashamed of *me*. The name given to me by my parents was Katryn Kauffman, Katie for short. When they died and I went to live with my mother's cousins, my foster mother was also a Katy. To avoid confusion, she remained plain Katy and I became—for reasons irrelevant to this discussion—Coffee Katie. Coffee Katie Kauffman. The reversal of my name"—once again her attention was directed solely to J.D. Shale—"was meant to save my people from being embarrassed by me, not vice versa."

She kicked back her chair and walked over to the buffet table. When she returned several minutes later with another heaping plate and a fresh glass of champagne poured over strawberries, her face was glacially calm. She sat down without so much as a glance at J.D. Shale and concentrated on her food and drink, quietly listening to Princess Elena's slightly slurred and extremely libelous remarks about the wealthy and overweight women who came to her upstate retreat to starve themselves expensively into slimness.

J.D. listened to Princess Elena's rambling dissertation with an all-too-readable expression on his face. He would not attack the Princess, Katryn knew, because—for all her wealth and power—she was just another haggard, elderly woman who drank too much. But her clients were another story. He could allow his scorn of middle-aged women in frantic pursuit of beauty to appear openly on his face.

"Princess," Katryn asked at the first opportunity, "I believe that *men* as well as women come to your retreat, do they not?"

"Men as—as w-well as w-women," hiccupped the Princess.

"I rest my case."

"I don't," said J.D. grimly, turning slightly to his left. "Princess," he asked urgently, "approximately what percentage of men to women do you have at your retreat?"

Princess Elena stared down into her champagne glass, baffled. She seemed to be counting bubbles, rather than clients. Sorry for the Princess, sorry she had allowed herself to start this silly fracas, Katryn shrugged and told J.D. sharply, "I am willing to concede that far more women than men can be found there."

The smirk of triumph on his face was too much for her. "Still, speaking of sex bias . . ." she began, only to have him interrupt, with a weary shrug of his shoulders, "Oh, put a sock in it, Katie. I liked you better on your milk stool than on your soap box."

Katie's hand clenched about the stem of her champagne glass. Her head was going round and round, round and round. She was no longer in the Macedonian Tea Room, a restaurant for the rich and fashionable. Like Dorothy transported to Oz, she was being whirled back to Pennsylvania. Farm odors were in her nostrils. Instead of roast lamb, onions, and green peppers, she smelled hay and horse manure and the steaming scent of fresh-filled pails of milk.

She rubbed her forehead with the hands that had once been called a healer's, trying to return to the here and now.

"I've just realized something, J.D.," she said slowly, experimenting with the novel thought as well as with the words. "In all those times we spent together, we never got to be friends. Wouldn't you say that means I've never liked *you* at all? Truth to tell, I like you even less now as the pompous, self-righteous, asinine know-it-all you seem to have become. Here, have some strawberries." She leaned forward again to toss her remaining half-glass of champagne, strawberries included, into his face.

The strawberries bounced off his nose and onto the table. The champagne dripped down his cheeks and chin and onto his sweater.

After one moment, during which the whole table seemed to be frozen in time, J.D. carefully wiped his face dry with a napkin.

"If we're going to take the gloves off to speak of pompous, self-righteous, asinine know-it-alls," he said almost casually, "how about Katryn Kauffman Coffee? Never been married, but she sets herself up as an authority on men and sex. Never had a child, but she tells all the women who do have them how to bring them up. Not noticeably successful in her own relationships, but she presumes to speak for all American women on love and marriage, divorce, widowhood, birth control. You name it; Katie from the farm knows it."

He stood up and stared across at her dispassionately. "I don't think I like *you* either, Coffee Katie. Here, have some fruit salad."

It was just a small cup of salad, but dumped on the top of her head, it somehow seemed to be much more. There was a shriek of dismay from the usually poised Dodie, and dead silence from the men. The Princess Elena beamed benignly on the proceedings; Katie sat stiff and still, fearing that the slightest movement might start an avalanche of fruit salad sliding down her face and clothes.

Unpredictably, Lars Gunderson rose to the emergency; he must be used to dealing with them at the U.N., thought Katie hysterically. He seized a serving spoon and slowly, solicitously, scooped each clinging bit of fruit off Katryn's head and dumped it into an empty water glass.

"Chust a bit of chuice left," he said with a comforting touch of his hand on Katryn's shoulder before he returned to his seat.

Katryn toweled her hair vigorously with a napkin, removing the last of the "chuice." A waiter promptly handed her a clean napkin and under the concentrated glare of the cameras, which caught the display at every angle, she wrapped it, scarf-like, around her head, with a casual double knot at the back of her neck.

J.D. Shale got up and bowed slightly in Dodie's direction. "Ladies . . . gentlemen . . . my apologies. I think, perhaps, you could all dispense most comfortably with my presence."

"Walking out, J.D.?" Katie asked him mockingly. "As usual?"

His eyes and lips narrowed. "No," he said briefly, "I'm running."

"Typical." Katryn shrugged. "You were always great at running out, leaving the women and children behind."

J.D. opened his mouth, encountered a fiery glance from Gregorio Grieg, and closed it again. His contemplated retort, *The hell with you, too,* changed to a genuinely amused laugh.

"K-K-Katie," he said amiably, "I think we've made fools enough of ourselves for one day, and on national TV yet. *Hasta la vista.* Mrs. Mitchell, Mr. Mitchell, thank you for an interesting morning and a delightful meal. Better luck with the next batch of guests. I hope I didn't screw up your ratings."

"You probably enhanced them," said Dodie with rare humor. Chuck merely grinned.

Sketching a salute to one and all, J.D. walked across the Aegean Room, pursued by the cameras until the door closed behind him.

He stopped at the check room to retrieve his khaki windbreaker and, turning toward the exit, collided with a small, dark-haired girl in a grey quilted coat.

They both stepped back, murmuring apologies, as the young stockbroker darted forward. He had been hovering in the doorway of the Delphi Room for the last ten minutes, dividing his time between waiting for Julie and watching the TV which was set up there for the benefit of patrons who wanted to see "Celebrity Brunch."

The young stockbroker seized the girl's hand without any of his usual shyness. "Julie, come along; I have a great table," he told her eagerly. "You missed most of the fun, but there may still be some more. I'll tell you all about it."

J.D. brushed by the two as they turned around, and the young stockbroker saw his face for the first time. "Good God!" His penetrating whisper reached J.D. as well as the girl. "That's him, Julie. J.D. Shale; he just walked out on Katryn Kauffman Coffee."

"Goodness," J.D. heard the girl Julie say with earnest intensity. "I shouldn't think any man in his right mind would want to walk out on Katryn Kauffman Coffee."

J.D. slammed through the double doors of the Macedonian, walked east till he reached Fifth Avenue, and then started hiking uptown.

He had—*they* had, as he'd pointed out to Katie, made right smart fools of themselves; but he had been in the world of communications too long to let it bother him. They would be a choice morsel of gossip, a target for silly stories, only till a newer and more fascinating scandal came along. It was nothing to lose any sleep over.

Of everything that had happened . . . all that had been said . . . he suspected he would lose sleep over only one little question and two short statements.

Walking out, J.D. . . . as usual?

You were always great at running out, leaving the women and children behind.

I shouldn't think any man in his right mind would want to walk out on Katryn Kauffman Coffee.

So brittle and poised she was, Katryn Kauffman Coffee, so opinionated and cocksure. Only for a fraction of a moment had he seen a chink in her armor. Her mouth had quivered; her eyes had flickered for a moment in what seemed like pain when he had taunted her. *Never been married . . . Never had a child.*

I shouldn't have said that, J.D. thought to himself, sticking his ungloved hands under his armpits to warm them a little. It wasn't . . . gentlemanly.

He stood stock-still on Sixtieth Street, astonished to hear that word echoing in his mind. He had always prided himself on being anything but gentlemanly! In the tough Brooklyn neighborhood where he grew up, it would have made him dangerously vulnerable. For J.D. Shale, particularly, it might have spelled disaster.

Still, there were those other rules he'd grown up with . . . the one about picking on a smaller kid . . . about not hitting a guy when he was down.

Just for a moment there, with the pain in her eyes and the fruit salad on top of her head, she had looked small . . . stricken . . . defenseless . . . not like Katryn Kauffman Coffee at all, but more like Katie.

Sweet, simple, forthright Katie of Strawberry Schrank, Pennsylvania . . .

One

The Sugarcreek Budget
National Edition
Serving the Amish-Mennonite Communities
Throughout The Americas
Published Weekly at Sugarcreek, Ohio

Strawberry Schrank, Pa.

May 15, 1976 *Church was held last Sunday at Levi Smucker's by home ministers; to be held at Lester Stutzman's next.*

Now I have news of mixed joy and sadness for all of you who remember Ada (Stoltzfus) Oberholtzer. Her only daughter Martha married Paul Kauffman, neither of whom took Baptism, and they moved to Sarasota.

When last seen at Ada's funeral, Martha and Paul Kauffman looked to be a healthy couple, but Paul died last year of cancer and Martha supported her four children by doing home massage. Now comes word that Martha is gone, too.

So there are four orphaned children, past ten years old down to one and a half. The oldest two are girls, Katie and Annie. There is a boy of four, John, and the baby, also a boy, is Gideon.

The closest family these children have now is right here

*in Strawberry Schrank, our own Amos and Katy Stoltzfus,
second cousins. It's well known that they live by the Word
and would never turn away a soul in need of help. Having
only one child of their own, a son John, aged twelve (before him Katy had the misfortune of three stillbirths), the
Stoltzfus family is prepared to accept the Kauffman orphans into their hearts and home and our Fellowship.*

*God does indeed move in mysterious ways His wonders
to perform!*

Mrs. Christa Bontrager

Sugarcreek Budget
Strawberry Schrank, Pa.

May 29, 1976 *Before starting the news, I just want to
mention (so many have asked) that my original geranium
plant belonged to Aunt Mary Yutzy, who passed away
thirty years ago.*

*Katy Stoltzfus got a letter from her husband Amos in
Sarasota, where you remember he went to bring home his
cousin Martha Kauffman's children, now orphaned. It's
not proving so quick a business as Amos had hoped, because he has to deal with lawyers and social workers and
such-like to make all the arrangements, and he worries
about his farm. But he has faith his hired worker Chris
Beiler will not let him down, and his son John, though
he's only twelve and small for his age, is still a good
worker. Also, Amos' father, Bishop Jacob Stoltzfus, who
retired six years ago and lives in the* grossdaadi haus *with
his wife Mary, says it's as good as any hospital drugs for
him to spend some time in the fields again. So it looks
like the doctors will be out of business for a while so far
as Jacob Stoltzfus is concerned and Amos can rest easy*

*about the farm. The daily chores will not be shirked and
his crops will be planted.*

All her life Katie would remember her first sight of the
Pennsylvania-Dutch countryside after the nightmare of the
two-day train trip from Florida.

Day and night the teething baby had fretted and fussed,
almost as though he sensed the turmoil as well as the pain
threatening his young life.

Katie had circled around the tiny roomette till she was
dizzy, rocking him in her arms. She had walked with him
through the train aisles hour after hour to try to keep him
amused.

In the Club Car a helpful barman had suggested rubbing
a little whiskey on Gideon's sore gums, and he had kindly
provided a minute amount in a small glass. The remedy
brought the little sufferer brief relief, but Katie had been
unable to repeat it. Her cousin Amos had been horrified
when she lugged Gideon back, asleep in her arms, and he
smelled the alcohol fumes coming from the baby's mouth.

Annie could hardly be coaxed to talk at all. She sat
wherever she was told, dressed, undressed, slept, and ate
as she was directed. She had been that way ever since
their mother's funeral, and Katie had neither the time nor
the energy to coax her out of her condition of frozen fear.

Even John, usually the most even-tempered little boy,
whined and complained so ceaselessly that Katie, while
she tried to be understanding, felt a strong yearning to
shake him silly.

Toward the end of their first day of travel, her cousin
reprimanded John for his behavior. Several minutes later,
he reprimanded him a second time. At the third offense, he
leaned forward in his seat, speaking sternly to John, though
Katie had a notion his words were meant for all of them.

"In an Amish home a child learns young to obey, to

show respect, and to refrain from sulking or bad humors. Those who do not heed admonishment must accept what comes to them."

Then he took John's pudgy little hand in his own big calloused palm and dealt it four sharp slaps.

John, unused to such treatment, dissolved in noisy wails.

After five minutes Amos thundered, "Enough!" and John was shocked into stillness.

All the rest of the hideous journey, Amos had only to look at him or utter that one word, "Enough!" and John behaved.

Katie found herself torn between fury that this man—this stranger, cousin or not—should dare give her brother a smacking, and relief that the whining had stopped.

There was the nuisance of changing trains mid-way through the journey before they arrived in Lancaster on the second day. They were met at the railroad by a man with a horse attached to a strange closed black carriage, which Cousin Amos said was an Amish buggy. He was introduced to them as the hired man Chris Beiler.

Her cousin and Chris did not shake hands, just nodded. Amos asked him, "At the farm all is well?"

"At the farm all is well," Chris replied.

The two men lifted the children into the buggy, and for what seemed a long time they traveled along ordinary highways. They passed many buggies just like theirs going in both directions, and frequently cars passed by them, with horns blasting a loud signal.

Then suddenly they turned off the highway, and it was like entering a new world, a world of green hills and clean pine-scented air. They went along dirt roads and pebbled roads and stretches of tarred roads, but wherever they went there were trees: great oaks and pines, graceful white willows, sweeping weeping willows, all kinds of evergreens the like of which Katie had never seen outside the pages of a book.

For the first time Katie understood why her father used to look at the stunted palms in their tiny back yard and shake his head wryly. Whenever Mommy saw him do it, she would grin the impish grin that made her look about Annie's age.

"I think that I shall never see, a poem lovely as a tree," Mommy used to recite.

It was one of the many private jokes her mother and father shared between them. The younger children couldn't understand most of them. Katie had never understood that one before, but now she did. Why, Mommy and Daddy had come from this place, from this wonderland of plentiful trees and greenery! Florida, where they had lived, was flat and brown by comparison, and the roads smelled mostly of melting pavement and gasoline.

We have the ocean, of course, she told herself loyally, and the houses are bright, pretty colors. But even pink and pale green and beige stucco didn't seem to compare to the spanking-clean white-painted farmhouses dotting the landscape, most of them nestled against mountain backgrounds like in a picture postcard. Even the flat fields, which Cousin Amos pointed out laconically as "Corn" or "Tobacco" were at the top or the bottom surrounded by hills.

"Pennsylvania is beautiful," Katie admitted to herself most unwillingly. She had been determined to hate everything about it.

Her cousin Katy was waiting on the front steps of a house even more dazzlingly white than most. It was two stories tall on one side, long and low on the other. On the long low side, right against it, was what looked like a miniature duplicate of the big house.

Amos saw her puzzled look. "That's what we call a *grossdaadi haus,"* he said, pointing with his pipe. "It's where the parents live for peace and privacy when the younger ones take over the work. My *mutter* and *fodder* live there. Someday *my* son will run the farm, and it will be my turn to go."

He was interrupted by his wife's rushing down the steps to greet each of the children as they were handed down from the buggy. She was a small, plump woman but very light of step. "Welcome, welcome," she said to each one, her pretty, round face all wreathed in smiles. Only she pronounced it *Will komm*.

She took the sleeping baby from Katie's arms and into her own as though she were hungry to get hold of him. "Ach, the little angel, look at the rosy cheeks. See how even in his sleep he takes hold of my fingers."

"He only looks like a little angel when he sleeps," Katie told her. "He's teething, and as soon as he wakes up, you'll see he's more of a devil."

"Sha sha, such a thing you shouldn't say," her cousin Katy murmured with a quick look up at her dark-bearded husband.

"She'll learn," he said calmly; and, reassured, Cousin Katy broke into smiles again.

"So where's Johnny?" asked Amos, as Chris drove the buggy to the side of the house and the rest of them trooped up the steps together.

"He was with me in the kitchen, but he went off to the fields. He said *grossfodder* was waiting and he had a lot of work to get done before supper," Katy explained.

Amos frowned. "So if he had so much work to do, why was he in the kitchen with you?"

"Now, Amos—"

"Don't start with the 'now Amos.' I smacked little John on the train when he needed it. Would I do less for my own son?"

"So maybe he won't need it," Cousin Katy said soothingly.

Amos snorted. "I only wish."

"Come, children. I'll put the baby down in the cradle and show you the house and then your rooms."

The outside of the house was so inviting that Katie couldn't help but be shocked when she went indoors. All the rooms were painted the same color grey, and not a single window had curtains, just dismal dark green shades. There wasn't a picture or mirror anywhere, nor so much as a single photograph. All the chairs in the parlor as well as in the kitchen were of wood. There was nothing comfortably soft and upholstered to sink down on.

After Cousin Katy left them upstairs in the room that she said was to be theirs, Katie and Annie looked around silently at the two small iron bedsteads with their gay hand-sewn quilts the only touch of color, at the single wide chest of drawers and the one wooden rocker and one straight-backed wooden chair. That was all except for a great walnut chest under the window.

In Florida their bedroom furniture had been painted white, and their wallpaper was all covered with flowers and birds. Annie's stuffed animals and dolls had overflowed the room; Katie had her own desk and bookcase. For each of them, there had been a separate little fake-fur rug beside her bed.

"Why don't they have lace curtains, Katie? Where's the TV?"

"Amish people don't watch television; it's got something to do with their religion."

"I don't think I like it here, Katie. I don't want to go to the bathroom where you can't flush."

Katie tried hard to swallow her own misgivings. "Now, Annie, you've got to give it a chance. I feel a little strange, too, but Cousin Katy seems awful nice and Cousin Amos was very kind."

"He slapped John."

"Just between you and me, Annie, John had it coming.

He was being a regular pain in the neck. You can be sure Cousin Amos won't slap you; you won't give him any reason to."

"Don't be too sure of that," said a mocking voice from the open doorway, "not unless she's a saint."

Startled, both girls whirled around. The boy standing there had to be their cousin Johnny, Katy and Amos' only son. He would be pretty nice looking, Katie decided, if only he got that nasty sneer off his face. He had wavy light brown hair and brown eyes like his mother's; he was on the tall side for twelve, but kind of skinny.

"You're in Amish Land," that same jeering voice continued, "where the Lord and His Anointed here on earth expect you to be perfect. And if you're not—" He smacked his right fist hard against his left hand—"Pow! Whom the Lord loveth He chasteneth," he taunted them. "And how my father can chasteneth!"

Annie began to cry.

"Annie, come on, stop it, he's only teasing." She looked coldly over her shoulder at their tormentor. "You know how overgrown baby boys like to tease. Go away!" she ordered her cousin John. "You ought to be ashamed, a big boy like you trying to frighten a little girl."

He clasped his hands before him in mock penitence.

"Forgive me, Lord, I know not what I did."

Katie walked across the room and started to close the door in his face, but he put his foot inside. "This is not an idle visit. I was told to call you down to supper."

"We'll be there in a minute," she said, and slammed the door against his foot.

A few minutes later when Katie and Annie went downstairs, Amos was already seated at the end of the long dining room table, his son John on his right and their brother John next to him. The hired man Chris Beiler sat at the other end of the table.

Their happily flustered cousin Katy explained the seating arrangements to them.

"For family, with only four of us, it was simplest before this to eat at the small table in the kitchen. Now, with a fine big family, we'll have our suppers, at least, in the dining room. You'll sit here, Katie, next to me. No Annie, *mien kindt,* that's my place on the right of *him.* You sit there between your sister and Chris at the end. Gideon will sit across from you once he's old enough to be at table with us."

Curiosity overcame Annie's shyness.

"Do we always sit in the same place?"

Cousin Katy looked surprised. "But, of course, *als.* We—" She interrupted herself as Cousin Amos cleared his throat. "Hush now, children. It's time for the silent prayer before the meal."

"What do we pray for?"

Cousin Katy looked genuinely shocked. Cousin Amos shook his head, as though he were asking himself, *What else could you expect,* which Katie felt was a reflection on Martha and Paul Kauffman. Even as she bristled, prepared to defend her parents hotly, Cousin Amos answered mildly, "Just thank the Lord in your hearts for His blessings and the bounty of this table. Later you'll have instruction in our ways."

Halfway through the meal, which Katie had to admit *was* delicious and bountiful—bean soup, both chicken and ham, fried potatoes, pickled beets and cucumbers, tomatoes that were the biggest and the best she had ever tasted—she decided that Amish eating was as silent as Amish prayer.

Considering that Cousin Amos had been away from his small family for several weeks, the members seemed to have little to say to one another. Katie decided a bit righteously that they weren't a loving family like *hers* had been. Then she saw the occasional warm glances that passed between husband and wife, the mother's hovering worry and the father's gruff concern that their son didn't seem to eat much, and she changed her mind. Their ways were just different. Different in a way she could hardly comprehend.

Her heart sank at the thought of years and years of them. Oh God, she wanted her own mother and her father and her old life back. If it weren't for the younger children, she would have burst into tears, sobbing out her anguish and her longing.

But she was the oldest. She had to be strong. Weren't those almost the last words her Mom had ever said to her? "Katie, you're the oldest. You'll have to be strong for the younger ones, my poor darling."

She stiffened her spine and said calmly, "This chicken is awfully good, Cousin Katy."

Just then Chris Beiler, who obviously agreed with her, bit down into his third portion and the room echoed with his loud belch. A second later there was a second, slightly different, explosion of sound from him.

Annie giggled nervously and Katie looked down, red with embarrassment, while little John, sitting opposite her, leaned across the table and said in a loud whisper, "Katie, he didn't say 'I beg your pardon' for belching or f—"

Chris looked surprised, their cousin John snickered, and Katie gave a shake of her head violent enough to keep her brother from finishing.

"John!" said Cousin Amos in his authoritative way.

Both Johns swiveled their heads round in quick attention.

"A belch in appreciation of good food is only natural, nothing to apologize for. It is for sin and error we must beg to be pardoned, not for natural acts. *Fer schtay?* I mean, do you understand?"

"Yes," said John, looking utterly confused.

"I'll explain to you after supper," Katie said to him softly.

Another culture shock, but instead of being even more downcast, Katie suddenly felt light-hearted. Her ever-ready sense of humor had come to her aid. The Amish were different, all right, she thought, tickled.

Cousin Katy addressed herself suddenly to her husband. "It's going to be a *druwwel* having the two Johns."

"No problem," Amos said genially. "We'll change one."

"I'm not changing my name for *him,"* John Stoltzfus proclaimed belligerently, getting up from the table.

His father gave him what Katie had already come to call one of his "Enough" looks. "The meal is not over," he said, and John Stoltzfus sat.

"It's no problem," Amos said again, turning from his son toward his wife. "Our Johnny will stay the same, but the new John in our family can be called after his own father; he's Paul's John, so we'll call him Paul John. Would you like that?" he asked little John Kauffman, who smiled at the attention from all the table and nodded a vigorous yes.

"So that's settled," said Amos in his patriarchal manner, "and now to the matter of the two Katies."

Everyone looked at him expectantly, and Katie's heart sank. She didn't want to be Martha's Katie; she just didn't. Martha had been Mommy, and though both names were special, she was herself!

"It strikes me this way," Cousin Amos continued. "Whether the name is Stoltzfus or Kauffman, it doesn't matter, we are all one family now; and *she"*—he indicated Cousin Katy—"and *I* are the mother and the father. Your own, I know, you called Mommy and Daddy in the Englisher style, and I wouldn't take that away from them or from you. Our Johnny calls us Mem and Pap, the Pennsylvania-Dutch way. This should be what you call us, too."

The instinctive rebellion in Katie's heart was just a brief flame, quickly extinguished by her own good sense.

Cousin Amos was right. *Mem* and *Pap* had nothing to do
with Martha and Paul Kauffman, and it would be better
for the little ones (not her, never her, even though she
would do it) to use names for these two good people who
had taken them in that would make them seem like the
mother and father they were going to be.

Her brother and sister were looking at her, a little dis-
turbed and uncertain. What Katie said now would be important to them.

"I think that's a fine idea," said Katie, loud and clear.
"Mem. Pap." She looked first at Katy Stoltzfus, then at
Amos as she pronounced each name.

Across the table she encountered a look from Johnny
Stoltzfus that made her shiver suddenly. His lips were set
in their usual sneering smile, but his eyes were fiery and
frightening. How could the soft brown eyes, so like his
mother's, cast such a look of dark hate? She had a crazy
impulse to cross herself the way she had read they did in
the Middle Ages to ward off a curse from the evil eye.

Two

Sugarcreek Budget
Strawberry Schrank, Pa.

June 5, 1976 *Published to be married are Daniel Miller,
son of the Jacob Millers of Maiden Falls, who assists Levi
Luke Fisher in his carriage shop here in Strawberry
Schrank, and Lena Miller, the daughter of our recently
deceased Deacon Reuben Miller and his wife Molly. The
Reuben Miller farm has been sold, and after the wedding,
Molly will go with the newly-wed couple to live in Canada. Levi Luke says he is sure sorry to lose the best assistant he ever had, but he wishes Daniel all the best. His
new assistant, named Mark Gruber, will be coming here
in August from somewhere in Indiana. In the meantime
Levi will use temporary local help.*

*They're not here yet (at my time of writing this) but by
the time the* Budget *comes out and this is being read, the
Kauffman orphans will most likely have arrived home to
Strawberry Schrank with Amos Stoltzfus, whose Katy got
a letter from him yesterday, which caused her some concern. It seems her four new children, not having been
brought up in the Plain way, have to have all new clothes,
which doesn't give her much notice to get such a lot of
sewing done. Anyone who can help out, it will be greatly
appreciated. The little boys, John and Gideon, are four
and one and a half. The two girls are Annie, six or seven,*

*and Katie, who's ten and a half, but nothing said about
their sizes.*

Less than three weeks remained until the end of the
school semester, so it was decided that Katie and Annie—
especially without the proper clothes—need not attend
classes until September.

Told of this decision the morning after their arrival by
the cousin who was now their new Pap, Annie scampered
outside, wild with delight, but Katie had to struggle hard
not to rebel.

It wasn't that she minded so much missing a few weeks
of the new school, but already on her second day in her
new home she was beginning to be hungry for something
to read.

While she and Mem did the dishes together after a
hearty breakfast, she asked where the books were kept.

"In the parlor," Mem told her, looking surprised.

Katie couldn't remember seeing any books the night
before, but she had probably been too tired and upset to
notice. She excused herself for a minute and rushed to
the front room.

There wasn't any bookcase there . . . and as far as she
could see, there were only three books: a big, worn leather
Bible and a huge Prayer Book, which she guessed from
the few words she recognized must both be in German . . .
an enormous, unpromising-looking volume called *The
Martyrs' Mirror.* It had over fifteen-hundred pages, and all
of them, Katie realized, skimming quickly through it, were
devoted to tales of the martyrs who had suffered horrible
deaths or torment for clinging staunchly to their Anabaptist faith. The Amish, deduced Katie, shuddering over the
story of a man buried alive, must be the descendants of
the Anabaptists.

She went back to Mem in the kitchen. "I could only

find an old German Bible and Prayer Book and a horrid book about all kinds of martyrs."

"Mein kindt!" said Mem in horrified tones. "Never say so. Those are the sacred Books of our Faith."

"But where are the books for reading?" Katie burst out.

"You want to catch up on your studies? I guess Johnny could lend you his school books. He keeps them in his room."

"That's all there are in the whole house?" Katie asked in desperation.

"That's right, Cousin Katie." Johnny Stoltzfus had entered the kitchen, himself ready for school after his early-morning chores. "Once classes are out," he said righteously, while his eyes laughed at her, "we're much too busy on the farm for foolishness like books."

"That's the truth." His mother nodded eagerly. "There'll be the work of the house and vegetable garden, feeding the chickens, help with the milking, the cooking, the baking, the sewing, the mending, tasks for the needy, games with new friends. Never *brootz,*" she assured Katie comfortably. "You'll be so busy, you won't have time to read."

Katie ran out of the kitchen.

No time to read. A house without books. How could she bear it?

At home in Florida, there had been a bookcase in every room, a magazine rack even in the bathroom. There had been books on every table, even sometimes piles of them on the floor.

Martha Kauffman used to tease her husband that he never read less than four books at once, even though she was an avid reader herself. Whenever Paul tried to smuggle a book into the house that he wasn't supposed to have, she would greet him with pretended severity. "What's that? The new jacket you were going to buy yourself?"

"I don't need a new jacket," he'd say, "but I couldn't resist this, Martha, you wouldn't want me to. It's the poetry anthology we wanted . . . I found it on a half-price shelf."

"Oh, well." Martha would flick eagerly through the anthology. "At half price, I suppose . . ."

Katie could remember like it was yesterday the very last book he bought before he got so sick.

"I suppose that's the roast beef I asked you to pick up," Martha said, eyeing the square parcel under his arm.

"No, my sweet, it's the new biography of Kennedy. Food for the soul, darling, food for the soul. Besides, you know very well," he continued, poker-faced, "that I cannot comprehend the neglect . . ."

" '. . . of a family library in such days as these,' " Martha finished for him.

It was what they always said about their book-buying, another of their famous jokes that didn't sound so funny to anyone else, though the two of them would always burst into uproarious laughter when they made their shared remark.

Katie had demanded an explanation once, and her father had told her it was a quotation from one of the most beautifully crafted novels in the English language, *Pride And Prejudice*.

Katie had promptly gotten *Pride And Prejudice* out of the bookcase and taken it to bed with her that night, but she gave up on it after only four chapters.

"You're too young to understand it," her mother reassured her the next day. "Wait—oh, six or seven years; then you'll love it."

She had five out of that seven left to go, and here she was in a house where there was no time for reading and only three books, two of them unreadable.

She wanted to attend the last few weeks of school because she had counted on being able to borrow some books from the school library. She could have asked her cousin Johnny to get some for her, but the way he felt toward her and she toward him, she would have died an Anabaptist martyr's death before asking him for a favor.

Under her breath, she called him all the bad names she could think of to relieve her rage and frustration. *Snotty-nosed brat. Mean little bastard.* And other things far worse.

Johnny was gone when she went back to the kitchen. Mem hadn't realized anything was amiss.

"Katie, I'd like you to dust the parlor and polish the furniture. You know how?"

"Of course, Cous—Mem. I always did it for my Mom."

"Good," said Katy Stoltzfus heartily. "Because I want to get on with the baking. I wouldn't be surprised if we'll have plenty of visitors coming, all wanting to get a look at you. You'll be careful of the china in the corner cupboard, ain't?" she mentioned anxiously as Katie gathered up the cloths and polish set out on the kitchen table. "I got most of those pieces from my *grossmutter* and even some from her *mutter.*"

"I'll be as careful as can be," Katie promised.

When she returned to the kitchen, Mem was rolling out the dough for pie crusts. A dozen of them, she said in answer to Katie's question, as though making a dozen pies was no big thing.

"What else do you want me to do, Mem?"

"Well, it's enough for the first day. You still look tired from the traveling and the change. Maybe you'd like to go outside?"

"That would be nice," Katie agreed eagerly. "I'd like to take a walk and see the countryside . . . it's so green and pretty."

Katy Stoltzfus looked toward the big uncurtained window, vaguely surprised. *"Ja,* I suppose it is. Florida's not green?"

"Parts of it," said Katie, torn between loyalty and truth, "only not too much where we lived." Then she burst out from a heart full to overflowing with homesickness, "But there's nothing like walking barefoot across a sandy beach on the edge of the ocean with the water splashing around your ankles . . . especially when it's almost deserted. Daddy and I used to do that lots . . . before he got too sick to walk."

"Ja," repeated Mem on a soft sigh. *"Ich wutt . . .* it would be something to see before *es dode."*

"You feel free like a bird in flight."

Mem seemed to come out of the bemused state in which Katie's words had cast her.

"So, run outside," she said in her usual kindly, practical manner. "You'll see plenty of birds flying among the trees. And remember, *mien kindt,"* she added as Katie opened the kitchen door, "even the birds have to come often down to earth."

Katie understood but didn't answer the oblique message.

Closing the door, she walked in the direction of the barn and saw Annie and John—no, her brother was Paul John now—standing there with the hired man Chris Beiler, who held what looked like a calf in his arms. Ordinarily, she would have charged eagerly toward them, with her usual insatiable curiosity about anything new to see or learn.

But now she felt a desperate need to be alone. She wheeled about toward the front of the house, hurried through the gate before her sister or brother could spot her, and went hurrying down the mountain road.

She walked for hours, up hill and down hill, on straight paths and some that seemed to wind round and around. When she was hungry, she climbed over fences and helped herself to blueberries and strawberries and another tart kind of berry she had never tasted before, filling the long dark apron that Mem had given her to wear.

The apron strings, tying in back, also served as a belt to pull up one of Mem's dresses, which she had lent Katie till her own new clothes were ready. Since Mem, though a short woman, was still inches taller than Katie, the ugly purplish dress would have dragged on the ground if she hadn't been able to bunch it up under the apron.

Having eaten her fill of berries, Katie scrambled up, up, up as high as she could manage into a giant oak, using the heavy, low-hanging branches as steps. She settled herself comfortably against the trunk of the tree and looked down over in one direction to a scene of domestic tranquility—a snug farmhouse with a herd of cows ambling in all directions over a wide stretch of grassland—and then across the other way to a scene of more rugged grandeur, a succession of rolling green hills topped by a tree-covered mountain.

Her mother—her *real* mother—had been enough a product of her early upbringing to remind her, "Count your blessings," whenever Katie fussed about something unimportant.

So now she started counting them out loud.

"It's beautiful here," Katie told herself. "I'd be silly to call it a prison just because it's different. We're all together. Mem and Pap are giving us a home. Without them we'd be in an orphanage . . . or even separated, put in different homes." She shuddered at the very thought of it.

"July and August and part of June without books. Big deal. If I can't manage that somehow, something is wrong with me. It should be *fun* learning how to milk cows. Maybe I can get lessons in driving the buggy, too, and riding a horse. The time will pass fast, with all Mem said there is to do."

She was silent for some moments, chewing reflectively on a leaf.

After a while, she earnestly assured a red-breasted robin who suddenly alighted on the branch below her swinging feet, "The main thing is that it doesn't have to be forever."

Unimpressed by her reasoning and alarmed by the sound of her voice, the robin darted off.

Entranced by the bird's graceful flight, Katie laughed in sudden joyful exuberance. "I'll be like you!" she called out after the robin. "When the time comes, I'll fly away home. And Annie can fly with me, and the boys, too. This is just a stopping-off place till we're grown."

She climbed down from the tree, snagging the bunched-up skirt of her dress on one of the branches and tearing it rather badly at the back.

"No loss," muttered Katie, craning her neck to study the jagged rip. She hoped uneasily that Mem would be equally philosophical.

Once on the ground, she walked breathlessly up the hill she had recently run down, only to find a new worry. She didn't know which path to take next. She was lost.

"Oh, well." She could stop at the nearest farmhouse—there was one just a few yards away—to ask for directions. She walked quickly toward it and had actually knocked on the wooden panel of the screen door before a sudden thought struck her.

She uttered one soft expressive word, which would have earned her the same quick whack from Martha Kauffman, Mom, as it would have from Katy Stoltzfus, Mem.

Then she said aloud mournfully, "I'm an idiot!"

"Surely not?" laughed the young man in blue work shirt and denims who answered her knock.

"Oh, yes, I am," Katie assured him. "I wanted to ask directions because I walked so far, I didn't know how to get back. Then I just realized I don't know where I'm going back to. I forgot to notice the name of the road the house is on. Am I still in Strawberry Schrank?"

"No, hon, you really did walk far, didn't you? You're nearer to Intercourse."

Katie looked at him to see if he were making fun of her. He obviously wasn't.

"You'd better come in." He opened the screen door and at the same time bawled from the depths of a pair of powerful lungs, "Ma!"

It was a reassuring sound. Katie came into the house as Ma came down the stairs. Carpeted stairs. Carpeted hallway. Pictures on the wall. Papered walls. And Ma's dress was of a cotton covered with bright red poppies that hung just a few inches below her knees. Obviously, not Amish.

"The poor kid's lost," said the young man, and Katie's indignant look at this description was not lost on Ma. "She's from somewhere in Strawberry Schrank, but she doesn't know the address."

"How about the names of the people?"

Katie brightened. "They're Amos and Katy Stoltzfus." They both shook their heads. "They have a son named Johnny, and the hired man is called Chris Beiler," she added helpfully. "They're Amish."

Ma turned to her son.

"What you'd better do, Tom," she told him, "is go get the car while I give . . ." She looked down questioningly.

"Katie."

"While I give Katie a glass of lemonade and some cookies. Then you can drive her back to Strawberry Schrank and stop at houses there till you find one that can direct you to the right place."

"Okay. I'll get the keys," he said cheerfully, taking the steps two at a time while his mother shooed Katie toward the kitchen.

Forty-five minutes later, when Tom came to a stop in front of the Stoltzfus gate, the entire family, including Amos' aged parents from the *grossdaadi haus,* the hired man, and even Gideon, holding onto Mem's skirts, were all assembled at the front door.

Tom whistled. "The troops are out, kid, and looking pretty grim. Want me to go along and help to explain?"

"I have a feeling it would only make matters worse," said Katie glumly, opening the car door. "Thanks a million, billion, Tom."

"Nothing to it, kid. Hope everything works out okay."

Katie stumped through the gate and up the path as the car drove off, spraying pebbles in all directions.

The elders all looked at her with varying degrees of displeasure.

"I went for a long walk and got lost," she blurted out. "Then I didn't know what road you lived on, so I stopped at a house, and Tom's mother told him to drive me home. He asked at lots of farms till he found a family to direct us."

As though she hadn't spoken—as though she weren't even there—Amos looked past her to his wife. "I'll go back to the fields to make up my lost work. Set supper back an hour. Chris. Johnny. *Koom.*"

For a moment Katie thought she saw a look of sneaking sympathy on her cousin Johnny's face; then he saw her looking after him, and he grinned back maliciously over his shoulder, as though saying, *I told you so.*

Mem sent the children out to the yard, putting Annie in charge of Gideon. She sent Katie upstairs to wash and change out of the torn dress. "And put on your *kapp.* Your hair is all *stroovlich.* An Amish girl, from the time she wakes, is never seen without her *kapp.* Then come down and help me with the supper," she directed.

As she went upstairs, Katie put her hand to her head. She had never even noticed the *kapp* was gone. She must have lost it climbing up or down the tree.

When she came back to the kitchen, wearing another of the older Katy's baggy dresses and a clean *kapp,* Mem turned and faced her.

"Katie, you have caused worry and trouble and wasted work time. You behaved as heedlessly as someone Paul John's age, and here you are the oldest. In an Amish household, you do not stay away from meals without a word or leave your chores for others to do. You're not that bird you spoke about, free to do as you please, but part of a family that shares all . . . the work, and the freedom, too."

She paused, but Katie didn't answer, and Mem continued in a softer voice but just as firmly, "The young man who brought you home . . . it was kind of him to take the trouble, but he is not *unser Satt Leit*—our sort of people. Our ways may seem strange to you yet, but as long as you live here you must abide by them. We do not mingle with *anner Satt Leit*—the other sort of people. We know that our ways are best. And though it is not forbidden for an Amishman to ride in an automobile, so long as he does not own one—for ourselves, your Pap and I agree, we do not want a daughter of ours to ride in cars with Englishers."

"Englishers?"

"Gay people. Fancy people. Outsiders."

"You mean," said Katie, a whole new vocabulary opening up to her, "not Amish?"

"Ja," agreed Mem in self-satisfied tones, "not Amish."

The wave of desolation that swept over Katie brought a pain that was sharply physical. With a wisdom beyond her years, she detected the blindness in Mem that prevented her from seeing that Katie herself not only was but would always be *anner Sait Leit* . . . the other sort of people!

Three

Sugarcreek Budget
Strawberry Schrank, Pa.

June 19, 1976 *There has not been enough rain. All the farmers are waiting on rain.*

Alma Hochstetler of Lancaster, who is a widow since her husband Slim Sammie Hochstetler died of tuberculosis last year, will be the new schoolteacher here in September.

At the quilting party last Wednesday at the home of Nancy Hirtz, all the ladies laid aside their quilting, and instead it became a Kauffman clothing party, and they made plenty trousers and dresses and aprons and shirts, so the Kauffman children, living now with Amos and Katy Stoltzfus, will have enough clothes to start off with.

All who want to pay their respects to Amos on his return will see him with the children at the Preaching on Sunday at the home of the Eli Masts. . . .

Anne Kauffman lifted big, solemn brown eyes to her sister Katryn.

"Is it for a Hallowe'en party, Katie?" she asked, fingering the white organdy cape and apron tied on over the strange, shapeless, bright green dress that fell all the way to her ankles. She stood on tip-toe to examine Katryn's new pleated white head cap. It was identical to the one that had been pinned on top of her own red-brown hair, after her curls were carefully straightened out, scraped back, and bundled beneath the *kapp*. "Is that why we're dressed this way?"

"No, honey, don't you remember how Mommy explained to us once about the Amish way of dressing? It's the way *she* dressed when she was a girl growing up here."

Anne's face puckered up, tears threatening any minute to spill down her cheeks. "I would rather be with Mommy and dress the way we did in Florida."

"We can't, Annie." Katryn knelt, the better to put comforting arms about her small sister. "We have no family except the Stoltzfuses, and they're Amish, not Mennonite like Mommy and Daddy. We have to do what they say now," she advised the younger girl, even as her own heart rebelled. "When we're grown up, then we can please ourselves."

"Do you *like* to dress this way, Katie?"

I hate it, Katie wanted to rage, *it isn't me!*

But for a long time, with their father sick and their mother sometimes working outside the house, and then through the year of Martha Kauffman's illness, she had been forced early into the role of mother to the younger ones, especially Anne.

The truth would not set Annie free but only make her unhappy. Properly handled, her mood could shoot up from distress to delight with the speed of quicksilver.

Katie managed a big, bright smile. "It's like you said, we have to pretend we're dressing up for a Hallowe'en party." She nodded her head, then circled around Annie in a gay little dance step, dark skirts whirling. "These are our costumes."

She stretched out her hands and Anne took hold of them. They danced around together, joyfully singing their father's favorite old folk song about a man who got bewitched by a bear.

When Katy Stoltzfus entered the room on this scene of breathless, laughing merriment, the singing and dancing stopped abruptly at first sight of her horrified expression. "Katie! Annie! *Denk schond!* It's the Sabbath." She took each girl by the hand, looking earnestly and not unkindly into their faces. "It wonders me"—she shook her head—"your mother didn't lesson you against such *sindhoftich.*"

Anne's face puckered up again, but Katryn pulled away her hand, red and wrathful.

"My mother was *not* sinful!" she shouted. "Don't you talk about her like that."

"Annie, go downstairs to your brothers," said Katy Stoltzfus.

Annie looked quickly at her sister, who nodded. When the two Katies were left alone, the older one said in a quiet firm voice, "I keep telling myself you are here only a short time, Katryn, and not so used to our ways, but still you know, for I have admonished you many times now, what is and is not right. You must know it was *letz*—very wrong of you to speak to me in that loud, rude, rebellious way. If he had heard"—*He,* Katryn had already learned, spoken of in that respectful voice, signified her cousin Amos, the head of the house—"He, I fear," Amos' wife continued, "would think you deserved more punishment than just words."

Katie hung her head; not in shame, but because she didn't know what to answer. The older Katy accepted the bowed head as an act of contrition. *"You,* the eldest, must be well-mannered, quiet, humble, and obedient, or how can you help teach the younger ones?" She went on, greatly encouraged. "How are we to raise them in the way that they must go if they cannot look to the example set by their older sister?"

"I am sorry," murmured Katie, which she was, not for what she had said, but because she recognized that she had truly grieved this woman who was of such remarkable goodness that she could readily accept four strangers as her own children.

Just the same . . . *I don't belong here . . . I won't ever belong here . . .* The sudden realization struck Katie with such blinding force that with it came another of those waves of incredible panic she had been experiencing. Her quickened heartbeats sent stabs of pain shooting up through her chest; a lump of such threatening proportions lodged in her throat that she began to cough and choke, turning first white, then red, as she gasped for breath.

From what seemed like far off she heard her cousin calling her, raising her hands above her head, rubbing her back. Gradually the pain subsided, the lump melted, the mists dissolved . . .

She didn't belong . . . but they must never know. For all their sakes . . . her sister and brothers, her cousins, even her own. . . .

Pale and shaken, she nevertheless managed a small reassuring smile for Katy Stoltzfus.

"I am all right now."

"Do you get much sick, *mein kindt?*" Mem asked gently.

"No, I'm very healthy."

"Donk Gott." She put her head tentatively on the girl's head, a rare gesture of affection. "It is my duty to admonish you as it is yours to take my words to heart, but not so that you become ill."

Katryn nodded solemnly.

"Come then, let us go down. *He* will not be pleased if we are late."

Johnny stood by the horse's head next to the Stoltzfus buggy, the customary scowl on his face. Mem mounted the buggy seat and Amos handed little Gideon up to her. She set him happily on her lap. When Katryn and Anne and little Paul John Kauffman had climbed into the back of the carriage, Amos nodded to his son, who followed them. As usual, he had nothing to say to his cousins.

While the buggy rattled along the road, they could hear Mem talking to Pap.

"Did you ever see such a fine, stout boy?" It was obvious she was speaking of Gideon. "So big and brown. Look at the strength of his little hands. And these sturdy legs."

Amos shook his head, tightening his grip on the reins. "You must not fall into the sin of pride, wife."

"I was not being proud," Katy Stoltzfus protested, "only thankful to God that He finally sent us so many strong, healthy children. This one will surely make a fine farmer," she added slyly, knowing Amos' weakness. Not to have fathered more farmers had been his great grief.

Katie Kauffman, who had been staring at her cousin John's face, saw a sudden spasm contort it for a moment. The expression was quickly gone, and his usual sullen mask slipped back; but Katie was not fooled.

How could his mother, all goodness to the orphans, have no notion of the pain she inflicted on her own son with such comparisons about their size and strength, their health and abilities?

Johnny Stoltzfus was jealous . . . and he dared not say so. To be jealous was to be wicked, to be worldly. He must either confess his sin or keep it locked and festering inside him, thereby increasing the agony.

Katie, who in just this short time had learned that to be Amish was to strive ceaselessly for an almost-impossible perfection, rocked back and forth in silent sympathy for her all-too-human cousin. Oh, it must be terribly hard on him.

It would have been difficult—no, she corrected herself impetuously—it would have been *devastating* for her suddenly to share the attention and affection of *her* parents with four complete strangers, and to hear their praises sung while her own were never mentioned.

Katie, two years the younger, tried not to look at John Stoltzfus. He would only resent her compassion.

Poor boy. Poor boy.

Even though she could not quite take to him, all the way to the Preaching she keened quietly to herself for his pain.

By the time Preaching Service was over, all compassion was gone and Katie had the sorry satisfaction of disliking her cousin as much as before. He had done his best to make her uncomfortable from the moment they arrived at the Eli Mast farm.

When the buggy stopped and she was about to be handed down from it, she looked about, her mouth opened in surprise at finding herself in another barnyard.

"I thought we were going to church."

"Our services are held in our homes," Johnny's mocking, sanctimonious voice came from behind her. "We don't need fancy buildings to worship our God."

Katie jumped down from the buggy, ignoring him; and he and his father drove off to get the horse unhitched while the Kauffman children followed Mem, staying shyly close to her.

"Everyone's staring at our clothes," Annie whispered uncomfortably.

"Of course they're not," Katie whispered back, just as uncomfortable. "Why would they stare when everyone's dressed the same?"

"Then why are they staring?"

"I suppose because we're strangers."

Mem overheard the last question. "Don't be embarrassed, *mien kindt*," she said soothingly to Annie. "Lots of people here knew your mother and your grandmother, so they want to meet the children of Martha and the grandchildren of Ada."

She pushed them forward to greet a dizzying number of people. In a little while, Katie could scarcely match any names to faces, especially as so many names were the same. Soon, though, she noticed and began to resent a certain attitude, a congratulatory air about the four children having been returned from the perverted outside world of disobedience to the purity of life in the community of Brothers.

"God moves in mysterious ways His wonders to perform," she kept hearing again and again.

It took her disagreeable cousin to put into words what she felt was the insulting nature of this pious pronouncement.

"His wonder, in this case, being to get rid of your parents so you could return to the Chosen," said Johnny's voice close to her ear.

Katie swung around to him, fury in her own face and voice, even as she remembered to speak quietly. "You rotten little bastard!"

"Hey, I'm not saying what I think . . . it's what *they* think."

She walked swiftly away from him, from them all, till Mem called her over to meet yet another of her grandmother's dear friends.

Then it was time for services to begin, and though Katie and Annie sat with other young girls on one of the backless benches transported by special wagons from the place of the last Preaching, she could see Johnny, right across from her, sitting with the boys.

Even worse, *he* could see *her.*

Whenever he caught her eye, he made all kinds of funny faces; and though she tried to look away, her eyes kept going back to him. The faces were so ridiculous that several times she couldn't help laughing out loud, and had to pretend that she was coughing. Everyone was staring at her again. Once, the Preacher even stopped in the middle of a droning discourse and looked her way.

Katie turned bright red, and a girl down the bench

passed her a cough drop. From the kitchen, going through a dozen hands on its way to her, she received a glass of water.

So many of the prayers were in German, she was understandably bored. Not only little children and babies on their mothers' laps fell asleep, she noticed: after the midway point in the service, when small moon-shaped pies were passed around to the young ones, Katie alleviated the tedium by counting how many adults fell asleep. Her total count by the time the three-hour service was over came to three women and four men. Her favorite was the stout man who had to be shaken awake by a friend when his snores grew too loud and prolonged—louder even than Katie's coughing.

Going home again in the buggy, after the hearty snack that followed the Preaching Service and another hour of socializing, Katie looked at her cousin, wondering if he would try to be funny again. But he had fallen back into his sullen mood; he just sat, wooden-faced, acting as though none of them were there.

Katie played word games with Paul John and Annie and ignored him as thoroughly as he ignored them. He was impossible!

She was very surprised when he deliberately walked over to her later that day where she was standing outside the kitchen filling a pail with well water.

He looked around quickly, saw that no one else was there, and told her in a low, rough voice, "Look in the chest in your room. I put something there for you under the pile of quilts."

"What?" asked Katie suspiciously.

"Never mind. You'll see. You better take good care of them and don't let anyone see." He swaggered away.

Katie set down the pail, went through the kitchen, and ran upstairs to her bedroom. She knelt and threw open the chest, then hesitated. She didn't really trust him. She wouldn't put it past that nasty boy to have hidden a toad, maybe even a garden snake, under the quilts. Torn between dread and expectation, she lifted the quilts by their very edge, gingerly, slowly, so she could snatch her hands out of harm's way if she had to.

She sucked in her breath.

Two books lay under the last quilt: *Little Women* by Louisa May Alcott, and a slim volume, *American Poems*.

Katie's eyes filled with tears. She hugged *Little Women* to her. She had read it, of course, but it was a wonderful book for re-reading. She set it down and opened *American Poems*. The very first poem sent a thrill shooting through her; it was "Trees," by Joyce Kilmer.

> *I think that I shall never see*
> *A poem lovely as a tree. . . .*

She had never known there was more to Mommy's and Daddy's joke than those two lines, that they were part of a poem, a beautiful poem. She read it three times, repeating the last lines lingeringly aloud:

> *Poems are made by fools like me*
> *But only God can make a tree.*

A sound outside in the hallway brought her to her senses. She hurriedly returned both books to the walnut chest and covered them with the quilts again.

She would do her reading at night by the kerosene lamp after Annie fell asleep, which thank God she did pretty quickly. She was a *sound* sleeper, which was cause for even more gratitude. Not that Annie would ever *deliberately* betray her, but she might forget and make a slip of the tongue.

Katie bounded to her feet, happier than at any moment since she had left Florida. What she couldn't get over was that her cousin Johnny should be the cause of that happiness. He was a strange one, that boy. He acted as though he hated her, he was always making fun of everything, even his own family, so how come he of all people had done something so nice? So *understanding?*

She got to her feet and determinedly crossed to the bedroom she knew was Johnny's. The door was open; she could see at a glance that he wasn't in the room.

"Looking for me?"

Katie spun around. He was at the other end of the hallway, standing in the doorway of the room that Mem had called the "spare."

She walked over to him. "Yes, I was."

"Come on in."

Katie followed him into the room. It was nice and big, the usual grey color but somehow more cheerful and interesting than the other bedroooms, maybe because it had more windows and a big four-poster bed and a little corner cabinet filled with little cotton-stuffed animals.

Johnny followed her glance. "They were my Aunt Mattie's," he said. "My great-Aunt Mattie's. They let her have some toys because she lived in this room."

"Lived?"

"Yeah, lived." He shrugged. "Okay, so ask me about the books."

"Okay, I'm asking. Why?"

"Don't get the wrong idea. I don't like your prissy sister and I don't like your whiny little brother and I sure as hell don't like *you*. But"—he shrugged again—"I can feel sorry for you just the same, or don't you believe that?"

"I believe it, all right; it's how I feel about you."

"Who asked for your pity?"

"Who asked for yours?"

"You wanna give the books back?"

"You mean," Katie asked him, "if I want to read the books, I have to let you feel sorry for me?"

"Yeah," said Johnny, "you want to borrow my books, it has to be on my terms."

"Okay," said Katie. "Where did you get them?"

"I bought them," said Johnny. "Oh, not myself. Levi Luke Fisher—he's the carriage-maker here in town—he gets them for me at auctions. They can be picked up real cheap. Once we got a boxful for just five dollars. Your *Little Women* came in that batch."

"And your parents don't know?"

"You kidding?" He looked horrified. "There'd be a big bonfire if they ever found out. All ninety-seven of my books right up in smoke. Levi Luke keeps them for me in a bookcase at the back of his shop. I helped him build it."

"Levi Luke's not Amish?"

"Yeah, he's Amish, but he's not like most, maybe because he never married or had kids of his own. Anyhow, he seems to understand people feeling *different*. He lives with his mother; she's real old and blind, and I know he reads to her in the evening and it's sure not from the Bible."

He looked at Katie, and his voice got gruff again. "When you finish those, I'll smuggle them out and bring you some more."

"Thank you," said Katie meekly. "I'm very grateful."

"Who asked you to be?" snapped her prickly cousin, then suddenly grinned. "We *different* people have to stick together."

His grin faded. He went over to one of the windows and stood there, a fist clenching on the sill. Over his shoulder he flung at her, "Go on, nothing's keeping you here. You know what you came to find out."

"What did you mean," Katie asked softly, "about your Aunt Mattie *living* in here?"

"C'mere."

Katie went.

He pointed to a stone ledge outside the window. "See those grooves?"

Katie nodded.

"Feel them."

Obediently, with his hand guiding hers, she ran her fingers across the ledge.

"Those grooves are holes they filled in with cement after they took the bars off the windows."

"Bars?" Katie said uncertainly, a little frightened now of his strangely glittering eyes and the fierce grip on her wrist.

"Bars on the window and an outside lock on the door. She died when I was seven, but I can still remember. Great-Aunt Mattie had bats in her belfry. Harmless, they said, but utterly loony. They used to walk her like a dog in the morning and at night."

Katie finally got her wrist loose. She rubbed it gently, edging toward the door.

"I don't see why you stay in here if it upsets you," she told him frankly. "It's like frightening yourself with ghost stories."

"The bars are in the store room," Johnny told her in a trance-like voice. "Nicely tucked away in a mattress of straw. All ready in case of need."

"Why do you keep going on about it?"

"Pap says a fellow is never too young to start thinking about the future and planning a home." Johnny's sudden smile was more chilling than his scowl. His voice fell to almost a whisper. "More than one Stoltzfus hasn't had all his marbles. Maybe this is what's planned for me. Bars on the windows and an outside lock on the door. Maybe this is my future home."

In a panic, Katie fled from the room.

Four

Sugarcreek Budget
Strawberry Schrank, Pa.

November 19, 1977 *Ruth and Hiram Hochstetler have visitors from Virginia, the youngest daughter of Hiram's sister, who came with her husband and baby boy.*

All carriage orders taken in the last eight months by Levi Luke Fisher, and therefore not filled by the time he closed up his shop, have been referred to Ben Beiler, the carriage-maker in Maiden Falls. Those not wanting their buggies from Ben Beiler can get their money refunded.

A quilting bee will be held on Friday next.

Amos had been silent all through Saturday lunch, a silence which infected the rest of the family. Everyone—even Mem—was secretly wondering what he or she had done to displease him.

"Johnny, I have to see you in the parlor," Amos said after the silent prayer that ended their meal.

"Sure, Pap."

His mother looked at him anxiously, and he pantomimed, *I don't know.* He followed his father into the parlor, and Amos carefully closed the door after them.

"Johnny, I have to ask you some questions which maybe will seem strange to you." For the first time in the son's memory, his father looked uncertain and embarrassed. "It's about Levi Luke Fisher."

"Levi Luke!" Johnny's voice, which had recently started to change, rose to a squeal. His heart sank. Had his father found out about his books?

"Levi Luke," affirmed Amos grimly. "There's something I have to find out before Sunday's Preaching. You worked for him lots of times these last couple of years. Did he ever approach you?"

Johnny wet his lips. "Approach me?" he repeated, his voice descending low again and sounding strangely flat. He looked his father in the eye. "How do you mean?"

Amos was sweating as though he were at work in the fields.

"It's a terrible thing to have to ask, but did he ever make immoral suggestions . . . even immoral overtures to you?"

"Of course he didn't!" Johnny flared. "Levi Luke's my friend. He wouldn't do that."

"Johnny, I know you admire Levi Luke. I respected the man myself—a hard worker, a good son, and always willing to give to the needy or lend a helping hand—but I'm sorry to tell you it turns out he is not the righteous, godly man he always seemed. This Sunday at Preaching, he will be put under the *meidung.*"

"The *meidung!*" Johnny breathed. His father spoke of the awesome weapon of the Amish for avoiding contamination with the impure. "Levi is being excommunicated? *Why?*"

"The truth will be told at Preaching," Amos said simply, "when he is asked to confess his sin. But we know already that he has been guilty of impure acts, abominations in the sight of the Lord." He put his hand on Johnny's shoulder in so fleeting and rare a gesture that his son almost thought he had imagined it. "I can only be thankful that his sin stopped short of approaching you."

"So that's what you meant by immoral overtures? I tell you, Levi would never have done that. He's not a bad man, he's a *good* man."

"Johnny, you must believe I wouldn't say this if I didn't know . . . but they were seen, Levi and his hired man, Mark Gruber. They were engaging in an unnatural act."

"What's unnatural about it if the animals do it, too?" Johnny's voice cracked; his eyes teared; he wiped his nose with the back of one hand. "They're both grown men. They didn't harm anyone."

"You don't know what you're saying, Johnny. Man, made in the image of God, is far above the animals. And they could have contaminated the pure with whom they came in contact . . . like you."

"Pap, it's the way they were made, and it ain't catching. If it were, I'd have caught it years ago."

"Gott in Himmel, Johnny, you *knew?"*

"I didn't know. I suspected."

"And you didn't tell?"

"What was there to tell? I only suspected. I wasn't sure. It was none of my business."

"Johnny, it was everybody's business who belongs to the Faith. You should have come to me."

"And maybe borne false witness against my neighbor— my friend. I tell you, I was never *sure."*

Amos tugged at his beard, then shook his head. "You're maybe right, I have to think on it. It's true you can't take away a man's good name for only suspicion."

His father might be rock-hard in following the Faith, but Johnny had to admit that he always tried to be just. "What will happen to Levi Luke, Pap?" he asked in a softened tone.

"The *meidung* doesn't have to be forever. If he confesses and repents openly and doesn't sin again, he will eventually be taken back into the fold."

But Levi Luke did not confess or repent. He stayed

outside at the next Preaching, and the *meidung* was put
on him without his being there. His mother, blind Sarah,
sat tremblingly alongside her niece Lucy Weiss as she
heard her son be excommunicated.

"But he's waiting outside for me in the buggy, Lucy,"
she cried piteously.

"You must not accept a ride or any service from him,
Aunt Sarah. It's best you come home with me."

"I'm not comfortable away from my own home. I know
where everything is placed, so I can walk around without
getting hurt. Levi fixes my meals, he serves me. He talks
to me while I eat, he reads to me while I sit in the evenings.
He never makes me feel like a burden. He's been a good
son to me. No woman here can say she has a better."

Deacon Strubbs came around and took her hand. "We
all feel for you, Sarah, and we'll all pray that soon he'll
be restored to you in the Faith. So long as he's under the
Ban, I think it might be better if you went with Lucy."

"Abandon my Luke in his trouble?"

"He has abandoned godly ways."

Sarah rose from her rocker in the front row. "Then you
must put the *meidung* on me, too, Deacon, because I cannot—I will not—leave my son. A lamp, he has been to me
in my years of darkness; perhaps now, I can lighten his."

Without care for those in his way, Johnny pushed his
way forward from one of the backless benches. He went
to the side of the gallant old woman, took one of her
hands, and put an arm around her. "Sarah, it's Johnny
Stoltzfus, Levi Luke's friend," he said. "Let me take you
out to him. I saw him before from the kitchen window.
He's waiting in the buggy on the roadway."

As he guided her stumbling footsteps, everyone made
way for them. Both men and women wept. Katie sprang
up from her bench when the two reached the door, and
ran after them. She and Johnny together brought Levi
Luke's mother to him.

Five

January 11, 1978 I will try to gather a few lines this cold winter evening, though I have been down four days with the fever and plenty around here are involved with the flu.

Isaac Schrock was to Lancaster, took twenty-six teeth out and got his new dentures in. His son David is doing his chores.

Amos Stoltzfus' adopting of the Kauffman boys (his second cousin Ada's grandsons, John and Gideon) is all legal, and they are now Paul John and Gideon Stoltzfus, his sons as God-given as though by birth. Since Katy and Amos already have their own son, John, aged thirteen and a half, the younger boy is called Paul John, Paul being his dead father's name. The Kauffman girls, Katie and Annie, are being raised like daughters, too, though not adopted. Amos says they will change their names soon enough in marriage.

With two Katies as well as two Johns in the family, it was pretty confusing there for a while until the Sunday breakfast when young Katie accidentally poured coffee from the pot instead of milk from the pitcher over the cornmeal mush and gave everyone a good laugh (especially the hogs that got to eat the cornmeal mush). Ever since then she got called Coffee Katie.

*With five children now calling her Mem, Katy Stoltzfus
says God has been mighty good to her.*

*A quilting bee is planned at Susie Hochstetler's, Wednes-
day for the women and Thursday for the girls.*

Chris Beiler, the Stoltzfuses' hired man, wiped his feet
automatically before he came into her spotless kitchen, but
Katy knew by his face that there was no good news for
her; and no news was bad news.

"I'm sorry, Katy, we talked to Teacher and all his
friends and looked everywhere yet."

Katy rubbed her work-roughened hands against her
black apron. "You tried your all," she said dully. "Where
is Amos at?"

"He took the buggy to town to talk to Deacon Strubbs.
I rode on the mule."

Katy looked out the window. "It's coming on to *spritz*
again; all last night it made down too. He's so thin, all
bones, and his chest is weak; Johnny gets colds settled
on his chest so easy."

As Chris backed out awkwardly, muttering that he
would see to the livestock, Coffee Katie asked her foster
mother, "Do you have one of your headaches, Mem?"

"Ja," Katy Stoltzfus admitted, "my *kopp* hurts."

"Would you let me try and help you?"

"I tried my pills already; they didn't do me no good."

"How about trying a small dose of Katie Kauffman?"
Katie suggested. "Something my mother taught me. She
didn't believe much in pills, you know. She used to work
with her hands to help people in pain." She added a bit
diffidently, "Mommy said I had better hands than hers.
She said anyone could be trained in the work, but that I
had natural healer's hands, which were a gift."

"You never mentioned such a thing before."

Katie reddened, then mumbled, "It just never came up.

Lots of people think it's mumbo-jumbo." With renewed confidence she ordered, "Sit right down in this chair, Mem."

Katy Stoltzfus sat. Her head *was* throbbing with pain, and she didn't think Coffee Katie's treatment could make it any worse.

Coffee Katie stood behind her and put each of five fingertips on either side of Mem's head, spreading them from below her jawline across her temples, gently at first, then pressing harder and harder and finally sweeping her fingers back and forth across the forehead, with her two thumbs exerting pressure on the closed eyelids.

Gradually, under these ministrations, Mem relaxed a little. "Oy, anyhow," she told her foster daughter gratefully, "it really hurts good."

Seeing some of the pain ease out of the tired face, the younger girl ventured an opinion. "You know something, Mem, I think you're wrong about Johnny's chest being weak. He hasn't had a cold in a year, and if he's thin, it's because he's shooting up like a beanpole. When we first came here, he was almost a head shorter than Chris Beiler. Now he's almost a head taller. He's a healthy boy, Mem, and it wouldn't hurt him to get caught in a little rain, but I bet he didn't. I bet he slept nice and snug last night in somebody's barn."

"Coffee Katie, do you know something you're not telling?"

"No, Mem, cross—I give you my word, I don't. But I can't help noticing how unhappy he's been."

"My Johnny is not a happy boy," said Mem sadly.

"He still feels very bitter about Levi Luke Fisher," Katie reminded her, resuming her stroking movements. "He resents that Levi was pushed out of his home and his business and had to go far away to start a new life. And he misses him; they really were friends. Johnny could talk to him in a way . . ." She hesitated.

Katy Stoltzfus smiled faintly. "In a way that he couldn't talk to his own. You think I don't know that?"

She turned in her chair and looked up at Katie. "Did Levi save Johnny's books for him before he left?"

"Wh-what?"

"Coffee Katie, I'm Amish, I live by the Faith, I obey the *Ordnung*—mostly. But I'm a mother, as well as a believer and a wife. You think I don't know my Johnny is different? Without the books, he couldn't—I won't say he couldn't exist, but something in him would snap. I knew that farming would never be enough for Johnny. So I sinned a little . . . if there can be such a thing as a little sin. I looked the other way when he brought the books in and I helped him conceal sometimes—though he never knew it—when he carried them out. I made sure, God forgive me, that *he* never found out. So where are the books now?"

"You know the falling-apart stone house on the east border of Levi Luke's property, right near that old cemetery?"

"*Ja.*"

"When Levi rented out his farm, he didn't include a few acres with that house and the cemetery. The books are there."

"Won't the cold and damp—"

"No," Katie interrupted eagerly, "Levi fixed everything. The windows are boarded up, and he mended the roof so there's one big room that doesn't leak. And he hung insulation all over that room and even put an old sofa in it and a lamp and table. He re-hung the front door and put a lock on it and gave Johnny a key. And he—"

"Don't tell me any more. I found out what I wanted to know, and for Johnny it's *gude.* For me, it's a sin on my conscience—another one. As for Levi Luke . . . I can't make Johnny less unhappy about him. I can't even say that I think the *meidung* was wrong. It may seem cruel, but these are the rules we live by, the same rules for everyone."

"But everyone's not the *same!*" Coffee Katie cried out passionately. "Did you ever think that Johnny minded about the adoption, too? He's jealous, and he's been taught jealousy's wrong, so he's ashamed."

"Why would he mind the adoption? What difference to him?" Katy pulled away from the ministering hands and stood up, looking at her foster daughter in genuine puzzlement. "He's my *soohn.*"

"He was the only kid till we came along. Now he has to share with *us* what belonged only to him for all the years before."

"My Johnny is not so selfish. He may not accept the Faith like I wish he would, but he would never begrudge a home and food and clothing for—"

"Of course he doesn't begrudge us *that.*" At any other time Coffee Katie's rude interruption would have earned her a reprimand. "It's your love he doesn't want to share, yours and Pap's. He'd rather do anything but farm work, but look how hard he works for Amos—how he'll do anything for you. You fuss so over Gideon, but never over Johnny."

"Gideon is a little one, Johnny is near to being a man."

"Oh, Mem!"

For the first time ever, before her foster mother hid her eyes behind her apron, the girl saw tears in Katy Stoltzfus' eyes. She was dry-eyed when she spoke again.

"Maybe I did wrong," she admitted uncertainly, "not to fuss over him too much, even when he was little. I didn't want to get too wrapped up in him; he was so small and sickly, like the three before him who died. The midwife and the doctor both prepared me that I wouldn't get to raise him neither, and I believed them. I never stopped believing or being scared."

"Well, they were idiots," Coffee Katie told her bluntly,

"and you can stop believing them now. He's not little; neither is he sickly. You've raised him to be a strong healthy boy, nearly fourteen. So you can let yourself show you love him."

Before Mem could answer, a heavy step sounded in the hallway. Woman and girl both turned anxiously toward the door. Amos Stoltzfus stood framed in the doorway, unsmiling.

"I just stopped by to tell you your son John is out back, unhitching the horse from the buggy."

Coffee Katie's face became one big wide grin. Katy Stoltzfus murmured a prayer of thanks, then, "Where?" she began. "How—?"

"He hitched rides—in automobiles, yet—all the way to Maryland. Last night he slept in a barn. Today he decided to come back."

"Did he tell you why he left?"

Amos snorted. "I asked him, 'why did you go?' He answers, he doesn't know. I ask him then, 'so why did you come back?' He doesn't know that, neither. So I asked, 'did you know what would happen when you came back?' and that question he didn't answer so *doomb;* to that one he answered, yes. So now you know he's safe, *layg's uff der dish,* put supper ahead—I had no lunch— while I go back to the barn where he's waiting for what he earned."

As Amos turned away, Katy hurried after him.

"Amos, don't . . . Maybe you shouldn't be too hard on the boy?" she urged softly.

He looked at her, astonished. "You mean I shouldn't whip him?"

"Maybe just this once . . ."

"I have a rebellious, disobedient son. He shames us by running away—and you think he shouldn't be punished? What kind of father would be so neglectful of his duty? For far less, let me tell you, my own father thrashed me soundly and I lived to thank him, as God willing, my own son will one day thank me."

Katy bowed her head submissively as he strode out. Coffee Katie muttered audibly, "Don't count on it," and found herself on the receiving end of a smart smack on the bottom from the older Katy's calloused palm.

"Better *me* than *he,* but next time you won't get off so easy. Now no more smart talk; the table set."

There was no talk at all at the supper table that night beyond what the needs of the meal dictated. *Help yourselves to the chicken . . . Reach me the bread . . . Is the apple sauce all? . . . Pass the salt . . . Some more fried potatoes, ain't?*

The children were all aware that more than John's empty place on his father's left—he had been sent supperless to bed—was responsible for the uncomfortably quiet supper.

Amos kept darting strange, searching glances at his wife in her usual place on his right. It was as though he were trying to make up his mind about the worth of a new acquaintance. Katy quietly saw to the needs of the children as well as of Chris Beiler, the hired man, who wolfed down the meal in his usual way, uttering occasional loud belches of appreciation, too wrapped up in his food to be aware of the others' discomfort.

Toward the end of supper, Gideon started fussing and Paul John, with an anxious look at their Mem and Pap, shushed him.

Amos finished a large helping of shoo-fly pie, then signified by a quick look around the table that the meal was over for everyone. He bowed his head for the silent prayer of thanks following a meal, and immediately every other head was bowed respectfully, too.

The moment supper was over, Katy Stoltzfus was first up from her seat, but not as usual to do the clearing and cleaning.

"Coffee Katie, see to the kitchen. Annie, help your sister. Paul John, carry the water to the sink and take out the garbage. Tonight is the quilting party, but first, before I change my apron"—She raised her voice to make sure that Amos, on his way to evening chores, was bound to hear her—"I stop by his room to see my son."

Amos turned back, frowning. "Your son is being punished."

"To spend five minutes with his *mutter* won't make sitting any easier for him."

The children all stared in shock. No one had ever before heard such a note of sarcasm in Katy Stoltzfus' voice, particularly when she spoke to her husband.

It was a shock to Amos, too. Katy was a good Amish wife, her first loyalty to God but otherwise obedient to him. She was boss of the house, true, but his own word was law, and never had she shown herself unwilling to submit to his authority, especially after he had used strong silence to show displeasure about her conduct.

Since it was not meet that a man and wife air their differences in public, certainly not before their children, the nearest Amos could bring himself to do so was roundaboutly.

He looked from his wife to Coffee Katie and then to little Anne. "A good thing it was Paul advised us, 'Let the woman learn in silence with all subjection,' " he remarked heavily and left the room, satisfied by the look of his red-cheeked wife that the last word belonged to him.

He would have been less satisfied about the last word if he had watched his good, submissive wife mount the stairs.

"Paul, yet," she muttered to herself. "It's wonderful strange how a man without a wife always gets commended to know the most about marriage."

Half an hour later Coffee Katie and Annie watched

Mem come out of Johnny's room, wiping her eyes with the backs of her hands even while she smiled. She was ready for the quilting bee in a clean black dress and bustle, a fresh apron, and a big scoop bonnet over her *kapp*.

When there was no longer the sound of her footsteps going down the stairs, and they heard the noisy closing of the front door, Coffee Katie whispered to her sister, "Go to bed, Anne; I'll be back soon."

"If Pap finds out, you'll get a smacking like he gave Johnny."

"He never hits us as hard as the boys. Besides, he won't find out. Go to bed now."

She pushed her sister inside, closed the door, and with a shawl thrown over her arm to cover the basket she carried, slipped noiselessly into Johnny's room.

He was lying on the bed on his stomach, fully dressed, and she could tell—even in the dim light of a single kerosene lamp—that he had been crying, but he didn't look sulky or sneering—not even particularly unhappy.

"It's a regular convention going on in here. What do *you* want?" he asked in the gruff voice he always used with her.

"I brought your supper."

"Did Pap say you could?"

"Of course not, idiot." She looked around the clean bare room, and seeing no better surface, told him, "Shove over, so I can spread the napkin on the bed."

He moved over but still watched suspiciously as she carefully lifted a big dinner plate out of the basket and placed it on the napkin. He swallowed hard, his eyes never leaving her as he watched her place on the plate a piece of fried chicken, a thick slice of ham, some cold boiled potatoes, and a tomato already cut in half. From a separate package came a quarter of an apple pie and a jar of apple cider.

"Aren't you hungry?" she asked as he half-sat, half-lay, still staring up at her.

"Hungry? I'm starving."

"So?" she said, like his mother. "Eat, then. Reach and help yourself. *Dee schnide opp ge numma.*"

It was invitation enough. He fell on the simple meal like a ravenous beast. There was no conversation between them till every crumb was gone and he had thrown back his head to pour the last drop of cider down his throat.

Like a careful *hausfrau,* Coffee Katie folded the napkin and returned it to the basket with the plate, then brushed a few stray crumbs off the bed.

She noticed when John stood up that he winced slightly.

"Did he hurt you bad?"

"Hurt? A *schtrap,* with Amos Stoltzfus wielding it like the right hand of God?" he asked sarcastically. "How could such a thing do more than tickle?"

"Take off your shirt. Lie down on your stomach. I'll help you," she said.

"You! How?"

"Do it."

He did it.

There were half a dozen red welts on his back and shoulders, but no broken skin. Amos was a concerned father who would hurt but never harm.

To John's surprise, Katie's hands were winter-cold when she laid them on him but quickly warmed, almost as though each spot she touched on his body was a separate small furnace providing its own heat. With the heat came an easing of the pain.

After ten minutes, Johnny rolled over, swearing an oath that, if Amos had heard it, would have earned him more of the same. "I hardly feel it anymore!" he exclaimed in wonderment. "In Salem, Massachusetts they would have burned you for a witch."

Katie said happily, "Does any place else on you hurt?"

Johnny got off the bed and actually grinned at her. Other than the two books that appeared at the bottom of the walnut chest every week, it was his first sign of friendliness since she had stepped across the Stoltzfus threshold.

"Only the couple of licks that landed on my backside," he said, "but I'd better keep my trousers up and your hands off *there,* because it would take a lot of explaining if anyone walked in on us."

"Johnny Stoltzfus!" Coffee Katie bent over the basket, her face beet-red. She hadn't known he was capable of any such natural kind of bawdy humor.

She turned toward the door, her basket once again covered by the shawl.

"Coffee Katie?"

"Yes?"

"Thank you."

"You're welcome."

"Katie," he said again, sounding so subdued, her hand dropped off the door knob and she turned around.

"Something else?"

"You know why I went away, don't you?"

"Because the Kauffman kids won't go away and Levi Luke did?"

"That was part of it . . . the smallest part. I thought out there . . ."

"I can't hear you."

"I thought," he mumbled, "I wouldn't have to worry out there about bars on the window. But the bars kept pulling me back."

"Oh, no, they didn't, Johnny Stoltzfus. Whether you admit it or not, the people you love pulled you back."

"Maybe. Well, yeah." He shifted awkwardly around on his feet. "My *mutter* stopped by for a minute." He was mumbling again "She—she said she wanted me to know she loved me and that it would break her heart to lose me. We would never talk of it again, but just this once, she had to say it." He gave Coffee Katie a small, apologetic smile. "She said she loves me more than the rest of you put together."

"I know."

"She told you, too?"

"Of course not. It was plain to anyone who ever watched her."

"I didn't realize, not ever. Do you know, Katie, she blushed all over when she said it, like she was confessing a sin at Preaching?"

"She's been Plain all her life; it's hard for her to say such things. *Your* mistake was thinking that because she didn't say them, she didn't feel them."

"I guess."

"Are you happy now, John?"

He took his time answering. Then, "Happy and miserable both," he said slowly. "She freed me and she trapped me all at the same time. I don't belong, and she made it harder for me when I leave."

"I know," said Coffee Katie, her own face reflecting the pain in his.

"Coffee Katie, at least let's you and me be friends."

Basket and all, she flew across the room to hug him briefly. "You *glutz kopp*. From the day you gave me those first two books, I've always been your friend, Johnny Stoltzfus."

Six

Sugarcreek Budget
Strawberry Schrank, Pa.

April 15, 1980 *Over two hundred attended the wedding of Louise Beachey and Levi Hertzler, where there was more excitement than even the wedding when Susan Stuzman's baby decided in the middle to come early and no time to get her to the hospital, so there was a wedding and a birth in the same morning. Susan and her husband Henry John are the parents of a little girl, now in an incubator at the hospital, but doing fine.*

Showers

We wish to announce a household and tool shower for our (former) hired man Chris Beiler, who was for five years a member of our household and always dependable, cheerful, and hard-working; so he deserves the good luck that came to him with his uncle in Canada's legacy that allowed him to buy his own farm on the Beltville Road, but no money left over for much else. We will start the giving with a plow, a manure spreader, a bed, a kitchen table and four chairs. Anything else, large or small, will be greatly appreciated.

Mr. & Mrs. Amos Stoltzfus

* * *

Amos and Katy Stoltzfus never admitted to each other how much they enjoyed their lunch time after Chris Beiler left. With the five children all at school, the half hour— sometimes willingly extended by talk to forty minutes— was a pleasant break in the day. They could make plans, discuss problems, talk over family news without the noise of gobbling and belching, which was Chris' way of show-ing appreciation for good food, and without a pair of sharp ears listening in on what were, after all, purely Stoltzfus concerns.

The privacy of their talk was sweet, almost like being in bed, Katy reflected one day. She jumped a little as Amos cleared his throat. Had he read her thoughts, maybe, and could such thoughts be wrong?

"I have been thinking about something, and already I discussed it with my father. He gives me the right I can manage without another hired man. When I took Chris on, I had only one son; now I got three."

"But Gideon isn't even six, and Paul John is just past eight. How much help can they be to you?"

"Enough, enough for now," Amos answered in high good humor. "You forget, in a couple of weeks our Johnny will be sixteen, and then soon it's goodbye to the school books and he's a full-time farmer. When I need, I can hire by the day instead of permanent. I told John already, for his birthday he can have a new calf or heifer to raise for his own."

"Did he mind about leaving school?"

"What's to mind? I gave permission he could stay on through end of term, that's an extra three months. I can manage without till then."

Katy sighed. Amos was an Amishman, not only heart and soul but to his very fingertips. He loved his fields, the earth he walked on, the same soil his fathers had tilled one hundred years before him. He disdained all book-learning beyond what a farmer's daily life required and the law dictated. He could not see—*would* not see—that he had fathered a son in every way different from himself.

Katy sat silent for a minute, then spoke up with unusual firmness.

"It's too late for this birthday," she said, "but it won't be too late for his next if we put in the order *recht opp*. I think we should give him a courting buggy, yet, and the new grey horse."

"The new grey horse!" Amos looked at her as though she had lost her mind. The new grey horse was a fine, spirited animal, the best in their stable. "A courting buggy, I give you the right," he conceded, "though I never seen our Johnny has much interest in the girls yet, but why the new grey horse?"

Katy debated only a minute the thought of answering honestly, "Because our Johnny needs something to take his mind off the grief of leaving school." It was no argument to use with her husband.

Instead, she shrugged elaborately. "Since when does a father know till the last when his son has his eye on a girl? And what's so strange John should get a courting buggy next year? It's usual, ain't, for a father—if he can afford it," she put in slyly, "to give his son, when he reaches sixteen, an open carriage and a good animal?"

Amos would have thought it sinful to allow worldly pride to influence his actions, but nevertheless he was not pleased with the notion that anyone should think he could not afford to give his older son what other boys his age received.

"The grey horse, then!" He pantomimed expressively with raised hands and raised shoulders, as though he were giving in to an unreasonable request from his wife.

"Women!" he muttered with unusual humor. "Any man who claims to understand one, I can tell you, has a misunderstanding right there. Are you anxious to get rid of your son, you're pushing him off onto the girls so young?"

"No," Katy blurted out, "I'm trying to push him off a little from Coffee Katie."

"Coffee Katie! *Our* Coffee Katie?" It was plain the idea had never dawned on Amos.

"Haven't you noticed how wonderful close they are?"

"Would it be so bad, Katy, once they got older? They're not Swartz-cousins."

"No, not Swartz-cousins, but you were second-cousin to her mother, and we were second-cousins to each other; and with the Kauffmans, and on both sides our parents, it was the same." Her voice broke. "Three babies I lost, and Martha and Paul died young. Better for Johnny and Coffee Katie they should both marry from outside the family."

Amos cleared his throat loudly. "I think maybe you *drowel* for nothing. They're close, like brother and sister, but not for courting." His big, rough hand touched Katy's briefly. "So, if it will make you feel better, I'll go to the shop tomorrow to order a courting carriage, and in the meanwhiles Johnny can borrow the closed carriage from us pretty much always when he needs, and drive the grey horse."

"You're a *gude mon,* Amos Stoltzfus," Katy told him softly.

"Well, well, I'd better go, ain't, the work doesn't stand still," said Amos, ignoring her remark.

He left the kitchen without another word, but she could tell by his step that he was pleased, though he would have considered it improper to acknowledge it.

Two months before his seventeenth birthday, John was proudly driving his spanking-new open carriage with the grey horse, and Coffee Katie was most often the girl riding beside him when he took off from the Stoltzfus farm.

His mother was not alarmed at this, however, for it was

Amish custom to be highly secretive about *rumspringa*—running around. If a boy planned to be with a particular girl at a frolic or singing, he would never dream of escorting her there. Instead he would bring his own sister, while the girl he had his eye on would be brought by her brother or another relative. Once arrived at the social event, an unobtrusive change of partners could take place.

Katy and Amos never discovered that when their son and foster daughter went to an auction, a softball game, or an apple-peeling party, there was no change of partners. Johnny Stoltzfus, reluctant farmer and unbelieving Amishman, after his one abortive run-away, had bided his time about leaving his home and family. Next time, he would do it right. Without consciously formulating the decision, he avoided any action that might get him tied up to a proper Amish girl. To do so would be to chain himself forever to Strawberry Schrank.

Coffee Katie—his sister, his friend—was not only a safe companion, but their minds were in harmony. Unknown to anyone except Katy Stoltzfus—and even she never suspected how often it was used—they had created a private home, a secret school of their own in the big downstairs room of the old falling-down stone house that Levi Luke had made habitable for them before he left Strawberry Schrank.

When they were supposedly using Johnny's courting buggy for *rumspringa,* more often than not they were at the Fisher property in what they laughingly called the Levi Luke School House.

During good weather the grey horse, Einstein, was tied to the willow in the ancient cemetery a few yards in back of the house. When it was cold, they brought him right inside with them.

The room still had the same old sofa and scarred table that Levi Luke had left for them and, of course, the precious bookcase, with a piece of oilcloth thrown over the front for extra protection of the books. Over the years they had added more kerosene lamps, wooden chairs to push to the table so it could be used as a desk, and a small chest for their papers, notebooks, pencils, and pens. Her framed honorable mention from a short story contest and the medallion Katie had gotten from the American Legion for second prize in a patriotic essay contest hung lopsided on nails in the wall. Johnny's big trophy of a geometric figure on top of an atlas stood in the center of the crumbling brick mantel over the fireplace. He had won it for inventing a mathematics game that Mr. Hertz, the lapsed Amish man who had taught them during Johnny's last year of school, had sent to the state Science Fair.

Mr. Hertz had realized his very first week as schoolmaster that Johnny Stoltzfus was a natural mathematical genius, and he was appalled that such a mind was destined to be cut off from all education at age sixteen.

The teacher's first impulsive plan had been to go see Amos Stoltzfus and try to persuade the father that his son should not only continue with his education, but go on to college as well. Johnny's bitterly amused refusal that he should do this, and his own reflection on the inflexible Amish code, persuaded him that he would be wasting his time.

Without guilt, he suggested and arranged for correspondence courses that would allow Johnny to obtain a high school equivalency degree by the time he was eighteen.

Using Katie as a courier, Mr. Hertz smuggled American and world history and English literature as well as mathematics books to his former pupil. Since their plans were no secret to him, he also sent newspapers so both of them would know about the outside world they were one day going to be a part of.

Once in a while, Mr. Hertz would stop by the Levi Luke School House on a Saturday night and spend a few hours with the two. Those were magical evenings for all of them.

The moment he appeared, they produced the pages and pages that had been added to their never-ending list of questions. They discussed the books they had read, then listened, enthralled, while Mr. Hertz talked of politics and religion—all religions, not just the narrow world of the Amish. They spoke of theatre in New York, grape-picking in California, strikes in Detroit, hippie life in Boston.

For almost twenty memorable months, since they could not yet go out into the world, Mr. Hertz brought the world to them. When, to their grief, he accepted a teaching job in Cambridge, Massachusetts, he arranged for Johnny's correspondence courses to be mailed to Mike Maseratti, who owned the local garage.

Mike was no stranger to such arrangements. Half a dozen conforming, conservative Amish fathers were totally unaware that he stored cars owned by their young rebellious sons on the empty lot next to his garage.

Coffee Katie and Mr. Hertz suspected that Johnny Stoltzfus was unlike these other young men in their final season of sowing some wild oats. His destiny was different. They would eventually sell their cars, join the church, grow their beards, and become conforming and conservative in turn. Not Johnny.

Just as much as Katie (who had come from outside), he was a square peg in the round world of the Amish. The two of them lived a life they could never accept, preparing for the day when they were in a position to reject it.

Seven

Sugarcreek Budget
Strawberry Schrank, Pa.

June 10, 1982 *A second accident in a month has struck the Moses Smucker family. Not so long ago it was the middle daughter Deborah who fell downstairs and broke her arm; now we get word the youngest son Willy was involved in a buggy crash over Bird-In-Hand way and has three cracked ribs, a broken nose, and torn ligaments in his legs but, thank God, no internal injuries.*

About a dozen of our youths in the Lancaster area will shortly be leaving their homes to serve in different hospitals, some in other states than Pennsylvania, as alternative to registering for selective service. Among those who will be leaving is our own Johnny Stoltzfus, the son of Amos and Katy, who naturally wouldn't register for the army, but is happy to contribute doing hospital service. He has all our heartiest good wishes for the next two years away from home and for a safe return to his family who will miss him. . . .

* * *

Basking Reade Hospital
Maryland
July 2, 1982

Dear Mem and Pap and all the rest of the Family,

Well, I have been working here long enough to tell you truly that all the farm work has paid off for me. I am what they call a patient orderly in a ward for old folks, lots of them kind of childish. They mostly use us Amish and the Mennonite boys, too, for orderlies, because they say we've got the muscle it takes.

I have to do a lot of lifting of the patients (for bathing them, dressing them, making their beds, transferring them from beds to wheelchairs or tables to go to the operating room, or being someone to lean on when they walk). It may not sound like much, but it takes muscle, all right. You'd be surprised how heavy a little frail old man can seem when he puts his full weight on you.

I don't mind; in fact, I enjoy. They're so pitiful, some of them, and so alone and so grateful for any little help or attention. It makes me schtarn wedder base, *I can tell you, when I see the nurses impatient or sometimes even downright mean with the patients, as though they can help being old or sick or dropping their food. I have to admit I wasn't so sweet-tempered to one of those nurses yesterday when she yelled at Mr. Kellerman, as though he wet his bed on purpose. She shut up when I said, "What are you so mad about? I'm the one changing the sheets."*

Well, enough about that.

I live three blocks from the hospital in what's called a Garden Quad, which is a bunch of brick buildings that form a square outside which has a little bit of green and trees and a few flowers in it. Our particular building (apartment house) is owned by the hospital, so most of us who live in it are Amish or Mennonite, too.

I live in a two-bedroom apartment with another patient orderly, Jacob Lentz (he's from Lebanon) and Mark Perrot, who's a Quaker from Philadelphia. We drew lots, and Mark and I share the bigger bedroom and Jacob has the small one to himself. We have a big parlor (they say 'living room' here) and a small kitchen that doesn't get much use, since we eat most of our meals at the hospital, which between you and me is enough to make a well person sick. What I wouldn't give for some good home-cooking, Mem. . . .

Basking Reade Hospital

Dear Folks:

After all these months here, I can still say I find the work interesting and not too hard. If I'm losing weight, which Mem worries about, it's not because I'm over-worked, but under-fed. Not that they don't give you enough food, but who can stand this stuff when he's used to good Pennsylvania-Dutch cooking, to say nothing of baking . . . Mem, in my sleep I taste your apple pies and your shoo-fly pies and even those wonderful dry half-moon pies we used to have at Preaching when we were kids . . .

I know that you can't travel such a long way to see me, it being close to harvest time, but if you could maybe spare Coffee Katie for a couple of days and send her with the biggest basket you can find, all filled up with your home-cooked food?

Yesterday I had a funny experience on the Ward. There was. . . .

Basking Reade Hospital

Dear Mem and Pap,

You don't have to worry about Katie. I can make

arrangements for her to stay in the nurses' dormitory. I spoke to the head matron in charge here, and she said she would be glad to look after her. All I have to know is the day and time to meet her train.

I've told Jacob and Mark all about the food they'll soon be tasting and their tongues hung out. They can't wait. Neither can I. . . .

Katie came down the train steps, a huge basket over her left arm and an overstuffed cardboard suitcase dangling from her right hand. She wore her old blue dress, but her apron was missing and so was her *kapp,* both of them tucked somewhere out of sight. She'd probably gotten rid of them as soon as she was on the train.

Johnny grinned. That was his Katie, all right!

As soon as she saw him, she screeched out his name, and as he ran along the platform, she let go of the suitcase and put down her basket, the better to throw her arms around him. Johnny put his hands on her waist, forgetting his usual Amish reserve, and swung her round and around.

"Come on," he said presently, putting her down again and picking up the basket and suitcase. "My roommate Mark's waiting outside in his car."

"A car! Oh Johnny, a real live car again!" she sighed ecstatically.

While the basket and suitcase were shoved into the seatless back, Johnny introduced his friend.

"I'm sorry the car's so beat up," Mark apologized as the three of them squeezed into the front, Katie in the middle.

"If it's got four wheels and it goes, that's good enough for me," she assured him happily.

Mark stole a look into the golden face with the eager blue eyes; he noticed the odd-colored silky lemon hair, half piled on top of her head, half tumbling down her back. He gulped. What a contrast to that baggy dress, and how like a brother not to mention that this particular sister was a living doll!

"Are we going to the nurses' dorm first?" Katie asked, her eyes darting from one side to the other, anxious not to miss a single thing as they drove along a busy business street.

Johnny laughed uproariously. "Don't be a goop! You're not going to the nurses' dorm at all. I only said that to pacify the home front. You're staying with us. I'm sleeping on the couch, and Jacob's taking my bed so you can have his room. *Gott in Himmel,* Katie, get your elbow out of Mark's face . . . do you want to land us all in the hospital as patients?"

"Sorry," said Katie, continuing to hug Johnny impenitently, "but I must admit that a dormitory with a *matron* in charge sounded a bit—a bit—"

"Old Johnny said you wouldn't go for that," put in Mark, "but he thought it was a nice sober touch to pacify the parents."

Katie sat, chewing her lower lip, and Johnny, after a quick sidelong look, advised her quietly, "Katie, you have exactly two and a half days of freedom. Lay off the Amish guilt or you might just as well be back in Strawberry Schrank. When in Rome, and all that."

"You're right. Isn't it *awful,*" she asked them both, "how some of the very things I hate the most sort-of— of—"

"Seep?" suggested Mark.

"Yes, that's *exactly* it." Katie accepted the word gratefully. "They *seep* right into my own thinking without my even being aware of it. Well, I won't let it happen here."

Having disposed of that worry, she said in her usual buoyant way, "Do you have much time off while I'm here, Johnny? Have you made any plans?"

"I've got the whole time off, and the first plan is to

get you out of that awful dress. You can also forget about whatever ones you have in the suitcase—"

"The suitcase is more food, *glutz kopp*. It's so heavy my arms nearly came out of the sockets. All I've got is a change of stockings and things at the bottom of the basket."

"Good," said Johnny callously. "We can certainly use the food, and no one wants to see your clothes. I picked out a nurse your size, and everyone on the ward lent something, if not from herself, from a sister or a roommate. You've got a whole wardrobe to choose from, hanging in Jacob's closet."

Johnny hadn't exaggerated. Jacob's closet contained blouses, skirts, slacks, pants suits, party dresses, a plastic raincoat, a wool jacket with a fur-lined hood, and a dozen pairs of shoes, sneakers, and boots in assorted sizes because he hadn't known her shoe size.

Everywhere Katie went for the next two days, she was greeted with compliments:

Gee, those slacks look better on you than they do on me.

I knew that dress would be perfect for you when Johnny described your coloring.

You may as well keep my blouse. I'm tired of it anyhow, and it looks great on you.

The night of her arrival, there was a big party in one of the orderly's apartments across the quad. Katie wore a blue velvet pants suit with a white lace blouse and flat navy suede sandals that were just a little tight. Not knowing what else to do with her hair, and for the sheer pleasure of not having it all scraped back under a *kapp*, she had combed it out loose and free.

Mark's eyes bugged out when he saw her. "You look stunning, Katie," he told her sincerely; then aside to Johnny, "How old did you say she was?"

"Sixteen . . . maybe almost seventeen, now I come to think of it."

"Wow! A few more years . . ."

As his voice died away, Johnny looked at Katie with new eyes. He'd packed a considerable lot of living into the months at Basking Reade. Mark was right. In a few more years . . .

But right now she was still his own little foster sister . . . his best friend . . . good old dependable Katie. "Come on, the fun's waiting."

Katie adored the party. Maybe the music was kind of loud, but oh, the dancing! The room was heavy with smoke, but the apartment had a balcony; she could always run out there for a few minutes and fill up her lungs with fresh air. Everyone seemed to be having such a good time. When they weren't dancing, they were singing; and she hadn't come across so many talkative people in years. It was wonderful.

The best part of it all was the laughter. Life didn't seem to be real and earnest here, but one long continuous joke. It was marvelous. Katie's laughter trilled out as often and as infectiously as anyone else's. What matter if every boy seemed to have as many arms as an octopus? They accepted gracefully the firm way she fended them off. So what if they drank a bit too much? Tomorrow, Johnny assured her, they'd all be sober.

She was shocked to discover her most insistently amorous swain, Reuben Glitz, was from a strict Old Order Amish fellowship in Ohio. Still, Johnny, having rescued her from the clasp of Reuben's muscular arms and the wet rubbery kisses he was dabbing all over her neck, said not to mind; old Reuben always got like this when he had a joint or two . . . he'd apologize nicely tomorrow.

The next day their picnic plans were rained out, so she and Johnny, Mark and Jacob and a few other girls had lunch at a seafood restaurant; and then they all took Katie to see her first James Bond movie, a revival of *From Russia With Love*. There was another party in the quad that night, but the lustre of the boys who had seemed so glamorous the night before had been a little dimmed by her first encounter with Sean Connery. Especially the panting, palpitating Reuben.

"If you put one hand on me again," Katie told him firmly, as he made his fourth attempt to do so, "I shall kick you. Right in the *bolla*," she added sweetly, looking him straight in the eye.

Reuben's jaw dropped; his perspiring face turned rosy. He looked around, as though wondering what a nice Amish boy like him was doing in such a place. He was next seen hastily exiting the party.

Katie happily danced on till the small hours of the morning.

"It's the best time I've ever had in my life!" she said to Johnny at the railroad station when they were saying goodbye on the third day.

"Well, don't turn on the waterworks, we'll do it again soon. Every couple of months or so, I'll send out an SOS the way I did this time and get you here on a visit."

"Promise?"

"I promise. For God's sakes, stop all that carry-on in public."

"A little sisterly hug and kiss," jeered Katie, "and you kid yourself, you don't act Amish."

> *1160 Garden Court*
> *Basking Reade, Md.*
> *March 9, 1983*

Dear Mem and Pap,
  Sorry not to have written for a while, but I wasn't feeling so well for a few weeks, and now it turns out I have a bad case of the flu. The hospital offered me

a bed when it was diagnosed yesterday, but the truth is, when it comes to hospitals, I would rather be an orderly than a patient. So I'm in bed at the apartment, and Mark and Jacob look after me in their spare time.

Yesterday one of the older nurses sent me something they call 'Jewish penicillin.' (That's a joke for home-made chicken soup, which happened to be good, almost as good as yours, Mem.)

I ache from head to foot and everywhere in between. I'm sorry for all the times I laughed at her about them because, boy, could I use Coffee Katie's healing hands. . . .

"Mem couldn't wait to speed me on the way after your letter came, but why on earth did you say you were at home when you're here in the hospital?"

"Katie, use your *kopp.*" Johnny coughed raspingly. "If I said I was in the hospital, why would they think I needed *you?*"

"My heroic brother! Thinking of me even on your bed of pain. So what can I do for you?"

"Go away. I'm tired. I ache. Your voice hurts. All I want is sleep. Mark's off today; he's going to take you out to lunch and a movie. Jacob's in charge tomorrow. Your clothes . . ." He started coughing again.

"Shut up. You're straining your throat." Katie put her hands against his cheeks and then slid her fingers through his hair and across his forehead. "You *sent* for my healing hands; you're going to *get* my healing hands."

"You better *had* get out of Strawberry Schrank," muttered Johnny, "because you'll never make a proper Amish wife, you bossy little shrew." But even as he was talking, her fingertips seemed to find the exact points of pain at his temples and pick out and work on the precise sore spots just above the backs of his ears.

When a nurse came into the room with his sleeping pill, he was blissfully unconscious; and he slept all through the argument between Katie and the nurse about the folly of awakening him for the purpose of swallowing a pill that would put him back to sleep again.

"I already knocked him out for the next few hours," insisted Katie.

"How?" asked the nurse with deep suspicion.

"With my magic fingers and my magic words," Katie said in a sepulchral whisper, waving her work-red, work-roughened hands in the air and wriggling her fingers while she recited a meaningless mumbo-jumbo of Pennsylvania-Dutch words in the manner of a witch-woman delivering an incantation. Pill-cup in hand, the nurse fled to report to her superior.

Katie jumped at the sound of light applause from the doorway. Mark stood there, laughing. "Ready for lunch?" he asked.

"You bet."

He tiptoed over for a look at Johnny. "Will he really sleep for a couple of hours?"

"We'll ask him tonight when we get back from the movies. You *are* going to take me to the movies after lunch, aren't you?" she wheedled.

"While your brother's on his bed of pain."

Katie just grinned.

"You heartless little minx. Okay. Okay." He grinned back. "We're going to the movies."

> *Basking Reade Hospital*
> *October 15, 1983*

Dear Family,
    It sure was good to see you all and to see and smell the Pennsylvania countryside again. There's no

place as pretty as home, and filling the silos, working in the fields, and stripping the tobacco sure seemed almost easy after the work here. To say nothing of eating like a king!

In just the short time I'm back in the hospital, I feel as though my energy is more drained here than by anything I did on the farm.

After a three-week holiday like I've just had, it's impossible for me to get any more time off for Thanksgiving or Christmas. Besides, holiday times they're always short-staffed at the hospital. It sure would feel good if I had someone from home with me then—or even in the new year. . . .

December 17, 1983

Dear Johnny:

I'll be in Basking Reade the day before Christmas. My train gets in at four-forty P.M. Besides all the usual sustenance, your mother is expecting me to bring—I swear to you—a full dozen *apple pies! I've been practicing walking with* The Martyrs' Mirror *on my head like the African maidens. Since I have only one pair of hands, that's the only way I figure I can carry them.*

Would you be a darling and ask Rita Slade to buy me a new blouse, preferably pale blue or cream, to go with the pants suit she gave me? Size twelve. No more than fifteen dollars. I'll pay her back when I get there. I have lots and lots of egg money saved, plus some of my salary from my mawd *jobs this past winter that Pap gave me before he put the rest away for my dowry.*

I get nervous when I think how soon I'll have to tell him there will be no need of a dowry.

Listen, Johnny, I love the parties and all that, but put aside just a few hours this time so we can talk,

*just the two of us. We'll have a whole ten days this
time, which is plenty of time for both.*

*I can hardly wait, and in the meantime say hello
to Mark and Jacob for me and . . .*

On the fifth day after her arrival in Basking Reade,
Johnny came off the night shift at 6 A.M. and was unsurprised to find Katie waiting for him in the hospital lobby.

They went down the block to the twenty-four hour diner
and, having given their orders to the sleepy waitress,
Johnny lit up a cigarette. "So you've finally got me
alone," he said, smiling faintly. "So talk."

"I wish you'd put out that foul cigarette!"

Johnny made the clucking sound that his mother always
used to express mild irritation. "My, don't we sound righteously Amish!" he said mockingly. "Katie, doesn't it ever
strike you how hypocritical that rule—among others—is?
Pipes have the Lord's blessing and tobacco is one of our
chief cash crops. To smoke a cigarette is a sin, but producing what corrupts others is allowable."

"I'm not concerned with your sinning," Katie said
crossly, "but you happen to be smoking right in my face,
and it makes me cough. It also stinks. Do you think it's
going to be easy just breaking off the habit when you go
home?"

"I'm not going home," said Johnny quietly.

"Not at all?"

"Not at all." His voice roughened suddenly. "What are
you looking so shocked about, as though it comes as some
great surprise? When my time at the hospital is up in
June, I'm going straight to Boston. Mr. Hertz has arranged
for me to rent a room with a friend of his who teaches
at Boston U. With my experience here, I shouldn't have
any trouble getting night work at a hospital. I've been

making applications for college scholarships these last six months."

"Don't you have to take college tests?"

He crushed out the offending cigarette. "I flew up to Boston and took my SATs last winter. Mr. Hertz arranged that, too. I did pretty well on the verbal and I got one of the highest math scores ever recorded," he said matter-of-factly. "I won't have any trouble getting in somewhere for the September semester. Just as soon as my plans are definite, I'll write home. I don't want to do it too soon, because you do realize, don't you," he asked with a kind of savagery, "that *you* won't be allowed to visit me anymore once I do?"

"No, I—"

"Christ, Coffee Katie, did you think it was just complete cowardice on my part? Okay, I admit it's going to be easier in a letter than face to face. But if I go home to do it, they'll put the *meidung* on me."

"Johnny, they can't. You never took Baptism."

"I'm not talking about the official Church *meidung*. I'm talking about Amos Stoltzfus' private excommunication," he said excitedly. "You know my father, Katie. You know the code he lives by. You're a dreamer. Come down to earth. Do you think that if I told him in person he would give me his good wishes and say, come home whenever you can, fellow. Like hell he would! I'd be cut off from them, Katie. In my heart I know it's going to happen. But I thought if perhaps I don't give him a chance to say the words he'll be too stubborn to take back . . . if I maybe just keep on writing every month, as though nothing had gone wrong between us—even if I don't get answers—after a year or two I might come on a visit and see if they can accept me. Anyhow, it's worth a try."

"I'm sorry, Johnny," she said softly. "You're probably right."

"How about you?" he asked. "You'll be eighteen soon. Will you leave when I do? Do you still want to write?"

"Yes to both questions. I still want to write more than anything, but I'll have to take any kind of job that will pay the rent and try to go to night school."

"You do know I'll help you any way I can. Do you want to join me in Boston, just in the beginning?"

"I don't think so, Johnny. I think I'll take the plunge right away and go straight to New York. I have to see . . . and . . . well . . . I have to talk to Annie, see how she feels, if she wants to go there."

"Coffee Katie Kauffman, talk about *glutz kopps!*"

"What's that supposed to mean?"

"Your sister Annie is just where she wants to be. She's a contented little prig. She out-Amishes any Amish-born I ever met."

"You've always been unfair about Annie!" Katie flared.

"And you've always been blind, wilfully blind."

"We've got so little time together, perhaps for a long while. Don't let's waste time arguing, Johnny." She smiled at him with just a hint of tears in her blue eyes. "Friends, Johnny?"

"Ja, Katie, with you, friends *als."*

Katie Kauffman
c/o Maseratti Garage
Main Street
Strawberry Schrank, Pa.

April 15, 1986

Dear Katie:

I got my letter of acceptance into the Horton Business College today. A full scholarship—room, board, and tuition. I won't have to stay with Mr. Hertz's friend, and I won't need a hospital job. I can make ends meet nicely with what I have put by now, and working in the summers. It's like a dream come true. I've never been so happy in my life, so I had to sit right down and tell the person who means most to me and who has shared all my happier times.

You know, don't you, Coffee Katie, that the hard part is still to come? In a couple of weeks, I'm going to write my letter home, telling Mem and Pap. I just wanted you to be prepared for when it comes. . . .

"What's with you, Coffee Katie?" Mem asked in exasperation as the coffee pot slid from Katie's dishcloth onto the linoleum-covered floor. "For the last week you're acting like a cat on a bed of hot coals."

Before Coffee Katie could answer, Annie came flying down the steps and into the kitchen. "Mem, there's a police car at the fence and two policemen walking up to the house."

Mem dropped the plate she was washing back into the pan of soapy water. "Dear *Gott!* He's been in a buggy accident on the way to market."

They all three ran to the front of the house and got the door open as the two policemen came up the steps.

"Ma'am, is this the house of Amos Stoltzfus?"

"Yes. He's been in an accident?"

"No, ma'am, we got a call from the state police in Maryland asking for a message to be delivered about a John Stoltzfus."

"He's my son. He's hurt?"

"There was a fire, ma'am, in an apartment across the way from him, and he and some friends saved the lives of an elderly couple. But your son was injured."

"Is it serious?" Katie demanded fiercely.

"They said to tell you that his life is in no danger. We were to assure you of that," he addressed the older woman, whose color seemed to be returning. She had gone dead-white for a minute.

"Thank you, you're very kind," she said in the Pennsylvania Dutch.

The two policemen nodded awkwardly, and the three women retreated inside the house. Annie was sobbing noisily.

"Stop that!" her sister told her firmly. "Go help Mem pack a suitcase. They'll want to leave as soon as Pap gets home."

"Where are you going?"

"To pack for myself. I'm going, too. Johnny will need me."

Amos thought she should stay home with the younger ones, but Katy Stoltzfus agreed that their Johnny would want Coffee Katie. So a neighbor widow woman moved in, and the three left by railroad within a few hours.

They went straight to the hospital, where Johnny lay, his hands and arms all wrapped in bandages. He was conscious but all drugged up, and after a short visit they saw they were only tiring him, so they accepted the nurse's tactful suggestion that the visit be brief.

As they turned to go, Johnny called hoarsely, "Katie, K-K-Katie."

She hurried back to his bed.

"L-letter," he told her low and huskily. "L-lying on the t-table. D-don't let them s-see n-now."

She nodded her understanding. "I'll take care of it, Johnny." He looked up at her gratefully, then his eyes closed.

The moment Mark—given time off to do it—brought them from the hospital to the apartment, she started looking for the letter. It wasn't in the bigger bedroom, being given over by the boys for the use of Mr. and Mrs. Stoltzfus. She found it on a small end table next to the couch, attached to a clipboard.

When Amos and Katy went to bed, she read it
swiftly . . .

Dear Mem and Pap,
   *Writing this letter to you is the hardest thing I
have ever done in my life because I know that what
I have to tell you will bring you deep grief.*
   *I am not coming home, not to live. I'll never make
a farmer, Pap. I don't want to be one. Just as I'll
never make an Amishman because I don't accept the
Ordnung or the way of life. I can never take Baptism.*
   I intend to go to college in Boston, but I hope . . .

That was as far as he had gotten, but it was far enough,
Katie knew, to break his parents' hearts. Someday he
might still have to do it, but not now with him lying in
the hospital . . .

She tore the letter into shreds and flushed them down
the toilet.

The next day when Mem and Pap went to the hospital,
a nurse came hurrying to show them a sheaf of newspaper
clippings.

"It was a front-page story," she told them, sure they
would be pleased and proud. "See—this is him on the
stretcher being put in the ambulance. You can see his face
clearly."

"Our Johnny's face in a newspaper picture, yet!" cried
Katy Stoltzfus in distress.

"But he saved those old people's lives. He and his
friends made a human ladder, but Johnny was the one to
get them through the window. And then he went back for
the cat. The City Council already voted him a medal. It's
all there in the story."

Amos returned the clippings to the nurse. "My son did
good, his family's content. Medals he doesn't need, nor

newspapers to puff him up with pride," he told her brusquely.

"He couldn't help having his picture taken unconscious, Pap." Coffee Katie tried to tease him out of his displeasure. "And he doesn't have to accept the medal. They have different ways here," she said excusingly.

"Oy, anyhow." Amos shook his head in disdainful disbelief. "They sure do."

It was hard while they were at the hospital to fend off the newspaper people who wanted follow-up stories on the orderly that one reporter had dubbed the "Conscientious Hero." It was even harder keeping his parents from discovering that the offending medal had already been awarded at his bedside when Johnny was half asleep. A nurse hid it in his bedpan when his family came in close on the heels of the City Council.

Mark and Jacob missed their TV and stereo, which had been hastily moved out to their next door neighbor's apartment. Everyone breathed a sigh of relief when, after two more days, certain their Johnny was mending though still in pain, his mother and father went home.

Eight

Sugarcreek Budget
Strawberry Schrank, Pa.

May 10, 1984 *Baptism classes started last week for our Fellowship with Deacon Moses Strubbs giving instruction to an even dozen of our youth, exactly six girls and six boys, ranging in age from sixteen to twenty-one.*

The good news from Basking Reade Hospital in Maryland is that Johnny Stoltzfus, son of Amos and Katy (who are home again) is making a good recovery from his burned hands and won't even need skin grafts. He'll have just a few faint scars.

Coffee Katie Kauffman, Johnny's foster sister, is working as a nurse's aide at the hospital, so this way Johnny always has a family member nearby. . . .

Katie tossed aside the copy of the *Sugarcreek Budget* that Mem forwarded faithfully every week.

"God, it makes me feel guilty!"

"What now?"

"Sure, I stayed to be near you, but I'm having such a good time—movies and parties, dates and dances . . . to say nothing of a whole new wardrobe. Just wait till you see my new denim skirt with the patch pockets."

"Boy, oh boy, the Stoltzfus influence sure rubbed off

on you. Would it help any if you were having a miserable time? You *are* putting in a forty-hour week, you know. And you are a comfort"—his mouth turned up mockingly and he held out his hands—"to your poor, scarred hero brother."

"Oh, you!"

"Listen, before you go hog wild with all your money, you got any to spare?"

"Sure, Johnny, lots—well, not really, maybe about two hundred." She looked at him, puzzled. "What do you need money for?"

"How about waiting till next week's salary and giving me two-fifty?"

"If you need it, Johnny, I can manage."

"I don't *need* it, I want to match it with some of mine and invest for us."

"Invest? You mean like on the stock market?"

"Just like on the stock market."

"Johnny, that's crazy, it's like throwing it away."

"Bite your tongue. What do you think I've been doing with my *Wall Street Journals* and *Barron's* and *Richland Report*s all the last two years? Playing games? I studied the market for a whole year before I made a move. Then the last eight months I did my investing with paper money." He pointed to the bedside stand. "Get the little black book out of the drawer for me."

She got the little black book out of the drawer. "Your girlfriends?" she said, handing it to him. "From what I hear it would take a whole book to list them."

Johnny ignored that crack. "Better than girlfriends," he said. "A list of all the stocks I bought and sold. The cost. The dates. When they rose, when they fell. How much I made or lost."

"How much did you lose?"

"Two thousand or so on Consolidated Dynamics and twenty-eight hundred on Peerless, Inc."

"A mere four thousand eight hundred dollars. Wonderful, Mr. Math Genius. I think I'll keep my two-fifty."

"On the other thirteen stocks I traded," Johnny went on, as though she hadn't spoken, "if I subtracted my losses, brokers' fees, and imaginary expenses like long-distance telephone calls, periodicals, etcetera, my net profit—if I'd used real money—would have been eleven thousand one hundred, plus."

"Eleven thous—Johnny, you're kidding."

"Kidding! On my sacred little black book, I swear it."

Katie jumped up and down with excitement. "Maybe I can manage three hundred. I can always borrow from my roommate till the end of the month if I run short."

"Three hundred each would be great for what I have in mind."

"What's that?"

Johnny lay back against his pillows. "I'm too tired to go into the details, but there's this outfit in Seattle I've been keeping an eye on . . . an unimportant little company, Titanium, Limited. Titanium stocks have been going lower and lower, and I think they're going to take even more of a dive. There's a funny pattern to the activity. I'd be willing to bet—let's face it, I'm willing to gamble both our bankrolls on it—that some time down the line Titanium's going to merge with another company, a big one. That means big profits to be made if I buy low now."

He looked up at her with slightly feverish eyes.

"Are you game? Remember, it's a gamble, I could be dead wrong."

"I'm game."

"I'll call a broker I met in Boston and put in the order tomorrow when I get back to the apartment."

"You sure you're ready to go home? You haven't looked so well the last few days."

"I'm just tired. Too much hanging around here. It'll feel good to be back in my own place. So it's a deal?"

"It's a deal."

He slid down lower on the pillows. "So, who's your date tonight?"

"An intern. Tom Slattery."

His whistle came out huskily, cut short by a grimace. "You're really hitting the big time."

"*Slattery* thinks so, but he can be fun. Johnny, what's the matter? Your hands hurt?"

"Nah. Just a little heartburn. Those hot dogs I had tonight, I guess, and I've done too much lying around. Run along, I want to sleep," he added contrarily.

She came over just to touch his shoulder by way of goodbye. However he might deny it, Johnny was embarrassed by the casual kiss.

She looked down at his face. Last week he had seemed fine, much more full of bounce. Now his skin was sallow. With a prickling along her spine, she noticed that his eyeballs were yellowish. The last time she had seen symptoms like that in a patient . . .

She went out to the head floor nurse.

"Mrs. Allen, could you get in touch with Johnny's doctor? He has some symptoms I'm worried about. Heartburn. Excessive fatigue. Eyes and skin yellowish."

"I'll call Doctor at home." She eyed the pacing Katie. "No use your waiting around," she told the girl in a kindly way. "Even if he orders immediate tests, it will be tomorrow before we know."

The blood tests the next day confirmed that Johnny Stoltzfus had contracted hepatitis.

"Is it bad?" Katie asked Dr. Morse, Johnny's doctor.

"Well, not to worry unduly, but there's no denying it isn't good, Katie. He's in just the early stages," Dr. Morse told her cautiously, "and ordinarily, I wouldn't be so worried—though it's a damned uncomfortable, unpleasant illness—but there's the dual impact of the trauma he's just undergone and the fact that his liver isn't in too good a shape to start. You need a healthy liver to withstand the assaults of hepatitis, and I'd say he's been abusing his a lot with alcohol the last year or so."

He pressed her shoulder. "Don't be so upset, Katie. A lot of the Amish boys go that route during their time here. They see it as their last taste of freedom and adventure before settling down. In the end, they go home and make model citizens," he said to try and comfort her.

"But Johnny's not . . ." She decided not to go into it. "Shall I—do I have to send for his parents?"

"No, certainly not. They have a right to know, of course, but you can write calmly and optimistically and simply state the facts—forgetting about the alcohol, if I were you. There's no reason yet to alarm them."

So Katie sat down that night and wrote a letter meant to inform but not alarm, though that single word *yet* had sounded a nasty warning bell inside her own mind.

Johnny seemed a little light-headed when she came off duty and went to see him the next day.

"Of all the damn luck!" he grumbled to her. "Dr. Morse says I'll be here at least another month, maybe two."

"Big deal. What's another month or two when we've waited years?"

"I expected to be in Boston by the end of June."

"And I expected to be in New York. So what? Stop fretting yourself into a fever and concentrate on getting well."

"Okay, Mama." He managed a weak smile. "You're going to wait, and leave when I do?"

"Yes, except that I think I'll go home to say goodbye. Maybe I could take your letter with me. You'll have to write another letter, Johnny."

He moved restlessly. "I know. I don't want to think about it now."

"Then don't. Don't think of anything except getting better. Rest, Johnny. Relax."

"Put your hands on my chest where it hurts."

She put her hands flat against his chest.

"Probably just self-hypnosis," he mumbled sleepily after a while, "but it helps a little."

"So does being babied," she said lightly. "Go to sleep, Johnny."

That was the longest conversation they had for several weeks. When he wasn't sleeping, he was tossing in discomfort or too utterly listless to talk. His face and his eyeballs seemed to get more and more yellow. It was, he informed her in crude detail one day as a nurse carried away his bedpan, a damned colorful disease.

He remembered on the fourth afternoon to tell her to give her money to Mark, who would wire it to his broker in Boston. He had bought the Titanium stock. In the middle of telling her about it, he fell asleep.

He was too tired to read the newspapers and books that Katie brought for him at first, too weak even to hold a book in his hands, too disinterested in anything except to lie hour after hour watching the TV or sometimes listening, eyes closed.

Katie had thought he would improve after a few weeks, but he seemed to be getting worse . . . his color, his listlessness, his fever, his pain.

There came a day when Dr. Morse sought her out in the children's ward where she was on duty.

His face prepared her for his blunt words.

"Katie, I think you had better send for Johnny's mother and father."

She bit down on the whitened knuckles of her clenched fists. "Is he so bad?"

"Send for them."

She telephoned Mike Maseratti's garage. Betty Mast, an Amish woman, a friend of Katy Stoltzfus, lived just down the block from Mike. Her son would drive her out to the farm. Better for a friend to deliver such a message than the police.

Katie stayed by Johnny's bedside, her strong hand holding firmly onto his limp one, trying with all her might to pour her own vitality into him, talking to him constantly whether he seemed to hear her or not, trying to infect him with her own strong will for them to live both their lives to the fullest.

"It doesn't matter if you have to go home to convalesce . . . six months . . . a year. It doesn't matter. I'll go with you, I swear I will. We'll see the waiting time through together. We're going to have a wonderful life, Johnny. You're going to make lots of money on the stock market. You're going to go to college. I'm going to write and make a name for myself. We're both going to live just the way we always planned. No beard and *mutze* for you, no head cap and *halsduch* for me. It's the great outside world for us, only you've got to fight for it. Fight, damn you, Johnny, isn't it worth fighting for?"

They switched him to a private room that the doctor thought would be better for him, and he opened his eyes, looked around bewilderedly, and started screaming. "There're bars at the window. Let me out, let me go. Unlock the door."

Katie motioned a nurse to close the curtains.

"You're dreaming, Johnny. There aren't any bars. No bars for you ever, I promise you. Hold my hand. Feel my hand. It's Katie, Johnny; we're at the Levi Luke School . . . your books are there waiting. Just think; soon you'll be able to get them shipped to Boston. You'll have bookcases in every room of your apartment. Did I ever tell you how my Daddy used to keep books even in the bathroom? You're going to be just like him."

When he quieted and seemed to be resting easier, she sat beside him. While the nurses and doctors came and went, she never let go of his hand unless they had to examine him. She prayed silently, as she never had at any meal time; she prayed hard, as she never had at Preaching.

She prayed to the gentler God of her mother and father. *Please let him live, God. Please, he's had so little that he wants out of life yet.*

She bargained with the sterner God of the Amish.

I'll do anything You want . . . I'll stay as long as he stays . . . I'll stay an extra six months after him, longer even, if You'll just let Johnny live.

Nine

Sugarcreek Budget
Strawberry Schrank, Pa.

August 9, 1984 *There is great joy in the Amos Stoltzfus house that all its members are home together again, especially Johnny Stoltzfus, the eldest son. He was away almost two years on hospital service when he was hurt in a fire in which he helped save two lives. Later when he was in the same Maryland hospital as a patient, he got hepatitis and was pretty sick there for a while. In fact, there was danger. But now he's home again, and with him Coffee Katie Kauffman, the Stoltzfuses' eldest foster daughter, who worked in the hospital to be near to him.*

We're told, though, that it will be a long time before Johnny will be in shape to do a day's work on the farm. He has to get back his strength slow and easy over the next year or two.

It's the middle of the tourist season when so many Englishers with cameras seem to think we're maybe like animals in a zoo, so it was appropriate that Bishop John Beiler preached to us last Sunday from Exodus. Thou shalt not make unto thee any graven images, or any likeness of any thing that is in Heaven above, or that is in the earth beneath . . .

It's a shame someone can't preach it to the tourists. . . .

* * *

Katy Stoltzfus was ready to serve up the family's Saturday lunch when Annie ran into the kitchen, her organdy *kapp* askew and her apron torn.

As they all stared at her, open-mouthed, Annie cast herself into Katy's arms, sobbing.

"Mem, I told him not, I tried to make them stop, but they wouldn't listen, and when I ran away, they chased after me."

Katy straightened out Annie's *kapp* and tried to quiet her, "Someone harmed you, child?"

The younger boys looked frightened, but Johnny jumped up in his place, fists clenched. Amos gave his son a single glance, and the fists unclenched. Then he turned to Annie.

"Annie, *schwetz uff,*" he said kindly but commandingly. "So what happened?"

The accustomed strong voice had a calming effect on Annie. "It was an Englisher boy, two of them in a car," she sniffled. "They were driving along the road, and I made myself small by the side, but they stopped a ways ahead and one of them got out with a camera and he offered me a dollar to let them take my picture. He said"—her voice grew tearful again—"that without the picture his friends wouldn't believe he had seen such a c-cute d-doll in such a G-God -f-forsaken sp-spot."

"Un so?"

"Was that all?" asked Coffee Katie in relief.

"No, he took the picture anyways before I could turn away. Then he threw the dollar at my feet, and his friend got out of the car and asked if I wanted a ride with them, so I ran away across the fields."

"You did no wrong," said Amos. "The Englisher did; let the *sind* be on his head. So make your dirt away, then sit and eat."

Comforted by this quiet common sense, Annie washed

at the sink, then sat down. As Coffee Katie put a bowl
of soup before her, the loud, raucous honking of a car
horn sounded outside.

"I think that's them," said Annie nervously, her spoon
clattering against her bowl. "They followed me along the
road right up to our gates."

"Eat," repeated Amos. "Pay them no mind. It's hard, I
know," he acknowledged a bit grimly to the table at large,
"but we've got to turn the other cheek and forgive them
their ignorance."

Soon Annie was talking and laughing with her brothers;
Coffee Katie sat silent, hardly eating. Amos, knowing she
had always felt more like mother than sister to the younger
girl, addressed her gently. "Coffee Katie, eat up. Nothing
so bad happened."

"I'm not very hungry today."

Johnny looked across at her sharply but held his peace.
Whatever was bothering her, she would tell him later.

"I'll get the meatloaf," said Katie, jumping up. As she
went toward the stove, she glanced out the window and
suddenly screamed out, "Damn his hide!"

Before Amos could reprimand her, she called to him
excitedly, "Pap, it's the Englisher. He opened the gate, and
the cows are all getting through."

Later, when he was not around to hear, the girls were
to giggle that Amos, too, in the heat of the moment, had
entirely forgotten about turning the other cheek and also
cursed the *fer doom'd Englishers*.

Leaving lunch to get cold on the table, the entire
Stoltzfus family sprinted for the door and made a mad
dash down the steps and along the path, where fourteen
wild cows under the mistaken impression that they were
horses, had started a galloping stampede for freedom.

One of the Englishers was still in the car. Another—the
one who had obviously caused the havoc—was standing
outside the gate.

"Gosh, I'm s-sorry," he stammered apologetically. "I—didn't realize—I only wanted to get through to—"

"Never mind the apologies, *doom koop*," Coffee Katie hurled at him unkindly. "If you want to undo some of the harm, stand *in*side the gate and don't let any more get out. What's the matter, city boy?" Her voice dripped with scorn. "You afraid of a cow's tongue? Just shove them away. Come on, Johnny."

She picked up her skirts and went tearing down the road, Johnny following after her, the Englisher staring at the flying figure, torn between annoyance at her contempt of him and admiration of her shapely calves and ankles.

The family members were all strung out at a distance, trying to encircle the cows, like Indians around a covered wagon. Even Grandfather Jacob came running from the *grossdawdy haus* and neighbor Hans Hershberg and his son Matthew from the next farm came hurrying to help.

It took an hour and a half until the last cow was finally rounded up and returned to its stall in the barn.

"Oy!" cried Katy Stoltzfus, brushing off the damp apron with which she had been busily shooing cows. "What will be with the lunch?"

"So it can warm in the oven or we'll eat cold," said Amos genially. "I could swallow a whole cow without help from anyone, especially one of those *doomb* cows of mine."

"You'll join us, Hans . . . Matthew . . . Granpap," urged Katy.

All three claimed to have eaten, but gave in when she mentioned coffee and apple pie.

"For *your* apple pie, Katy, I would herd twice the cows, ain't?" laughed Hans Hershberg.

The same invitation was extended to the two Englishers, whose car remained on the road while they stood at the gate.

"It was *gude* of you to give so much time to help us,"

Amos told them, trying to do penance for his shame at having cursed them.

They stared at him, bewildered. "But I caused all the trouble," one blurted out.

"So, you didn't mean to; no harm was done. Come into the house. Eat with us some coffee and pie."

More than willing, the two young men, having introduced themselves as Harvey Reardon and Tom Gillette, followed the Stoltzus family, the Hershbergs, and the two tempting little morsels they had heard called Annie and—it sounded like—Coffee Katie.

As soon as they were seated together at the end of the kitchen table, Katy set two full plates before them on the oilcloth covering and they reached eagerly for their forks.

"Is this that shoo-fly pie I've heard so much about?" asked Harvey.

"No," said Katy, bustling about and serving generous portions to the others while Coffee Katie filled the cups, "it's apple. You maybe prefer shoo-fly?"

"No, no," he disclaimed hastily. "I love apple pie. It's just that I've heard so much about the famous Pennsylvania Dutch shoo-fly pie, I was curious about it."

"I have a quarter left over from last night's supper, so maybe you'd like to taste a little of both," Katy suggested.

Before they could utter a polite protest, she was putting a piece of shoo-fly pie onto both their plates.

"I don't know which of them was better, they were both so great," Harvey told Katy when he had eaten his last bite.

"Fabulous," grinned Tom, looking at Amos. "Would it be all right, sir, for us to take the two girls"—he nodded at them courteously—"for a ride into town? There's a fair, I understand, and perhaps we could have some ice cream afterwards. We'd take the greatest care of them and bring them home whatever hour you say."

Coffee Katie looked at her sister and saw on Annie's

face the shocked dismay that their foster mother was trying more valiantly to conceal.

Amos got up from the table. "Our thanks to you for the offer, but our religion does not permit," he said decisively. "Our daughters"—he gave it the strong German pronunciation, *dochters*—"may not ride in automobiles with Englishers."

"We're Americans," protested Tom.

Harvey was quicker to understand. "You mean, not Amish, sir? For us to have a date would be against your religion?"

"To mingle in friendship, yes; but between a girl and a boy, it's courting, which the Bible forbids."

"The Bible!" Tom echoed incredulously.

"From Corinthians." The words rolled sonorously off Johnny's tongue. *" 'Be ye not unequally yoked together with unbelievers, for what fellowship hath righteousness with unrighteousness? and what communion hath light with darkness?' "*

Harvey pinched his friend's elbow. "We understand. Thank you very much, Mrs. Stoltzfus, for the delicious pie. Our apologies again, Mr. Stoltzfus, for the trouble we caused you."

With a last lingering glance of regret at Coffee Katie, Tom followed his friend out of the house.

There was silence for a while after the two young men left, then Katy and Annie started to clear the table while the men donned their buttonless black work coats.

"Danke, Katy," said Hans Hershberg, clapping on his flat-topped black felt hat and nodding to his son to do the same. He fingered his full dark beard thoughtfully. "Wonderful strange ways these Englishers have," the women heard him say as he and Matthew went out the door.

"Wonderful strange," piped up Gideon, like his brother Paul John a miniature version of the older men in his smaller brimmed hat and barn-door britches.

Coffee Katie suddenly put her hand to her mouth to hold back a cry of anguish.

"I've got a stitch in my side, Mem, from all the running," she said, getting up from the table stiffly, like an old woman.

Katy and Annie looked at her, surprised. Coffee Katie was tireless . . . she had always been able to out-run any boy for miles around.

"Go lie down, then. Johnny, maybe you should rest, too. You did enough for one day."

Katie went flying up the stairs, strangely fast for someone with a stitch in her side. She flung herself down on the afghan-covered bed in the room she still shared with Annie, and broke into a storm of weeping. The tearstains were still on her cheeks when Johnny came into the room without knocking.

The bedsprings sagged as he sat down next to her. Katie sat up.

"What's wrong, Katie? I'm sorry about making fun of the Word. I know you hate it when I get my kicks out of ridiculing them. But it wasn't that . . . and neither was it those town boys. You knew Pap would never let you go with them. You were acting strange from the time Annie came home."

Coffee Katie looked off into the distance, not seeing the rolling green hills outside the uncurtained window.

"I've been listening to Annie from the time that I came home, watching her with new eyes, maybe *your* eyes. I realized that I had been blind, wilfully blind, just the way you said. All those years I had been fooling myself with a kid's dream. She was never going to go away with me. Like the boys, she belongs here."

Johnny touched her hand lightly, comfortingly.

"You'd be surprised how quickly I adjusted to that fact," she added, shrugging. "So maybe in my heart I had known for a long time that she would stay and I would go. But listening to her today . . . I don't know . . . I had a feeling of—of revulsion. All that fuss because a guy said a few harmless words to her. And making a big deal about the sin of her picture being taken . . . She knew damn well it was no sin when it was without her consent."

"So she's a prig, like I always told you," said Johnny with unexpected tolerance. "She's only . . . what is it now, fifteen? She'll get over that, and about the other you shouldn't mind. She's happy in the Plain way. She's happy in a way that you and I may never be."

Katie reached out to him suddenly, and he took her two hands in a rare gesture of affection.

"She accepts," said Johnny, a bitter twist to his lips. "She knows who she is and what she is. Do you? Do I?"

Ten

Wall Street Journal

Seattle, Washington. April 3, 1985 *The SEC has approved the purchase by the Chicago-based Great Giant Corporation of the controlling block of Titanium, Limited, Seattle. The final purchase price was twenty million dollars, at twenty dollars per share . . .*

Sugarcreek Budget
Strawberry Schrank, Pa.

April 10, 1985 *Annie Kauffman, daughter of Amos and Katy Stoltzfus, was the first to sign up for the new Baptism classes; also, Eli Hertz, Joey Hochstetler, Lizzie Raber . . .*

The day that Annie started Baptism instruction, Amos, who had a fine strong voice, led them all in singing a special hymn of praise after supper. When he finally looked at the clock that night and said, as he always did, "Bed time comes. Tomorrow is a working day," the rest of the family jumped up.

"Johnny. Coffee Katie, a *minoot* stay."

Surprised, his son and foster daughter sank back on

their chairs. When the three were alone, Amos cleared his throat loudly.

"Johnny, Coffee Katie, there's trouble in my heart and maybe in yours, too, ain't?" His shrewd blue eyes stared at them from under beetling brows.

They looked at each other bewilderedly, then back at him. Both began to speak at once, then broke off, giving Amos the chance to go on.

He said heavily, "Annie is the youngest of you three, but already she has started Instruction. So why not her sister, past nineteen, and my son, past twenty-one? The Bishop, the Deacon, the ministers—from all sides I'm pressed. They all want to know why my eldest son and daughter haven't entered the Church. I want to know, too, ain't?"

He turned to his son. "Johnny, you think I don't know when a boy is young it's his time to rebel? So I gave you plenty of space. I reminded myself how we almost lost you. I told myself, it's time for you to *say die willder howwer.* So it's years now. Enough wild oats you've sowed. Now it's your season to settle down in the life of righteousness. I got money put aside, and all the wages you've earned with me, too, so you can have a fine farm of your own. And you, Coffee Katie"—he turned to her— "have a good daughter's dowry to offer any man."

He cleared his throat again. "You two have always been wonderful close; if it's each other you want—"

Once more they spoke together.

"I care for Katie like a sister . . ."

"Johnny's my brother . . ."

"I'm sorry, Pap," Coffee Katie told him in a voice husky with unshed tears. "It would be wrong of me to take Baptism, wouldn't it, when in my heart I don't believe all the way?"

"It's true," Amos agreed sadly, "you got to believe. And it must be my failure that you don't. *Und* you, my *soohn,* have I failed with you, too?"

Katie saw the way Johnny's shoulders squared before he stood up, the way his hands were clenching against his sides. She tensed herself, knowing the dread moment of truth had finally come.

"I can't take Baptism, Pap. I'm"—he gulped, and the words came out in a rush—"I'm going away again."

Amos stood up, too. "Going away? Going away where? What is it with the going away?"

"To Boston, Pap. To college."

There was a long, terrible silence. All that could be heard in the room was the ticking of the old grandfather clock and Amos's hard breathing.

"To Boston. To college," Amos repeated finally. "You're serious?"

"Yes, Pap."

"You didn't decide this overnight," Amos said, half to himself. "This has to be something you've been maybe planning a long time. You admit that?"

"Ja, I admit it."

"It won't change your mind that you'll be tearing out the heart of your *mutter* . . . your *fodder?"*

To Katie, Johnny's cry of response was torn from deep in his own heart, but Amos just looked at his son as though he had not spoken. "There is nothing I can say to change your mind?"

Johnny was too choked up to answer. He could only shake his head.

"Coffee Katie, go to your bed. I have something to say to my son alone."

Katie ran out of the parlor, her heavy shoes clattering on the wood floor; but instead of going upstairs, she lingered in the hallway, unashamedly listening.

She heard Amos' deep voice, strangely expressionless despite the solemn words he spoke. "When you were hurt in the fire and they sent for us, your Mem and I were frightened all the way on the train journey . . . suppose it was worse than the message said and we lost you. The second time, it was even worse; the second time we knew for sure there was a danger you might die. I thought I knew grief and pain from those two times, but it seems I knew nothing. To lose you in death *then* would have struck me less of a blow than to lose you *now,* by your own choice, to a world of sin and perversion."

In the hallway Katie stood, quivering against the lash of each word, knowing Johnny must be feeling a far greater pain.

She heard Johnny try to speak. "Pap, I—"

"No," Amos interrupted him heavily, "there's nothing I want to hear from you except that you've decided against putting us out of your life and being put out of ours. Because that is the way of it if you go. You know that, don't you? You could never come back, except in remorse to do penance and ask to be taken back into the Faith."

"I know."

"Spend the night thinking what you give up. *Gott willich,* you'll see the light."

Katie took off her shoes and ran in stockinged feet through the kitchen and up the stairs, reaching her room before there were sounds below, leaning against her closed door with a pounding heart.

Annie was in bed already. "What did Pap want?" she asked sleepily.

"Nothing much. I'll tell you tomorrow."

She put out the light in the kerosene lamp so Annie wouldn't realize she wasn't undressing. She sat on her bed, waiting for Annie to fall asleep. Twenty minutes later she was scratching lightly on Johnny's door, an old signal between them. The door opened at once; he had been expecting her.

"What took you so long?"

"That Annie," she whispered, "I thought she'd never

fall asleep, and now she did, you should hear her snoring. I feel sorry for her husband."

"You should tell Crist Raber," said Johnny. "Maybe he'll have second thoughts."

"Crist Raber?"

"Sure. They're *rumspringa,* I think."

"She never mentioned a word to me," said Coffee Katie, a little hurt.

"Oh well, you know how courting couples are. Till it's published, they keep their mouths tight shut."

"For God's sakes, never mind about Annie and Crist. What happened between you and Pap after I left? After he said you should think it over tonight . . . I listened in till then."

"If you heard that, you heard it all." His voice shook, in spite of a mighty effort to sound matter-of-fact. "I've got a simple choice. Stay and conform. Leave and be regarded as dead."

"Oh, Johnny!"

"Aw, c'mon, we knew how it would be. Don't start blubbering on me, Katie. I couldn't take it."

He knelt and pulled the suitcase he had used in Basking Reade out from under his bed. "For your last sisterly act here, wanna help me pack?" he cajoled her.

"Are you leaving tonight?" Katie asked, blowing her nose in her apron.

"No, I'll wait till first light and get away before anyone is up. I want to go see Mike Maseratti about packing my books and sending them on to me later when I have an address for him. And I have to wait till the bank opens in Lancaster so I can get my money out. Thank God for Titanium . . . I'll be able to rent an apartment and spend the spring and summer loafing and reading. I'll be in good shape for classes by September. Now about you—"

"What about me?"

"Why don't you leave now, too? We might just as well

both break their hearts at the same time," he added with a tinge of bitterness.

"I'll leave"—Katie counted on her fingers—"in October—six months from now."

"What's so damn special about October?"

Katie thought of the hospital room in which she had bartered with the God of Amos Stoltzfus for his son's life . . .

"It's a sort-of promise I made," she said lightly, dropping a bundle of socks into the suitcase. She took a pile of shirts out of his wardrobe. "Which of these do you want?"

"All. They're good enough to sit around the house in."

"Thrifty Amish."

"Extravagant Englisher. Don't spend all *your* money on clothes."

"I will if I want," said Katie pertly. And then, "Johnny, did I ever tell you—properly—how grateful I am for the money?"

"Forget it. It was *your* money; you took the gamble with me. I could have lost it all instead of making you . . ."

"All those beautiful thousands. Okay, Johnny, no thank yous. There." She flipped the two locks shut. "You're all packed."

"A lifetime in one medium-sized suitcase," Johnny said philosophically, slinging it onto the floor.

"Anyhow," he added, with his back to her, "you think I don't know that if there are any thanks to be given, they should all come from me to you?"

"Why, Johnny, what—"

"You think I don't know the best day of my life was when you came into this house?"

She couldn't speak for a moment, then she walked over and reached up, lightly tugging his hair. "Pretty speeches from *you,* Johnny?"

He turned round swiftly and gripped her raised wrist.

"No jokes, Katie, not tonight. All these years we've used jokes because we knew if we didn't laugh, we'd spend most of our days drowning in tears. But tonight we can be ourselves. Will you stay more with me tonight, Katie, and keep the fears at bay one more time?"

"St-stay with you?"

"I'm too stirred up to sleep; it's not that long till dawn. Will you sit up with me this one last time, Katie, my sister, my friend, my—the one I have always turned to—like tonight—even now when I'm leaving?"

"I've always turned to you, too, Johnny. Ever since the first time when I felt so lost and bewildered and you brought me the books, and especially after the time you ran away and we—why, Johnny . . ."

The face she lifted to him was full of a dawning wonder. "Maybe that's why I didn't mind as much as I thought I would about Annie. Because I had *you*. You came first. You were dearer than my own to me."

They were standing so close it seemed the most natural thing in the world for her to lean against him, her head turned into his shoulder. Johnny's fingers, trembling slightly, unpinned her *kapp* and then her hair. He pulled all her hair down a little at a time, twining each strand around his hands.

Johnny, thought Katie in a daze of delight, *Johnny.* All those boys in Basking Reade who had touched and stroked her, hugged her and tried so hard to kiss her on the mouth . . . and not one of them had ever made her feel so much as a tenth of the quivering delight that Johnny was giving her, just playing with her hair.

"Shall I tell you what you've meant to me, Katie Kauffman?" His voice was husky with unaccustomed tenderness.

"Please."

"Remember the day they put the *meidung* on Levi Luke and poor blind Sarah said she wanted it put on her, too, because she couldn't abandon her son?"

"I remember."

"She said he had been a lamp to her in her years of darkness. I never forgot those words. They describe how I feel about you, Katie. Whenever it got too dark for me, somehow you managed to light my way."

He looked down at her flushed face and gave a pleased little chuckle. "I never thought anyone could strike *you* speechless, Katie. Your eyes are round as saucers, and midnight blue, and your lips are parted . . . your lips are . . ."

His voice faded away as they stared at each other for an incredulous twenty seconds. Then her parted lips, under the pressure of his urgent mouth, were like the petals of a flower unfolding.

One lone cricket was chirping outside the window. It sounded like a thunderclap in Katie's ears. Or maybe, she thought when she was capable of thinking at all, that had been the clamor of her own shattering heartbeats mingled with Johnny's as the delight of that long first kiss went on and on, soft, then hard, savage, then sweet, achingly, intensely beautiful.

When Johnny lifted his mouth and stepped back from her, muttering, "Don't move," the loss of physical contact was so sudden and so shocking, she felt utterly bereft. She watched him swing the kerosene lantern off the dresser and place it on a wooden chair in the farthest corner of the room, leaving only a dim, eerie flicker of light, so that he was a shadowy blur when he returned to her.

"That's better," whispered Johnny, drawing her back into his arms. Like a starving man given a meal, he fell to kissing her again. Short kisses, long kisses, nibbling kisses, probing kisses, kisses so passionate her toes curled up in her shoes, and kisses so comfortingly tender she felt rocked in his loving embrace. This time his hands were behind her, below her spine, pushing her hard against him; his knee was slightly bent and lifted, wedged intimately against her legs.

"Let's get comfortable," Johnny said softly in her ear.

"Yes, let's," she agreed dreamily.

Getting comfortable, she discovered after she let him lead her, meant stretching out together on his bed.

"Johnny, we can't . . ."

"Don't worry." It was that new honey-soft voice she had never heard from Johnny's lips before. "I won't go all the way. I'll—it will half-kill me not to, but I promise. Only, the dawn will come so quickly, and I want to be close to you all of tonight."

They kicked their shoes off and lay facing each other, every part of their bodies touching, from the toes straining against toes to the mouth over mouth.

Presently they fell apart, gasping, lying on their backs, but their hands clasped tight together.

"Sister!" he said. "My God! I must have been out of my mind to believe that. My God, Katie, I love you! Why didn't I realize it before?"

She leaned over to plant light kisses up and down his face. "Because you're a big dumb Pennsylvania Dutchman."

"How about you?"

"I was dumb, too, not to realize it in Basking Reade when I was so jealous of all those little *hoors* you were running around with."

She could sense rather than see him smile. "Some of them were very nice girls. Dull compared to you, but very nice."

Katie propped herself up on her elbow to look down at him. "Were you jealous of my dates?" she asked hopefully.

"I guess. Though I thought I was just being big-brotherly."

"What you are doing right now," said Katie, slapping

away the hand that was lifting her skirt, "is not in the least brotherly."

"Katie, let me love you the way I said. I'll keep my promise. There are ways. I want this night. I want to feel close to you. No," as she started to speak, "closer even than this."

She sat up and turned her back, unpinning the modest frontpiece of her dress. She untied the apron and took off the dress and lay down again. Johnny gathered her to him and, using his hand and his mouth and wonderful, whispered words, he made wild, wonderful things happen to her body. Obviously, to his own, too, because presently his shuddering convulsions shook the bed, and when Katie whispered anxiously, "Is something wrong?" he managed to gasp out, "No, something's right."

He left her for a few minutes, and when he came back, he lay on his side, pulling her into the curve of his body. Then he spread the quilt over them and they slept.

"The sun is going to rise." Katie thought she was dreaming those words, but they sounded in her ear again and she was being gently shaken.

Johnny was standing over her. He was dressed in a denim shirt, his tight-fitting dungarees from Maryland, and the leather belt forbidden by the Amish dress code.

"Better get dressed. If anyone knows you spent the night here, the worst will be suspected."

Katie got into her dress, pinned the modesty piece in front, and looked around for her *kapp*.

Johnny pointed to the suitcase standing at the door. "One word from you, and I'll unpack it."

She didn't pretend to misunderstand him.

"By unpack, you mean, stay?"

"That's what I mean, Katie."

"Then I'll never give the word, Johnny. I'll never let you stay because of me."

"Why not . . . if you love me?"

"It's *because* I love you . . . and I want you to go on

loving me. You won't, if you stay. You might even wind up hating me."

"Katie, you're crazy. I—"

"Johnny, listen to me, listen, *please*. What happens if you stay? You take Baptism, we marry, and for a while we're happy because we have each other. Then one day you wake up and you're what you never wanted to be . . . a farmer, an Amish husband, then a father, living under the *Ordnung*. Your dreams would be gone and the life you wanted would be forever out of your reach. You'd hate me, all right."

"How can you be so sure?"

"I'm as sure as I was that before I came into this room last night you had a drink. You think you can take the taste and smell of it away by chewing mint; well, you can't . . . not any more than you could make the taste of life here less bitter when the first fine rapture of love wore thin. It would, you know. We would both resent a love that made us into prisoners."

She knelt on the bed, lifting her arms in mute appeal, while he stared down at her, white-faced.

"I don't want you one day drinking because of *me*, Johnny. And don't forget, I've got dreams of my own. I played my part here all these years because I had to survive, but I don't think Amish, I don't feel Amish, and I'm not going to be a farmer's wife. You're the best part of half my life, Johnny, and I don't want to wind up hating you either. If I lose my dreams, I very well might."

"You could come away with me to Boston," Johnny said suddenly as she started to pin up her hair. "No farm money, no dowry, but we have plenty between us for a start."

Katie slid off the bed and put on her shoes. "I thought of it," she said. "I probably thought of it before you. And don't think it wouldn't be the most wonderfully easy thing for me to do. Just walk out that door with you without once looking back . . . get on a train away from here today."

"So what's stopping us?"

"Common sense, maybe?"

Johnny snorted.

"Then call it a deep instinct," said Katie, rubbing her forehead. "We've used each other as crutches for so many years, I just think we should find out—separately—how we go it alone . . . without you leaning on me and me leaning on you."

She saw by his face that he understood. He didn't want to believe that what she was saying could be right, but his own intelligence went against his will.

"Wise little Katie," he said a bit unsteadily. Then, "Sunrise; it's time to go."

Her lips trembled as he walked toward the suitcase. When he turned back, holding it, she couldn't restrain the tears that rolled down her cheeks.

Johnny saw the tears and put down the suitcase and held out his arms. She flew into them. "Someday," he addressed the head burrowing into his shoulder. The head shook violently. "Someday," he repeated somberly.

"Never mind the someday. Look how much more we both have than we did when we came into this room," she said almost pleadingly, then ended on a teasing note, "ain't?"

Johnny's face seemed to open up. "You are right, Katie Kauffman," he told her, tender and loving, as he gently kissed her lips. "But I still say someday we're for each other . . . *tzu how wa un tzu* . . . to have and to hold."

Eleven

Sugarcreek Budget
Strawberry Schrank, Pa.

September 10, 1985 *Published to be married in two weeks are Annie Kauffman, daughter of Amos and Katy Stoltzfus, and Crist Raber, son of Thomas John Raber and his wife Rebecca, both families from here. Being the only son, after the wedding visits, Annie and Crist will make their home on the Raber farm. . . .*

Eight weeks before the August Preaching Service when the Bishop announced that Annie and Crist would marry, Coffee Katie had found her sister down on her knees in their bedroom one afternoon. She was praying aloud in a voice choked with tears.

Katie sat down on the bed and put her hand under Annie's chin to lift a face that was red and swollen with long crying.

"Annie, *liebling,* what's the trouble?"

"Oh Katie, I've been so wicked. I've sinned terribly, and now God's punishing me."

"You never did a wicked thing in your life."

"But I did . . . we both did."

"Both . . . ?" said Katie, beginning to understand. "You and Crist, you . . . ?"

"Yes." Annie's tears fell afresh.

"You love him?"

"Yes." It was a shamed whisper. "I'm—Katie, I'm *leebgronk* for him."

Katie suppressed a smile. "It's no sin to be lovesick for a man. Does Crist love you?"

Annie forgot for a moment that it *was* a sin to be proud. "He says he's *leebgronk* for me, too,"

"So it's simple. You get married and then it's no sin. You can both be as *leebgronk* together as you want."

"But we have to make confession of our sin first."

"I don't see why," said Katie, who saw only too well.

"Katie, we have to. We're in the Church and—and it wasn't just the one time. We—we—three times it was, and I'm—*mitt kindt.*"

"You're having a baby? Then you have to get married quickly!" said Katie determinedly.

"Yes, but first we have to make our peace with the Church."

Katie threw up her hands, defeated. "So let's tell Mem; that's the first step."

Hand in hand, like the long-ago time when they were two young sisters together against the world, they sought out Katy in her kitchen.

Annie cried so hard, it was Coffee Katie who wound up making the confession.

Katy Stoltzfus, who seemed to have aged years in the months since Johnny's leaving, was shocked to the core.

"You, Annie, I can't believe it, not of *you!*" she cried with unconscious emphasis. Coffee Katie had the feeling that Mem would have found it less hard to believe of her than of her younger sister.

"I never thought *you* would put such a shame on us, and so soon after joining the Church."

Annie cried so bitterly all through Mem's scolding, she

missed hearing most of it except the last ominous threat. "He will have to settle this."

When Amos was given the news and sent for Annie, she looked the very picture of the penitent sinner, following Coffee Katie into the parlor where he and Mem were waiting, head bent, eyes red and swollen, nose all puffy and pink.

"Look at me, Annie."

Fearfully, Annie peeked up at her Pap and encountered such a look of fiery rebuke, she burst into tears of fright.

"Crying won't give you back what you lost or take away the disgrace of what you've done, Annie Kauffman. If you were a few years younger and not with child, you would get from me the punishment you deserve."

Annie cowered away, as though afraid she might get it anyhow, and Amos' tone grew slightly milder.

"Coffee Katie tells me it's Crist Raber and he wants to marry you. Do you want to marry him?"

Annie's tears stopped flowing. "Yes, Crist does, and so do I."

Amos turned to his wife. "It's maybe best we go to the Rabers and discuss with them what is to be done."

"With a *bubbel* already on the way, the sooner, the better," Katy Stoltzfus agreed.

Amos called Paul John to hitch up the buggy while he put on a clean shirt and Mem went to fetch her bonnet.

The marriage was arranged that night, although both families knew it would have to be delayed until after the punishment given to Annie and Crist when they knelt at Preaching to make their confession for such a major offense.

It was inevitable that, for such a transgression, the *meidung* would be invoked against them. This excommunication would be temporary, of course, probably only for three or four weeks, after which, provided they were properly repentant, they would be welcomed back into the

Church without reservation and without any moral stigma attached to their names.

In bed that night, Katy Stoltzfus voiced a secret fear to her husband. "Amos, I'm more worried about Coffee Katie than I am about Annie."

"Coffee Katie!" Amos bolted upright. *"Gude Gott!* Always another trouble. What has that girl done now?"

"Nothing. Why are you so quick to judge?" Katy bristled in defense of the daughter she secretly loved most of the two.

"So what's wrong with my judgment? I married you, ain't?"

Katy moved a little closer to him as she lay down again. "You think you talk like that, I'll go soft on you."

He chuckled in the darkness. "I'm wrong."

"Nay."

He pulled her rather roughly against his hard-barreled chest, and a groan came up from the very depths of his body. "With little ones, it's little troubles; with big ones, big troubles." Something perilously like a sob sounded in his voice. "Our J—our oldest son is gone from us, lost to us maybe forever."

In spite of her own pain, Katy's hands comforted him.

After a while he said in his usual way, "Now our Annie is pregnant before the wedding, so tell me, what would be the new worry with Coffee Katie?"

"Annie will be shunned, *recht?"*

"Recht."

"Can you see our Katie shunning her sister? Not speaking to her, not eating with her . . . acting like she wasn't there?"

"Annie wouldn't mind; she expects."

"You think I don't know? She looks forward, almost. There's more than a touch of Anabaptist martyr in our Annie. She'll feel better getting punishment for her sin. It's Coffee Katie who will mind. Not only mind—she won't go along with it. Never did I think to say it, but thank *Gott* she's not in the Church yet because they'd put *meidung* on her, too, and *she* wouldn't accept gladly like Annie. We would lose her forever, and I couldn't stand."

"I give you the right there." Amos nodded his head, forgetting she couldn't see.

"She's so stubborn *und* so sweet," Katy said excusingly.

"By comparison," Amos agreed, "a mule is an easy animal; but to look at her face," he mused, "is to brighten the day. In the room where she is, you don't need a lamp."

"Amos! That sounds like a poem," declared Katy, greatly pleased.

"Coffee Katie's no poem. She's too much flesh and blood. And *Gott willich,* she'll settle down before she, too, has a *bubbel* in her belly."

"God forbid." After a minute of quiet concern for the future, Katy brought him firmly back to the present. "What will we do to keep her from getting in trouble with the ministers? Will it matter she never joined the Church?"

"No, it won't matter," said Amos. "She can't be mited, sure, since she was never baptized, but the ministers can decide she's a bad influence—that she might harm other members of the congregation, by her bad example, especially the young ones in her own family."

"So what can we do?" Katy's voice rose high in panic.

Amos got his arm around the plump, comfortable waist. "Don't look for trouble where there's no big problem, ain't? Let Coffee Katie go to a job away from Strawberry Schrank all during the *meidung* and not come home till Annie and Crist are published and it's time to help you with preparing for the wedding."

"Oy, Amos!" She pressed her lips quickly to his cheek. "That's wonderful thinking. I'll go to town tomorrow to see where there's a place she's needed."

"That's the best you can kiss a husband who pleases you so?"

"Amos!" But even as she said his name in pretended shock, she was offering him her mouth.

Amos chuckled in the darkness after their long hard kiss. "I had to laugh to listen to Annie and Crist tonight even while I had to cry shame on them," he told her. "A person would think they were the first two ever *tzu foll in leeb*. It made the years roll away. I mind the first time I saw you running in the fields. Your *kapp* fell off and your hair fell down; it was like golden threads spilling down your back. You made to feel ashamed, but oy, the sinful pride of you when my eyes came out of my head to see. From that day I couldn't eat, I couldn't sleep, I couldn't work. Talk about *leebgronk*. I was so sick with love, my father begged I should speak to the Deacon and get the date set. He couldn't wait we should get married so he could get a day's work out of me again."

There was silence in the room while his hands—the calloused, work-hardened hands of a farmer—moved over the familiar planes of her body.

"Amos," presently came a whisper from the darkness, "twenty-eight years we've been married, and in all that time you never till now said you loved me."

"So? You didn't know?"

"I knew . . . but it's not the same. It's something wonderful to hear."

"So maybe I'd like to hear, too."

As she whispered the words to him in German, Amos sighed gustily and pulled her underneath him. "So maybe actions speak louder than words." He gave this opinion with a bellow of a bawdy laughter loud enough to penetrate the wall to Coffee Katie in the next room. It was not by any means the first time she had heard that rich, private laughter. It sent shivers up and down her spine even as she pulled the feather pillow over her ears.

* * *

The next day, looking placid and sedate as ever in her dark dress and apron, Katy told Coffee Katie how much she was needed in Strasburg by the Mennonite Widow Miller, recently bed-bound with a broken leg while her ten-year-old twin daughters ran wild.

"I can't leave my sister when she's in trouble!" Coffee Katie rebelled.

Katy looked at her steadily. "Yes, you can, Coffee Katie," she said. "If you care enough for what *she* wants instead of what *you* want, you will leave her be now."

So Coffee Katie went to Strasburg to help the Widow Miller, whose daughters Becky and Sadie were known as the Terrible Twins. Their mother, a lapsed Mennonite, was delighted to have her, and the girls responded amazingly quickly to Coffee Katie's imaginative games, robust humor, firm directions, and an occasional brisk swat on the nearest backside.

In no time at all, Katie had the household running smoothly and plenty of free time on her hands. Occasionally she helped the hired man Flat Joseph Dietrich on the farm to work off her nervous energy, or took long hikes through the fields and along the by-roads whenever she was restless, which, increasingly, she seemed to be.

Soon Annie would be married and settled in a life of her own. Before long she would have a child as well as a husband. Her sister Katie was dear to her but not important in her life. If the Church put Katie under the *meidung* tomorrow, Annie would sorrowfully, but unquestioningly, shun her. Her first loyalty would always be to the Church, just as Katie's would always be to those she loved.

It was as well that October was the month set for her own leaving. She would tell Katy and Amos right after the wedding. In her heart she knew it was they, not her sister or brothers, who would most feel the pain of her going. And even Mem and Pap, Coffee Katie reflected, taking a rest beside a corn field one day and chewing on a stalk . . . even they had a secret life of their own.

She thought of the bawdy bedroom laughter that sometimes filtered through the walls between their rooms . . . She thought of Annie, *leebgronk,* lying three times in Crist Raber's scrawny arms. He looked such a nothing, yet Annie was pregnant!

Katie rolled over on her stomach, burying her flushed face in her hands. She was ashamed of her troubled thoughts.

It was sinful to be envious, said the Amish-influenced part of her even while the practical part reminded her, you know very well you wouldn't want to do *that* with someone like Crist Raber.

The trouble was that ever since the long night with Johnny, so many other nights had brought their secret restless longings. Johnny's halfway love-making had stirred up yearnings in her that for once could not be satisfied by books.

If it was just Johnny she yearned for, she could have forgiven herself . . . but it wasn't.

She must want to do *that* with someone . . . she just wasn't quite sure who!

Twelve

The Philadelphia Inquirer

August 2, 1985 *Continental Films has announced that J.D. Shale will produce and direct the last film of its public television series on the ethnic groups that make up America. Mr. Shale's film,* The Plain People, *will deal with the Amish and Mennonites, two sects which have both for two hundred and fifty years resolutely resisted assimilation into the American culture.*

Shooting of this episode has already begun in Strasburg, Lancaster County, Pa.

It was a typical country inn room—uneven hardwood floors only partly covered by the usual factory-made hooked rug, a chintz-covered rocker and four-poster bed, and a dresser and desk that might or might not be solid maple.

But the mattress seemed comfortable—J.D. had tested it with his bottom before throwing his heavy suitcase onto the bed—and the air conditioner had provided quick, quiet cooling.

Above all, he would be able—when he pleased—to seize evenings of peace and privacy away from the luxurious extroverted ghetto of the hotel-motel complex where the actors and the rest of the crew were quartered. All in all, decided J.D., throwing his last pair of socks into the top drawer, more than a fair trade.

He tossed his empty suitcase up onto the closet shelf, then started stripping, with a sigh of relief for the cool air against his sweating skin. He really ought to take a shower first . . . but he was too damn tired. There had been very little sleep sandwiched in between the last three days of traveling and conferences . . . California to New York . . . morning to midnight meetings there . . . New York to Pennsylvania . . . then an hour's wait for the rental car in Philadelphia and the drive from there to Strasburg.

He was bushed . . . beat . . . He would nap first, shower later, and have a leisurely dinner—alone—then a walk on that wooded path he had noticed when he parked the car. Tomorrow, rested and refreshed, he would drive around with the notes and maps provided by Chris, his location scout, spying out the lay of the land.

Most of the rest of the company would be in town by the time he got back, but by then he would be more in the mood to face everyone.

Strolling naked from the bathroom toward the four-poster, he suddenly caught a glimpse of himself in the long oval mirror over the desk. He stopped short, his California-tanned face contorting for a moment, then turning granite-hard and impassive—what his Aunt Marion called his "inscrutable look."

There wasn't any resemblance, he reassured himself. There never had been. Just that they both had black eyes and those close-cropped curls like the men in the old Greek statues . . . though God only knew why, since the Shale family claimed to be pure Welsh.

It had just been the set of his jaw, the tilt of his brows, only a momentary thing . . . a fleeting expression he sometimes noticed, like just now when he passed the mirror, gone as quickly as it had come.

He faced the mirror again squarely, letting out his breath

in relief. No—no resemblance at all. He was a full head shorter than that hulking brute Mike Shale. His shoulders were wide, sure, but Mike's had been a massive support for a great bullish neck. Shirtless, his enormous flabby beer belly used to hang repulsively over the top of his trousers.

J.D. swallowed and closed his eyes, but even with them closed, he could not shut out the sight of those freckled, ham-like hands lifting up the pale mound of flesh to get at the buckle of his belt.

"Ah, Christ!" J.D. swore softly. "Not again."

He opened his eyes and studied himself carefully. There wasn't an ounce of spare flesh on him; his sun-browned stomach was as flat as a surf board. He had a waist and hips, by God. So what if his eyes and hair were dark? Half the rest of the world's were dark, too. Hell's hounds, why couldn't he accept once and for all that there were nothing but dark memories connecting him to Mike Shale?

He got into bed.

"I've conquered the memories!" he said out loud, knowing even as he said it that he was whistling in the dark.

He lay on his back with his hands clasped under his head, staring across at the flowered wallpaper, afraid that now he would be too tense to sleep.

He took long, deliberate breaths, forcing his mind to empty, ordering each part of his body to relax, starting with his toes and working his way upward. After a while his breathing became more natural, his lids shuttered the dark, staring eyes, and J.D. slept.

He might have conked out for a few minutes or a few hours. He had no way of knowing how long he was unconscious when the dream came. Mickey was in the dream, calling out to him. Mickey was always in the dream, begging for his help.

J.D., hide me, save me, don't let him hurt me!

He cradled his kid brother protectively. *Of course, I'll*

save you, Mick, he told him. *No one will ever hurt you while I'm around.*

Then Mike Shale was in the dream, laughing the way he always did when he was stinking drunk, laughing the way he always did before he inflicted pain, laughing at the young J.D. for thrusting Mickey defensively behind him.

He never went after Mickey if J.D. was there; Mickey was too easy a target. J.D. provided far better sport.

"Come on, J.D.," Mike Shale taunted him, "Come and get me . . . go for me, you snotty little bastard, I dare you . . . you know you'd like to kill me. You think you're such a man, you think you're so gutsy, so go for me, you sniveling little son of a bitch. I'd like the chance to break you right in two."

Goaded, J.D. went for him in the wild frenzy of anger and despair that always ended the same way, with Mike Shale holding him helpless, sometimes dangling him in the air by his hair or the back of his neck or pinning him to the floor with a heavy foot on his stomach or spine, depending on how J.D. landed when he was thrown. Then the ham-like hands would be fumbling for the thick leather belt.

But not this time. Not in this dream.

In the dream J.D. grew taller and taller and wider and wider. It was Mike Shale who cowered away, Mike Shale who got swatted down like a fly. The ham-like hands hung helpless at his sides and J.D.'s own hands were around the bullish throat, squeezing, squeezing hard, his two thumbs flat against the corded windpipe, pressing mercilessly. Mike Shale's eyes bulged out—those damn dark eyes so like J.D.'s—his face turned scarlet, then purple, his breath was a series of wheezing gasps that faded away to soundlessness. Then the eyes turned over in the sockets, the body went limp, and what J.D. was holding between his hands was a great flabby lump of dead flesh.

Behind him, Mickey cried out joyfully, "You killed him, J.D. You saved me."

"Yeah, I killed the SOB," agreed the dream J.D., shrinking slowly back to normal size. He dropped the lump of flesh onto the floor and kicked it casually out of the way so he and Mickey could walk out of the dream hand-in-hand together.

He had killed his father, and he was gladly, fiercely proud!

That was how the dream always ended—with that overwhelming exaltation because he had wiped Mike Shale off the face of the earth.

Over and over through the years he had wakened to the painful truth that it was only a dream. The constant crushing disappointment in his life was the awakening from the glorious unfulfilled dream that he had throttled Mike Shale.

This time was no different. J.D. came suddenly up out of sleep and found himself lying on his stomach in the four-poster bed, his heart jerking like a runner's in the last mile of a marathon. He was half raised up, with the pillow crushed between his hands. The striped pillowcase was half off, and he was squeezing it so hard, he had popped a handful of feathers out of the ticking. It was the pillow he was making mincemeat of, not Mike Shale. In a sudden fit of self-loathing, he threw it across the room.

"Damn, damn, damn." He sat up with his legs crossed in front of him, pounding his fists against his knees. "Why didn't I kill the son of a bitch?" he asked as futilely as he had asked so many times before. "Oh God, if only he were alive so I could kill him now!"

A cigarette might have helped, but he didn't smoke, hating the smell that Mike Shale had always reeked of. He wouldn't have minded a couple of belts, but he didn't drink. Mike Shale had been a boozer. With shaking hands, J.D. reached over to the night table for his watch, then remembered he had left it in the bathroom.

He was just about to get out of bed when there was a loud, rapid tattooing on his door.

He was still so caught up in the dream, he reacted as though the knock were a danger signal. His mouth went dry, his hammer-stroke heartbeats quickened, his whole body broke out in a clammy sweat.

"Who—who is it?" he stammered hoarsely.

"It's me, darling. Taffy," trilled a sexy-sounding soprano.

"Oh, my God!" groaned J.D. "What the hell are you doing here?" he addressed the closed door.

"Trying to get into your room, darling."

"What for?"

There was a rising crescendo of laughter outside the door; then the voice purred even more than before. "Do you *really* want me to tell you from out here in a public hallway, J.D. darling?"

J.D. leaped out of bed and stalked over to the door, saying just before he turned the lock, "Give me a minute to get back into bed; I'm not dressed."

He had barely slid his bottom under the blankets when the door opened, then closed again, the lock was firmly turned, and Taffy Tremont had perched herself upon his bed.

She was a tall girl—taller than J.D.—with voluptuous curves, masses of violently-blonde teased curls about which only her hairdresser knew for sure; huge grey-green eyes; a small rounded rump which she was snuggling as close to J.D. as she could get it, and deliciously large breasts, which it was her habit to press against any man she was talking to.

She was pressing hard right now. The large diamond on a chain that sparkled from the middle of her cleavage almost landed in J.D.'s mouth when he asked her, "Do you happen to know what time it is?"

"Almost five." She snuggled a bit closer. "What difference does it make?" She bit lightly, lovingly, on his nearest ear lobe. "Would you like to let me under those blankets, darling? I'm snow-white pure, love . . . as well as sooo red-blooded."

J.D. pulled free of her clinging hands and glanced at the card she was waving in front of his nose. "Very reassuring, but I'm not in the mood. Jet lag still has me in its grip. Some other time, thank you."

Taffy shook her head mockingly. "You don't sound like the same J.D. I've heard about. Are you sure you don't have a headache, too, sweet?"

"As a matter of fact, I do."

In one fast fluid movement, Taffy rolled over and onto him. The diamond tickled his neck and her nipples tickled his chest.

"Can it be that your reputation as a stud is undeserved, J.D.?" she taunted him.

"Very possible," he grunted.

While her breasts continued their tantalizing rotation against his chest, deep in her throat she began to hum the first few bars of the "Hawaiian Wedding Song." At the same time her hips began rotating counter-clockwise against his blanket-covered body.

After a minute or two, one of her hands snaked under the blankets, crept up his leg, and took firm hold of what awaited her. Her mouth curved up in satisfaction; her eyes brimmed over with a mixture of malice and merriment. She stopped humming and started singing her own version of a golden oldie:

> Your lids tell me no, no,
> But there's yes, yes 'twixt your thighs . . .

This time it was J.D. who rolled over and onto her, the hands that had savaged the pillow—in gentle contrast now—caressing each ripe breast as his lips ground her lips against her teeth.

While he indulged in an orgy of touching, teasing, and

tasting, Taffy's laughter trilled out again and again. It had been easier than she expected. He was mad with passion for her, she decided, smugly triumphant even as she whispered of love and whimpered with pretended passion and writhed artistically in response to his roving hands and lips.

"Take off your damn clothes; I can't get past them," J.D. said presently, and Taffy promptly stood up, peeled off her knit shirt, and wriggled out of the skin-tight black skirt he had been unable to yank up.

She had nothing on underneath. She threw both shirt and skirt on the floor and returned to J.D., standing naked over him. He grabbed hold of one ankle and pulled her down, then under him.

He didn't smoke, he didn't drink, but he knew all too well the marvelous forgetfulness to be found in fornication. You didn't have to be in love to enjoy a lover. In fact, without love it was easier, and more satisfying. It had to be—if you were J.D. Shale!

Thirteen

"Hollywood Tidbits"
by Pamela Goode

Taffy Tremont, the blonde sexpot from the soap Love Is Forever *has a small featured role in* The Plain People, *produced and directed by J.D. Shale for Continental Films. She plays the part of a sweet young Mennonite bride, certainly not type-casting for the much-married Taffy.*

They slept for half an hour, and when J.D. woke again, Taffy was on her side, staring straight at him. A fluttering of the false curling eyelashes attached to her real ones quickly veiled the naked calculation in her eyes.

"Lover boy, you are really something else!" she told him in the deep-throated sexy voice she could summon at will.

"All testimonials gratefully accepted," said J.D., and then like a gracious host, "Thank you kindly, ma'am."

She sat up, yawning and stretching. "You know, I didn't have any lunch, I'm starving," she said plaintively.

He stroked her arm absently. "As a matter of fact, so am I."

At the first touch of his hand, she started bouncing her breasts provocatively in case he was interested in another round. She glanced over at him, prepared to please him any way she could.

"Starved for food, Taffy," J.D. told her dryly.

She bounded thankfully out of bed and pulled the blankets off him. "Get dressed, then, and take me out to dinner," she ordered, pirouetting around the four-poster. "Someone told me the restaurant in this inn is great."

"Speaking of someone telling," J.D. asked her, "how the hell did you know where I was staying?"

"That PR guy—Foley, Fellows, something like that—he told me."

"Follett," J.D. corrected in a voice that promised Follett a hard time even though he could imagine in just what fashion Taffy had used her velvet-gloved iron fingers to twist the hapless guy into knots.

He slid out of bed. "I'll just have a quick shower. Why don't you call down to the restaurant for a reservation?"

Taffy pulled the phone toward her as he started walking to the bathroom. She dropped it. "My God, what happened to you?" she exclaimed.

"Happened? Oh, you mean my back." J.D. screwed his head around for a casual look, as though he had forgotten the ugly network of scars across his back and shoulders. "War wounds," he said briefly.

"Oh, you poor dear. Vietnam?"

"I prefer not to talk about it."

She retrieved the phone and stumbled off the bed toward him. "You poor dear!" she said again with genuine concern. "How you must have suffered. Was it a mine explosion?"

"Taffy, hear me loud and clear. It's not something I want to talk about."

"Of course, darling. Forgive me. I'll call the restaurant."

J.D. proceeded to the bathroom. He looked into the mirrored door of the medicine cabinet with a death's-head grin plastered on his face. "Well," he told his image. "It was a *kind* of war."

When he came back from his shower with the towel tied around his middle, Taffy was sitting on the bed, once again encased in her shirt and the skin-tight skirt. Her feet sported a pair of transparent ankle-strapped shoes with rhinestone-studded spiked heels. The diamond twinkled at him from her cleavage.

She smiled up at him, a smile that tried to blend sexual allure and sexual satisfaction in one appealing package.

"Our reservation is in twenty minutes. I asked, and you don't need a tie." She pointed to the rocker. "I laid out clean clothes for you."

J.D. looked toward the rocker. His dark blue blazer was hanging over the back. Light blue wool slacks and a blue and white sports shirt were draped across the seat. She had even remembered undershorts and socks.

"Very wifely and efficient," he commented, and immediately wished the words taken back. It was just the opening she was waiting for.

"Speaking of wifely, darling, come over here a minute." She patted the bed beside her invitingly and gave him another of those Mona Lisa smiles.

"Wait till I get my pants on. You did say twenty minutes, didn't you?"

"Silly," she said flirtatiously, when he sat down next to her. "I didn't mean sex." She giggled. "At least not till after you feed me. No, it was"—she stroked his scarred back delicately with the tips of her fingers—"I just wanted to tell you about the absolutely marvelous psychic I went to before I left California—Madame Veronni. You've probably heard about her. She advises all the top studio people."

"Not *my* studio people, she doesn't. She's a fortune-teller, not a psychic."

"Oh, don't be stuffy, darling. She's really super. She told me that I'm going to be married again."

"Taffy, that *you* are likely to marry again hardly comes under the heading of news, let alone a psychic prediction."

"Not when she's absolutely specific about *when* and *where* . . . and even *who,*" she purred seductively.

J.D. looked at her in grim silence. He knew only too well what was coming.

"Darling, don't you want to know who the lucky man is?"

"I have a feeling you're going to tell me whether I know or not."

"Madame Veronni said I'm going to marry *you,* J.D."

"Just like that, without any prompting from you, she pulled my name out of her crystal ball?"

"Well, no, actually it was your initials, and your job and where you live and describing this TV movie we're doing, and your aunt and uncle who brought you up, and his being the head of Continental . . . oh, there was no mistaking it, it was *you* she meant, J.D."

J.D. got up and started pulling the shirt over his head.

"Her saying it doesn't make it so, Taffy."

"Why not?" She sounded like a high school girl just told she can't have a new dress for the prom. "I'd *love* being married to you."

"You'd love being married to the nephew-by-marriage of the president of Continental Films."

"It wouldn't hurt," Taffy conceded honestly, "but you know there's more to it than that, J.D. It was wonderful between us, wasn't it? It could be even better."

"Taffy, what we just had was a good old-fashioned lay, not love's young dream."

"It could be both."

"No, it couldn't. Listen, Taffy. You may be one of the sexiest-looking creatures in the solar system, but be honest. *I* know and *you* know you don't really like sex all that much, even if you do give your partner a rousing good time and an Oscar-caliber performance."

She jumped off the bed to fling her arms around his neck and press herself against him.

"I could give you even better times and better performances if you'd marry me."

He unwound her strangling arms and stepped firmly away from her jiggling breasts and grinding hips.

"Taffy, get this through your head. I don't intend to marry anyone—ever. In the remote event that I change my mind, I would wait till the sensible age of forty, which, in case you don't know, gives me nearly another eleven years of freedom."

He sat down in the rocker and started pulling on his socks. "For the final clincher of let's-be-cruel-to-be-kind week, if I married someone some time, let me make it absolutely definite—that someone would *not* be you."

She advanced on him, hands on hips. He wouldn't have been surprised to see steam coming from her nostrils.

"Why not? What's wrong with me?"

"Let's just say that for marriage, I'd want a partner, not a performer, and never mind all the other missing ingredients."

"You lousy, stinking, snobbish son of a bitch!"

Her arm reached behind her, giving extra force to a slug on his jaw with her balled-up fist. He could scarcely see her for his watering eyes as she stalked across the room, unlocked and opened the door, and slammed it closed so hard it rattled perilously on its loosened hinges. Chips of paint and plaster came flying through the air. The oval mirror over the desk came loose from the wall and crashed onto the desk, where it broke in two—with shards of glass scattering over the desk and floor and furniture—before hitting the floor. One little sliver lodged above J.D.'s knuckles, leaving a small trail of blood when he pulled it out.

Up and down the hallway, he could hear doors opening and people's voices, excited, questioning, all wanting to know, "What happened?"

"Was it a bomb?" asked a girl's voice, shrill with fright.

J.D. got up from the rocker, walked across to open the door, and poked his head out. "Just a falling mirror, folks. No harm done."

"Seven years bad luck for you, fellow," a voice floated back.

"So what else is new?" J.D. muttered, reaching for the phone.

"This is Mr. Shale in Room 824. I—there's been a slight accident. The wall mirror fell and broke. It's going to need quite a clean-up job. I'd appreciate your sending someone during the next hour while I'm down at the restaurant. Please put the mirror on my tab and let me know later who did the clean-up."

After he hung up the phone, he gingerly tested his jaw and checked his teeth. The humor of it struck him while he was putting on his blazer. As he slipped his wallet and keys into his pockets, he began to roar with slightly hysterical laughter.

Poor Taffy, he thought, walking down the single flight of stairs to the lobby and then across the lawn to the restaurant. All that effort, and she'd been done out of a dinner. All he'd been done out of was a dull dinner companion. Outside of bed, Taffy Tremont was predictably shallow and boring.

Nothing unusual about that, of course. In or out of the job, most of the women he spent much time with were the same . . . whether they were the sweetly ambitious little simpletons or the hardily mobile, on-the-make gold diggers.

Somewhere out in the world he knew there was a wonderful someone who did not automatically assume the horizontal position in order to climb the ladder of success.

Somewhere there was a special someone who did not

make love with the professional skill of a courtesan turning a trick.

Somewhere there was a girl warm and loving, funny
and interesting; someone he could laugh and talk and be
himself with.

He shrugged. What the hell? Even if he met that someone, she was not . . . she could never be for him.

Even if she existed somewhere, he didn't have the right
to a girl like that. He wouldn't dare take a chance.

He walked into the restaurant and stopped in his tracks.
Taffy Tremont stood talking to the hostess. She turned her
head casually as he came up. "They're holding our table,"
she told him.

"I had the distinct impression," J.D. said to her rather
formally, "that you had changed your mind about joining
me."

Her eyes sparkled wickedly down at him. "And miss a
free meal?"

He smiled back at her almost with affection, suddenly
glad not to be alone. "You're a good sport, Taffy. You
shall have champagne with your dinner."

"You're damn right I will, as well as all the most expensive items on the menu. And don't think," she added,
when they were seated opposite one another at a candlelit
table for two, "that I've given up on you, buster. I get
what I go after."

He grinned in genuine amusement. "Forewarned is fore-
armed."

Staring down at the book-sized menu handed to him,
he knew he would take her back to his room again if she
were willing. Or perhaps he'd drive the short distance to
hers.

He might have a great aching hunger for someone utterly different to share his life, let alone his bed, but he
must learn once and for all to make do with the Taffys
of this world. They were all he was ever likely to have.

Fourteen

Sugarcreek Budget
Strasburg, Pa.

July 18, 1985 Katie Kauffman of Strawberry Schrank is helping out Widow Jacob Miller, who broke her leg.

The movie people have started arriving in town and are getting ready to film. There is much excitement at the Abe Yoder Farm on Copper Hill Road, where the first filming takes place. . . .

Driving one-handed for a moment, while his fingers explored the passenger seat in search of his map, J.D. noticed a large figure in overalls in the field far to the right. He speeded up, then stopped and went into reverse. Out of the corner of his eye, he had spotted a much nearer figure over to the left . . . a young farm boy perched on a fence, totally absorbed in a book.

Before he could swing the car door open, J.D.'s elbow accidentally landed on the horn. At the static blast, the startled boy went backward over the fence, book and all.

J.D. scrambled out of the car and up the grass verge in a hurry. He leaned across the fence to ask anxiously of the figure sitting on the ground, "Are you okay?"

The figure was hugging the book close against a part of the body that even a less keen observer than J.D. could instantly perceive was not a chest but a breast. The boy was a girl.

"Are you okay?" he asked anxiously again, leaning across the fence and reaching down to her.

She accepted his hand unselfconsciously, letting go of it the instant she was on her feet.

"My bottom's sore, but I managed not to drop *Janice Meredith*," the girl said with simple pride.

J.D. looked at her blankly. "Drop who?"

"Janice Meredith." A tinge of impatience crept into her voice. She was still hugging it to her like a baby. "It's a first edition," she told him reverently.

J.D. looked her over with heightened curiosity. Under any other circumstances, he might have passed her by without a second glance. He could hardly see her face for the broad-brimmed straw hat that both shaded and shadowed her features. It was hard to guess what kind of figure she had because her denim work shirt was sizes too large, ditto her baggy blue overalls, which were tied around the waist with a short length of rope. She had cut off the bottoms of the pants with pinking shears so he *could* do a little favorable speculation based on the shapely curves of her calves and ankles.

Still, a farm girl in the middle of the Pennsylvania Dutch countryside talking about first editions . . . and any girl at all who was more concerned about hurting a book than herself!

Then the farm girl pulled off her straw hat, and his interest was well and truly caught. Her hair, carelessly pinned on the top of her head, was a pale lemon color. She had the biggest, bluest eyes he had ever seen, and they were alive with laughter and intelligence, as though she had guessed what he was thinking. The hands clutching the book might be strong and brown, but her face was a lovely, sensitive, pale golden oval. He would be willing to make a bet those white, slightly crooked teeth had never known an orthodontist's touch. And her mouth . . . those luscious full lips . . .

"May I see *Janice Meredith?*" he asked, holding out his hand.

Much to his surprise, she hesitated, looking him over far more thoroughly and thoughtfully than he had surveyed her.

Evidently she reached a favorable decision. J.D. was half amused, half flattered when presently, without speaking, she held out her book.

He turned to the frontispiece, muttering to himself, " 'A story of the American Revolution . . . Volume One . . .' " He turned the page . . . "Copyright, 1899 . . ." He figured out the Roman numerals below. "It's a first edition, all right. Is the story any good?"

"Yes, it's delightful. A little old-fashioned, I guess, but the historic parts are interesting, and even though Janice is a bit silly in the beginning, she's starting to mature."

While she was talking, she had climbed up on the fence again, curling her cute bare toes with the grass and dirt between them around one of the lower cross-posts. He stared up at her, bemused to be having this unusual conversation with a strange farm girl in the middle of the Pennsylvania Dutch countryside. Then he had a sudden thought and blurted it out.

"Are you a college student working here for the summer?"

She laughed out loud, having once again read his mind. "No, I'm a genuine part of the landscape, not a college student. I live in Strawberry Schrank, about eighteen miles from here, but I'm working in Strasburg for Widow Miller for a while." She grinned at him, looking less the fetching female and more the impudent urchin. "Is that what you stopped your car to ask me?"

A little nettled—he wasn't accustomed to being laughed at so openly by young women—J.D. said rather stiffly, "I wanted to inquire if this was the way to Copper Hill Road, which is where I'm supposed to be now. I think I took a wrong turn somewhere. I'm on my way to the Yoder farm."

"This is Pine Tree Road, though it can get you to Copper Hill. Do you happen to know which Yoder farm? There are dozens of them. It's a common name hereabouts."

"I think it's written down on my map."

He returned to the car and brought back his location scout's careful pen-and-ink map. Her light yellow head and his dark one bent over it together.

"Oh, here's where you went wrong," she said after a minute, pointing with one finger. "You missed this tiny little side turning . . . most outsiders do. What you should do now," she continued authoritatively, "is take the first right, about a quarter of a mile down the way you're going, then the next left, and after that just follow the map and you can't miss. Too bad you're not walking," she smiled. "It's just a mile, as the crow flies, past the Miller fields."

"Thanks a lot. I appreciate your help. And I'm sorry"— he started heading back to the car—"that I caused your fall."

"You are more than welcome, and no harm was done," she said with quaint dignity.

As he turned for one quick wave before he got into the car, he noticed that the intriguingly crooked teeth no longer showed through the bright smile. He turned on the motor and drove off.

Was it just his imagination that the blue eyes had looked wistfully after him and the lush lips had drooped downward in a rather pathetic way?

On an impulse he would never understand himself, he suddenly reversed the car again. This time when the vehicle stopped alongside her, she seemed to be waiting, solemn and expectant.

He leaned out the window. "Would you like to go for a drive and show me the way?"

Her face and her voice and her extraordinary eyes all came alive. "Oh, I would love that!"

She leaped down from the fence, hat and book in hand, and came running around the car. He leaned across to open the door for her, but she beat him to it. She scooped up all his papers and dumped them on her lap as she settled into the bucket seat with a joyful, puppy-like wriggle of her backside.

He thought of telling her he liked her utter lack of pretense, but instead suggested gruffly, "Better fasten your safety belt."

"Oh, yes." She fumbled around for the two parts of the belt as he started the car again. When she was safely strapped in, she gave another joyful wriggle. "Oh, this is fun. I love riding in cars."

"Is it such a rare treat?"

"Pretty much. It's forbidden among us to own them, you—oh, take this right."

He turned sharply right, grumbling, "I swear Lancaster County has some of the shortest, bumpiest, hilliest, curviest roads I've ever come across."

"I know." She laughed in happy agreement. "Hiram Hochstetler, one of our neighbors, once said our roads were God's atonement to us for Route Three-forty. Route Three-forty brings the Englishers *to* us, and the back roads help us to lose them." She giggled. "Hiram was reprimanded at Preaching. It was considered a blasphemous remark."

"Preaching," J.D. said, "and car riding not allowed. Are you a strict Mennonite?"

She shook her head, "My parents were, but they broke away from it. Then they died and we—my sister and brothers and I—came to live with Mem and Pap, who are our cousins really. They brought us up Amish."

"Amish. You!" He careened crazily into the left turn-off she was pointing to and stopped the car dead to stare at her. "If you're such strict Amish, what the hell are you doing here with me, and wearing that outfit you have on?"

"Playing hookey."

"I'm serious."

"So am I," she grinned. "While I live at home, I have to practice the Amish way of life. When I get away—like now on a job—I grab at the chance to be more myself."

"Would you be in trouble with your family if they found out?"

"Small trouble for *Janice Meredith,* bigger trouble for the clothes, and biggest trouble, I'm afraid, for car-riding with you. Hey, don't looked so scared." She smiled at him in a charmingly carefree manner. *"You* wouldn't be in any trouble, only me."

"That leaves me strangely discomforted."

"I hear a buggy coming. You'd better start the car again . . . unless you're minded to drop me off by the side of the road."

"If you want to know the truth, that's exactly how I'm minded," he retorted, starting the motor and squeezing the car as far as he could to the right side of the road.

As a horse and buggy came trotting along in the left lane, he noticed his companion put on her hat and glance out the opposite window, with her face carefully turned away.

"Did you think you might be recognized in this compromising situation?" he asked with gentle malice when the buggy was out of sight.

"It seemed unlikely," she returned with prim *sang froid* even as her eyes danced, "but why take a chance?"

"What form would the trouble take?"

"Don't worry, I wouldn't get beaten . . . Oh, right here, this is Copper Hill Road, just follow the twists and turns till I tell you to stop . . . To answer your question, I

would get *grieved* over and *prayed* with," she went on
chattily, ignoring the abrupt and total withdrawal, the aura
of desperate unease she felt coming at her in waves from
the man hunched over the wheel, his face a careful blank.

One moment they had been sharing a kind of laughing,
acerbic accord, and the next they could not have been
more separate if an impenetrable glass wall had suddenly
been erected between them.

"I get the silent treatment," she went on, pretending
unawareness of his constraint. "No one addresses a word
directly to me, not for hours, days, once a whole week. I
feel as though I'm invisible . . . I'm a ghost that no one
can see or hear or speak to even though I sit and eat and
work with them. It may not sound like much, but after a
few days, there's nothing—almost nothing—I'm not willing to do to make myself part of our family's life again.
I don't suppose you can understand, really; it doesn't
sound so terrible in the telling."

Slowly, silently, the wall of glass shattered. He said,
with what she felt was a tremendous effort, "I—I can
understand that would be hard to take . . . day after
day . . . for a sensitive person. Is it worth the risk?"

"Yes," she replied promptly. "So if you're feeling guilty,
please don't. You only invited me. I'm the one who accepted. I wanted to come, and I'm not sorry I did. We're
almost at the Yoder farm—it's the long low one over to
the right. You can park on the side of the road or pull
into the buggy entrance."

"I think at the side of the road would be better."

"I shall read my book and"—she smiled mischie-
vously—"if anyone comes by, I can pull the hat over my
face or get down on the floor and hide."

To her relief his answering smile was again as cheeky
as hers. "See that you do," he retorted, slamming the car
door shut and leaning through to add, "I don't want to

get jailed far from home for impairing the morals of a minor."

By the time she could think of a properly tart rejoinder, he was through the gate and going up the front steps.

She finished the last chapter of her book just a few minutes before he came back to the car slightly over half an hour later.

"I'm sorry I kept you waiting so long," J.D. apologized. "I had to check the interiors as well as the building and barns."

"It didn't seem long; I was reading."

"Do you know you're an extraordinary girl?" commented J.D., swinging the car wide for a u-turn.

"Are you buying the farm?" she asked him as they bumped back along Copper Hill Road.

Both of them laughed, then they both spoke together.

"Why do you think I'm extraordinary?"

"What on earth makes you think I might be buying a farm?"

"Ladies first," said J.D.

"Why else would you be inspecting it inside and out?"

"My company is renting the use of the Yoder farm—among others—for a week or so of shooting. I represent Continental Films. We're doing a TV movie about—come to think of it, about your people, the Mennonites and the Amish."

Her face lit up. "I not only read about it in the Philadelphia and Lancaster papers, everyone here's talking about it. Some of the Mennonites are cooperating with you, and the Amish, of course, won't have any part of it."

"That's about it."

"What kind of work do you do on the film?"

"Producer and director."

"Goodness, you're the one I read about."

He took his right hand off the wheel and held it out to her. "J.D. Shale."

She put her own hand into his. "I remember. I wondered at the time I read the article why they only used your initials."

"Keep right on wondering." He took his hand back. "Are you going to return the favor, or is your entire name a mystery?"

She giggled again, a delicious sound. He usually hated gigglers. "I'm Katie Kauffman."

"Katy with a *y?*"

"No, Katie with an *ie*. Why do you think I'm extraordinary?"

"Because I've never kept a woman—young or old—waiting thirty-five minutes and then been told she didn't mind because she was caught up in her book."

"Oh!"

"Disappointed?"

"Yes. I guess so. I was hoping it was something special about me."

"It *was* something special about you, Katie Kauffman."

She uttered a deep, contented sigh. "Thank you very much, J.D."

"You're welcome, Katie."

"J.D., did you happen to notice that you just missed the turn-off we were supposed to take?"

"Oh, sh—shucks. Do you think I can u-turn here?"

"If you don't mind living dangerously. Otherwise, keep going for about a mile, then we can get back to it roundaboutly."

They were quiet for the rest of the short drive except for Katie's directions.

"We're back on Pine Tree Road," she said presently. "You can let me off anywhere."

"At the front door," he said firmly, "unless it would get you in hot water."

"Oh, no, Widow Miller has strange—strange for around here, I mean—strange ideas. She thinks girls should date and have a good time. Her twelve-year-old daughters are known as the Terrible Twins. They're the holy terrors of Lancaster County."

"It sounds to me as though that should be *un*-holy terrors."

"I like that!" Katie declared happily. "I must remember to use it."

As the car stopped in front of the Miller home, she realized that her small adventure was over. Her smile faded and her little glow of joy was suddenly snuffed out.

"Thank you very much, J.D." She was gathering up her book and straw hat as she spoke. "I enjoyed meeting you and I enjoyed my outing with you more than I can say. Goodbye."

She was backing out of the car, not looking at him, when he reached out to take hold of her chin and turn up her downcast face.

"Why so valedictory a goodbye?" he inquired. "I was hoping to see you again. In fact, I was hoping you would do me a great favor."

"F-f-favor? Of c-course I would."

"Better hear it first," said J.D., laughing a little, but not unkindly, at her stammering confusion. "Katie, I'd like to have a copy of the script delivered to you. It would be a big favor if you would read it and give me your opinion."

"*My* opinion!"

"As a Pennsylvania Dutch girl, brought up Amish. You said it yourself, you're part of this landscape. We had a whole team of researchers on the background work—some of it I did myself—and we could still make basic mistakes that someone reared in the Amish or Mennonite world would spot in a minute. Do you understand what I mean?"

"I think so. I'd love to read the script for you, J.D."

"Fine. One of the crew will bring it along later today. Here. Show me where you are on this map, so he won't have any trouble finding the house." He handed her a pen.

"Better write in the address. Does the Widow have a telephone?"

"Yes, she does. I'll write the number down, too."

"How long will it take you? Direction, descriptions, everything—it's about two hundred typewritten pages."

"Oh, that's nothing. I'll start after supper tonight and be finished before I go to bed. Shall I take notes?"

"Whatever suits you. Notes would be greatly appreciated, but don't be in too much of a hurry, I'd rather you did a thorough job of it. Suppose I take you out to dinner tomorrow night, and we can discuss it then. Would the Widow approve that?"

"As long as she and the girls and the hired man eat first," said Katie, shining-eyed.

"What time shall I pick you up?"

To J.D.'s further amusement, Katie started calculating aloud. "Widow Miller's tray first, then supper at six for the twins and Joseph. Dishes and clean-up. Set out tomorrow's dough. Wash and dress." She looked at him eagerly. "Seven-thirty?"

"I'll make our dinner reservations for eight. See you then, Katie. *Arrivederchi*."

"*Arrivederchi*," Katie responded gravely, her spirits reined in but her heart skimming inside her like a skylark in flight.

Fifteen

. . . and so, of all the ethnic groups who came to the New World and were gradually and eagerly assimilated into the mainstream of American life, the Amish have been the sole holdout, maintaining and glorying in their difference, their isolation, and their own Plain way of life.

from *The Plain People*
A TV movie for Continental Films
written by Joshua Aaron Richardson
and J.D. Shale

The drive from the inn to Widow Miller's to bring back Katie Kauffman gave J.D. the chance to cool off after an altogether disagreeable session with Taffy Tremont.

He had known even while he was indulging that it was a serious mistake to spend a second night wining, dining, and reclining with her. The proprietorial rights she had assumed on the set today were proof of his lack of prudence, not to say self-protection.

At the end of the day's shooting, he had made it quite clear to Taffy that his evening was not free. She had smiled sweetly, gestured obscenely, and waved him off with "Ta, ta, you bastard."

He thought that was the end of it and had been glad to get off so easily. He should have known better.

Just as he was stepping into the shower, the tenacious Taffy turned up, knocking at his room door as she had done the first night. He had no choice but to let her in; with her flair for the dramatic, she would gladly have played her scene of rejected love as a benefit performance for the entire floor.

"I'm having dinner with our Amish consultant tonight," J.D. told her firmly.

"Take me along."

"It's business, Taffy."

"I'll be still as a little mouse."

"That'll be the day."

"He may be Amish, but he must still be human. I'll charm whatever it is you want out of him."

J.D. almost forgot himself that his appointment was with an Amish woman, not an Amish man. "Who are you kidding, Taffy? You'd be more likely to shock the pants off him."

Taffy moved close to him, hips wriggling amorously. "I'd rather shock the pants off *you,* J.D.," she whispered as her hands wandered below his belt.

Coaxing, cajolery, and seduction having failed to win him over, J.D. read the storm signals in her eyes and moved to block the oncoming Taffy Tremont temper tantrum.

"Any falling mirrors, damaged furniture, or broken windows will be charged to your salary, Taffy. There will be—to put it bluntly—no more screwing, since you persist in reading into it things that do not exist, and"—he opened the door, heedless of his naked state—"no more scenes, except those you play on the set."

As her mouth opened mutinously, he held up one hand. Quietly, calmly, deliberately, he told her, "That's a kindly warning from your boss."

Taffy's mouth closed; she cast him a venomous look,

then marched away. He could hear her heels clicking on the outside stairs as he double-locked the door.

When he got into his car to go pick up Katie, he was still more angry at himself than at Taffy, for having been so stupid as to thrust so much as one toe into her obvious trap.

The crawling lanes of traffic and snarling, horn-blasting drivers on Route 340 didn't help his mood any; so, since he was early, he stopped off at a small shopping center. By the time he arrived at the Miller farm, he had pushed Taffy to the back of his mind.

Before he could even knock on the door, it was flung open. Two faces peered out at him. They were identical narrow, freckled faces with thick manes of chestnut hair flowing down from plastic barrettes like horses' tails. The un-holy terrors, no doubt.

"Are you the fellow courting Katie?" asked one twin.

"No, I'm the fellow taking her out to dinner."

"You don't look so special to me," said twin number two.

"You don't look so special to me either," he shrugged.

They looked at him, then at each other, registering surprise. Evidently it was a shock to them when rudeness was met with rudeness.

"Do I wait out here for Katie?" he asked pleasantly, "or may I come in?"

They moved back, the door opened wider, and J.D. sauntered inside. He handed each short, skinny girl a small bulging bag.

"I was taught to say 'sweets to the sweet,' " he told them, "but in this case fudge seems more appropriate."

"What kind?"

"One maple, one chocolate nut."

Having opened the bags, they silently exchanged them. Twin number one stuffed a large chunk of maple into her mouth and muttered, "Thanks."

Twin number two pointed. "She's in there, in the dining room."

She turned out not to be Katie Kauffman but the twins' mother, the Widow Miller. The dining room had been converted to a combination bedroom-parlor. She was sitting up in a hospital bed with medicine bottles, cans of soda, an ice bucket, and a telephone on a tray table beside her. Magazines were scattered all over the bedcovers. She looked just like her Terrible Twins except that her horse's mane of hair was grayish and her skin was less spotted but more wrinkled.

"You must be Katie's young man," she said with a beaming smile.

Had someone put an announcement in the *Sugarcreek Budget?*

"We have a date. A business date, Mrs. Miller," he added a bit wearily.

"You can call me Widow Miller, everyone does. I just love being a widow," she confided cheerily. "Oh dear, that does sound shocking, but it's really not. I loved my Jacob, my, but I did; but one gets used to anything and it's been almost four years. After a while, it was such fun spending some of the money instead of just saving it all the time. Why shouldn't I hire someone else to do the kind of work I dislike when I can well afford it? Or order my bed jackets from Philadelphia, even if they're shockingly expensive? Do you like this one?"

J.D. examined the bridal-like confection of pink tulle and lace, which was pinned at her throat with a cameo.

"It's charming," he said sincerely.

"Oh, you dear man."

He handed her a box wrapped in cellophane and tied with a gaudy green satin bow. "I brought you some candy."

She inspected the contents of the box with rapture. "Chocolate creams and nuts. Oh, you dear man!" she said again.

"He only brought *us* fudge," said one twin, appearing suddenly. Her shadow followed, mumbling agreement.

"Rude ones," said their mother fondly. "If Katie were here, she would rap your behinds."

"Katie *is* here," said a severe voice from the doorway. "Thank Mr. Shale properly at once and apologize for your bad manners."

"Thank you, Mr. Shale," they both chorused demurely. "We're sorry we were rude."

J.D. looked at Katie with new respect. Then he looked at her again. No one could call her clothes smart; certainly they weren't costly, but by contrast with the too-large work shirt and the baggy jeans . . .

Her short-sleeved tailored blouse was almost the lemon color of her hair. Her short pleated white skirt hugged her small waist tightly, showing off a very fetching figure as well as the sturdy length of her legs. She wore flat-heeled white sandals with little string bows, like ballerinas' slippers; and when she turned to say good night to the Widow, he could see that her loosened hair was straight and soft and silky. It almost touched her belt.

"You look lovely, Katie," he said as they went down the front steps together.

"Thank you. Everything's borrowed," she said cheerfully. "I didn't bring anything from home for going out in, so Widow Miller sent out an SOS to all her friends today."

When they were in the car, he asked casually, "Would you prefer air conditioning or the sun roof?"

"Oh, the sun roof, please."

Amused by the reverence in her voice, he put on the car light before he pressed the button, so she could watch the sun roof slide open. Then he turned off the light, and they went bumping down the road.

"Do you need me to direct you?"

"No, thanks, I'm getting to know the roads fairly well."

"Well, good. Then I'm going to put my seat way back . . . where . . . ? Oh, here's the gadget . . . so I can look up at the sky and the stars and feel the breeze on my face all at the same time. I have your script here, and my notes"—she thumped the bulky manila envelope on her lap—"but do you mind if we don't talk about it till we get to the restaurant? In fact, do you mind if we don't talk at all? I want to absorb every wonderful moment without distraction."

"Be my guest," J.D. urged her with amiable amusement, wondering how many seconds or minutes it would be before she distracted herself with a running commentary. He had yet to meet a woman—even that pearl above price, his Aunt Marion—who could have a one-to-one encounter without a ceaseless flow of words.

By the time they reached the inn, he had to his astonishment discovered the first one. Obviously Katie Kauffman didn't regard silence as fatal to the health. From the moment of his consent till he stopped the car in a parking spot near the inn restaurant, she was absolutely still.

When he came around and opened her door, Katie still seemed to be in something of a daze. She came out of the car reluctantly, moving slowly as in a dream.

In the pale moonlight, her eyes were luminous. Her voice was a hushed whisper. "That was—I can't tell you how wonderful that was."

"You just have," said J.D., partly touched, partly discomfitted by her innocent sensuous ecstasy. "Better take my arm," he added prosaically. "The ground's uneven here."

"I can see fine," said Katie, and promptly stumbled over a loose cobblestone.

J.D.'s grab at a handful of pleated skirt prevented her from falling. "You can be independent without being a damn fool!" he told her.

"You're right," said Katie disarmingly, slipping her arm through his.

It was his third night in a row at the Franklin Arms,

and other Continental people had already done a lot of expensive eating and drinking on the premises. The hostess greeted him by name as soon as they came in, noting his change of dinner companion without the flicker of an eyelid.

"I have your table ready, Mr. Shale," she said, picking up two menus and leading him past half a dozen waiting guests, who looked indignant.

Katie hung back a little, and J.D. gave her a gentle shove to indicate that she should go ahead of him. They were seated solicitously at a cozy corner near the unlit fireplace, which was decorated for the summer with an arrangement of dried flowers in a big copper pot. The hostess handed them two of the book-sized menus and departed with a smile.

"Do you realize," said Katie, clutching her menu and looking raptly about, "that I've lived here—here in Lancaster, I mean, not Strasburg—half my life and never eaten in this place?"

"Would you like something to drink?"

"Just water, please. My mouth's all dry, I guess, the excitement. It's the food I can't wait for."

"Decide what you want, then," said J.D., opening his menu.

"I'll never be able to choose," moaned Katie happily after a few minutes.

"Take your time. The prime rib of beef is excellent, and—"

"Oh, beef sounds too ordinary. I want to experiment. I want a—a *cul*inary ex*peri*ence."

J.D. grinned broadly at this impassioned utterance. "Frogs' legs? Crabs' legs? Lobster tail?" he suggested.

Katie shook her head. "That's *too* experimental. I think—what about 'Savory Crab du Chef'?"

A short stocky apple-cheeked boy in black cotton knickers and an imitation homespun colonial shirt stopped at their table. "My name is Larry," he announced pleasantly. "I'll be your waiter tonight."

"Hello, Larry." Katie leaned toward him. "Tell me," she asked confidingly, "is your 'Savory Crab du Chef' really savory?"

"It's one of our most popular dishes, ma'am," he answered diplomatically.

"I'll try it, then."

"Any appetizer, ma'am?" asked the waiter at the same time J.D. inquired, "Would you like to try a shrimp cocktail, Katie?"

"Nooo, I think I would like to try one of the soups, only I can't make up my mind between the onion and the seafood."

"You could have our Soup Trio, ma'am. That's three miniature crocks, one of onion, and one each of the crab and lobster bisque. That way you get to try all three."

Katie nodded her approval of this solution, and Larry turned to J.D.

"Onion soup, prime rib, rare, baked potato, and salad for two."

"Wine, sir?"

J.D. looked at Katie, who shook her head. "No, no wine."

As Larry walked off, Katie made a slight sound of distress and half rose from her seat. "J.D., I left the script and my notes in the car."

"Sit down and calm down. I wasn't proposing to go over them in detail while we ate. We can go somewhere and do that afterwards. Could you just give me a general idea of what you thought, or would you prefer to do that later, too?"

"Oh, no, now, that's why I'm here," said Katie eagerly. "I really liked most of it," she went on in a businesslike way. "You handled it—*us*—with, well, with a tact and sensitivity most Englishers—outsiders—don't always show.

My main complaint is that you make everyone seem too black and white. The Amish aren't all saints, you know."

"But I thought the Amish way of life was a striving for perfection?"

"Exactly. It's a *striving*. But since the Amish are human, they frequently fall by the wayside, they often fail. They make mistakes, like anyone else, and fall short of their own high standards. On the other hand, this doesn't make the ones that *do* complete sinners. I can point to at least six or seven instances in the script where this isn't made clear."

J.D. nodded in satisfaction. "You've already paid for your dinner," he told her teasingly. "Anything else?"

"The character of the Deacon who agrees to the *meidung* on his own son. You made him appear too much the opposite of all the saints—hard, mean, cruel."

"But what he did was—"

"No," Katie interrupted in her eagerness. "It seemed to me your portrait of a naturally hard and ruthless man took away from his—well, his humanity. It would be much more real if you showed him as a man racked by pain, in anguish because of what his conscience dictates he do. His life-long beliefs tell him he must choose between his son and his God, which means that his son must be cast out. But never think he does it lightly, lovelessly. He's a father, for God's sakes; he's a soul in torment."

As she discussed the Deacon's character, she could tell by his face that he was eager, interested, and with her all the way till the last comment. Then his face closed up, and there went that wall of glass again. Once more, as though she hadn't noticed the distance he was suddenly putting between them, Katie rushed into speech again.

"I was awfully surprised when I first looked at the script to see that you had written it, or partly written it, as well."

"As well as what?" asked J.D. colorlessly.

"As well as producing and directing. I guess the truth is, I was more impressed by the writing than the other two."

"You were?"

"Uh huh. You see, I guess I'm a little in awe of anyone who writes professionally. It's—well, it's what I want to do more than anything else in the world. And I intend to try some day."

Once again she had shattered the glass wall between them, but it gave her less pleasure than she had expected, since J.D. was regarding her not from far away now, but closely and almost with distaste.

"I suppose," he said with an air of disdain, "you write absolutely wonderful letters?"

Katie looked at him in bewilderment. "I hardly write any letters at all."

"But you do keep a diary or a journal?"

"Well, yes . . ."

"Naturally. And the moment you have the time you will, of course, translate the story of your life, as set down in said journal, into one of the great books of our era?"

Their conversation was interrupted by Larry with their soup. As soon as he was gone, J.D. picked up his spoon, but Katie ignored the appetizing smell from the three miniature brown crocks in front of her and looked steadily across at him.

"Why are you being so disagreeable?" she asked him quietly.

"Because I am constantly irritated by would-be amateur writers who are convinced their peerless unpublished prose will set the world on fire."

"I never said any of those things," Katie pointed out. *"You* did. I don't write many letters. I've kept a journal—sporadically—since living in Pennsylvania, because I was a misfit in an Amish household and it gave me a chance to say things I could never say out loud. I am well aware that it takes talent, not time, to be a writer, because my father was one. Nothing as impressive as what you do, Mr. Movie Man," she told him, for the first time a cutting edge to her voice. "He was a writer-editor on a home crafts magazine, and the last two years of his life when he was dying of cancer—though I didn't know it then—he worked at home writing articles. He also corrected all my little poems and stories and encouraged me to believe I could write myself one day."

J.D. stretched his hand across the table to her. "Katie, I apologize. I'm utterly and abjectly sorry."

She sat, cheeks flushed and lips compressed, eyeing the hand but not taking it.

"Do I have to get down on my knees?"

"It would probably do you a world of good."

He pushed his chair back and started to bend his legs.

"For God's sakes, don't!" cried Katie, alarmed. "Everyone's looking. Sit down, please."

"Only if you accept my hand and tell me I'm forgiven for being a crass egotistical idiot."

"I forgive you for being a crass egotistical idiot. Now sit down."

J.D. sat. "Hand, too." He held it out again.

Katie extended her own hand, laughing in spite of her determination to be somewhat distant herself now. To her surprise . . . and the beginnings of another emotion she couldn't quite sort out . . . instead of shaking her hand, J.D. lifted it, palm up, and brushed it lightly, softly, with his lips.

He restored her hand to her. "Your soups are getting cold."

He applied himself silently to his own soup, but Katie kept stealing quick glances at him while she disposed zestfully of the contents of the three small crocks.

It was funny . . . he didn't look at all like Johnny; the two were as different as men could be, but just the same, when she was with him, he brought Johnny to mind . . .

Maybe it was the almost violent swing of his moods: Friendly. Pleasant. Kind. Boyishly charming. And then came that glass wall . . . and the icy distance . . . the sharp tongue . . . followed almost as quickly by warm contrition . . . easy laughter . . . the careless, wonderfully un-Amish-like indifference to what people thought of his behavior.

He really would have gone down on his knees if I hadn't stopped him, she thought, half wistful, half admiring.

"Good evening, J.D."

They had both been too wrapped up in their own thoughts to notice the swaying approach of Taffy Tremont, dressed in clinging black jersey that fit her like a snake's skin.

"So *this* is your Amish consultant, J.D.?"

J.D. stood up. "Yes, she is. What are you doing here, Taffy?"

"Having dinner with Myles and Edward. It *is* a public restaurant, darling."

"So it is. Well, you go back to Myles and Edward now, and I'll speak to you tomorrow."

"But I want to stay and hear about the business you have with your Amish*man*, J.D. darling. I'm sure I can give *him* a few pointers."

"Taffy," said J.D. in a low dangerous voice, "I'll pick you up at the hotel for an early breakfast and a heart-to-heart talk. Right now, get the hell back to your own table."

As Taffy flounced off, pouting and petulant, Katie and half the patrons of the restaurant stared in fascination at the retreat of her bouncing buttocks.

When Katie looked back to J.D., he shrugged slightly. "That's another apology you're owed. Sorry."

"You talked to her rather roughly."

"Did that offend your sensibilities? Sorry again, but

with apologies now to the canine world, Taffy Tremont's a bitch and doesn't respond to a gentle hint."

A bus boy took their soup plates and was promptly followed by Larry delivering their entrees and salad. The business of eating occupied them for the next few minutes. When Katie looked up again, J.D. was regarding her with a lurking twinkle in his eye.

"You're disappointed in me, aren't you?" Then, without waiting for her answer, "I suspect more of the Amish world than you realize has rubbed off on you, Katie Kauffman."

As they were both rounding off their dinner with coffee and strawberry shortcake, the hostess came by and set a single glass of champagne in front of Katie. "Compliments of the Franklin Arms," she said graciously. "I hope you enjoyed your dinner."

"Very much, thank you," said J.D.

"Oh, yes, thank you, it was absolutely marvelous," Katie assured her.

"What a nice thing for her to do." Katie took a tentative sip of the champagne. "But why didn't she give you one?"

"Because she's aware by now that I don't drink. I would say it was smart rather than nice. She's a good businesswoman, and film companies are big spenders."

"That's a terribly cynical outlook," protested Katie. "I prefer to think she was being nice." She took another, longer sip.

"You look at the world your way, I'll look at it mine," said J.D. equably. Then his face crinkled in amusement. "You know, if you don't like the stuff, you don't have to drink it just to be polite." He leaned across the table and suggested in a conspiratorial whisper, "We could pour it into the coffee pot and no one would ever know."

"I like it . . . sort-of . . . it just lacks something." She looked down at her plate, and her eyes lit up. "I know." One at a time, with her fingers, she plucked three strawberries from the top of her cake, carefully licked the whipped cream from each one, and deposited it in her glass of champagne.

J.D. watched, hypnotized, as she managed, with each swallow, to bite down on a strawberry.

"Now *that* was delicious!" said Katie, flushed and triumphant, setting down her empty glass.

J.D. shook his head. "Little Amish girl, you are something else."

Katie laughed happily. "It's a shame, but I'm too full to finish my cake."

"Thank the Lord for small mercies. I was beginning to feel slightly queasy watching you."

He signed his name in a careless scrawl on the bill tendered by Larry, wrote in his room number and a tip, and came around the table to pull out Katie's chair.

They passed the table where Taffy sat with Myles and Edward, who were friends of J.D.'s, but he just gave them a quick hello, without stopping. Myles gave him a friendly wink as J.D. propelled Katie quickly by them.

"Are you clear-headed enough to go over the script with me?" he asked jokingly when they were outside.

"Of course I am. I've had drinks before. At least five or six times."

"Practically an alcoholic! Hold onto my arm again. Do you mind going up to my room to work? The lobby doesn't offer much work space or privacy."

"No, that sounds fine."

They got in the car and drove to the other end of the parking area, then they walked up the outside steps to J.D.'s room.

Katie spread the script and her notes out on the bed, and J.D. pulled the rocker over for her and the desk chair for himself. They went through the script page by page, stopping whenever she had marked a piece of paper with specific corrections or suggestions.

She not only spotted a number of small but glaring errors and broadened his perception of the Amish and Mennonite views of the world, but also offered plenty of pithy comments on the action and the dialogue.

I just can't believe, after what he did before, that he would act this way . . .

The character you've described wouldn't say that . . .

This sentence doesn't ring true . . .

The girl would be at home when their intention to marry was announced at Preaching.

J.D. looked at his watch when they were done. "Only a quarter past eleven. I can't believe we got through so much so quickly." He patted her head like a fond uncle. "Katie, you've been—you *are*—a treasure. I'd better take you home now. Just one more thing. Sign this chit, will you?"

Katie looked at the slip of paper he had just brought from the desk drawer. "What is it?"

"An invoice stating how many hours of work you put in. What with your reading and notes, going along with me to the Yoder farm yesterday, and all of tonight, I made a rough estimate of ten hours. Ten hours of consultancy at twenty bucks per. That's two hundred dollars Continental owes you. You'll get your check next week."

"But J.D., I did it as a favor! Remember that's what you asked, would I read the script as a favor. You know I went to the Yoder farm because I wanted a car ride, and I came tonight for the pleasure of it." She looked almost ready to cry. "I don't want you to pay me."

"I'm not paying you, kid, the company is . . . the way it pays me."

"You get paid for taking me to dinner?"

"If it's part of my job."

"So." Katie inclined her head. "It's part of *your* job, but it isn't part of mine. My job is with the Widow Miller. I would like to be taken home now, please."

J.D. laid the chit back on his desk. "If you won't, you won't. Too bad. I really had hoped you would work on the set for me during the filming. Your suggestions have been helpful."

"Work on the set for you how?"

"Just the way you did on the script . . . as a consultant. Watching out for mistakes in dress and speech, inconsistencies, making appropriate suggestions."

"Why did you change your mind about my doing it?" she asked breathlessly.

"I didn't change it, you did. I offered you a job, Katie," he said casually. "Anyone who works on my film gets paid. No pay, no job."

Katie chewed furiously on her lower lip. "I guess that makes it different," she admitted cautiously.

With a mighty effort, J.D. restrained a grin.

"You understand I'm not free in the mornings? I have to get the house in order and the meals prepared. But from lunch time till about four . . ."

"Lunch time till four will suit me fine. Can you be at the Yoder farm tomorrow?"

"I think so. I'll call you here if I can't," Katie said airily, knowing all the while she would be there if she had to stay up all night to do her work and then crawl to the Yoders' on her hands and knees!

Sixteen

K-K-Katie, b-beautiful Katie
You're the only g-g-girl that I adore
When the m-moon shines over the m-mountain
I'll be waiting for you at the k-k-kitchen door.

"What do you mean, lunch time till four?" demanded Widow Miller. "Are you *narrish,* Katie? You get up before six in the morning; by nine, ten, you've got all your work done till it's time to put the supper on."

"I can't leave you alone all day, and I should be here when the twins get home from school."

"I won't be alone. I'll call my cousin Miriam Freed to keep me company after you leave in the morning. She's good company, Miriam is, and she can use the extra money since her husband's so sick. He has Parkinson's, you know."

"No, I didn't know, but in that case, you have to pay her the salary you've been giving me. The movie company will pay me really well."

"Whatever you say, just so you tell your young man you're available whenever he wants you."

Katie flushed. "He's not my young man. He's—"

"Well, if he isn't, he should be. You want to stay in Strawberry Schrank forever, with a *doppel* like I hear your sister's marrying?"

"Crist is a nice boy. Annie loves him."

"You want a *nice* boy, Katie? An *Amish* boy?"

Katie shook her head "No, not that."

Widow Miller eyed her with unexpected shrewdness. "You think I don't know what you want, Katie? You think I've forgotten what it's like to be young? Thank the Lord, I found myself someone different, a Mennonite not too strict, who was right here, but *you* have to make your own luck. For you, knights in shining armor aren't going to gallop over from Route Three-forty to hidden country roads."

"Do you think I don't know that?" Katie cried out passionately. "Any man on a Pennsylvania dirt road is a farmer in work shirt and suspenders, looking for a woman to share his bed at night after sharing the long day of chores. He wants his breakfast on the table at seven A.M. and a big supper after his work is done. He wants children——lots of them——to help on the farm, and a wife who sews and cooks and cleans and submits her will, not just her body."

"Well, is that the kind of life you want?"

"Hell, no!" said Katie, then clapped her hand over her mouth, aghast, but the Widow Miller just laughed.

"So, then? Don't fool with this opportunity God gave you. Hustle out there in search of what you want. Opportunity's sure not coming here to find you."

But J.D. *had* found her here, Katie reflected an hour later, taking the short cut across the fields. Of course, J.D. wasn't high romance. He was something better . . . a wonderful new friend, a companion with common interests, someone to talk and joke and laugh with, an exciting presence from that outside world she wanted so much to be a part of.

That was why her heart was beating so fast and she was all in a turmoil about seeing him again. Just as Widow Miller had said, he was opportunity knocking at her door. His business and his world might represent her future.

Friendship was all. High romance could wait, Katie decided even as she vigorously and unknowingly walked toward it.

At the top of a mountain road, she looked down on the Yoder farm and a spectacle she had only read about in forbidden books and magazines and newspapers . . . a movie company filming. There were half a dozen carriages and horses, dozens of milling people, many in Plain dress, Amish and Mennonite both, many in English dress. It was hard to tell some of the actors and workers from the residents and the tourists.

Katie watched, spellbound, for a time, then raced down the hill toward the scene of noisy, fascinating confusion. She came off the wooded path behind the farm, near to the almost-deserted barn. Even the workers were up front, watching—

She was just about to go up front herself and announce her early arrival to J.D. Shale when a man came around the corner of the barn. The sun was in both their eyes; she shaded hers with one hand to get a better look at him.

There was a long, timeless moment of looking, and her world turned upside down as she discovered that it wasn't friendship she felt—not at all. She knew now why her heart beat so fast at the thought of him and her knees knocked together at the sound of his voice.

In that one look she had found out that shining armor could be a short-sleeved loose-knit sports shirt with a broad zig-zagged grey and blue pattern and all the buttons unbuttoned.

College wrestling had broadened his shoulders, but it had never contributed to his height; even his biased Aunt Marion would not have called J.D. handsome. Still, Katie stood and stared at him with incredulous joy, almost as though she were seeing him for the first time. So this was how it felt to be struck *leebgronk!*

Friend? Companion? She must have been as *narrish* as the Widow had said, not to recognize at once that she loved everything about him . . . his eyes so wonderfully alive (how intriguing their snapping challenge!), the head of short-cropped black curls, and the chest of equally dark curly hair revealed by the unbuttoned buttons. Her eyes roved over him hurriedly, hungrily. It was wonderful how his jeans fit so tightly, so un-Amishly, around his legs (and even tighter over his flat stomach). She was fascinated by his strong hairy arms (so unlike Crist Raber's scrawny ones), his full mouth (Dear God! How come she hadn't known at once when he'd kissed the palm of her hand last night?), even the strange, massive ring with the colored stone on one of his fingers.

"Are you here for the milking?" asked the deep-timbred voice that sent a now-identifiable thrill through her body.

"I'm K-Katie," she faltered.

"Katie." He came out of the sun, blinking, then took her hand and pulled her into the shadow of the barn. "By God, you are!" He eyed her shapeless brown dress and apron and pleated *kapp* with disbelief. "What on earth are you doing in that outfit?"

"If—if I'm your Amish consultant," she said nervously, "I thought I should dress Amish."

"Your line of reasoning eludes me." He walked all around her, shaking his head.

Even in the throes of her newly discovered passion, Katie was capable of a spurt of anger against the beloved object of it!

"We Amish don't believe worldly appearance is of any significance," she proclaimed with self-righteous priggishness.

"In that case," said J.D. dryly, "you're a lot more Amish than you led me to believe because, take it from me, your worldly appearance at the moment would have no significance for anyone."

Katie felt a momentary stab of pain, and then she couldn't help being struck by the humor of it. She had planned to be thoroughly business-like, thoroughly Amish, to please him.

She began to laugh softly, then she began to laugh harder. Soon her laughter was ringing out warm and free. Her eyes crinkled up and her mouth opened wide, showing the full curves of her soft, kissable lips and the nearly white, slightly crooked teeth that had never known an orthodontist's touch.

"Touché," she said good-naturedly. "You've got me there."

J.D.'s eyes narrowed. "Touché," he repeated.

Coffee Katie of Strawberry Schrank was quick to catch the implication.

"Remember me? I'm the girl who reads banned books."

"I remember," J.D. said, flicking his finger along her nose. "You're the fresh one."

From the very first moment when he'd discovered that the boy sitting on the fence was a girl, she had posed a stimulating challenge. His interest had been fired by the wistful child, the impudent urchin, and the earthy quick-witted woman all combined in one Pennsylvania Dutch farm girl.

Last night he had been all too conscious of her physical attraction but even more aware—once they got down to work—of her easy humor, her pride and spirit, and her sharp intelligence.

From the moment she had started laughing, he was back again to thinking of her in physical terms. Even in that hideous drab dress, God, what a captivating minx she was!

Katie was looking at him inquiringly. While he was lost in his thoughts, she must have asked something.

"I'm sorry, Katie, I didn't hear you."

"I asked, what was that you said about needing someone for the milking?"

"One of the Mennonite girls from the crowd scene said she would help me out. I've never watched a cow be milked. I wanted to figure out camera shots and angles."

"I can milk a cow for you, city boy, so long as you don't take any real photographs."

"Why not, country girl?"

Katie looked embarrassed. "Oh, well . . . Pap, you know . . . it has to do with the Commandment about graven images . . ."

It was J.D.'s turn to laugh, which he did long and heartily. "And *you* such a proper obedient little Amish girl!" he chortled.

Katie, nose in air, left him alone to his glee and walked into the barn to look over the cows. Having selected a likely one, she set herself down on a stool, pail in place, and put business-like hands on the full udders.

When J.D. came close, she warned him, "Don't get too near; they can kick."

"Will you be all right?"

She cast him an amused glance. "After ten years of this, I could do it in my sleep."

Then she bent to her task while he stood with his eyes swiveling back and forth from the competent browned hands directing twin streams into the pail and the pale golden profile of the milkmaid.

God, what he wouldn't give to see her in really smart clothes. Or, come to think of it, without any clothes at all.

He shook himself. He must be getting sick . . . or prematurely senile . . . Katie was a kid, a smart but unawakened country kid. He should be shot for what he was thinking.

Then Katie came toward him, casually swinging the half-full milk pail. "Want a drink?" she invited. "There's a dipper over there. The milk's nice and warm."

He shuddered and gagged. "No, thank you."

"Do you care if I do?"

"Not at all." But he turned slightly green as he watched her throw back her head, showing the long lines of her throat as she literally poured down the dipper full of warm milk.

"That was lovely," she told him. "I was warm from the walk."

"You're lovely," said J.D. Shale, surprising himself as much as he surprised her. He had never intended to say any such thing. He hadn't intended to kiss her either, but her lusciously full red mouth (and she didn't even wear lipstick) was right there, laughing up at him. He was only human, after all, and even the Amish—hadn't she said so herself?—were allowed to be human.

His hands touched her shoulders lightly, exerting just the slightest leverage. Katie, still clutching the pail, lifted her face and he kissed her softly, sweetly, and briefly. She was still straining toward him when he removed his mouth from hers. With a grieved little murmur of disappointment, she let go of the pail.

"Damn it to hell!" snarled J.D. as milk spilled over and inside his leather moccasins, soaked his French lisle socks, and dampened the bottoms of his jeans.

Katie had jumped back in time to avoid more than just a slight spraying; he saw tears on her cheeks.

"Aw, c'mon," he joked, ashamed of his ill temper, "haven't you ever heard you shouldn't cry over spilled milk?"

"Of c-course I have. We s-say *b-brilla inwer f-ferschittie m-militch.*" She blew her nose in a corner of her apron. "That's not why I'm crying."

"Why are you, then? If it was the kiss, I'll apologize, though it would be a da—a big lie to say I'm sorry."

"It was the kiss," said Katie, avoiding his eyes. "I hoped— our first time—it would be a real one."

"A real one?" J.D. repeated cautiously.

"You know . . . the way a man is . . . he's supposed to know how to kiss a woman."

"Well, I'll be . . ." He suddenly doubled up with laughter. "That's hitting a guy where it hurts," he gasped, while Katie stared, slightly affronted at this inexplicable burst of merriment.

J.D. straightened up. "How old are you, Katie? Ten going on forty?"

"I just turned twenty."

"Twenty. I've almost forgotten what it felt like to be twenty. Well, K-K-Katie, there's something else you may have read." He moved close to her again.

> *" 'Then come kiss me, sweet and twenty*
> *Youth's a stuff will not endure.'*

That, in case you don't already know it, was written by a fellow named Will Shakespeare, and for your information, I'm more than nine years older than you in years and about double that in experience, but I have never been told that I don't kiss a woman like a man."

He took her by the shoulders. "Shall we try again?"

"Yes, please," said Coffee Katie, sounding so like a schoolgirl requesting a treat, that J.D.'s mouth was still spread in a wide grin when it landed squarely on hers.

Taking his time, his lips gentled hers for a bit until they were soft and pliant; then they rubbed and tasted and nibbled and devoured, all the while with his hands working their way across her head and neck in the strangest way, touching places she had never known to be so sensitive . . . the lobes of her ears and a spot just behind them, the nape of her neck, the pulse at the front of her throat, the parting of her hair underneath her *kapp,* even the arch of her eyebrows.

She leaned against him, visibly trembling, and he lifted

his face for a moment and gave her the quick, triumphant glance of a conquering male, then returned to the job at hand, kissing her temples and her forehead and slowly, one at a time, her eyelids. As a finale, he used his tongue to tease and tangle her lashes.

Presently, panting a little and painfully conscious that this was getting out of hand and that he might be the one to suffer for it more than she, J.D. put her away from him, silently cursing his tight-fitting jeans.

"Was that real enough for you, honey?"

"Yes, thank you," gulped Katie, at which piece of naivete, J.D. Shale, whose Hollywood-famed golden tongue had persuaded reluctant conservative Mennonites, including two ministers and a bishop, to cooperate with some of the more liberal ones in the shooting of his film, stood tongue-tied before a slip of a country girl in a dress that no other woman of his acquaintance would have willingly used for anything except a dust rag.

Coffee Katie's legs were cornmeal mush and her insides were *unner's ew erscht.* Other unidentifiable urges were quivering along the nerve endings of other unmentionable parts of her. So this was instant love, she told herself in innocent ecstasy.

She would have been shocked and horrified if J.D. had been as blunt about *her* present reaction as she had been about *his* first kiss. But J.D. had begun a teasing rendition of a familiar number from the *Book of Old Songs* in Johnny's Levi Luke collection:

> *K-K-Katie, b-beautiful Katie*
> *You're the only g-g-girl that I adore . . .*

Katie stood mesmerized, *leebgronk,* experiencing the casually carolled words as part of the magic and majesty of this moment, with no way of knowing that the correct spelling of the four-letter word for what she felt was not spelled l-o-v-e but l-u-s-t.

The sight of her tremulous uncertainty completely restored J.D.'s own slightly toppled self-assurance. He glanced down at his watch. "Break's over," he said. "Time to get back to work. Come on, Katie. I need my Amish consultant out front."

Seventeen

Continental Films has bought the movie rights to the comedy-mystery, It's Murder, She Sez *by James O'Dare. It will star Nancy Vail and Seth Edwards of the original off-Broadway cast. Auditioning for the other roles will take place in New York and Hollywood next week. . . .*

The first person Katie noticed when she and J.D. walked up front to join the rest of the film company was the girl he had been so "rough" with the night before. Even in her adaptation of Mennonite dress—much too modish and form-fitting to be authentic—how could one miss all those blonde curls spilling over the bodice?

She tugged at J.D.'s sleeve, "That girl . . . the one who was in the restaurant last night. Who is she? What part does she play?"

"That's Taffy Tremont. She has a small featured part— the Mennonite bride. We'll be finished shooting her scenes in a few days."

Katie hadn't meant to ask anything more. It was none of her business, and besides . . .

"Did you have breakfast with her this morning?" she

asked J.D., all the more abruptly for being ashamed of the question.

"Yes." J.D. smiled to himself.

He had feasted on a full Pennsylvania Dutch breakfast while Taffy—dieting, as usual—confined herself to black coffee and dry toast.

Their conversation had been short and to the point.

"Taffy, listen and listen well, because I'm not repeating this," he had said, setting down his empty juice glass. "I'm fed up to the teeth with your shenanigans. You have two choices: I can throw you off the set, or you can behave here and leave in a few days to audition for the role of the drowned model in *It's Murder, She Sez*. It's a small but very juicy part, which is likely to be yours if I make just one phone call to Bunny Wren in casting. Well, which is it going to be?"

"J.D., you darling, I adore you, I'll be an angel from now on. When will you call Bunny?"

"The day you leave here."

"Bless you forever, you adorable man. I'll go call my agent."

She darted away, coffee and toast untasted, leaving J.D. to finish his own breakfast in peace. It was his recollection that Taffy had shown more genuine ecstasy about the prospective movie role than she had ever exhibited in bed, which now made him smile, but Katie was not to know that.

"Her dress is much too tight and her hair's all wrong," Katie said waspishly. "It should be pinned up and scraped back under her *kapp*."

"That much we know," said J.D. easily. "She just takes it down between scenes. Says the pins give her a headache. But go right on noticing. That's what I want you to do . . . spot any discrepancies. Keep taking your notes. By the way, you ought to have—Tommy, over here. Get me a clipboard and pen for Katie, please."

J.D. left her while Tommy was fetching the clipboard. People kept running into her, so after a while Katie wandered over to a big weeping willow, out of the way of the shooting but near enough so she could see and hear everything.

She sat under the tree with her clipboard, observing all the action but watching J.D. the most intently. Occasionally he used a megaphone to shout his orders, though his voice was so powerful, Katie thought proudly, he hardly needed it.

There was a short lunch break when Mrs. Yoder and her daughters served sandwiches and coffee at tables set up outside. Then the work continued.

It was interesting at first; then it got to be tedious. Katie marveled at the patience of J.D., who had not seemed to be a patient man . . . the way he went over and over the same little bit.

In the late afternoon J.D. called a halt. He issued a series of instructions to the camera crew, and the dismantling of their equipment was executed swiftly and smartly. He called out to a handsome young man in Mennonite garb, who had casually peeled away his beard, complaining that it itched, "Remember, Paul, no late night tonight. We start the wedding scenes first thing tomorrow. Taffy, that goes for you, too."

Taffy Tremont came running up to him. Her hair was down again—she seemed to have enough of it to fill a haystack.

"J.D. darling," she teased as she kissed him theatrically. "A pity it can't be *you* that I'm marrying tomorrow."

Coffee Katie Kauffman, sitting under her tree, clipboard in hand, experienced a primitive burst of fury at the sight of those pouting lips planted on his cheek and the possessive way the blonde actress was clinging to his arm.

Almost as though her thoughts and feelings had been

transmitted to him by telepathy, J.D. glanced at Katie for the first time in nearly three hours.

"Run along, Taffy," he told the blonde, propelling her forward with one hand on her bottom. "Get plenty of beauty sleep," he reminded her. "Tomorrow you're a blushing bride."

She looked languishingly back over her shoulder. "Two times a bride so far, darling, but never a blush," she simpered and ran off, laughing.

Katie, who had risen and left the shelter of her tree, looked after the Taffy creature with eyes that darted fire. How dare that Jezebel touch and talk to him so intimately? And what was his hand doing on her bottom?

J.D. looked over at the flushed cheeks and furious eyes of his little milkmaid and had much ado not to break down laughing. The proper little Amish girl was jealous, frantically jealous, of the casual attention he'd paid Taffy, he realized with smug enjoyment. She should only know—and he had no intention of telling her—he wouldn't have the blonde bitch as a *gift!*

He should be ashamed of himself, getting a kick out of what was probably the Katie girl's first crush, but he couldn't help it. Some stolid Amish farmer, he decided half-regretfully, was going to wind up with a surprising bundle of passion.

In spite of the many departures, there were too many people around to suit Coffee Katie. She was wild to be alone with J.D. again, and as soon as his day's work seemed to be over and he came strolling up to her, she asked, "Would you like to go for a walk and look at my notes?" in a tone that she hoped sounded casual.

J.D., who was tired and in no mood for a walk, found himself yielding to the pressure of those pleading eyes. He agreed to walk a short way with her, and they went up one hill and down another till they came to another weeping willow with a patch of grass cleared beneath it.

"Let's sit down here," J.D. proposed, sliding down with his back against the trunk of the tree. Katie sat beside him and handed over her clipboard.

"There wasn't so much today," she said apologetically.

While J.D. studied her nòtes, Katie studied him, her mind and heart equally confused.

She felt humbled, she felt shamed, thinking of how soon after he left—only these few months—she had forgotten her love for Johnny.

Then she corrected herself. No, it wasn't that . . . Of course she loved Johnny still; she would love him always. She just wasn't *in* love with him, as she had thought.

There was a wide world of difference between what she felt for Johnny and what she now felt for J.D. Shale. This was what Annie had meant by being *leebgronk:* passion, adoration, and the overwhelming desire to be with the one special man who made every other want and desire in life pale by comparison.

No wonder she had been able to deal so sanely, so logically, with Johnny's proposal that she come to Boston with him. . . .

She was fiercely aware that if J.D. Shale were to say, come with me somewhere, *any*where, she would willingly go at once. She would follow him across a jagged mountain, barefoot; over a burning plain, naked; through a flooding river, without a life jacket.

Anything, anytime, anywhere, so that they arrived together.

"These are fine," J.D. said abruptly, putting the clipboard aside.

He looked at her, and Katie looked at him, waiting to continue what they had begun a few hours earlier. Waiting to be kissed. Waiting to be loved.

Just look at her sitting there, J.D. said to himself, all ignorantly sexy and innocently ready. A twenty-year-old girl in this day and age . . . unbelievable! And with no idea of the trouble she could be asking for if she fell into the wrong hands. He shuddered just to think of it. Not that the wrong hands would ever be *his,* of course.

Even as he preened himself on how safe she was with him, he started remembering the feel of her in his arms and began to sweat as he hadn't when the sun was high.

The world was full of pretty, eager, available girls. It would be only right, as well as smart, to throw this small vulnerable fish back into the pond. Telling himself so, he felt a desire for her so far from casual, it almost amounted to a craving. He wanted to hold her close again, feel her body molded to his like a second skin.

He closed his eyes, trying to shut Katie out, but there was no driving away the memory of warm lips and burning thighs, the naive and quivering readiness of her response. Suddenly, impetuously, he reached for her and pulled her into his arms.

Some time during the wild kissing, Katie found herself lying on the ground with the top of her dress all unpinned and the two white globes—that any decent Amish girl was expected to conceal under extra layers of cloth—completely bared to his touch and his taste and—what she found even more mortifying—his sight.

"Don't look," she whispered in an agony of embarrassment, trying to cross her hands over her breasts.

"Don't be silly," said J.D., taking hold of both her wrists and moving her arms down against her sides. "They're beautiful," he said matter-of-factly. "They were meant to be looked at."

He continued to look and then to do much more, and Coffee Katie, after a few tentative wriggles of protest, relaxed into passive acceptance and from there into dazed delight.

Her eyes were closed; her body was pulsating under his. He could do any damned thing with her he wanted to, and that very awareness stopped him cold.

"Katie!" he said sharply.

She opened her eyes slowly, looking up at him like a sleepwalker.

"Get up," he told her roughly. "Pin yourself together."

"Wh-why?"

"It's time you went home, isn't it? You'll be late, won't you?" he asked savagely.

Katie stumbled as she rose, but he didn't reach out a hand to help her. Shamed by the cold merciless eyes now raking her with what she took to be contempt, she turned her back, fumbling with the pins as she got her dress together and tied the cape around it.

Tears filled her eyes and rolled slowly down her cheeks. "Wh-what d-did I d-do?" she asked piteously.

"Too much. Didn't anyone ever warn you about making yourself too easy? Too cheap?"

She winced under the lash of his scorn, not realizing it was directed far more at himself than at her.

"I am not any of those things," she told him, her head held high. "I have never behaved this way before."

"Well, you shouldn't have behaved this way now," he proclaimed, self-righteously forgetful of who had initiated this particular intimacy.

"Why not?"

"Because"—telling himself he spoke this way for *her* sake, his answer was brutally blunt—"nice girls don't take quick tumbles in the hay with any passing stranger—strangers who, for all they know, might pass on a dangerous illness or even a fatal disease. You didn't even ask if—"

"I had no need to ask where there was trust."

"That kind of trust is plain idiocy when AIDS is an ever-present possibility. You didn't even ask," he repeated angrily. "And if you had, and I'd said I was clean, you shouldn't have believed me just like that. Not without certain proof."

For years to come, there would be sleepless nights when he would lie awake and listen to the echo of her strange little wail of anguish. She turned so deadly white, J.D. thought she might be going to faint. He put out his hand to support her, but Katie shied away from his touch.

"For you it might have been a tumble in the hay," she said with quiet dignity. "For me, it was not. There is no such thing as a passing stranger when a girl sees the man for whom she feels *leeb* . . . but, obviously, you know nothing of that. Nor do you need to tiptoe so delicately about the subject of the HIV virus and venereal disease. Our people are not that ignorant of the threats of the outside world . . . and I worked many months in a hospital. So, let us just say it is over between us and no lasting harm has been done. As we agreed earlier"—her voice faltered the least bit—"there's no use crying over spilled milk."

His hand went out again as she brushed by him. "Katie, I'm sorry. I never meant to hurt your feelings."

She turned her head a little to give him a long, candid look. "You lie," she told him dispassionately. "You showed a great need to hurt me. Perhaps, Mr. City Man, you should ask yourself why."

She was gone without another word, running so fleetly, he knew there was no way in the world he could catch up with her.

He called out her name a few times, loudly and demandingly, and finally, when it was too late, coaxingly. Coffee Katie never looked back or slowed her steps.

When she reached the end of a corn field and disappeared through a stand of trees, J.D. bent to pick up the clipboard. He was surprised to find that both his hands were shaking.

He had tried to behave according to the rigidly imposed code he had set for himself half a lifetime ago . . . yet somehow he felt ashamed.

He had known, even if she would not admit it, that in rejecting her, he had acted to protect her . . . so why did he now feel as though he had taken advantage of some poor defenseless creature?

He had resisted her for her own sake . . . It was crazy for him to have wound up feeling rejected.

Carrying her clipboard, he trudged back to the Yoder farm, back to his car. He was used to the bad moments . . . accustomed to knowing he was one against the world.

There had been worse times for him, God knew, and yet . . . and yet . . . he had never felt so damned alone in his life.

Eighteen

"Hollywood Tidbits"
by Pamela Goode

Taffy Tremont, back from Pennsylvania, where she played the young bride in Continental's TV movie, The Plain People, *is much more vocal about her coveted role as the slain model in* It's Murder, She Sez *than about her former ambition to make producer-director J.D. Shale her next husband . . .*

Every afternoon during the week after Coffee Katie ran from J.D. Shale's crushing rebuff, she had helped Flat Joseph with the farm work. It kept her from thinking too much during the day and left her tired enough to sleep at night.

On the eighth day they worked side by side in the fields for a few hours, hardly talking; then he tended to the mending of some harness, while she walked, barefooted still, to the barn to feed the livestock.

Presently he came to help her.

"You sure are *narrish* to be a *schoff frau,* Coffee Katie," he said in a rare burst of sociability.

Coffee Katie shrugged. "Better to *arawid* than *denk.*"

Flat Joseph laughed heartily. "I hope the next *schoff mon* who works for me feels the same."

Someone else joined in the laughter, and at the sound of that voice, Coffee Katie spun on her heel to confront J.D. Shale.

"Hello, Katie," he said gently.

"Hello," she said, unsmiling.

"Would you mind enlightening my ignorance? What did you two just say?"

Seeing that Coffee Katie intended to ignore these questions from the outsider, Flat Joseph good-naturedly obliged. "I said she's crazy to be a working woman," he explained, "and Coffee Katie—she said it is better to work than to think. So I said"—he laughed comfortably again—"I hope the next working man I get feels the same."

"Thanks. That makes perfect sense." J.D.'s hand shot out. "J.D. Shale," he said. *"Wee—er—gayt's?* Did I get that right?"

Flat Joseph cleaned his hand surreptitiously on the seat of his worn denim overalls before they shook. *"Ja, ja. You got it right. Wee gayt's."* He repeated in English, beaming, "How do you do? I'm Flat Joseph Dietrich."

"Would it be all right, Mr. D——" Remembering that when in Rome, he corrected himself. "Flat Joseph, would you mind if I took Katie for a walk?"

"Sure. Sure. Coffee Katie's her own boss."

J.D. slipped his arm through Coffee Katie's and felt resistance in every fiber of her being. He drew her along anyhow, rightly counting on her unwillingness to make a scene before the farmer. She walked quietly with him toward a field out of sight and out of hearing of Flat Joseph.

Once arrived, she pulled her arm free and let him feel the lash of her tongue. "I didn't want to see you again," she said untruthfully. "You should not have come."

"I wanted to see *you,"* said J.D. "Why on earth is that man called Flat Joseph?"

Taken off-stride by the unexpectedness of the last question, Coffee Katie said stiffly, "It's a nickname."

"Well, I didn't think he was christened—"

"On his first day of school his teacher asked him if he thought the world was round or flat, and he said any fool could see that, except for the *blutzes*—bumpy places—it was flat. He's been called Flat Joseph ever since."

"And why are you called Coffee Katie?"

"Because Mem—my foster mother is a Katy, too."

"But why *Coffee* Katie?"

"Why are *you* called by two letters of the alphabet?" she countered. "Don't you think *that's* strange-sounding?"

He conceded her point with a shrug. "My mother was a romantic. She named me for the hero in a book she was reading the day before I was born." He grinned at her. "I'll tell you what the names are if you promise on your sacred honor never to tell."

Torn between curiosity and the inclination to say she didn't care, Katie hesitated. Curiosity won.

"I promise."

"Jocelyn Daryl."

"Jocelyn Daryl." She rolled the names over on her tongue, carefully drawing out each syllable. "They're pretty," she pronounced.

"Pretty," he groaned. "Sure they are. But I grew up in a multi-ethnic neighborhood in Sheepshead Bay, Brooklyn—" Noting her puzzled expression, he interrupted himself to explain, "Italians, Irish, and Jews. It was tough enough being one of the few WASPs . . ."

Seeing her bewilderment, he again paused to translate. "That means white Anglo-Saxon Protestant . . . anyhow, like I said, it was tough enough for me to fit in there without a killer of a name like Jocelyn Daryl. Hence, J.D."

"Where was your father when the naming was going on? Didn't he have a say?"

To her surprise, J.D.'s face went absolutely blank. "In those days . . ." He stopped and started over again. "He was supposed to have been—fond enough of her to let her do as she pleased."

Katie stared at him doubtfully, sensing something peculiar in his choice of words, as well as in his stony expression. Then suddenly he was smiling again, saying to her easily, "Now that you've heard a small part of my life story, will you listen to my apology and explanation?"

"I would rather not."

"I don't believe that," said J.D. shrewdly. "If you're female—and I know damn well you are—you would give a year of your life to hear me explain and at least two to see me grovel."

Coffee Katie considered his words carefully, then nodded in agreement. "I have to admit you're right," she told him with reluctant honesty. "Very well. You want to talk . . . I'll listen."

"Can we sit?"

Without waiting for her to answer, he pulled her toward a distant fence.

When they were seated side by side, with their backs against the fence, Katie said primly, "I saw you that day with your hands on the actress with all the blonde hair . . . Taffy Tremont . . . and she had her hands all over you. I suppose for a while with me you forgot she was your woman."

"My woman! Taffy Tremont? You've got to be . . . what was that word Flat Joseph used for crazy?"

"Narrish."

"Yeah, *narrish.* You, Katie honey, are as *narrish* as they come if you think I would have Taffy Tremont as my woman any time before hell freezes over."

"But your hands—"

"My hands were a lot more over you just a short while later. Did you think that made *you* my woman? Good God!" He stared at her, stunned. "You did think so."

He leaned across her, taking hold of both her hands,

explaining urgently, "Katie, a man can want a woman without having any deeper feeling for her than just that— wanting. Any response I made to Taffy Tremont, in the course of work, was the kind she encouraged and expected and—the more fool I—I responded to."

He paused, studying her face, and Katie said thoughtfully, "I see. So what you are saying is that you responded to me in the way *I* encouraged and expected that you would."

"Don't be a fool!" he counseled her sharply. "I started making love to you just a little, for our mutual pleasure . . . only it turned out to be not so little. It was beginning to get out of hand. For *your* sake, God knows, not mine, I had to call a halt."

Katie continued to stare at him, her face impassive.

"Do you think it was easy?" he growled suddenly, his teeth grinding together in such unmistakable sincerity that the great weight that had been turning her insides leaden all week was suddenly, for the first time, eased a little.

"But why did you want to call a halt?"

"I didn't want to," J.D. shouted at her, forgetting this was supposed to be an apology. "I did what I thought was right."

"Why?"

"Because if I had stayed with you for another few minutes . . . things were getting out of control."

"So?"

"Damn it, Katie. Do I have to spell it out? I would have made love to you all the way. Do you understand what I mean?"

"You keep thinking of an Amish girl as a creature from outer space. Of course I understand what you mean. Possibly better than most city girls. I grew up on a farm . . . among only farm people. What I do *not* understand is that *you* wanted what *I* wanted, too, but you sent me away."

He swore. Then he groaned.

"I am not the nicest guy in the world," he bellowed so loudly that a nearby robin fluttered away in fright. "I am almost ten years older than you. *You*," he stated bitterly, "were probably still in grade school when I had my first girl. To use a well-worn phrase, I've been around . . . not so much in recent years, for prudent reasons—I was protecting myself."

He clamped his teeth shut. "But this one time, I was really thinking of *you*. The fact is that a man of my age and experience doesn't take advantage of a corn-fed country innocent unless he's completely lacking moral character, which at the moment"—he jumped up and started wearing out the patch of grass with his rapid footwork— "I feel is close to being the case."

There was a short pause while he continued his tigerish pacing. "If you didn't intend to make love to me, then why did you bother to come here?" Katie demanded outspokenly.

"I told you. I wanted to explain . . . and apologize. You looked so . . . No matter what you think—" His hands seemed to have a mind of their own. They were busily roving around in her hair. "I never intended to hurt you, K-K-Katie," he said, both teasing and sincere.

She looked up at him, not speaking, and he groaned aloud. "Oh, damn it all, Katie, I'm lying again. For days I've struggled with my better self, which said to stay away. I came—" He half-knelt to her. "I came simply because I couldn't stay away."

Her hand went out and tangled itself in the dark curly hair so different from her own. "Why did you struggle so hard?" she asked softly.

"Because there was no point in coming here to torture myself with wanting you . . . knowing I can't have you."

"Why are you so sure of that?"

"How many times must I tell you—a mature man doesn't take advantage of a young virgin."

"Who said I was a virgin?" asked Coffee Katie.

He sat back on his heels. "Of course, you're—you're not?" he asked uncertainly.

Katie shook her head. "In all honesty," she said carefully, "I haven't been able to call myself one since I was fourteen."

"My God!"

"Does it make a difference?"

The words were barely off her lips before her mouth was crushed under his. How they got there, she never remembered, nor did he, but several minutes later they were lying together in a small cleared section in the middle of the corn field. The stalks on the fields around them were high and concealing, but he was past caring. He had the dazed feeling he would have behaved in the same way if they were lying together in the middle of a major highway.

The lush little armful in the demure Amish gown was twined around him like an ivy vine, and they were kissing madly.

"Did you learn to kiss like this at fourteen, too?" he murmured into her ear.

"No, of course not. Except for one night of kissing with Johnny, I have never been kissed the least like this by any man but you."

"You surely do have a natural aptitude for it then, Coffee Katie," he said against her throat, starting to unpin the cloth at the breast of her dress. "Who is Johnny?"

"Thank you," said Coffee Katie dreamily. "Johnny is my foster brother," she told him between more kisses. "He lives in Boston now, but we were brought up together, and I thought I was in love with him—until I met you."

They were stretched alongside one another, and she never stopped speaking, not even when he turned her on her back and lay across her, propped up on two elbows so she wouldn't feel his full weight all at once. "He's always been my best friend," babbled Katie as J.D. released his elbows and slowly lowered himself. "He . . . ooooh."

"What's the matter?" he whispered in her ear. "Am I too heavy?"

"No, no, I was just startled by the—you know, I felt the—the—your *bolla* and—and—"

"My what?" he asked, lifting his head and chest.

"Your *bolla*," said Katie, slightly flustered. "You know . . . some of the—the private parts." She tugged at him. "Please don't move. I feel so—so complete when you are lying on me."

Willingly J.D. lowered himself again, his arms going under her, his lips nuzzling her neck. Wordlessly they embraced, kissed, and fit against one another in the ritual rhythmic motions of love-making. She was quiet now, but he could feel the wild throbbing of her heart as though it were inside his own body.

He knew that she was more than ready, and his hands left her breasts to lift her skirt. All at once a thought that had been vaguely teasing the back of his mind catapulted to the forefront.

He lifted his body again to look down at her "Why should it startle you so? Haven't you done this since the man when you were fourteen?"

"Well, I—I'm experienced enough. There was Johnny . . ."

"Was it Johnny when you were fourteen?"

"Of course not!" she said, horrified. "Johnny wouldn't . . . it was—er—"

"You're a very bad liar, Coffee Katie Kauffman. Now tell me the truth . . . damn it, what's the matter *now?*" as Katie once again uttered a prolonged "oooh" sound and tried to pull him back to her.

"You—it feels as though you have gone away from me," she whispered. "I think you have lost your—your firmness."

"You're damned right I've lost my firmness!" he roared.

"I am not accustomed to discussing the mechanics of the process and the state of my organ while I make love . . . while I *try* to make love. Answer my question, Katie!"

"There was no man when I was fourteen," she said forlornly, a lone tear slipping out of one eye and down her cheek. "I'm not a virgin, but it wasn't because of a man. I said that so you wouldn't have all those attacks of conscience about being with me."

J.D. rolled all the way off her. As he stood, he hauled Katie up with him, not caring that his handling of her was more than a little rough.

"Before I go completely round the bend, let's straighten this out once and for all." His hands left their vise-like grasp of her elbows in favor of a pincer-grip on her shoulders. "It's got to be one or the other. You're either a virgin and have never done this before, or you're *not* a virgin and you have. Which is it?"

"Neither," protested Katie, trying to wriggle free. "You're hurting me."

"Sorry," he said without conviction, letting go of her. Then, just as implacably as before, "Answer me, Katie."

"I had an accident in the barn," Katie flung at him. "It was mating time and our cow Alice was f-feeling wild. She kicked out, and I tripped backwards and sat down h-hard on a m-milk pail, which is how . . . well, technically, it was then I stopped being a virgin."

While he listened to this artless clarification, J.D. clutched at his head with a truly heart-rending sound of suffering. "My God, are you telling me you lost your virginity to a milk pail?"

Coffee Katie nodded. "I understand *now* how poor Alice felt!" she said defiantly.

Without answering her, J.D. started walking back across the fields. Coffee Katie hurried after him.

"J.D., where are you going?"

He didn't answer, just kept walking.

"J.D., are—are you leaving me again?"

A low, guttural snarl emerged from his throat. Nothing more.

"J.D."—she was running to keep up with him—"I don't see why you're behaving this way. You know—"

She stopped because she was too breathless to go on speaking. He had seized her by the shoulders again and was shaking her with passion. "You don't see!" he cried hoarsely. "You don't know! Damn it, how many times do I have to tell you that I don't seduce virgins almost half my age, even impatient virgins like you."

"P-p-please, J.D., st-stop it."

He released her so suddenly, she took three staggering steps backward. He caught her by one elbow again and kept her upright. "All we need is another milk pail," he said sardonically.

Katie whimpered ever so slightly, and J.D. growled, "Don't cry."

"I won't," said Coffee Katie in a hard, cold voice. "Believe me, I won't. I'm just trying to understand why my virginity or lack of it makes the difference. I thought it was how we felt about one another that counted."

"You were wrong."

"I—I even thought that you might take me with you when you leave Pennsylvania."

"Take you away with me! Are you crazy? Maybe you'd like to have me arrested for abduction as well as seduction. Of course I won't take you away from your home."

"I'm leaving anyhow," Coffee Katie told him steadily, "so it wouldn't be any of those things you said. The day after tomorrow I am going back home to Strawberry Schrank to help with my sister's wedding. The day after she marries, I intend to leave. I planned it long ago."

"Just where were you intending to go before I came on the scene?"

"New York . . . to try to be a writer. But I changed

my mind after meeting you. I'm sure I could do just as well in Los Angeles."

"Just like that? Overnight you'll turn Hollywood from Amish?"

The elaborate sarcasm was not lost on Katie, but she ignored it and gave him a deliberate, careful answer. "Naturally, it won't happen overnight, but certainly the moment I leave here, I'll cease to be Plain."

"Good for you. *When* you cease to be, and *when* you get to Los Angeles, by all means look me up. I'm in the Beverly Hills phone book. S-h-a-l-e . . . you know the first name. It's been interesting getting *not* to know you, Coffee Katie. God save me from any such future education."

He resumed his rapid walking, and this time Katie let him go. Perhaps it was just as well; there was so much to do here in the little time left. Later she could concentrate only on him.

Poor J.D. He didn't believe in her complete willingness to go away with him any more than he was able to accept that *he* might really want her to come, so he used that biting sarcasm and the cutting wit as his ultimate weapon.

Poor J.D., Katie repeated to herself, almost pitying him. Well . . . let him run away from her for now.

J.D. Shale of Hollywood, so much older than she in both years and experience, his learning so much greater . . . but it was Coffee Katie Kauffman of Strawberry Schrank who understood far better than he that good sense and good intentions were no match for such feelings as she felt . . . as he felt.

Twice he had forced her away from him and twice he had come after her, she reminded herself, half terrified, half triumphant. If love cast out fear, it also cast out pride. This third time she would go after *him*.

"Beverly Hills phone book," Katie said aloud as she started running toward the Miller farm.

She danced as she ran, she circled, skipped, and spread her arms wide. She hummed, she sang, she uttered hymns of praise.

The intensity of the feeling might be frightening, too, but above all, it was a wondrously marvelous sensation— this one of being *leebgronk!*

Nineteen

The social avoidance practiced by the Amish to avoid a drift toward worldliness may bring an erring member back into the fold. It may also work in reverse, driving him entirely out of the community and out of the Faith.

from *The Plain People*

On the morning after Annie's wedding, when the newly married couple had departed on a round of family visits, Katie broke the news of her own plan to leave home.

Katy Stoltzfus uttered a single piercing wail, then sat down in her chair, face buried in her hands as she rocked back and forth in time to a soft keening. It was more of a reproach to the now-weeping Katie than anything else Mem could have said or done.

"If you go, Coffee Katie," Amos told her, his voice as hard as his expression, "you are lost to us."

"Pap, please, I—"

"You are lost to us," Amos repeated implacably, "as surely as though you were taken in death."

Without another word to her, he called Paul John and Gideon to go out with him to the barn. When they came back for breakfast, he would not speak to Katie, nor accept food from her hands. He looked not at her, but through her, as though she did not exist. Her brothers acted scared and uncertain. Katy Stoltzfus served them, then sat staring straight ahead, not eating. As always, when Amos showed displeasure, silence prevailed.

Katie had thought, for Mem's sake, to stay on another day or two to make her going easier, but *this*—this was only prolonging the agony for all of them.

She had hardly any packing to do. Her suitcase full of the clothes she had worn in Basking Reade stood waiting in the bride's chest upstairs. She had only to add to it the two-volume set of *Janice Meredith*, which was her parting gift from the Widow Miller, and all her journals and school essays.

Out of regard for Mem's feelings, she did not change out of her Amish dress but carefully scraped her hair back and pinned on her *kapp* one last time. Then she descended again to the kitchen, suitcase in hand.

"It's best that I go now," she told her foster mother.

"Ja," Katy Stoltzfus acknowledged dully, " 'S *bescht."*

"I—I—you know how much you've meant to me," said Katie in a voice clogged with tears. "I don't want you to think—"

Mem tried to smile, but it looked more like a grimace of pain. "From the day my son left, I knew I wouldn't keep you long either. Always I understood you two better than you could see."

"I want to thank you for—"

"Thanks, I don't want."

"I love you, Mem."

Then Katy Stoltzfus wept and accepted her foster daughter's fiercely loving hug. "I don't care what *he* says, write to me, *mein kindt,* so I know always you're safe and well. And if you get the chance, look after my Johnny."

Katie walked down the road without looking back. Half a mile away a buggy stopped to offer her a lift, and she hitched a ride as far as the Levi Luke Fisher place.

She didn't need her key, someone had broken the

lock . . . but it didn't matter. There was nothing inside to harm. She had sent Johnny's books to him months before. Lifting the oilcloth covering, her fingers moved almost caressingly over the empty top shelf of the bookcase.

Her framed honorable mention and medallion were still hanging crookedly on their nails. She slipped them off, opened the suitcase, and tucked them among her blouses.

Then she undressed, shedding every piece of Amish clothing, stripping away the last vestiges of Coffee Katie.

The girl who left the Levi Luke School and walked down the road, a suitcase in her left hand, a navy bag slung over her right shoulder, might have been an Englisher tourist. She wore fitted jeans tied around her waist with a red print silk scarf instead of a belt. The top three buttons of her tailored blue cotton shirt were unbuttoned and the long sleeves rolled up above her elbows. She had brushed out her hair and it felt wonderfully light and free, bouncing against her back with every step.

She had no trouble, once she got to the highway, hitching a car ride into Lancaster. In Lancaster she went to the bank where she and Johnny had both opened accounts when he sold their Titanium stock. She emptied her account and converted all the money into traveler's checks. Between the Continental Films check mailed to her at Widow Miller's and her earnings, she also had over five hundred dollars in cash. That should be plenty.

Feeling rich, she took a cab to the railroad station, and while she waited for the next train to Philadelphia, she had two cups of coffee and some toast to make up for her uneaten breakfast.

In Philadelphia she took another taxi to the airport.

She could not get a reservation to Los Angeles until a late night plane. Hours and hours of waiting. It seemed a shame to waste all that time, which she could have used sight-seeing in Philadelphia, but it was too late now.

She checked her suitcase, carefully tucking her ticket

into the shoulder bag along with her money and traveler's checks. She walked around the airport, holding tightly onto the top flap of her purse.

She wandered in and out of attractive little stores, enjoying the knowledge that she could buy whatever she wanted . . . and soon she would. All she bought immediately, feeling the need, was a cheap digital watch.

In one gift shop she spent an enjoyable twenty minutes choosing three paperback books and then headed back to a restaurant she remembered seeing.

The leaden lump of guilt and misery that had lodged in her stomach most of the day seemed to be dissolving, and she was feeling amazingly hungry.

It was wonderful to sit back, order her food, and let someone else serve it to her. She thought of the last time . . . with J.D. at the inn. Not that this coffee shop was any Franklin Arms; it couldn't even be compared to some of the restaurants in Basking Reade, but it was the start of her new kind of life.

Katie sighed contentedly as she opened one of her paperbacks and settled back in the booth, waiting for her soup and sandwich.

She spent most of the next four hours curled up in a seat in the waiting area outside the gate where her plane would be taking off. She was not the least bit impatient. She either read or watched the passing scene.

Half an hour before the scheduled boarding time, the loudspeaker announced an "unavoidable two-hour delay, due to technical difficulties."

The waiting area had crowded up considerably in the last hour. The sounds Katie heard on all sides varied from light moans to lengthy curses. She couldn't help but be amused by some of the more picturesque language she was hearing!

A slim blond man with a wispy moustache and rather long legs, who had arrived at the gate only five minutes before and was stretched out in one of the few empty seats opposite Katie, seemed to share her amusement. He caught her eye and they exchanged wry smiles as a saintly-looking white-haired lady uttered a blistering denunciation of the airline, the airport, and the possible illegitimate beginnings of the personnel of both.

As people crowded around the counter, angrily demanding an explanation, the blond man unfolded his long legs, stood up, and walked over to Katie.

"It's going to be awhile," he said, indicating the counter, "before most of those impatient fools realize their complaints won't make the plane fly any sooner, at which time they will all decide at once that a restaurant is the logical place to kill most of the two hours. Then there'll be a mad stampede. May I suggest we beat them to a table and the first choice of food?"

He pretended to look pained when Katie burst out laughing.

"My name is Arnold Jay Richter," he said. "I didn't know that to know me was to laugh at me."

"I was laughing at your approach, Arnold Jay Richter, not at *you.*"

"Not sufficiently subtle, you think, Miss . . . Ms . . . Mrs . . . ?"

"Kauffman, Katie Kauffman. But Katie will do. Your approach was about as subtle as a bulldozer, Arnold, but don't misunderstand, I liked it. And I think you're absolutely right, in addition to which I happen to be hungry."

She stood up and tucked the paperback she had been reading into her shoulder bag along with the two others. She gave him a much wider smile than her first one. "Shall we go?"

Instead of taking her to the coffee shop, he led her in the opposite direction to a much more elegant restaurant. Carpeted floors. Dim lighting. Elaborate menus.

Katie's eyes widened at the price list. After they or-

dered, she said, trying to be tactful, "I will pay for my
own meal, of course."

"No, my dear," said Arnold Jay Richter paternally, "you
will not. When I ask a lady for her company, *I* pay. As
a matter of fact," he grinned in answer to her haughtily
raised eyebrows, "my *company* will pay. I'm returning
home from a business trip. Dinner is on my expense account."

Katie had learned all about expense accounts from J.D.
"But I'm not business," she pointed out.

"How do you know? Do you really think I invited you
to share my meal because you're an exceptionally attractive girl and—since you appreciate my wit—obviously
have a great sense of humor? Nonsense. I'm always thinking in terms of prospective clients. Who knows that you
might not be one? Everyone needs an accountant. Have
my business card."

He whipped out his wallet and handed her a card. It
showed his name in fine script and a string of letters after
it. Underneath was the name of his company . . . Aloro,
Roth, and Halloran . . . and in the corner, a Los Angeles
address.

"Is this anywhere near Beverly Hills?" Katie asked him.

"Near enough in distance . . . far in other respects."

Katie looked at him, puzzled, and he explained, grinning. "Beverly Hills is posh and expensive; downtown
L.A. is more for us peasants."

Katie nodded her understanding. "Oh, then maybe that's
where I'll get my own apartment," she told him cheerfully,
"even though I'm going to Beverly Hills first."

"You're looking for an apartment?"

"I will be."

"If you're willing to share, perhaps I can help you. My
firm is crawling with secretaries and bookkeepers who always seem to be trading in their roommates for husbands
or other roommates. Would you like me to ask around?"

"I'd be very grateful." She looked down at the card again. "May I keep this so I'll know where to phone you?"

"Certainly. Why do you think I gave it to you?" He paused a moment as a waitress served their salads. "So that you'd trust me, of course," he went on. "There's something eminently respectable about a business card."

"As a matter of fact," Katie confided, popping an olive into her mouth, "it happens I may need an accountant. This is the first year I have to pay taxes."

"See? I told you this dinner was properly deductible. I hope you won't feel you have to give your business to a Beverly Hills firm."

"And pay higher prices for the same service? I'm too Pennsylvania Dutch for that!" laughed Katie.

"Are you really Pennsylvania Dutch?" he asked with interest.

"If living in Strawberry Schrank for more than ten years qualifies me, I am."

He eyed her flowing hair and unbuttoned shirt and remembered the way her jeans fit over her hips. "You certainly don't look it."

"If you had seen me early this morning in my Amish dress, you wouldn't be saying that."

He looked at her suddenly shadowed face. "You don't really want to talk about it, do you?"

"No, not now, if you don't mind. I'm feeling too good."

"In that case, let's make everyone happy and talk about me," he said gravely.

The waitress set a platter of veal parmigiana with spaghetti in front of Arnold and gave Katie a plate with baby broiled flounder, baked potato, and spinach.

"Your name is Arnold Jay Richter, you're an accountant in Los Angeles, you talk a great deal of nonsense and are as subtle as a bulldozer, but you're also a very kind man, I think."

"You haven't left much for me to say about myself," Arnold complained. "Shall we start with my schooldays in Philadelphia?"

"Oh, so you come from Pennsylvania, too?"

"Until I went to college."

"Do you still have family there?"

"Oodles of family . . . practically all gathered together yesterday and today for my Uncle Dan's funeral."

"You went to Philadelphia for your uncle's funeral?"

With his mouth stuffed full of spaghetti, Arnold only nodded.

"Then why," demanded Katie triumphantly, "is this an expense-account dinner?"

He looked at her, and though his eyes grew bright with laughter, he answered in the most sober of voices, "Because, when we were in the waiting area, a single glance at your glorious face and figure told me that you might be in the market for a California accountant."

As Katie began to giggle, he continued serenely, "I was on the basketball and track teams in college—Berkeley—I play a mean game of handball, and I jog seriously. I'm convinced there is other life in outer space; and I believe I am what is known in the personal ads of the magazines as an eligible Jewish single."

Katie sighed exaggeratedly. "Just what I might be looking for if I didn't have someone in mind already. Did you know that the Amish identify with the Jews, sort-of?"

"How sort-of?"

"Well, I guess they believe they've both been chosen to be persecuted."

They exchanged wry smiles again. Then Arnold got back to the point. "Were you trying—subtly, of course, Katie—to tell me that you already have a guy?"

"Well, he's *there,*" said Katie a bit ruefully. "I'm not quite sure—in fact, I'm rather *un*sure—that I have him."

"He must be nuts," said Arnold with prompt and flattering conviction.

"Nooo," Katie said slowly. "He's just—cautious." She shook her head. "No, that's the wrong word. J.D. is . . . he's prickly."

"Well, hold onto my card," said Arnold. "I still want to be your accountant. And if the prickly J.D. doesn't fall in line, I'd like to date you. I'd like to date you even if he does."

"I still want you to find me an apartment," Katie reminded him. "And I certainly want us to be friends."

"Thanks a lot, kid."

"Now, now," Katie chided, "show more respect to your clients."

They continued to laugh, chatter, tease, and enjoy one another all through the rest of the dinner, including coffee and dessert, over which they lingered despite the line of people now waiting for tables.

"I have no guilt about it," Arnold pointed out virtuously. "They could all have been here as soon as we if they hadn't stayed to grumble and swear."

When the plane finally took off, they were seated far apart but met occasionally in the aisle, between cat naps, for brief chats. When the plane landed, Arnold escorted Katie to the baggage claim area, stopping on the way to look up J.D. Shale's address in the Beverly Hills phone book.

After both their bags arrived safely—a minor miracle, he informed her—Arnold took Katie outside and put her into a cab.

"I'll phone you at Shale's place, Katie, as soon as I get a lead on an apartment," he said through the open window. "It should be soon."

She felt strangely loath to say goodbye to this friendly

face. "Perhaps"—her smile wavered a little—"I'll call you first."

"I hope so."

She looked back to wave as the cab pulled away, then sank back against the seat. She looked eagerly around for a bit and then, since it was just mile on mile of cluttered wide highway, closed her tired eyes.

"Beverly Crest Apartments, miss," the driver said a second time, raising his voice.

Katie came out of her half-sleeping state, opened her pocketbook to pay him, and stepped out on the sidewalk.

A doorman offered to take her suitcase as she went inside the tall white stone building, but she shook her head. A second doorman inside the elegant lobby was more successful; he took hold of the case while Katie was questioned by the grey-haired woman behind a round marble desk.

"Whom did you wish to see, miss?" Her nasal voice blended surprise with disdain.

Katie lifted her chin. "Mr. J.D. Shale," she announced firmly.

"Is Mr. Shale expecting you?" She checked the watch on her bony wrist. "It's only six in the morning."

"I'm aware of that," Katie said sweetly, glancing at her own new watch. "Man proposes but God seems to dispose of the arrival of planes."

"What name shall I announce, madam?"

Katie had hoped to announce herself, but she said quietly, "Katryn Kauffman."

The grey-haired woman pressed a button and spoke into a machine. "Good morning, Mr. Shale, sorry to disturb you . . . yes, I know the time, but there's a young woman here to see you . . . a Miss Katryn Kauffman . . . Mr. Shale? Mr. *Shale!*"

She turned to Katie, the rouge standing out in bright

red patches on her cheeks. "Apartment Fourteen F. Go right up."

The doorman with the suitcase escorted Katie to the elevator and pressed the button for her. "Shall I carry your suitcase up, ma'am?"

"No, thank you, I'll take it," said Katie firmly.

She looked about uncertainly when she got out on the fourteenth floor, but only for seconds. A door was flung open and J.D. Shale came out into the hallway.

Katie's heart beat fast as she ran to him, the suitcase bumping against her knees. His eyes were heavy with sleep, his dark curly hair all disordered. She suspected he had just pulled on the black swimming trunks and t-shirt which were all he wore.

She dropped the suitcase at her feet; it fell between them.

"I don't believe it," he said in a hollow voice. "You really came."

"You invited me to look you up when I got to Beverly Hills," Katie reminded him mendaciously, knowing full well that his so-called "invitation" had been more of a sarcastic dig.

"How could you take such a chance? I'm often away on business. Suppose I hadn't been here? Suppose I—"

"J.D., calm down," Katie told him, exceedingly calm herself. "I'm a big girl. I have money. I even have other friends here." Arnold Jay Richter made that not too much of a lie. "If you were away from home," she told him smilingly, "I would have gone straight to a hotel until I found an apartment of my own. I came here first because I was eager to see you again." With her left foot, she nudged the suitcase off to one side and came closer to him. "I thought you might possibly be glad to see me, too."

They stared at each other, and her stomach churned till

a sudden rueful grin split his face, somewhat restoring the
J.D. she had traveled thousands of miles to see.

"I think maybe I am, K-K-Katie. Come on in."

Twenty

   . . . and in marked contrast, the crème de la crème of the industry will flock to Malibu on Saturday night for the annual Open House hosted at their weekend beach retreat by Nate Sherman, President and Chairman of Continental Films, and his charming wife Marion . . .

Two nights of sleeplessness took their toll the moment Katie sat down at the kitchen counter while J.D. made them both a breakfast of bacon and eggs, toast, and coffee. As he cooked, he lectured her again on her foolhardiness in having come to California without first informing him.

When his long-winded monologue died down without a single tart response from the object of his lecture, J.D. turned from the stove to find Katie fast asleep, with an arm across her placemat and her face cradled in the crook of her elbow.

"Katie," he said softly, then much louder, "K-K-Katie!"

Katie slept on.

J.D. shrugged, then turned off the heat under both frying pans and set his electric coffee pot on warm.

Katie never stirred as he heaved her up—not without some difficulty—and carried her into the guest bedroom, but her eyes did open for a moment when he dumped her onto the bed and pulled off her shoes. She seemed to be having some trouble focusing.

"Get some rest, Katie," he said, touching her cheek briefly. "I have to go to the office for a few hours, but I'll be back by lunch time."

"Mmm," murmured Katie as he threw a light quilt over her, then she promptly closed her eyes again.

When he came home shortly before twelve-thirty, Katie was sitting in his living room, very much at home. She had sprawled out on the couch with her bare legs propped up on extra cushions as she watched a vintage John Wayne western on TV.

She had changed to a nubby light wool skirt and a fleecy matching sweater, both the deep blue color of her eyes, which were now bright and clear.

"You look a little more animated than you did this morning," said J.D. in some amusement, noting her wistful look as she turned off the television.

"Oh, I feel *won*derful. I slept and slept. Then I took a shower and washed the travel dirt out of my hair."

She swung around to show him her lemon-yellow mane, and for a moment J.D. was back in a field in Pennsylvania with the combined scents of corn, mown grass, and flowering trees all around him and his hands entwined in that luxuriously soft and soap-clean mass.

He blinked and came back to Beverly Hills and the sound of Katie's voice finishing, ". . . just love your square tub and that whirlpool effect."

"I came to take you out to lunch," he said somewhat gruffly.

"You weren't listening," she reproached him. "I told you I made myself some breakfast after my shower, and that was less than an hour ago."

"Then you can keep me company at Mama Amalie's while I have mine. I—thanks to your sunrise arrival—had breakfast earlier than usual. Put on your shoes and let's go."

Katie knelt and fished a pair of navy leather pumps from under the couch. Her head poked out like a turtle's, she asked J.D., "Do I need to put on panty hose?"

"Not unless you want to."

"Good." She slipped her bare feet into the pumps. "I'll just get my purse."

The bare legs flashed by him; in seconds she was back, her navy bag slung over her shoulder.

"What's Mama Amalie's?" Katie enquired on the way down to the garage level.

"My favorite Italian restaurant."

"Italian!" Katie's eyes opened wide with interest. As the car moved smoothly along the roadway, she mentioned confidingly, "I've never had *real* Italian food before. There were a few places in Basking Reade, but Mark—he's from Philadelphia—said they weren't very good and the food wasn't authentic."

"I can assure you, Mama Amalie's is authentic. Are you by any chance working up an appetite?"

"I think perhaps I am. Especially if it takes awhile to get there."

"Sorry to disappoint you but"—he turned into an open parking area—"we've already arrived."

"I can't believe this," Katie told him, scrambling out of the car herself as he came around to help her. "All the trouble of taking your car out and the nuisance of parking for just a five-minute drive. Why, we could have walked it faster, it can't have been more than seven or eight blocks."

"Only six." J.D. smiled broadly as he steered her toward the back entrance of Mama Amalie's. "The first thing you had better learn about Californians is that their legs aren't made for walking; driving is their way of life, especially in Beverly Hills. I'll never forget the first week I moved here . . . I got restless my first night and went for a walk. Five blocks from the house a police patrol car stopped right alongside me. A teenager walking on the street was regarded as highly suspicious. They picked me up."

He opened the door of the restaurant and they went through a dark narrow corridor, then came out into a big cheerful room with wooden tables crowded together and more roomy booths off to the side.

A smiling young host greeted J.D. by name and led them at once to a booth.

"What happened?" Katie demanded as soon as they were seated.

J.D. looked up from his menu.

"Huh?" he asked vaguely.

"You were picked up by the police patrol car. What happened then?"

J.D. shrugged. "Nothing much. I gave them my uncle's name and they drove me back to the house. Uncle Nate had gone out, but the housekeeper called my Aunt Marion to the door and she vouched for me."

Katie was staring at him, a strange glazed look in her eyes. "What's the matter now?" J.D. asked patiently.

"Our lives. It's as though we came from two different worlds. Yours is as foreign to me as mine must seem to you. A place where the police pick you up for walking . . . oh, my goodness . . . your Aunt Marion!"

"What about her?"

"I forgot to tell you—she called this morning just as I got out of the tub."

"I forgot to tell *you*—well, actually you were too sleepy to be told anything—to ignore the phone. I have an answering service that picks up on the third ring."

"But she asked me to remind you that you're expected at their party on Saturday night."

J.D. grimaced.

"She also gave me her phone number, in case you don't

have the new one since they moved, I wrote it down. It's on the wood block next to the kitchen phone."

J.D. grinned. "That's Aunt Marion's little joke tied to a not-so-gentle hint. The move she referred to happened three years ago and the phone number, I assure you, is engraved on my heart. It's just her way of letting me know that I haven't called her lately, which means all of four or five days. Aunt Marion is a worrier. If I don't report in at least twice a week, preferably three, she's convinced that I'm ill or indigent, or otherwise sorely in need of her tender loving care."

"How very nice," said Katie gently, "to have someone care for you so much."

"And how very nice a girl you are, Katie Kauffman," J.D. riposted lightly, "to offer that interpretation of what many another young lady has sat opposite me in a restaurant and described as smothering love."

"The question is," Katie asked him seriously, "which young lady do you agree with?"

"The *nice* young lady, of course," answered J.D., unsmiling. "For more than half my life the one steady, stable element in it has been Aunt Marion. My uncle, too, of course, but mostly her."

"They brought you up?"

"After fourteen. That's how old I was when my parents were—they were killed in an accident." His laugh sounded forced. "Talk about culture shock. From an apartment in Sheepshead Bay, Brooklyn to Truesdale Estates, Beverly Hills."

She gripped his hands across the table. "How terrible for you, J.D. . . . suddenly . . . *both* at once . . ."

"Hey, Katie, come on . . . I admit, at the time . . . but it's fifteen years or more; I'm not exactly still in mourning."

Katie slowly let go of his hands. "Did—did you know your aunt and uncle well?"

"No, not at all. My father wouldn't let my mother have anything to do with Aunt Marion—who was her younger sister—because she married a Jew."

"That's sounds like the *meidung!*"

J.D. looked grim. "No, not really. Not if the way you explained it to me is right. Your people are supposed to shun a sinner out of faith . . . they want her or him back, repentant. My father did it out of hate. He hated all Jews . . . not that there was anything strange in that. He also hated Hispanics, African-Americans, Asians, Italians, Poles . . . you name it, if it was different from him, he hated it."

"And you," said Katie soberly, "hated him."

"With all my heart."

She took his hands back and pressed them again, hard and briefly.

"You know," she said consideringly, "Pennsylvania Dutch country or Beverly Hills, perhaps our lives and worlds were not so different, after all. We both lost our homes and families at a rather young age and had to move to far-away places to live with absolute strangers. Strangers who turned out to be special people."

"A glass of white wine for the young lady, plain tonic with lime for me," J.D. told the red-aproned waiter hovering over them. "We'll order later."

He was quiet until the waiter returned with their drinks. Then he said, smiling faintly, "I doubt that you were spoiled in that Amish household the way I was. Aunt Marion couldn't have children; she and Uncle Nate proceeded to madly indulge their late-come solitary chick."

"It doesn't seem to have harmed you any."

"You think not, K-K-Katie? Others might dispute that. They say that without Uncle Nate's coattails to cling to, I wouldn't have risen higher than a gofer on any production, let alone be a producer-director."

"It seems to me you work very hard and know your

craft . . . I saw you on the set, remember? And I read your script as well. Do you really give a damn what jealous people think?"

J.D.'s laugh rang out, genuinely amused. "Katie, my love, you wise little owl from out of the sticks, you're a constant refreshment to me. And you're right, of course. They *are* jealous, and I don't give a damn. Let's order lunch."

While they were eating—Katie with as much appetite as though she hadn't had a late breakfast—J.D. asked her, "Seriously, have you made any plans, Katie?"

"Seriously, I have, J.D. My first priority is to get an apartment. A friend of mine—an accountant in Los Angeles—expects to have a roommate for me soon. Actually, within the week."

"In that case," said J.D., "would you like to stay on at my place till he comes through?"

"I would like it a great deal," Katie said, very prim and polite, "if you're sure I won't be any trouble to you."

"Not," said J.D., setting down his empty glass, "unless you try to seduce me. The rules here are the same as in Pennsylvania. I don't seduce, or get seduced by, virgins."

Katie finished the last few drops in her glass. "I won't—if you won't," she said with wine-induced bravado.

"I *beg* your pardon?"

"Well, you came pretty close for a guy with such high-sounding principles . . . *and* rules."

"Okay. Okay." Faint color tinged J.D.'s face. "So we're both agreed about *this* time. After the apartment, then what?"

"Job-hunting. Preferably one that has something to do with writing . . . but, if not, I'll work my way up or down or around to it."

"Even with contacts like yours—meaning *me*—you don't come to Hollywood and get a writing job right off the bat . . . not unless you're a name or have some kind of track record. But I could probably get you some odd jobs doctoring really bad scripts. It would be a foot in the door. Would you be interested?"

"Of course."

"I'll look into it. And by the way, as long as you're staying with me this week, you may as well come to my aunt's and uncle's party Saturday night."

"I can't go without being invited!"

"My dear girl, if it matters that much to you, I'll call Aunt Marion and get you properly invited, but it's not the least bit necessary. The party is one of those shindigs more business than social. There are going to be about one hundred and fifty guests, many unknown to the host and hostess even though quite a few of them work for or with Continental Films. It'll be a mad scramble of people trying to make beneficial contacts, not there to have a good time. Who knows? You may even make a few yourself."

"It sounds kind of—kind of—"

"Exploitative? Mercenary? Unappealing?"

"Actually, all three."

"It is, believe me, it is. I only go because my aunt and uncle count on me; I'm a secondary host. But *you* should go this once because it's a fascinating first experience . . . the chance to see the Hollywood performing animal in its natural habitat. Do you have a dressy dress?"

"Well, yes"—Katie wrinkled her nose—"but acceptably dressy in Basking Reade, Maryland might be a bit different from dressy in Beverly Hills."

"More than just a bit. I want you to look—" he gave her a kindly but critical once-over—"the knockout I know you will be in the proper get-up. There's a rather special boutique just down the block. Let's skip dessert, so you won't gain any extra pounds, and see if we can find anything suitable. I'd like to treat you to your first really glamorous dress."

"Thank you very much," Katie told him firmly and formally, "but if I find something suitable, I'll treat myself."

The word "boutique" had prepared Katie for a small intimate shop. What J.D. led her into was an enormous room covered with lush green carpeting and lit by several crystal chandeliers that looked as though they might have provided the illumination when Marie Antoinette and a few hundred guests dined at Versailles.

A saleswoman approached, wearing a gown of clinging silk jersey the same shade of green as the carpet. Jade earrings dangled from her ears and a jade necklace was wrapped three times around her swan-like throat.

"May I help you, sir—madam?"

"We're looking for something rather special for the young lady . . . dressy but not too much fluff . . . cocktail length, I think."

"Mmmm." The saleswoman walked around Katie, studying her from all angles. "Size eight?"

"I've always been a ten," Katie offered meekly.

"In our establishment, in a quality garment, you would be size eight," the saleswoman said loftily.

J.D. snorted with laughter as she flitted off. "And that puts you in your place, Miss Pennsylvania with clothing out of Maryland."

"I don't think I like this place," whispered Katie. "It's . . . it's . . ."

"Intimidating?" suggested J.D. "You've just got to learn to give as good as you get. Then you'll see who intimidates who."

The saleswoman came back with her arms full of dresses, which she bestowed on the back of a chair. The first gown she held up for their inspection was of a metallic gold cloth.

She looked first at J.D., who shook his head.

"A little too brassy, I think," he said. "Not Miss Kauffman's style."

"Bras-sy," repeated Katie, prolonging each syllable. "My dear J.D., it's positively garish. I thought you told me this shop rose above the usual Rodeo Drive vulgarity."

As J.D. choked on a laugh, the reddening saleswoman held up a cloud of green chiffon. Katie inspected it with her head to one side.

"Pretty," she pronounced finally. "Definitely pretty, but just a wee bit insipid, don't you think?"

"Whatever you say, madam."

The third dress produced was of a red satin material cut in Chinese fashion with a Mandarin collar and a straight skirt slit on either side.

"I really like the style," said Katie, who was now enjoying herself enormously, "but it's just not my color."

In grim silence, the saleswoman held out her final offering, a silk chiffon in muted colors of the rainbow, with a low-cut cowled neckline and a watered taffeta petticoat that showed through the separated halves of the many-layered front-slashed skirt.

"Oh!" exclaimed Katie, unable to play her game any longer. It was the loveliest dress she had ever seen. She said so out loud and the saleswoman thawed visibly.

"Would you like to try it on, miss?"

"I'd adore to," said Katie fervently. "Where's the price tag? How much is it?"

The saleswoman, about to pull the tag out from under a cap sleeve, intercepted J.D.'s frantic sign language just in time.

She swallowed. "Well, it *was* five hundred dollars . . ." She looked hard at J.D., who was signaling at his side with the fingers of one hand.

"Five hundred dollars!" shrieked Katie, drawing the attention of two other salespeople and all eight shoppers in the boutique.

"But it's on half-price sale," the saleswoman added hurriedly, praying that she had read the man's signals correctly. She gave a sigh of relief when J.D. nodded vigorously. "Because we're making room for our new inventory."

"But that's still two hundred and fifty." Katie shook her head mournfully. "It would be sinful."

"You're buying it for my party," J.D. told her. "I want it to be my present."

"Absolutely, not," Katie answered decidedly. "It's one thing for me to live in your apartment, J.D. It's quite another for you to buy me a dress. I have plenty of money to buy my own; I just don't think I should squander it."

"Whatever little money you have, you need to save. If it makes you feel any better, you can pay me back some day when you have a decent bank account."

Katie lifted the flap of her shoulder bag and took out three folded books of traveler's checks. She slapped them down into J.D.'s palm. "Count!" she said tersely.

J.D. counted. "My God! You've got over eight thousand dollars!" he told her, eyes bulging. "Where in hell did you get that much money?"

"Johnny—my foster brother—made it for me on the stock market. He's a math genius. As soon as I have an apartment and job, I'm going to send him more to invest."

"I think I'll join you," said J.D. dryly, handing back the books of traveler's checks. "But since you're loaded now and are obviously going to be wealthy in the future, you can allow yourself to splurge on one special dress. Go try it on."

"Okay," agreed Katie cheerfully. She put the checks in her bag and tossed it over to J.D. "Take care of my treasure, please."

Over her shoulder, as she followed the saleswoman, she

flung back at him, "I'm not doing this because you told me to, Mr. Movie Man. It so happens I've conceived a mad passion for this gown . . . in Lancaster, they might even say I was *leebgronk* for it."

Twenty-one

. . . she never told her love,
But let concealment like a worm i' th' bud
Feed on her damask cheek; she pin'd in thought,
And with a green and yellow melancholy
She sat like Patience on a monument,
Smiling at grief. . . .

Twelfth Night

"Aunt Marion."

J.D. came up behind a regally tall, slim, grey-haired woman in a black and silver net evening gown, and planted a firm kiss on her cheek. "You look glamorous as all get-out, aunt of mine."

"Thank you, dear." She studied him searchingly. "You look tired, J.D. And I think you've lost a little weight."

"I'm fine, darling." He put one hand against the cheek that he had kissed. "Truly," he added softly.

To Katie, standing a little behind him, the words seemed to have a significance far beyond their casual meaning . . . or was she imagining things?

"Aunt Marion, I'd like you to meet the friend who wouldn't come without your specific invitation. This is Katie Kauffman."

Aunt Marion turned to Katie at once. Her glance was kindly, but once again searching. Evidently she was satisfied by her brief scrutiny. "My dear, I'm most happy to have you here." She looked at Katie's rainbow-colored chiffon. "What a beautiful gown."

"Thank you, Mrs. Sherman." Katie smiled a bit shyly. "It's my first Beverly Hills dress."

"Where's Uncle Nate?" J.D. asked.

"With his lawyer and accountant." Aunt Marion shook her head ruefully. "He might just as well be at the office. I wish you'd get him over here, J.D. He really ought to be receiving with me."

"I'll try to pry him loose, and if I can't, then I'll receive with you . . . just as soon as I get Katie settled."

He dragged Katie away while she was still protesting that she could take care of herself and would love to sit outside and listen to the ocean.

"You did not invest two hundred and fifty dollars at one of the poshest boutiques in Beverly Hills to hide that dress outside," he advised her. "You're going to stay here where it can be seen. Later we'll walk along the beach together."

"Two hundred and fifty dollars in a Beverly Hills boutique. What was it . . . a fire sale?" asked a voice just behind them.

They both turned around, Katie in surprise, and J.D. with a big, widening smile.

"Tony! I'll be damned."

"Long time no see, J.D."

They shook hands, still eagerly talking.

"Vienna, wasn't it?"

"No, that was the year before. Rome, I think."

"You're right."

They both broke into loud guffaws and fell to pummeling one another.

"Will you ever forget Bill Travis in his undershorts trying to swim in the Trevi Fountain?"

"Looking like a beached whale!"

"And Gregorio trying to talk the police out of arresting him?"

"Out of arresting the bunch of us."

"All that eloquence . . ."

"And you just waved your magic wad of lire . . ."

Katie laughed aloud in delight; they were so animated, so excited, and they made such a startling contrast. J.D., trim and smart in black tie, pleated dress shirt and a dinner jacket snug over his stocky shoulders, was almost dwarfed by his six-foot-two friend. Tony had a quarterback's body, arms as long as a chimpanzee's, and an Amish-like bushy black beard that half hid his clever narrow face but not his bright sharp eyes. He looked as though he would be more comfortable in overalls than the three-piece navy pin-stripe he was almost bursting out of.

Katie's laughter reminded both men of their manners.

"Tony Burney. Katie Kauffman."

Katie held out her hand and found it swallowed up in Tony's great paw, but his shake was thoughtfully easy.

"How do you do?" she said, liking him enormously.

"I do very well. And you?"

"Marvelously. Have you two been friends a long time?"

"We were at the University of Southern California together. Then J.D. went into the movie business seriously while I only played around with it for a while."

"What do you do now, Tony?" Katie asked with genuine interest.

"I'm a free-lance photographer. I do advertising layouts for magazines, mostly high-fashion, and my favorite of all—cover art. My studio is in New York, but I have camera and will travel."

"Speaking of which, what brings you to California this time, Tony?"

"A business meeting with the Holland Maid cheese people in the Valley. They're starting a big promotional campaign. I intended to call you, but a couple of hours after I got here yesterday I ran into your uncle. I was having lunch with my client, and it turns out they belong to the same club. Your Uncle Nate said I'd catch up with you at his party, so I just came. Besides which, who knows . . ."

"You might make some business contacts," Katie giggled. "J.D. told me that's what everyone is really here for."

"J.D. is right. That's why I emigrated to New York, three thousand miles from the seat of corruption. Look at me here tonight. See how painfully easy it is to fall back into the trap."

His grin set his beard jiggling up and down and stretched his lips so wide, the chimpanzee look grew even more pronounced.

"Look, Tony," J.D. said, "I have to speak to my uncle and then help Aunt Marion receive for a bit. Why don't you and Katie get some drinks or food and sit and get acquainted and I'll join you as soon as I can?"

"I'd be enchanted," said Tony promptly, and J.D. took off.

"But *I'm* not a good contact," Katie told him, eyes dancing, and they both laughed.

"Which shall it be?" Tony asked. "Food, or drink?"

"Food. Definitely food."

"A girl after my own heart. Let's go."

They squeezed onto the line at the buffet table and filled their plates liberally; then Tony found two unoccupied chairs in a far corner of the living room.

Katie spread a big linen napkin over her lap to protect her dress and sat silent for a few minutes, absorbed in tasting and trying. "Mmm," she said after a while, spreading more chopped liver on a piece of rye bread. "This is fabulous. Tell me about your work, Tony."

"You don't by any chance want to be a photographer's model, do you?" he asked, looking alarmed.

"Why?"

"Well, frankly, sweetie, I don't see you making it. You'd have to lose about fifteen pounds for the cameras, which would be a crime, because your figure as it is constitutes one of nature's works of art. In view of your appetite—which, believe me, I admire—dieting wouldn't come easy to you. In short, you look too damn—too damn—"

"Too damn what?" Katie asked serenely when he didn't finish.

"Healthy, I guess. You just don't have that so-called sexy anorexic look the camera loves," he told her, shrugging, then peered anxiously up from his plate. "You're not going to cry, are you?" he asked.

"Why should I cry?"

"Girls have been known to shed buckets on hearing the kind of verdict I just gave you. Not that I couldn't be wrong. I am occasionally," he mentioned modestly.

"Don't worry, I have no desire to be a model," Katie assured him.

"Bless your unambitious little heart."

"Oh, I'm ambitious all right, but not to model."

Tony wasn't listening. "You could make it with your hands, I think. Give them to me a minute, will you?"

Katie laid her fork carefully across her plate and extended both hands. Tony stretched them out impersonally across his own. "Beautiful," he said matter-of-factly, "but great God, have you ever abused them! What do you do . . . dip them daily in lye?"

"What I've done for years is bake and clean and scrub floors and clothes and pick and plant vegetables. But not anymore. They'll soon be soft and smooth, with no burns, no cuts, no calluses."

"Well, when they are"—Tony let go of her hands—"they'll be good for modeling, if you're ever interested."

"I'll keep it in mind," said Katie, spearing a piece of

crab and a bit of avocado. She looked up, feeling the intensity of his look. "What's the matter?"

"Your hands," he said. "They were very cool when you gave them to me, and a moment later I seemed to feel warm—and I mean *really* warm—vibes coming from them." He laughed uncomfortably. "Almost like I was getting a message. Has—has anyone ever told you something like that before?"

"Only people I'm very close to . . . or who are deeply intuitive."

They smiled into each other's eyes, and Katie picked up her fork again just as J.D., circling the room with a full plate of his own, located them. "Duty done," he announced. "I'm free to enjoy myself."

"Well, take my chair while I go get seconds," said Tony, standing up.

"What were you two talking about?" J.D. asked Katie, taking Tony's chair.

"Modeling mostly."

"The way you were looking at him . . . Katie, listen, it's no secret so I'm not telling tales out of school, but you're such an innocent that I think maybe—before you get any ideas—"

"J.D.," she said so compellingly he broke off, blinking.

"I know what you're trying to tell me about your friend," Katie said, "and it isn't necessary."

"How do you know?" J.D. bristled defensively. "He doesn't appear gay."

"No, he doesn't, but I knew. It has nothing to do with the way he looks or acts."

"Well, all right . . . it's just . . . the way you were looking at him," he said again. "I don't want to see you get hurt."

"Honestly, J.D.!" Katie exclaimed, exasperated. "If there is an innocent around here, it's you, not me. Just because I looked at Tony more than casually, you're already seeing me falling in love with him. Do you think I do that every week? Every month? Or perhaps three times a year? You don't have much faith in your own power of attraction, do you? Or have you by any chance forgotten that it's *you* I fell in love with?"

"For God's sakes," said J.D., very red in the face. "Not that again. You're only—"

"I know. I know. I'm only twenty and you're twenty-nine, so I'm supposed to know nothing about love while you know everything. Did it ever occur to you that age hasn't a thing to do with it?"

"Did it ever occur to you that for your pride's sake—"

"Oh, stuff it!" Katie interrupted rudely. "I'm not interested in preserving either my pride *or* my damask cheeks."

"Come again?"

"You heard me."

"I thought I missed something in between. It didn't make sense."

"You were the one who first quoted Shakespeare at *me*." She recited rapidly:

> . . . *she never told her love,*
> *But let concealment like a worm i' th' bud*
> *Feed on her damask cheek* . . .

"That's not me, J.D. It never will be, but don't worry. Neither will I be Patience on a monument smiling at grief. I've got a life to live—with you or without you. Now, if you'll excuse me." She rose and put both napkin and plate on her chair. "I forgot I wasn't supposed to be having a good time. I'm going to circulate in my two-hundred-and-fifty-dollar dress and see if I can make some important contacts."

Tony had returned unseen. "That," he said, trying to juggle his full plate and Katie's empty one and sit down all at the same time, "is a hell of a lot of woman, friend."

"She's a kid," growled J.D., still staring after Katie, bemused.

"Christ, J.D., I never thought *I'd* be telling *you* about a woman. Kid, my eye!"

Having said which, he tactfully dropped the subject, and they reminisced for the next hour or more with only a few interruptions. Then Tony took off and J.D. went in search of Katie, whom he eventually found out on the enclosed patio dancing with an aged character actor. She was dancing with a great deal of verve . . . not to say abandon. Every few steps the white tops of her breasts pushed up out of the low-cut cowled neckline, then subsided as her movements grew more sedate . . . only to rise again. Damn! he fumed silently. She should be wearing a bra.

The moment the music ended, he was at her side. "My dance, I think, Katie?"

"Yes, of course, J.D." She smiled dazzlingly at the actor. "Thank you, that was lovely."

They danced to a slow ballad, so the parts of her anatomy he preferred hidden stayed where they were supposed to stay.

"I'm sorry if I hurt your feelings, Katie," he said after they had circled the room twice, not talking.

"You didn't," she told him crisply. "You annoyed me, but I'm becoming accustomed to that."

J.D. laughed softly. "That dress needs a bra."

"I hate bras. They cut underneath and across the shoulders. Why do I need one?"

"So you won't show everything you possess to the general public. Or did you enjoy doing that?"

"I didn't mind," said Katie sweetly. "It made me lots of—contacts."

She gasped a little as his arms tightened around her. "Such as?"

"Oh, actors and agents and one man who said he could help me with a writing job."

"Name of . . . ?"

"Carruthers. He gave me his card."

"Quentin Carruthers?"

"I think so."

"Better throw the card away, unless you like wrestling matches," J.D. chuckled. "He's known in the trade as Casting-Couch Carruthers, and he couldn't help you to get a job as an errand girl, but he likes 'em young and nubile. Disappointed?"

"Not really," said Katie. "I already tore up the card."

J.D. laughed. "That's my wise girl."

She slanted her eyes up at him, asking a question without words. J.D. answered it with another question. "Would you like that walk on the beach now?"

"I would love it."

"Follow me, then; we can go down through the side entrance."

In what J.D. called a "mud" room at the bottom of a flight of steps, they took off their shoes and put on rubber thongs and then donned waterproof jackets, laughing at the comical effect of them combined with evening dress.

The beach was deserted as they walked along, but on one side she could watch the awesome pounding of the ocean with its never-ending roll of waves, while on the other side, the bright lights of small beach houses and large mansions twinkled or glittered hospitably.

They walked hand in hand, neither needing nor wanting conversation. J.D.'s face in the moonlight looked calm and serene, and Katie's heart swelled inside her.

She had never felt so happy in her life!

Twenty-two

"Hollywood Tidbits"
by Pamela Goode

. . . Unconfirmed rumor from Continental Films has it that Mike Henry is out as director of It's Murder, She Sez, *and J.D. Shale is in. The long-running off-Broadway play will start filming on location in San Francisco before the end of the month . . .*

They arrived home at four in the morning, with Katie sleeping all the way from Malibu to Beverly Hills. J.D. had to hold her upright from the garage to the elevator and then the few yards to his apartment.

In the guest room he unzipped the back of her dress for her, dropped a chaste kiss on one shoulder, and left, closing the door behind him.

A few minutes later he was knocking on her door again, message pad in hand.

She opened it, wrapped only in a towel, her yellow mane of hair flowing around her shoulders.

"Yes, J.D.?" she yawned.

"My answering service had a message for you, Katie. I thought you'd want to know. Your friend Arnold Richter called, and he has two possibilities for apartments to share. He'll be glad to show them to you tomorrow from three

on, and he'd like to take you out to dinner afterwards.
Call him any time after eleven in the morning to confirm.
Oh, yes, and you're not to worry, you're deductible. He
emphasized that."

"Thank you. I'd better get to sleep if I have to call him
at eleven . . . it seems like it'll be here any minute." She
tumbled backward onto the bed, exhibiting enough bare
flesh to overcome an even greater exhaustion than J.D.
was feeling.

Hastily he removed himself, carefully closing the door.

After getting up to call Arnold a little past eleven, Katie
went back to bed and slept for another two hours. When
she awoke again, she was alone in the apartment. A note
left by J.D. on the kitchen table said he was spending the
day with Tony and some other USC friends.

Katie treated herself to breakfast in front of the TV,
then bathed and dressed carefully but casually in a navy
cotton shirtwaist dress with a red, white and blue stretch
belt and a broad sailor collar.

When reception buzzed her that Mr. Richter was waiting, she threw a bulky white sweater over her shoulders
and picked up her navy bag.

"Beverly Hills seems to be treating you well," was Arnold's greeting, accompanied by a kiss on one cheek.
"You look delicious, Katie."

"Thank you kindly, sir," said Katie. "So do you."

After maneuvering herself with some difficulty into his
low-slung car, she laughed, "Why do tall men get such
short cars?"

Safely inside, she began to thank him, but he cut her
off ruthlessly. "Never mind all that. How's your prickly
boyfriend?"

"Prickly still," said Katie, "but—"

She thought of their beach walk last night, that wonderful silent hour when they had walked hand in hand,
communicating in every way but with words. Then, before

they went back to the party, there had been that single kiss. Just one, but so long, so achingly sweet, so tenderly passionate, she had hardly been aware of the water lapping at her ankles or the chill of the air when her jacket fell from her shoulders.

"But—" Katie began again, and Arnold interrupted, "Yeah, that's what I thought." Then, as briskly as usual, "Let me tell you about your choices of accommodation. One of them is a house with four bedrooms. Three other roommates. Nice residential neighborhood. Big yard. Lots of space."

"Which roommate do you know?"

"Olivia Randall. Sweet, serious, about twenty-nine, I'd guess. She's a bookkeeper with my firm. The roommate you'd replace is getting married next week."

"How about the other?"

"An apartment. Not as nice an area, but almost on top of shopping, nearer to theatres, restaurants, etcetera. A car wouldn't be important. Two small bedrooms. One bath. And I think, a very compatible roommate. Crystal Karn. She's around twenty-four, bright, pretty, sense of humor, a paralegal for a firm of attorneys we share office space with."

"I think Crystal and her apartment sound more like what I'm looking for."

"I thought so, too, but I figured you should make the decision. Okay, on to Crystal's first."

Katie found Crystal so compatible on first meeting that she skipped going to see the second possibility. A statuesque, cream-skinned redhead, Crystal was as bright and attractive and funny as Arnold had said.

In fact, Katie couldn't help wondering why they weren't interested in each other. Then she intercepted a fleeting glance from Crystal's hazel eyes in Arnold's direction as she was plying him with drinks and dips while Katie prowled around the apartment and realized that one of them, at least, was not indifferent.

Crystal and Katie agreed to split rent, electricity and gas, basic phone, and twice-a-month maid down the middle, with Katie contributing an extra fifty per month for the use of Crystal's linens, kitchenware, and furniture.

"Lila—the maid—is coming in tomorrow to fumigate the place after my last roomie, who was a slob to end all slobs," Crystal told Katie frankly. "So you could move in the day after that, if it suits you."

"It suits me fine. I don't have a bank account yet— would you like me to sign over some traveler's checks to you for the first month's rent?" She poked around in her purse. "Or I could give you one hundred cash for a deposit?"

"She would probably be better off with the cash," Arnold interposed. "You write out a receipt, Crystal, on a piece of stationery that has your name and address."

Crystal looked relieved. Katie nodded approval. While her new roommate had her back to them, bending over her desk, Katie pointed to her, then pantomimed eating and drinking. Arnold raised his eyebrows, and she clasped her hands under her chin, mouthing, *Please.*

When the money and receipt had changed hands, Arnold, as though it were his own sudden brilliant notion, said, "Well, ladies, hitching up to a roommate is the closest thing to marriage; I think this calls for a celebration. How about a Chinese dinner, family style, which means that no one is allowed to have a meal to him- or herself? Share and share alike."

"The best idea of the day," Katie applauded quickly.

Crystal's feeble protests were soon set aside, and she ran happily into her bedroom, winning Arnold's approval by returning in record time, her baggy dungarees changed to tailored slacks and a denim jacket.

A good time was had by all at dinner, Arnold as much as both his "dates."

Katie, sampling the broccoli with crab sauce in silent ecstasy, watched and listened to the other two laugh and joke about office affairs. Arnold might like her, Katie, quite a lot, but not so much that he would cherish a hopeless passion or couldn't be diverted to Crystal, provided she played her cards right. Katie resolved to help her play them.

Katie was back at J.D.'s apartment by nine, and to her surprise, J.D. was home before her, sitting in the living room with the TV on, though he didn't seem to be watching it. Newspapers were scattered all over the floor. He was leaning back in his big tweedy recliner reading a script.

"Did you have a nice day?"

They both asked it together and both burst out laughing.

"A lovely day. I got an apartment, J.D., and my roommate seems great. You'll be rid of me in less than two days. I'm moving Tuesday evening."

"Is that my cue to say I'll miss you?"

"Will you?"

"Sort-of. You know, the way I might miss pressing my tongue against a tooth that aches."

"Miserable creature," said Katie fondly. "The world won't come to an end if you break down and say something nice."

"Okay, I'll miss you."

"I know you will," retorted Katie smugly. "I'm counting on it. How's Tony?"

"Tony is fine. He sent you his love."

"How come you're home so early?"

"It was fun, but I was tired, and eight hours of college days' nostalgia seemed sufficient. When they started bar-hopping after dinner, I decided I'd had enough. Besides, I have a full schedule at the office tomorrow. The director walked out on *It's Murder, She Sez*. Artistic differences, it will say in the papers. Actually, he got miffed because his girlfriend got turned down for a starring role. Uncle Nate phoned just a while ago. He wants me to take over," he added casually.

Katie was not the least bit deceived by his offhand manner. "Oh J.D., would this be the first time you'll direct a full-length feature?"

"Yup."

"That's wonderful. I'm so happy for you. I wish we had some champagne. I—" She stopped suddenly, gave him a hostile stare, and muttered something below her breath he suspected to be a Pennsylvania-Dutch curse.

"That was a pretty quick switch from sugar to vinegar. What's the matter now?"

"Isn't *It's Murder, She Sez* the movie that Taffy Tremont has a part in?"

"Yes, it is. She has a very small part. She gets killed off early in the film and disappears from view quite soon. How many times and in how many languages do I have to tell you that Taffy Tremont is no threat to you and of no interest to me?"

"There aren't enough," said Katie darkly. "I remember the way she used to drape herself all over you."

"Did you ever see *me* draping myself all over *her?*" Then he asked in a voice of baffled disbelief, "What the hell are we arguing about? Katie, if I were interested . . . seriously interested . . . in any girl, it would be . . . Hell!" he finished violently. "I don't want to get involved at all!"

He sat upright as he spoke, and the back of the recliner came with him, rising so suddenly that he was thrust forward. The script fell onto the carpet, and as he bent over the arm of the chair to pick it up, he gave a yelp of pain.

"What's the matter?"

He straightened slowly and with difficulty. "I threw my

back out the other day, lifting a piece of camera equipment. Now I guess I bent wrong; I've really fixed it."

"If you'll lie face down on the couch, I'll give you a treatment that will help."

She caught his skeptical look, "Honestly, I can, J.D. I had some training, first from my mother years ago, and then at the hospital in Maryland from the physical therapists."

J.D. accepted her hand to help him get up out of the chair. Seeing his wincing, tentative walk, Katie said, "Maybe you ought to go to bed. You could relax more there. Let me just change out of this dress into something easier to work in. Oh, and take off your shirt and pants."

She answered his quick suspicious glance with a sweet saintly look of her own. "I'll pull up the blanket or use a big towel to preserve your modesty," she promised kindly, "and I swear not to take advantage of your helpless condition."

Then she ran, laughing, to her own room while he hobbled, swearing, to bed.

When she came into his room a few minutes later, wearing a loose short cotton robe and carrying one of the big fluffy bath sheets from the linen closet and a jar of her own oil mixture, he was lying in his queen-sized bed, face down, with the quilt pulled up to his waist. He had taken off his sports shirt but was still wearing an undershirt.

She yanked at the undershirt. "Let's get rid of this, too."

His head swiveled around and he started to sit up. "Why?"

"Because I'm not just going to use manipulation, I'll be massaging you with oil. It would be pretty ridiculous to do that through a shirt. Why on earth are you so damned suspicious?"

J.D. suddenly turned brick red all the way from his

throat to his hairline. She would have sworn it was with embarrassment; but almost immediately the color faded, and a look of sullen despair settled over his face. It was a look she knew only too well. How often had she seen Johnny's face take on that same angry, hopeless mask?

"You dig and you dig, Katie Kauffman, and you leave no room for privacy," J.D. said with almost weary indifference. Then he shrugged himself out of the undershirt and lay back again, face down.

Katie stood for a few seconds, staring. Then she sat next to him on the bed, and her calloused hands began to move gently over the network of scars that went from his shoulders down his back as far as she could see . . . right to his legs, she suspected. They were faded pink scars in all kinds of sizes and odd forms, short, long, narrow, wide, round, straight, and jagged, scars overlapping other scars, and each and every one the symbol of a past agony!

"What reticence! What restraint!" J.D.'s muffled voice mocked her. "Not a single question. No sympathy for a gallant hero's war wounds."

Katie poured a small amount of oil onto her hands and spread it over his shoulders and the bunched muscles at the back of his neck. Her strong fingers worked at loosening the muscles. As she rubbed and stroked, pinched and probed, she spoke softly.

"I worked in the children's ward in Basking Reade Hospital. The battered kids were brought there, toddlers as well as teenagers, even babies. They had broken bones, concussions, burns and bruises, and bloody cuts. They'd had belts and baseball bats as well as broom handles used on them, hoses, lamp bases, anything you can name. One other thing they had in common . . . the old scars of their past beatings. Now I know why you hated your father."

"*Hate,* Katie, not hated. Present tense. I hate him still."

"He's dead, J.D. You told me he's been dead for fifteen years. Maybe it's time you buried him."

"I doubt that day will ever come."

"Only if you don't want it to. Only—" Her voice was suspended for a moment; her fingers dug in harder, but J.D. twisted around suddenly as some of the scalding tears streaming down her face dripped onto his back.

"Hey!" He grasped her wrists. "What the hell are you crying about?"

"What the hell do you think?"

"If it bothers you to look at it . . . then don't."

"God, J.D., sometimes you can be so incredibly dumb! It doesn't bother me to *look* . . . it bothers me that it happened. Don't you really understand that I can feel some of your hurt . . . a little of your pain? It's what you once suffered I find unbearable, not the sight of your scarred back. Now shut up and lie down, will you?"

Obediently, J.D. shut up and lay down again. For half an hour Katie manipulated and massaged, finally drawing a few grunts of pain when she worked on his lower back.

"Ah, that's where your trouble is," she said, not without satisfaction, and a moment later, "Lord, what a stubborn sacrum!"

He was moved to protest only when she whisked his undershorts down a trifle, but she slapped his hand away and draped the towel modestly over the rest of the unexposed area.

"So I'll see a half-inch of your backside. Big deal. You feel better, don't you? Would you trade that to preserve your macho modesty?"

"No, ma'am."

"Then lie still and relax. There's no benefit if you tense up."

When she finished, he was half-dozing. She drew the sheet and quilt up to his neck, and her hands lingered, tucking him in.

"Thank you, Mama," he said, rolling over and opening his eyes just when she thought he was fast asleep.

"You're welcome," said Katie.

She found herself suddenly pulled down by the wrists; she was lying on him, separated by the quilt. "K-K-Katie, you are something else. I feel great, and your hands are—"

Words seemed to fail him. He seized the aforementioned hands instead and started kissing them, one finger at a time.

When all ten fingers had been saluted, Katie reluctantly wriggled off him. "Go to sleep, J.D.," she urged softly. "You're going to feel much better in the morning."

She planted both hands, palms down, on his chest, feeling his hair curling between her fingers and his heart beating strongly against her thumbs.

"Your hands—feel—like—heating pads," J.D. told her sleepily. "Whatcha doing?"

"I'm trying to help heal you."

"That's not . . . where . . . scars are."

His eyes closed again. He didn't hear her whisper; she didn't mean him to. "Oh, yes, it is, J.D. Oh, yes, it is."

When she straightened and walked to the foot of the bed, he was deeply and quietly asleep. He lay with one bare arm thrown over his chest and one raised above his head. He looked so very vulnerable.

Her heart ached with the new knowledge that he was indeed so much more vulnerable than she would ever have believed back in Pennsylvania.

She had seen him first as someone clever, sophisticated, and fascinating from the envied outside world, someone challenging to talk to . . . even fight with . . .

And then had come that moment of blinding realization, followed by her jealousy of Taffy Tremont. She had been suddenly *leebgronk* . . . love struck, lovesick, lusting after the seemingly god-like creature who had appeared to her out of nowhere on a lonely country road . . . her knight in shining armor!

How shallow that early emotion!

He wasn't a knight at all . . . nor even the least bit god-like. He was a man, and a very human man at that, a prickly, hurting, vulnerable man to whom much harm had been done.

There was such aching pity and tenderness mixed in with her love for him now. She wanted him, she desired him, yes; yet even more, she longed to make him happy.

She wasn't *leebgronk* anymore. To be lovesick, she now felt, was to experience only an undernourished, child-like sort of love. Her love for the J.D. who lay sleeping was whole and healthy, a dream of shining splendor, waiting only for fulfillment. Fulfillment for the both of them.

Twenty-three

*"My sweet," quoth the tempter, "what have you to
     lose?"*
She longed to resist, but what was the use?
He had made her an offer she could not refuse. . . .
     from *Other Poems Of Love* by Lady Martibelle

When Katie came into the kitchen a little after seven
in the morning, J.D. was there before her, sitting at the
counter, crunching dry toast and drinking coffee while he
made notations on his script.

"Top of the morning, K-K-Katie."

"How's your back?"

"Incredibly improved. Want some coffee?"

"Please."

He poured a cup for her while she checked the refrigerator for orange juice. After filling a small glass to the
brim, she took the stool next to him.

"Katie?"

"Yes?"

"Something funny happened last night," he said, not
looking at her. "I dreamed about my old man after you
left me."

He seemed to fall into a reverie. "Yes, J.D.?" she encouraged after a while.

"It wasn't funny that I dreamed about him—I've been

doing that regularly most of my life . . . the same dream. He beats me up, and suddenly I'm big and strong and I wind up turning on him, killing him. Then I wake up and I'm sorry. Not sorry he's dead, you understand, but sorry I wasn't the one to kill him in reality." His lips twisted. "I suppose you think that's pretty sick?"

"No, J.D., just bitter."

"Last night's dream was different . . . more like an old memory, one I'd almost forgotten. He was sitting on the couch next to my mother, crying about not being a man anymore. I remember vaguely overhearing them once, a year or so after he was first hurt." He laughed uncertainly. "Are you sure you want to hear all this ancient history?"

"I want very much to hear it. Go on, J.D."

"He was head of a construction crew working on a high-rise office building in New York when he had a bad fall from one high ledge to another two floors below. There were a couple of operations, but they never could put his back and left leg quite right. I guess he was in pain most of the time . . . and he couldn't work construction anymore. They gave him an office job; he wasn't much more than a filing clerk. It didn't give him half the money he'd been earning, and he wasn't entitled to disability—well, he always said he was cheated out of it, but the firm had proved his blood content at the time of the accident was half alcohol, and some of the other workers admitted a bet was involved . . . he had no business being out on that ledge.

"Anyhow, our house got eaten up by medical bills and we had to move to the apartment in Sheepshead Bay. My mother got part-time work nights as a supermarket checker. He let her because we needed the money, but he couldn't stand it. Looking back now, I can see he was one of those super-macho types who doesn't feel he's a man unless he's bringing home all the bacon, and only by manual work.

When he failed at both, he took his bitterness and frustration out on all our hides."

"So you feel sorry for him now, J.D.?"

"Hell, no! I understand, perhaps, but he'll never have my sympathy. He *chose* to wallow in self-pity and booze instead of trying to make a new life. Only, I think you were right last night . . . it's about time I buried him. So maybe the new dream means the hate is easing up."

"I'm glad, J.D."

He looked at her shrewdly. "Smug, as well as glad."

"Mmm . . . maybe."

"Because of you . . . and your hands, you think." But he stroked one of them even as he spoke the jeering words.

Then, as though ashamed of his moment's softness, he hastily finished his coffee and jumped up from the stool. "I've got to run. Take you out to dinner tonight?"

"I expect you to make it a special splashy farewell one. Tomorrow I'm eating with Crystal."

"I'll make a reservation at Mama Amalie's. What are you doing today?"

"Walking, wandering, shopping . . . I may not be at leisure long, so I should enjoy it while I can."

"See you tonight, then." He grabbed up the script and the last piece of toast and left at a run, but halfway to the door, he changed his mind, came back, yanked Katie's head back by the hair, and gave her a quick hard kiss on the lips. "Wise ass," he muttered in her ear.

Two sweeter-sounding love words had never been heard, thought Katie joyfully, stowing the coffee cups into the dishwasher.

The telephone rang, and she answered it, still in a happy daze.

"Is that you, Katie Kauffman?"

"Arnold?"

"No, it isn't Arnold. It's Tony Burney. You remember . . . we met at the Sherman party."

"Of course I remember you, Tony. I'm sorry, but you just missed J.D. He's on his way to the office."

"As a matter of fact, you're the one I wanted."

"Me?"

"This is pretty embarrassing in view of all the things I said, but would you be willing to pose for me today? At top price, of course?"

"Doing what?"

"Well, in the layout I'm shooting for Holland Maid cheese, I was using four non-Holland presumably-Maidens . . . healthy looking types, all beauties, of course . . . but the top man took exception to every single one of my four. Too starved-looking, too skinny, he said. He wants a more sturdy, wholesome type . . . so I thought of you right off."

"Thanks a heap."

"Now, now, take it as a compliment. All you have to do is skip around for a few hours in a peasant skirt and blouse and—so help me—wooden clogs, clapping your hands and looking as though life held no greater bliss for you than eating Holland Maid cheese. You said you like new experiences."

"Okay," said Katie blithely. "Where and when?"

She told J.D. all about it over their "farewell" dinner at Mama Amalie's. "I would *hate* to be a model," she confided. "The lights were so hot I thought I'd melt, and the clogs were a couple of sizes too large; they had to stuff the toes with paper. I didn't walk in them . . . I clumped. Between shots I had to go into the dressing room and unlace the blouse so I could breathe. I was wearing the skinny girl's outfit, and she was undoubtedly flat-chested. Then I had to practice smiling just so . . . not too big a smile, that would be grinning, but not such a skimpy smile that I didn't look overjoyed about eating their blasted cheese, which wasn't real anyhow . . . or rather, they'd covered it with some kind of coating so it wouldn't melt. Tony told me not to dare taste it. And all my life I've read that modeling is a glamorous profession!" she wound up disgustedly.

J.D. laughed enjoyably. "I think the glamor tag refers to the perks, not to the actual work."

"Well, they can have it, perks and all," Katie told him firmly. "I plan never to model again."

She had been living with Crystal slightly more than a month when she got her second call from Tony.

"Katie, I know you don't like modeling and you swore you would never do it again," he said after the usual polite preliminaries, "but I may have an offer you can't refuse."

"I hate modeling, but neither can I refuse to listen to any offer," Katie conceded. "I haven't exactly been swamped with them."

"No job, kid?"

"Well, I helped a little with two horrible B scripts at Continental . . . but it was charity because of J.D. . . . and I do so want to make it on my own."

"Well, you made this one on your own, I can swear to it. They're scrapping the original layout you did for Holland Maid because there's been a major switch in their campaign plans. They want just *one* Holland Maid—you."

"Me!" squealed Katie.

"The head guy was crazy about—and I quote him exactly, so don't gag—your 'healthy glow of natural bloom and beauty'—and the new promo idea is for a series of magazine ads, with the Holland Maid girl going to different exotic cities, proclaiming everywhere that her cheese is so much better than the local product. Katie, I'm talking Paris, Amsterdam, Venice, Madrid, and Copenhagen."

"You mean I'd get to go to all those places?" Katie shrieked.

"All expenses paid and incredible fees—if you're willing to pose as the one and only sweet and simple Holland Maid."

"I will hate posing as the one and only sweet and simple Holland Maid, but you're absolutely right. To get paid to travel around Europe is the one offer I can't refuse!"

"Bless you, my child. I knew I could count on you. Listen, Katie, could you get your a—self to New York this week? We have to set things up in a hurry."

"Well, I—I suppose so. Sure. Why not?"

"Take down my phone numbers . . . studio during the day, home at night." He waited patiently while Katie rummaged in a drawer for paper and pencil. "Call me back and let me know the minute you can leave and I'll get you a hotel reservation and arrange to have your ticket pre-paid so you can pick it up at the airline office. Don't forget you'll need warm clothes. It will be winter-cold where we're going. Any other questions, call me any time. Ciao, kid."

"Wait! How long will I be gone?"

"Three weeks . . . maybe four. Does it matter?"

"I suppose not," said Katie in a small voice, thinking of J.D., which was ridiculous, really, she scolded herself. The only time she had seen him, since he had left to direct *It's Murder, She Sez* in San Francisco, was on Thanksgiving when he flew down for the day, gathered her up and took her to his Aunt Marion's for an enjoyable, festive, but not very private dinner, and then flew right back again.

She would be no farther apart from him in Amsterdam or Copenhagen than she was right now in L.A., she told herself. Nevertheless, she dialed his hotel room and left a message that Miss K. Kauffman would like to say goodbye to him before she left for Europe.

* * *

*On a TWA jet somewhere over the Atlantic
Ocean halfway between the eastern coast
of the United States and the west coast
of Ireland. Dec. 9, 1985*

Dear, darling Johnny,

I think it's Dec. 9th, though at this point I wouldn't
swear to it. I am positive, though, that I'm on a jet
plane, and I can definitely see the ocean below . . .
but halfway to Europe . . . who knows? As far as
I'm concerned, we could be halfway to the moon. In
short, brother mine, I am—Tony's words, not mine—
sloshed to the gills, which is his fault for filling me
full of a marvelous drink called Campari. When I
saw all that water below and realized there was no
place to fall but into it, my stomach turned unner's
ew erscht. Tony said I was the first green person he
had ever seen; but when he realized I was truly pet-
rified, he called the stewardess and they both started
pouring the Campari into me, and now my insides
are calm as a pond, and I feel wonderful, absolutely
wonderful. Isn't life a dream?

Tony is snoring away magnificently in the seat next
to me. Every time he gets to the highest octave in a
snore, his beard bounces around in rhythm. He's
wearing a denim work shirt and the kind of overalls
you used to put on to shovel manure. Just looking at
him makes me feel like I'm back home in Strawberry
Schrank.

I went to New York from Los Angeles sort-of roundaboutly, flying up to San Francisco first on Sunday
morning. J.D. picked me up at the airport and we
had most of the day together before I took an early
evening flight to New York. He drove me around all
afternoon. I saw the cable cars and the seals on the
rocks of the Pacific, and we went up and down those
scary steep streets of San Francisco. I still don't see

how cars stay at the top of them; I was convinced we were going to slide down backward. We ate at a seafood place on Fisherman's Wharf—very touristy, J.D. said—but so what, I was a tourist.

About J.D., Johnny . . . you were so sweet and understanding that now I can tell you that I cried all over the letter you sent me after I first wrote about him—just as I cried all over your last one (which is in my purse right now) telling me about your Suzy. I'm so glad for you, Johnny, so very, very glad. No matter what, you'll always be my dear best friend.

My handwriting seems to be like this plane . . . it keeps going up and down, Excuse it, please, it's the drink, not me; and speaking of drinking, I am exercising my sisterly privilege of nagging. You aren't doing any, I hope? It's different for you than this teensy necessary bit for me.

Remember how I once told you that when I left Pennsylvania, I was through forever with being Coffee Katie? Well, a funny thing happened on my way to Europe. In New York, at one of my meetings with the Holland Maid people, they told me they wanted a slightly more exotic professional name for me than Kauffman. You'll never guess what name I took! Why should you have to guess, when I can tell you?

Your loving sister,
Katie Coffee

Amstel Hotel
Amsterdam, Holland

Dear J.D.,

Your flowers were in my hotel room when I arrived, all beautifully arranged in the Delft bowl, which, of course, I shall bring home with me. It looks very like one that Mem has in her kitchen cupboard *back home. Hers came from a great-great-grand-mother.*

It was dear of you and made me feel very important, sort-of like a movie star.

We started the shoot yesterday, and the work is just as dreary as I expected, but at least this time I have my own size costume and clogs that fit, so I don't clump (or not quite so much) and I can breathe without breaking the bodice laces.

Outside of work, I'm having a marvelous time. Tony said I must get some culture, so he took me to the Rijksmuseum, where there is the biggest collection of paintings by Dutch masters. Rembrandt's Nightwatch, which has a whole room to itself, was the most impressive, but I sort-of liked the landscapes by van Goyen and van Ruisdael better—they were more like the Holland I had pictured to myself before I came. I bought some prints for framing for both of us. (That's how come I spelled the artists' names right!)

Before we leave we're going to take a train ride into the countryside so I can get a good look at some dikes and windmills; I would feel cheated to leave this country without so much as a glimpse of either. I know, I know. I'm a tourist. I'm also going to see Anne Frank's house. I bought a copy of her Diary in Dutch and was pleased that I can understand quite a bit of it.

You'll be amazed to hear that I have finally discovered some food I don't want to eat . . . something called Rijstafel, which it seems the Dutch imported from Indonesia when it was their colony. It consists of twenty-six different dishes, each one more highly spiced than the one before. For an hour and a half my mouth was on fire; my hair stood on end! I wound up taking a tiny taste of this and that and drinking cup after cup of tea while all the Dutch photographers we were with gulped down all twenty-six offerings with unbelievable gusto. When dinner was over, Tony took pity on me, and we went straight to the Hilton, where I had a hamburger and a milk-shake.

From here we go to Paris and after that to Venice. Tony's roommate Gregorio Grieg, a pianist—do you know him?—is meeting us in Venice. He's half-Italian, half-Greek, and he's been on a three-month fellowship studying with some famous maestro—*I forget his name—in Rome.*

Tony has been trying for days to explain to me that Gregorio is more than just his roommate, but each time he starts, he gets sort-of panicked and steers away from the subject. I think he's afraid my innocence is not up to the shock! Whatever in the world did you tell him about me to make him think I'm such a fragile flower?

Well, au revoir *till Paris, mon cher J.D. (I've been studying a French phrase book).* Merci beaucoup *again for* les fleurs.

> *Don't forget* je t'aime,
> *Katie* Café

Twenty-four

. . . why this myth of virginity still prevails today, though it is not so much a physical condition as a state of mind. The married virgin, as always, still abounds . . . while many a schoolgirl, still in full possession of that frail membrane modestly referred to as a maidenhead, can perform on a man with the skilled virtuoso of a Heifetz playing the violin.

from *Once A Virgin, Twice A Virgin*
by Katryn Kauffman Coffee

Tony took her to supper at his favorite restaurant on the Left Bank their second night in Paris. Katie wore her rainbow gown and Tony his pin-stripe, which was not only his best suit, he admitted unabashedly to her, it was his only suit.

"With my height and build and beard, I look like a clown in dress-up clothes," he told her,

"You do not," Katie said heatedly. "If you wanted to, you could look impressive."

Tony grinned. "I don't want to," he said. "It's too much trouble, and it's far too expensive."

"Why do you have to economize so? It seems to me you make good money."

"I do, but the Morgue eats it up."

"The Morgue?"

"A brownstone I own in the east twenties . . . in partnership with my bank, of course, till the end of the year two thousand when the mortgage will be paid off."

"Why on earth do you call it the Morgue? Is it so gloomy?"

"Nah, actually it's a cheerful, homey place," said Tony with simple pride. "The last owners spent plenty re-doing it, and there's a big garden out back—can you picture it, a real garden in the heart of Manhattan?—but in the 1920s it used to be a funeral parlor, so even after it was featured as a New York beauty spot in *Garden Homes,* the name stuck."

"Honestly." Katie lifted her eyes heavenward. "J.D. always says that in California the smog gets in everyone's brain, but New Yorkers seem just as crazy to me. Calling a beautiful home the Morgue. Tony, what made you buy an expensive house?"

"I guess with five generations of farmers in my background," Tony admitted a bit sheepishly, "I can't help myself. Nebraska or New York City, I don't feel secure unless I own a little chunk of land. Besides, I rent out three of the second-floor bedrooms to help with expenses. All people in the arts, so it's by way of being a rather special rooming house. There's a lot of coming and going; it's noisy and crowded and fun."

"I wish I had seen it when I was in New York."

"You can when we go back."

A waiter placed a plate of hors d'oeuvres before each of them, and five minutes of complete silence reigned, with both of them absorbed in their food, before Katie poked a small object on her plate with her fork.

"What's this?"

"That?" Tony's face was carefully blank. "A French delicacy," he said diplomatically. *"Escargots."*

Katie speared one and chewed it thoughtfully.

"I don't think I like it."

"Most Americans aren't partial to snails."

"Snails!" Katie grabbed her wine glass and drank deeply. "Ugh!" she shuddered.

"Now, now, don't be small-town."

Katie muttered in Pennsylvania Dutch.

"What did you say, Katie dear?" Tony grinned. "It's rather noisy in here to speak so softly."

"I merely expressed some doubt about whether your mother had been faithful to your father," Katie told him with vast dignity.

Tony grinned again, but not quite so pleasantly.

"My father," he drawled, "when he found out about his only son's sexual proclivities, wondered the same thing."

"Tony, don't—"

"I think you know that I'm gay," he said. "I want you to understand before we get to Venice and he joins us for a few days that Greg, who shares the master suite at the Morgue with me, is gay, too. I've been trying to tell you for some time."

"Tony, what you call your proclivities—and your friend Greg's, too—are none of my business. We're friends. If I ever manage to get J.D., into bed, I don't expect *you* to start judging *me*. Here, I'm finished. Have my snails, too."

"You mean, you haven't bedded him yet?"

"No, but I'm working on it."

"Holy sh—smoke! You're a virgin."

"Would you like to get up and announce it to the whole restaurant?"

"Sorry, Katie, I don't suppose it's any more startling than my being gay."

"That expression, used that way, always seems so strange to me. You know, among the Pennsylvania Dutch, going gay means you've joined the wicked non-Amish outside world. You get excommunicated for it."

"So do we, Katie. In a good part of society, so do we. When, in a glorious burst of youthful idealism, I told my father the truth about myself, he threw me out. No more Burneys to perpetuate the line, you see, besides which I had tarnished his masculine image. He would have preferred a lie."

"My foster father would never want a lie," said Katie thoughtfully, "but he, too, insisted that his son and I must conform or never come home. We are what we are, Tony; we can't lead our lives to suit others. I don't see any particular virtue even in trying to—"

She interrupted herself, waiting, while their waiter set down two plates of venison and deftly served their vegetables. "Smell that sauce!" she murmured.

"I'd rather eat it."

"Tell me more about the people in the Morgue," Katie said, picking up her fork.

"We're kind of an odd bag," answered Tony with his mouth full. "Besides Greg and me," he said, swallowing, "there's Celestine Forrester. She's an actress, just bit parts so far, and between parts she works at Barnes and Noble—that's a big book store on Eighteenth Street. She has the face of a Christmas angel—you know, one of those cotton candy blondes—and a mouth like a sewer. She could shock the pants off a stevedore."

"But you like her," Katie said shrewdly.

"Her mouth may be big, but so is her heart. Yeah, I like her."

"Who else?" prompted Katie. "Any more girls?"

"No, the other two are both guys. Brian Scully, a writer, mostly freelance trade journal articles while he produces the great American novel in his spare time. A bit stuck on himself, but not a bad guy. He plays a mean guitar, which is fun at our parties. Nobby Rose is a sculptor. He has the smallest bedroom, but he uses the cellar—where the bodies were kept in the old days—as his studio. You two should have a lot in common," he added provocatively. "He's a male model."

"In that case, we have nothing in common."

"Now, now, don't be a bigot. I told you he's a sculptor, but sculpting doesn't pay his rent any more than writing pays yours."

"You're too painfully right," said Katie. *"Mea culpa.* I apologize to the unknown Nobby."

"As a matter of fact, he rather shares your viewpoint, but he's got one of those pumping-iron physiques the fashion magazines go for, so what can he do but capitalize on it?"

"Anthony Burney! I had no idea you were in Paris." The voice addressing Tony spoke in heavily accented English, but it was a deep, sonorous voice and the accent was romantically French.

Tony stood up, looking not at all pleased.

"Katie, may I introduce Jacques Blanchard. Jacques, my little cousin, Katie Coffee."

"Your little cousin, Katie Café," repeated the deep, velvety voice with obvious amusement. "But how charming!"

The big dark melting eyes in the lean handsome face swept Katie from her waist all the way up to her forehead. She had a strong notion that he was X-raying her lower half through the table. "But how very charming," he repeated softly. Then, "I must not disturb your meal . . . eating is a serious business . . . but you must join me in the bar when you are finished and be my guest for your liqueurs. No, no"—though he had not given Tony a chance to speak—"I insist. You must not be selfish and keep this delightful young lady all to yourself, Anthony."

With a last lingering look at Katie—she was convinced he could describe her underthings, even to the lace edging on her panties—he departed, and Katie immediately demanded, "Who on earth is that man and why on earth did you say I was your cousin?"

"I thought it might keep him from making a pass at you," Tony told her gloomily, "but I should have known better. Jacques Blanchard, my dear, is the owner of *Les Belles* and *Paris Modistes* magazines. His internationally famous nickname is the Virgin Scalphunter."

"The Scalphunter?"

"Virgin Scalphunter. He wasn't so discriminating before the AIDS crisis, but now he insists on virgins. Quantity, not quality, is his aim. And he leaves a trail of desolate demoiselles behind him because quite a number would like a re-match, but he won't risk it. Unfortunately he can sniff out a virgin at fifty paces."

"A man who wants only virgins," Katie mused.

"You've got it."

"And never bothers the girl after just one time?"

"Exactly."

"Well, well, well." Katie looked quite thoughtful. "This should be rather interesting. I think I'm going to enjoy our after-dinner drink."

"I think *I* would enjoy ducking out through the rear exit."

"Don't be a spoilsport. I'm looking forward to Monsieur Blanchard's technique. Did you ever see anything like the way he rolled those bedroom eyes?"

"If you'll recall," said Tony wryly, "the lecherous son of a b had his back to me when he was rolling his eyes at my little cousin."

Katie giggled. "Finish your dinner, please. I want to get to the bar."

A few minutes later they were seated at a small round table in the bar, Tony's rigid back denoting outraged propriety, while Jacques Blanchard once again rolled his bedroom eyes at Katie, and Katie responded with cloying smiles and kittenish batting of her eyelashes.

"I know it's not a proper after-dinner drink," Katie simpered, offered a liqueur or a brandy, "but I just love your French champagne."

Jacques promptly ordered a bottle of champagne.

When Katie had finished her second glass and held it out for a refill, Tony said pointedly, "Katie, I hope you haven't forgotten that our shoot starts early tomorrow. We should be getting back to the hotel."

"In what hotel are you staying?" Jacques asked casually.

"The Bristol." The attempted fluttering of her lashes was more like a blink, but there was no mistaking the soft, seductive murmur of, "I'm sure you know how to get there."

Having gotten her message across, Katie put down her glass. "Tony is right, the slavedriver. Time for beddy-bye." She turned toward Jacques again, holding out her hand and puckering up her lips in a most un-Katielike pout. "It was lovely to meet you, Monsieur Blanchard. Thank you for the champagne."

As he brought her fingers to his lips, he whispered, "Shall I bring champagne to the Bristol, *ma belle?*"

"Mais oui," Katie whispered back with a smile that hid a calculation every bit as cold-blooded as his own.

He was handsome, charming, personable, disease-free and eager . . . above all, according to Tony (who should know), selfishly partial rather than full of qualms about virgins. It was decidedly a plus that he wanted only one night with her. It made him, decided Katie, bubbling over with champagne and determination, ideal for her own purpose.

She would be able to return to J.D., unemotionally involved from one night in Paris, but with her distressing— to him—state of virginity erased. They could go on from there!

When the soft knock sounded on her hotel room door, she was waiting calmly. She had showered, brushed her teeth, and dabbed cologne behind her ears before slipping into her new peach nightgown and matching robe.

Katie opened the door and blushed slightly when a room-service waiter preceded Jacques into the room, pushing a cart on which a spray of white orchids, a bottle of champagne in a bucket of ice, and a plate of canapés were beautifully arranged on a silver tray.

The waiter opened the champagne so matter-of-factly, Katie's blushes subsided, but she was relieved when Jacques finally pressed a tip into the man's hand and locked the door behind him.

Jacques seemed in no hurry. He served Katie champagne and urged more canapés on her, helping himself at the same time.

"You know," she told him presently, brushing an orchid lightly against her cheek, "I have never done this before. I hope you don't mind."

Since his answer about his pleasure in being the one to initiate her into the joys of *l'amour* was murmured caressingly in French, Katie saw only the smile and the charm and was enchanted by the warm, romantic-sounding words.

Presently he stripped to the waist, allowing her time to admire his broad-shouldered, bronzed body with its powerful chest, flat stomach, and taut muscles. He was as fully aware as Katie that he could have posed for the statue of a Greek god; there was no doubt that in a contest for masculine beauty, side by side with Jacques, J.D. wouldn't have stood a chance.

But just the fleeting thought of J.D., all dressed in casual sports clothes or lying with his scarred back exposed, brought a catch to Katie's throat, while Jacques Blanchard, standing there stripped and gorgeous, did not so much as quicken her heartbeats.

She forced herself not to think of J.D. but smiled and sipped more champagne, and when Jacques lifted her up in his arms, she found his kisses quite acceptable and clasped her hands around his neck the better to enjoy them.

The champagne had made her light-headed, almost lighthearted. She was ready when he laid her on the bed and divested her of the robe and gown with the speed and skill of experience. It might be rather pleasant, she thought fleetingly. If not, it would soon be over with. Then she could go back to J.D. After all, she *was* doing this for him!

"You did *what* for *who?*" Tony thundered at her.

They were riding in a gondola in Venice . . . the two of them and Gregorio Grieg, who had flown in from Rome two days before for a short vacation before the shoot began.

Katie, who had expected the half-Italian, half-Greek Greg to be dark-haired and dark-skinned, was surprised by his fair hair, ruddy skin, and blue eyes. He had a round, cheerful face, a flashing toothy smile, and when he sat down to the piano—which he did in the hotel lobby their first night together—she was overwhelmed by the majesty and power of his performance.

"He's magnificent!" she had gasped to Tony.

Tony nodded. "He's a genius," he said simply and proudly.

Katie had tried to make herself scarce during their few days of liberty, but neither man would permit this exercise in tact. They went sight-seeing together during the day and ate all their meals together, and their rapport was so great that she somehow found herself telling them both about Jacques Blanchard.

Now, in response to Tony's shouted question, she repeated, "I said I did it for J.D."

"Then take my advice and don't tell him so," Tony told her rudely. "He'd probably belt you one, and I don't know that I'd blame him."

"*I* think he would understand," Katie stated with injured dignity.

"If you believe *that,*" Tony retorted in disgust, "you're unbelievably naive . . . as well as an idiot."

"Greg?" Katie appealed to him.

He shook his head slowly, his ready flashing smile strangely absent. "I pass," he said.

"I don't," said Tony. "Take my advice. Forget it ever happened. *We* both will. Don't ever tell J.D."

"He called from San Francisco the other night to say he would be going home soon," said Katie in a small voice. "I mentioned that I have a big surprise for him."

"Did you tell him what the surprise was?"

"Nooo."

"Good. Buy him a really nifty gift and let him think that's the surprise."

"I don't want our—our relationship to begin with a lie."

"I'm not telling you to lie, Katie, just not to offer gratuitous information."

To the Katie raised by Amos and Katy Stoltzfus, there didn't seem to be much difference. On the other hand, she realized the rules of the world she now lived in were different.

When she remembered that night with Jacques Blanchard, however, her confidence returned. It wasn't as though she had enjoyed herself . . . or him. Thanks to the champagne, it hadn't been too disagreeable . . . just rather boring. In fact, she'd had a panicked moment of wondering what all the fuss was about and if she would feel the same way when J.D. and she . . .

Then, just his name echoing in her mind stirred her senses more than all of Jacques' practiced moves, and she relaxed again. Tony and Greg didn't know all the facts, so they couldn't understand, but when she explained it fully, J.D. surely would.

Twenty-five

. . . so that the unsanctioned gift of her virginity by a woman was regarded more as a crime than a sin. She had robbed her father of a valuable property that was his to sell, and her husband of a privilege that was his to take. Never was it a woman's right to give!

from *In Bed Unwed*
by Katryn Kauffman Coffee

At the Beverly Crest Apartments, the doorman registered instant approving recognition of the smart new Katie in the cloak of Scottish plaid she had treated herself to at Orly Airport.

"Is Mr. Shale in?" she asked as he took her bag.

"He got in about an hour ago."

Katie looked at her Movado watch, another gift to herself, this one from Amsterdam. Eleven-fifteen. If he hadn't been home since morning, he would be in the den going though his mail and listening to the late news at the same time. If he had been home any time this evening, then he'd still be listening to the news . . . but from his bed . . . with a little snack beside him.

"Oh, please, let it be his bed," Katie prayed, grateful that J.D. had never asked to have his key returned. It would be so much easier, so much more natural, just to appear in his bedroom.

At the door of 14 F she took her bag in exchange for a dollar bill, then waited for the doorman to step back into the elevator before turning her key in the lock.

The lock turned smoothly, but she had forgotten that J.D. sometimes used the chain. Tears of disappointment stung Katie's eyes as it barred her way and she had to ring the bell.

Nothing happened. After a while she rang again.

"Who is it?" barked a sleepy-sounding voice from far away. Sometimes when he'd had a hard day, he dozed off during the late news.

"It's me. Katie."

Suddenly, in a reprise from the past, the door was flung open and J.D. appeared in his old black swim trunks, just pulled on. Katie almost threw herself against the deliciously hairy chest.

There was one big difference from that earlier occasion, though; this time he didn't put her gently away from him. Instead his arms closed around her hard, harder, caving in her ribs, cutting off her oxygen supply.

She was glad of that tight hold when his mouth descended on hers. It was no sweet soft nibbling kiss he gave her, but one of such searing passion that Katie's knees buckled under her. She felt faint, dizzy, bruised, and deliriously happy. With joyous and generous abandon, she returned him kiss for kiss.

They stood in the open doorway for five minutes before J.D. thought to kick her suitcase through and slam the door shut, replacing the chain again. Then he returned to Katie, holding her less urgently this time, his hand slipping under the cloak to span her waist, his cheek resting against her hair.

"God, but I missed you!"

Katie's hands, lotion-soft now, came stealing inside his

swim trunks from behind. He uttered a sound somewhere between a gasp and a groan, then pulled her down to the carpet.

It was over almost before it had begun, with the two of them wrapped up in Katie's cloak and still lying tangled around one another on the floor.

"I'm sorry, Katie," he said into the curve of her neck. "I'll do better by you next time."

"I can wait."

J.D. rose slowly to his feet and reached down to her. Katie took his hands and let him draw her up beside him.

"Come into the bedroom," he said.

They walked there hand in hand, Katie still in her rumpled dress and cloak, J.D. naked, the swim trunks forgotten on the floor of the hallway.

The TV was still on in the bedroom, and he turned it off. There was a dish of crackers and a glass of grapefruit juice on his bedstand. He carried them into the bathroom.

When he came back, Katie was still standing in the center of the room, hands clasped, unashamedly studying his nude body.

"Why don't you take off your cloak?" asked J.D., and then did it for her. He unbuckled her belt and unbuttoned her dress and slipped it over her head. He reached behind her to undo her bra, and after he took it off, he pressed his body against her bare breasts and slid her petticoat off, standing back so she could step out of it.

"Lie down," he said, and, without taking her eyes from him, Katie went over to the bed.

She lay still and quiet while he gently removed her beige lace briefs; her panty hose had been discarded earlier, near his swim trunks. She turned to him quite naturally when he joined her.

"This time will be for you," he promised softly.

Katie looked at him with big shining eyes. "I can wait," she said again.

He kissed the tip of her nose and then the tip of each breast. "You won't have to wait very long. Tell me, what's my surprise?"

"I am," said Katie solemnly.

"And a very delightful one, too, even if you have caused the overthrow of my most cherished principle."

Before Katie could begin to explore this topic, it became quite obvious to both of them that she need not wait for him so much as ten seconds. Despite this, he was slow and deliberate in his approach, his hands roving over her from head to toe, exploring and enchanting. Finally, she turned to him, holding frantically onto him, whimpering, "Please, oh please," and he lowered himself onto her.

They fell asleep in each other's arms, with the bedside lamp still on, and did not wake till six in the morning when J.D. found himself staring up at the light and turned it off.

When he looked down at her, he saw that Katie was awake and that he had pulled the blanket almost off her. He slid down in the bed, covering her with himself.

"K-K-Katie," he whispered the way he had in the night. "K-K-Katie from Strawberry Schrank, you're something else. I just can't believe you're real."

"I'm real," Katie said with a smile of pure mischief. "Shall I prove it?"

When her wandering hands had supplied the proof, he gathered her to him with a smothered groan. They made love again and slept through half the morning, to be awakened by the ring of the phone.

"No, you'll have to take care of it, I can't come in today," Katie heard him grunt into the receiver. "Yeah, it's the bug all right. I've been felled"—he rolled his eyes lasciviously at Katie—"by a very peculiar virus."

"Virus, indeed!" said Katie with pretended indignation when J.D. managed to get the receiver back on the cradle. "A fine thing to call me."

"The K-K-Katie virus," he crooned, lying on his back, hands clasped underneath his neck. "It's addictive. I've never been one for back-to-back performances, but you—" She had sat up and he snatched her down to him. "You, I can't get enough of. Come here."

Around four in the afternoon, they were rested enough to venture leaving the bed and hungry enough to make breakfast a matter of some interest. J.D. took a quick shower, pulled on his swim trunks and a t-shirt, and went into the kitchen first while Katie took a leisurely bath.

When she was finished, she walked naked to the living room to get a complete change of clothing from her suitcase, choosing a pair of thin black wool slacks from Venice and a loose cream silk shirt from Copenhagen.

"Breakfast is served, Madame," said J.D. as she strolled into the kitchen. She sat down at the table and he sat opposite, setting a plate of pancakes and the coffee pot between them.

They were quiet until they were both feeling a little less hollow. Then Katie happened to look up and encounter J.D.'s eyes, and her entire body became one gigantic blush.

"D-don't," she stammered foolishly.

"Don't what?" asked J.D. as tenderly as he had ever in his life spoken any two words.

"Look at me like that," Katie said so low that he understood, rather than heard, the words.

"How am I looking at you?" he teased.

"As though you could eat *me* up instead of the pancakes," Katie retorted.

"I already have."

"J.D.!"

"Katie!"

Mercifully, he changed the subject. "Tell me about your trip."

"I'm too tired now. It would take hours. Days. But it was wonderful, and it's thanks to the trip that I'm here with you like this . . . that we had . . . what we had."

"You mean absence made the heart grow fonder, and all that?"

"Did it, J.D.?" she asked wistfully.

"I thought I'd answered that one pretty explicitly. Of course it did, you goose. Stop blushing. All my resolutions to be of noble character crumbled to bits while you were away. Couldn't you tell when you surprised me?"

"My surprise was that you didn't *have* to be of noble character anymore. Did you realize right away?"

J.D. looked up from spreading butter on his last pancake.

"Realize what?"

"That I'm not a virgin anymore?"

"Not again," he said wearily.

"I'm not talking about the milk pail," Katie denied indignantly. "I know better now. I'm talking about a real live man."

J.D. put down his knife and fork. "What real live man?"

"The one I—you know—"

"No, I don't know. Tell me."

There was something in his voice . . .

Katie said a little uncertainly, "I did it for you, of course. You felt so strongly about seducing a virgin."

"Exactly what is it that you did for *me?*"

"In Paris . . . there was a Frenchman," Katie swallowed. "Everyone told me that Frenchmen . . . and they said that *this* one stuck strictly to virgins and only wanted one time because he's scared to death about AIDS . . . so I . . . so I went out with him."

"Does 'went out,' by any chance, mean 'went to bed?' " J.D. inquired in a deceptively sleek and silky voice.

Katie swallowed again. "Yes. Only once, of course. So he could—free me for you."

She wondered how what had seemed such a sensible plan in Paris could shrivel into crass stupidity under the electric glare of J.D.'s kitchen lights and J.D.'s blazing eyes.

Almost echoing her thoughts, J.D. snarled, "You bloody little fool!"

Katie pushed back her chair.

"Maybe, if you feel so strongly, it wasn't as good an idea as I thought at the time, but I still won't be talked to like that," she told him stoutly, though her heart was pounding in panic and her hands and face were clammy.

"I'll talk to you any way I please."

"No, you won't. Maybe I was wrong. Still I did—what I did—to please you. I wasn't interested in Jacques. I didn't even like it with him. But he was experienced and—"

"And no doubt he taught you all the delightful little tricks I thought were natural passion!"

"They *were* natural passion."

"To believe *that,* I would either have to be as incredibly stupid as you or . . . would you prefer me to believe," he asked politely, "that you're a slut at heart? God knows you've been flinging yourself at me often enough since we met."

"And God knows," said Katie, cold with fury, "you kept claiming it was my virginity that stood between us. So I decided, mistakenly perhaps, but for your sake, to remove that tremendous barrier."

"You'll forgive me for not being overwhelmed with gratitude at the knowledge that you were hopping into the sack in Paris while I—like a prize jerk—was enduring the longest period of celibacy I've known since the age of seventeen."

"You'll forgive *me* for not being overwhelmed with gratitude and remorse at your terrible sacrifice."

J.D. lifted his hand.

So Tony had been right. He wanted to belt her. Katie stood her ground, staring at him unflinchingly. It was J.D. who looked in horror at his half-raised hand and took three steps back from her.

"I think you'd better get the hell out of here!" he told her hoarsely.

Silently, she turned and walked out of the kitchen. It took just a moment to collect her suitcase and cloak from the bedroom, her purse from the living room couch. She came back to the kitchen, where J.D. still sat at the table, drinking coffee, his face the same frozen mask.

"You're perfectly right, you know," she told him calmly. "From the first moment we met, I did fling myself at you. Three times now, you have thrown the love I offered to you, *only* to you—never anyone else—back in my face. Three times . . . but never again. There won't be any more flinging, I promise you that."

There were no goodbyes; she just walked out, and the doorman called a taxi to take her to the airport. She changed her Saturday return ticket to New York for a plane that would be leaving in just over two hours.

Tony had gotten her an admission pass to the airline's VIP lounge. After checking her suitcase, she went up to the lounge and found herself an isolated seat next to a picture window. She watched plane after plane take off and land, comprehending nothing.

Half an hour before she was due to board, she aroused herself to go to the back of the room and telephone her roommate.

"Crystal, it's Katie. I'm at the airport."

"Hi. You've just landed?"

"No, I'm just leaving. I came in this morning for some

unfinished business, but I have to go back east right away."

"I got a couple of your postcards. God, was I ever envious!"

"There'll be some more cards, and I'll mail a little present I bought for you in Paris. Listen, Crystal, I'll send you a check for next month's rent as well; it'll be by way of notice. I've had such good offers out of New York that I've decided not to come back to California."

"Some people have all the luck," mourned Crystal. "I'll miss you, Katie, but I'm glad things are going so great for you. You don't really have to send another check. It's ten days till your month runs out; I can probably find a prospect by then."

"No, it's only fair. You should have time to look around, find someone you like. And I need to keep my clothes there a while. Oh, and Crystal . . ."

"Yes?"

"If Arnold Richter calls . . . stop acting noble . . . he can be all yours."

"You devil! I didn't think you knew. I'll do my damndest. How about J.D.?"

"*He* won't call. But if he does, I've moved and you have no idea where. Tell him I left no forwarding address."

"You're sure?"

"Very sure. But I'll let *you* know my address when I settle somewhere. Perhaps you can come east to visit me on your next vacation."

"You're on. I'll be camping on your doorstep."

"Crystal," said Katie, blinking guiltily at the lie, "I have to go. It's time to board my plane. Goodbye. Thanks for everything."

"Goodbye, Katie. Best of luck."

* * *

The flight attendants started taking drink orders as soon as they were airborne. Katie asked for a brandy. She had felt shiveringly cold before she drank, and it provided comforting warmth; it also calmed the sick trembling in her stomach.

She held out her empty glass as a flight attendant went by. "Another, please." The words came out in a husky croak, and the middle-aged man in the brown business suit seated in the window seat alongside her gave her an appraising glance.

He probably thinks I'm an alcoholic, Katie decided without a flicker of humor, pouring the brandy into her glass from the miniature bottle with shaking hands. She resisted the impulse to tell him, What's wrong with me, sir, is that I fell in love with a dog-in-the-manger bastard, and I feel sick to my stomach because of him.

When the hors d'oeuvres cart was wheeled down the aisle, Katie shook her head. "I'm going to try to sleep," she told the flight attendant. "I don't want any food, and I'm not interested in the movie, so you needn't wake me up for anything."

After the cart had rolled by, Katie stood up and opened the overhead compartment. She helped herself to two small pillows and a blanket.

"Would you like to change seats?" the man in brown asked her. "I *am* interested in food and the movie; it might be easier if I took the aisle seat."

"Of course," Katie agreed politely. "Thank you very much."

The exchange was made; she put her seat back as far as it would go and curled up, with her face toward the window. She stared out into the blackness of the night, and images of J.D. danced before her eyes . . .

J.D. nude, his hand in hers, walking toward his bedroom . . . J.D. naked and sweating, making love to her . . . J.D. clamping her to his side after love, his eyes adoring

her . . . the frozen mask of his face when he rejected
her . . .

Damn J.D.! This would have to stop.

She pulled down the window shade with an angry snap
and closed her eyes. Fairly soon, the brandy did its work.
Along with the spreading warmth came relaxation.

Katie slept.

Twenty-six

"*It's strange how often, when it comes to women's rights, the male chauvinist and the male who espouses liberal causes on other issues suddenly become blood brothers.*"

Interview with soap actress, Celestine Forrester from a survey of prominent women in
Mucho Macho
by Katryn Kauffman Coffee

Tony looked her over critically when he found her waiting for him the next morning, sitting on her suitcase in front of his New York studio.

"Three days early and only two days since we went our separate ways at Kennedy Airport. Not such a good two days either, judging by your looks. I'm glad I don't have to put you in front of a camera today." He reached out as she stood up, and lifted her heavy suitcase as though it were a paperweight. "What in hell did you do to yourself?"

"Just what you predicted I might if I opened my big mouth too much," Katie answered, following him into the studio, "but if you dare say 'I told you so,' I swear the Holland Maid will never smile her vacant smile or clump in her wooden shoes again."

Tactfully refraining from either questions or 'I told you

so,' Tony busied himself with the fixings for coffee. When he handed Katie a large mug of the steaming brew, along with a slightly stale doughnut, he asked gruffly, "Wanna talk?"

"No," said Katie, "what I really want is a room at the inn."

"Say that again, please."

"I've come to New York to live, Tony. Can I rent a room at your Morgue?"

"There's nothing empty fit for habitation," Tony said, somewhat dismayed. "The attic bedroom has no heat, and you'd have to go downstairs to the bathroom. I couldn't put you in there, Katie, it's . . ." Suddenly his face brightened. "If you wouldn't mind gypsying it for about seven weeks, you could take the little den off the living room. There's a couch that makes up into a bed, and you could use the powder room in the hallway and shower upstairs . . . we'd manage something for your clothes. It's not ideal, but—"

"It's ideal, believe me, it's ideal," Katie interrupted thankfully. "I accept for the seven weeks. What happens then?"

"Brian is leaving for an editorship in Toronto. You can take over his room; it's the nicest after mine. Big, bright, and a garden view."

"That sounds wonderful." Katie flung her arms around him.

Tony detached her arms and went to the phone. He came back as she was rinsing out her mug, to inform her that Celestine and Brian were both at home, and one of them would show her around. "Leave your suitcase," he suggested. "I'll bring it tonight. It's walking distance from here in good weather, otherwise ten to fifteen minutes by bus; but until you know your way around, you'd better take a cab." He handed her a slip of paper. "Here's the address."

Katie got out of the taxi at Twenty-sixth Street and looked around. At the end of the block she could see a tall apartment house, but mostly there were narrow brownstones in varying stages of renovation, squat, flat little brick homes and even a few imposing white stone town houses.

The Morgue was a turn-of-the-century brownstone with a 1950s face-lift. Three steps down took her to a Spanish-style wrought-iron gate. When she lifted the latch and went through it, there were more steps leading at right angles to a heavy wooden door with a lion's head knocker in the middle and a bell to the side.

The doorbell rang out like church chimes, but no one answered. Katie lifted the knocker and let it fall with a lusty thump.

"I'm coming, I'm coming," a deliciously throaty voice shouted from inside. "Hold your friggin' horses."

Katie gulped, then giggled, remembering Tony's description in Paris. The sewer-mouthed Celestine, no doubt.

The door was flung open. Even in a baggy sweatshirt and torn jogging pants, she was beautiful . . . a cotton candy angel, all right.

"You must be Katie," she said cordially. "Want to go straight to the den? Tony said that you needed sleep and sympathy. By the looks of you, he was right. Your ass is sure dragging, kid, but Christ it's good to have another woman in this nest of male chauvinists!"

"Tony isn't a male chauvinist."

"Don't kid yourself, Katie. When it comes to the nittygritty of women's rights, the male chauvinist and the so-called male liberal are brothers-under-the-skin. I love the horny little darlings in my bed. Anywhere else, I'm wary of two-legged creatures whose pants need a fly."

Katie followed Celestine along a hallway and through the big living room, convulsed with laughter.

"I can tell you . . ." Celestine flung back over her

shoulder as she pushed open a sliding door, "that bastard Freud has a lot to answer for. Men were stuck on themselves enough before he came on the scene to set them all gloating over a stick between their legs that any four-legged animal knows how to use just as well."

She faced Katie. "Well, this is it. A bit crowded, but I guess you can manage for seven weeks. And you don't have to struggle so to pretend you're not in stitches. I'm effing glad you haven't got a stick up your backside; I'd hate to see Miss Goody Two-Shoes moving in. Want to go to a meeting of WOMAN tomorrow night?"

"Women?" Katie said uncertainly, her head spinning.

"No, capital W, capital O, capital M, capital A, capital N, WOMAN. It's a national organization that fights for women's causes in this damned youth-adoring, virgin-worshipping, male-oriented society of ours."

Katie's first impulse was to refuse. She wanted to hide in the den for a few days and quietly lick her wounds. But why *should* she shut herself up and brood? she asked herself suddenly. That kind of self-indulgence was exactly what she *didn't* need. She was damned if she would wallow in self-pity or regrets . . . and Celestine's speech had somehow struck a responsive chord . . .

"Hell, yes! I'd love to go to your meeting!" Katie said loud and clear.

"Okay, okay, you don't have to sound so effing belligerent about it. It's a date."

The following night when they left the church social room where the meeting had been held, Katie was not only a member of the local chapter but had also joined the national organization. She carried a shopping bag full of interesting pamphlets she had picked up to read and a list of books to get from the library.

"The books you want to buy to keep I can get for you

where I work at forty-percent discount," Celestine offered, well satisfied with her new recruit.

By Friday of the next week, Tony had completed the final shoot in the series for Holland Maid. Everyone had moved their jackets and coats out of the hall closet to make way, temporarily, for Katie's dresses, skirts, and blouses. Two bookshelves had been emptied to accommodate the rest of her clothes. She had written to Crystal to make arrangements to have everything she'd left in California boxed and shipped to her.

Before she started job-hunting in earnest, she decided to take the shuttle up to Boston to see Johnny.

When he met her at Logan Airport, his clothes were casual and careless, but his car was shiny and new.

"I'm impressed," said Katie lightly, which was a lie. She was worried. The smell of mint leaves on his breath when they greeted had been unmistakable.

"I thought Suzy might have come with you," she ventured after he had put her overnight bag in the back of the car and they were skimming along the highway.

"Suzy's a very tactful girl," he said off-handedly. "You can meet her tomorrow, but she thought we might like a few hours alone tonight. I made a dinner reservation at your hotel . . . the Ritz Carlton . . . it's right around the corner from Newbury Street and my apartment."

"Tell me about Suzy."

"She's a second-year drama student at Emerson College. Technically, she lives in the dorm there." He shrugged. "Most of the time she's here with me. Tell me about J.D."

"There's nothing to tell. J.D. is over."

"Is that why you moved to New York?"

"It seemed best." She pushed back the bucket seat and closed her eyes.

He reached out and touched her shoulder. "Relax. We'll talk when we get to the hotel."

Over dinner, Katie went straight to the point. "Do you

finally have what you want? Are you happy, Johnny?" she asked, knowing the answers. A contented man, with a history of hepatitis, didn't have to start dinner with a double Scotch.

"Happy?" Johnny repeated, as though he were experimenting with a strange word. " 'Happy' is not exactly the right word for how I feel. Are *you* happy, *Coffee* Katie?" he mimicked.

Katie shook her head, suddenly numb with pain. "No, not right now, but I expect to be in the future. Since I left home, my life has been full of wonderful experiences. I've made some good friends and done things I never expected to do, and been to far-away places I never dreamed I'd see."

"Do you remember how we used to talk, Katie? Our *dogs drawma?* Over and over, it was the same thing. If we could get away from Strawberry Schrank, out into the real world, life would be wonderful, we would be free. So here we are, the two of us, with plenty of money and living just the way we dreamed; and I don't know about you anymore, Katie, but I sure know about me. I have such satisfaction in my classes, in what I learn and how I study at home and play the market. But there isn't a day when I don't feel, just like I did back at the farm, *I don't belong here, I'm not one of them.* It's like the curse of Cain, Katie, except that that mark's not visible. God, but it scares me, the thought of going through my whole life feeling that I don't fit in."

The waiter set their platters of roast duck with orange sauce in front of them. Johnny, shivering visibly, ordered another Scotch.

"Please, Johnny," Katie said softly, and he gave her a sad, impatient sort of smile but canceled the order.

"How about Suzy?" Katie asked him.

"She's a lovely girl, a wonderful girl . . . but I'm so

much more 'plain' than I ever realized, Katie. You don't kill the Amish in a man because you take off the clothes."

He hesitated for a moment, ashamed, and then his difficulties poured out as they had always poured out when he spoke to Coffee Katie. "She gives herself to me, this beautiful girl, and I make love to her——how can I not? Then comes the guilt and the shame. I asked her to marry me, but she's a lot smarter than me; she said no. She said she loved me, but she couldn't marry me to take away my guilt over our living together. She thinks she's too young, and she's not ready, and she says I'm not ready either."

"She sounds like a very special girl. Have faith, Johnny. It will work out. You spent most of your life Amish; you can't expect to change completely in less than two years."

She reached across the table to squeeze his hand. He flushed and glanced quickly around the restaurant to see if anyone was observing them.

"It's all right," Katie teased. "Outsiders do a lot more in public than just touch hands."

Johnny grinned sheepishly. "See what I mean?"

"I see, but I still say it's just a matter of giving yourself some time," said Katie more confidently than she felt. "Listen, I fell in love with a supposedly liberated man, and in some ways he was even more rigid and strait-laced than any Amish fellow who tried to court me."

This time it was Johnny who reached impulsively across the table to take her hands.

"They still give warmth and comfort," he said wonderingly.

Katie smiled at him, misty-eyed. "See how easily you did that," she joked before gently withdrawing her hands. "Johnny, listen to me; if you believe in my hands, believe in my words, too. I'm not sure of many things in this world, but I am sure that all our *dogs drawma* will come true. Someday, you and I will both be happy."

* * *

Shortly after her weekend in Boston, on the basis of her record of work for Continental Films—somewhat exaggerated by the employment agency which sent her out after she took a quickie typing course—Katie got a research job on the staff of *Love And Marriage* magazine. It wasn't exactly what she wanted, but the work was interesting and it was a step up the ladder.

She had been in New York a little over two months when what seemed like a mild but persistent virus prompted her to see a physician. Her department head at work recommended a Dr. Philip Gordon on Park Avenue.

She left the office early one afternoon for an appointment with him, and when she left Dr. Gordon's office some time later—a card with a gynecologist's telephone number and address tucked inside her wallet—she walked all the way from Sixty-eighth Street to the Morgue on Twenty-sixth.

As she walked in the freezing March cold, snuggled down in her fake-fur coat and fur-lined boots, a wool scarf wrapped around her head and ears and lower face, she tried to believe the unbelievable. She was pregnant . . . pregnant with J.D.'s baby.

She knew it was J.D.'s because she had gotten her period in Venice, a week after being with Jacques Blanchard. She was glad that, no matter what had happened afterward, her baby had been conceived in love.

Of course there were all kinds of problems involved, but somehow they didn't seem important—not compared with the wonder of the baby growing inside her.

As soon as she entered the Morgue, she could hear Greg playing. He had returned from Rome three weeks before, and Katie would sit for hours listening to the wondrously beautiful sounds that he was able to coax from the old upright piano. She could imagine how gloriously he made music during the day when he practiced on a grand Steinway at one of the Carnegie studios.

"From the Peer Gynt Suite by Greig—no relation to me," Greg said without turning his head when she came into the living room. He educated as well as entertained her.

Katie sat and listened dreamily, joined for a few minutes by Celestine, who then drifted off again to dress for her dinner date. Tony and Nobby came from the kitchen and sat down to their never-ending game of gin rummy.

After a slight pause, during which Greg flexed his fingers, his hands seemed to ripple gently across the keys. "Here's something suited to your sleepy state," he told the half-drowsing Katie. "Brahm's 'Lullaby.' "

Katie's eyes opened wide. Instinctively her hands caressed her stomach, feeling it full of baby, fancying its flatness rounded. She didn't notice Tony eyeing her.

Fifteen minutes later she was in her bedroom—formerly Brian's—changing into the cotton warm-up suit she wore for lounging, when Tony knocked and called her name.

"Just a second." She zipped up her jacket and opened the door to him.

Tony walked in, looked around, and commented favorably on the new blue curtains and matching bedspread. Then the springs squeaked their protest as he deposited his bulk on the bed.

"You're pregnant, aren't you, Katie?"

Katie stood on tiptoe and peered into the oval mirror over the dresser. "You mean I show already?" she asked with eager curiosity.

"No," he said, grinning at her disappointment, "but I spend most of my days photographing women, studying the lines of their bodies. I know yours pretty well, and you simply don't have the same one I photographed two months ago. It's a lot fuller. You're still small behind, but you're straining out of your bras—I'll bet you need a larger size—you've got the least suggestion of a belly, and you're hippier. Your skin tone is different, too, and the way you walk. The possibility has been in my mind and on my mind the last week or so. How far along are you?"

"Just beginning my third month. I only found out today."

"Do you plan to get an abortion?"

Katie shook her head vehemently. "No, even though things went wrong for J.D. and me, I still want the baby. I'll make it up to her for having no father. I'll give her enough love for two parents."

"You're sure it's J.D.'s?" Tony asked uncomfortably.

"I had proof positive."

"That's no problem then," said Tony, relieved. "J.D. will marry you."

"Who asked him to?" retorted Katie, affronted. "This is *my* baby; I'm not telling J.D."

"Je-sus Christ! Why not? Are you afraid he won't believe you?"

"J.D. believes a lot of unpleasant things about me," said Katie, grimacing slightly, "but *not* that I'm a liar. It's just that I have no intention, because I'm having his baby, of whining to him for a wedding ring. It's too late, Tony," she told him earnestly. "It was too late from the moment I told him about Jacques and he stood staring at me as though I were some loathsome object. I'll never forget that look he gave me just before he told me to get the hell out. I'll never forgive it, either."

Tony tried to speak and she forestalled him. "Even if I were weak enough to go to him," she pointed out quickly, "can you see J.D. in a *forced* marriage? It would be like caging a wild animal and trying to tame him. He'd never get over the feeling that I had put something over on him. No, thank you," she finished decidedly, "marriage to J.D., even if I could get him to offer it, is out."

"Okay, Katie."

She looked at him searchingly. "And no going behind my back—for my own good—to tell him, or getting someone else to do it. It's my right to decide what's in my own best interests."

"Okay, Katie."

"I want your word of honor that you won't betray me— not to J.D., not to anyone."

"Word of honor. Can I just tell Greg?"

"If he'll promise, too." She hesitated. "Tony, will I be able to stay here after the baby is born?"

"Stay where? In New York, you mean?"

"No, here—at the Morgue."

"Why shouldn't you?"

"You won't mind having a baby in the house?"

"I think it could be fun." He held up a warning finger. "I'll babysit, but I don't do diapers."

"Did anyone ever tell you you were a beautiful man?"

"Yeah, yeah, beautiful, that's me."

"My daughter will think so, too."

"Did it ever occur to you," queried Tony politely, "that your *she* might be a *he?*"

"It's not that I favor one or the other, honestly," Katie assured him, "just that I think a girl might be easier with a baby that doesn't have a father. A little girl Jocelyn."

"Jocelyn! Holy shit! Is that J.D.'s name?"

"Yes, but never let on—if you see him again—that I gave away his dark secret. And if we're going to have a child in the house, you'd better practice cleaning up your language."

"Don't look at *me,*" grinned Tony. "Celestine is the one you'll really have to work on."

"Celestine . . . oh, my God!" Katie groaned. "If the baby learns to speak from her, I'll probably have the first toddler ever expelled from nursery school!"

Interlude

And now, the Chancellor Card. Corporation, makers of fine greeting cards for every occasion, is proud to present our hostess, Elizabeth St. Clair, who will introduce her first guest . . .

The camera focused on Elizabeth St. Clair, casually smart in a simple grey silk dress and pearls, her black hair brushed back from her face, which was lit up by the familiar warm smile known from Maine to California.

"Good evening, ladies and gentlemen. I am sitting in the living room of the Fifth Avenue condominium owned by Katryn Kauffman Coffee. Ms. Coffee is beside me . . ."

The camera panned to Katryn Kauffman Coffee, looking pleasantly comfortable but hardly elegant in a matching pair of blue cotton slacks and shirt, leather loafers on her feet.

"Katryn will do, please. I get uncomfortable being constantly Ms.-Coffeed."

"My pleasure, Katryn, and I would again like to express my thanks to you for permission to be here in your home with you today. For years you have been quite firm in your refusal to let any interviewer or TV camera, as you put it, 'invade the privacy of your sanctuary.' May I ask what induced you to change your mind?"

"Circumstances," Katryn laughed. "I don't think it is

any secret"—She stared straight out at the television audience—"The media has certainly made much of the fact that I more or less invaded my own privacy and, incidentally, made rather a fool of myself in the process, during my guest appearance on 'Celebrity Brunch in the Big Apple' last month. Since I didn't seem to have much privacy left"—she carefully erased a crease in her slacks with one finger—"when you renewed your offer, this time I decided to accept."

"For any particular purpose?" Elizabeth St. Clair nudged her gently.

"I suppose to set the record straight on certain points."

"One of those points being your change in name?"

"Not really." Katryn shrugged. "I never considered," she added challengingly, "that I *had* changed my name."

Elizabeth St. Clair smiled encouragement. "Could you explain the confusion about it?" she continued to prod in the gentle way that somehow incited the most reluctant subject to open up.

Katryn was no exception. "I was named Katryn Kauffman but always called Katie by my family. When my parents died and I moved to Pennsylvania, my foster mother was named Katy, too. To avoid confusion, as is frequent in Amish families, I was given a nickname. Mine was Coffee Katie. Coffee Katie Kauffman. All I did years later," she seemed impelled to explain, "was to reverse the name."

"So you come from an Amish background?"

"My mother and father both left the Amish community before marriage. They became Mennonites, extremely liberal Mennonites. When they died, my brothers and sister and I were taken in by Amish cousins."

"It must have been a difficult adjustment for you all," Elizabeth said with eager sympathy.

"Not for my younger brothers, and only in the beginning for my sister. They soon fit right in, and our foster parents—I must make it clear—were the most wonderful people in the world. Unfortunately, I was already too much a product of my early years in Florida. I never really felt as though I belonged, so, yes, there were times when it was—difficult."

"How did you happen to leave the Amish life?"

"I had always planned to. When the time seemed right," Katryn said quite lightly, "I just went."

Elizabeth seemed disappointed at this prosaic reply. "No problems . . . no adjustments in the brave new world you joined?"

"Of course there were," Katryn returned unhelpfully.

The charming smile Elizabeth was famed for slipped a little.

"Would you care to elaborate on that?" she inquired graciously.

"No," said Katryn quite baldly, "I would not. My feelings on the subject," she added just as graciously, "are rather private. We did agree beforehand, did we not, that I would not answer any questions I considered too private?"

"That was our agreement," Elizabeth admitted. "I had hoped, however, that—"

"Would you like some coffee and pie?" Katryn interrupted, and the camera immediately panned to the long low glass coffee table just in front of the couch on which she and Elizabeth sat.

Katryn poured a cup of coffee from the pot and placed it on a small tray, then filled a plate with a selection of pastries, chattering as she did so. "This has an apple butter filling, and this is the famous Pennsylvania Dutch shoo-fly pie you've probably heard about. These are half-moon pies. They are usually served to the younger children during Sunday Preaching Service to ease their restlessness."

She passed the small tray to Elizabeth St. Clair, who drank and tasted, exclaiming in delight.

"You baked these yourself? They're marvelous. Somehow"—her pleasant trill of laughter invited Katryn to join in—"one doesn't associate Katryn Kauffman Coffee, feminist leader, with cooking and baking."

"'I enjoy baking occasionally. It gives me time to think."

Pleasant chit-chat, decided Elizabeth St. Clair, but it was getting them nowhere. The large TV audience had not tuned in to learn that Katryn Kauffman Coffee could bake a mean shoo-fly pie. What they were panting to hear about out there were the juicy details behind her quarrel with J.D. Shale.

She set her coffee cup down on the tray and put the tray back on the table, deciding it was time to take off the gloves.

"You mentioned making a fool of yourself on 'Celebrity Brunch,'" she offered in provocation. "That doesn't seem to be the general opinion about what happened, although, of course, there has been some speculation . . ."

Katryn raised her eyebrows in derision. "Speculation is rather a kind word for the public reaction," she said curtly. "I had to take my telephone off the hook the next day because it never stopped ringing. I was so harassed by reporters and paparazzi as well as all the other vultures who gathered in the street just downstairs—that I had to move to a friend's for a week in order to get some privacy."

"Do you feel bitter towards J.D. Shale?"

"Bitter?" Katryn rolled the word about on her tongue, repeating it again. "I don't think so," she said thoughtfully. "Not anymore. Once I may have, but that was long ago. I am annoyed at him, of course . . ." Her voice trailed off deliberately, artistically.

"Annoyed!" exclaimed Elizabeth, disappointed. She had hoped for something a great deal stronger than annoyance.

"Well, he used to do research for documentaries," said Katie, smiling sweetly at the camera rather than at Elizabeth, her eyes very hard and bright. "I think that if he's going to state facts so arbitrarily, he should be a great deal more careful to get them straight."

"You're saying he made incorrect statements?"

Katryn spoke as blandly as though she were mentioning the time of day. "Why, yes, some of his statements were incorrect as well as biased. A number of his accusations were downright untrue."

Elizabeth concealed her jubilation beneath a look of inquiring concern. "I have the transcript of the 'Celebrity Brunch' program somewhere here with me." She started fumbling through a sheaf of papers.

"Don't bother." Katryn laughed merrily. "I'll supply questions and answers." She leaned back against the couch and crossed her legs. "J.D. Shale accused me of anti-male bias, which I find especially strange, since the five best friends I have had in my lifetime are all men."

"And they are . . . if you don't mind telling us?"

"I don't mind at all. Anthony Burney, photographer; Gregorio Grieg, pianist; Johnny Stoltzfus, stockbroker; Cable Canatelli, ex-football player and cookbook writer; and Arnold Jay Richter, presently my business manager and married to my former roommate."

"Quite an impressive list. And are—"

"But that's just incidental," Katryn broke in. "After all, I could be accused of using my friends as red herrings." She made a wry face, misquoting in a voice of mimicry, *"Some of my best friends are men.*

"What I really take exception to are J.D.'s *provably* untrue statements," she went on, reverting to her normal voice. "He said I sounded off on subjects I had never personally experienced, such as marriage, divorce, widowhood, birth control, babies . . . I'm not sure if that's the complete list. He didn't seem to think I had the right to talk about men or marriage, sex, or children, without having been married or borne a child.

"Which is ridiculous!" She paused for a deep breath.

"He knows very well that writers and lecturers can talk and write about subjects they have studied and researched or become involved in without any personal experience. But there is no need, as it happens, to debate Mr. Shale even on such flimsy grounds. For his information, and anyone else's who thinks it of interest, I *have* experienced marriage—twice. I *have* been divorced and I *have* been widowed, and during my first marriage I had a child . . . a daughter."

As Elizabeth St. Clair leaned forward, obviously about to unleash a spate of eager questions, Katryn Kauffman Coffee turned from the camera to face her.

"And that," she said finally and firmly, "takes care of all personal issues. . . . Now, if you please, I would like to deal with public ones."

Yet even as she spoke with practiced ease of the murder of a pro-Choice doctor, she was swept up in a maelstrom of memories.

The years melted away, and she was back at the Morgue on Twenty-sixth Street. She had washed her face and combed her hair and come downstairs to go to the movies with Tony and Greg, glad now that these two good friends shared her secret.

The two were at the card table, but as soon as they saw her standing in the doorway, Greg flashed his toothy smile and rushed to the piano.

"This is for you, Katie," he told her, and began to play. "Name the tune," he flung back over his shoulder. Then both men began to sing. . . .

Twenty-seven

Even when there was a lack of passion, a great incentive to bundle in an unheated colonial house was the lack of warmth. It was better to bundle than to freeze—and far more pleasurable.

from *Bundle In The Trundle*
by Katryn Kauffman Coffee

"*Dum dum da dum
Dum dum da dum,*" chanted Tony in a gravelly bass monotone.

Greg swung around on the piano stool. "Please," he implored, shuddering exaggeratedly, "the tone deaf should not sing."

He swung back to the piano. "This, my dear Katie," he said, above the crashing triumphant chords, "is the 'Wedding March' from *Lohengrin,* which my poor deluded friend thought he was singing. And this"—the music changed—"is from Gilbert and Sullivan:

> *Hail the Bridegroom—hail the Bride
> When the nuptial knot is tied . . ."*

They both burst out laughing.

Katie looked from one to the other in bewilderment. "What's the joke?"

"Tony drew the high card, three out of five," said Greg.

"So I'm the one who gets to marry you," Tony told her.

Katie looked from one to the other. "That's not funny," she said with hurt dignity.

"It wasn't meant to be. We're serious, Katie Coffee," Greg told her, looking very serious indeed. "We just drew cards to decide which of us would be the daddy—that was high card—and which the godfather—that was low card."

"Look, Katie," Tony explained kindly, "we've all of us at the Morgue got this in common; we're woefully short of family, all except Greg, and most of his is in Europe. So we decided it would be fun to share the baby. That way she—or he—would belong to all of us. And since we think the kid should have a father, too, the best solution seemed for you to go through a marriage ceremony. Like they say in all the books," he grinned, "a husband in name only. After a decent interval, there would be a quiet divorce."

Katie looked from Greg, who was flashing his toothy smile again, to Tony, who was peering at her anxiously. Quite suddenly she began to cry.

"I know I'm not much to look at," Tony said with unwonted humility, "but most kids like me, honest they do, Katie. After the divorce, I'd still be a real good father."

As her tears increased rather than lessened at this unusual bit of comfort, he asked disappointedly, "Would you rather have Greg? I could be the godfather."

Katie smiled with the tears still dripping down her face. "Tony, you'd probably be a wonderful father. Either of you would be. You're both so damn kind, you make it easy for me to be selfish, but I know I would be taking advantage of you. Of both of you."

"You couldn't be more wrong," Tony insisted. "It was our own idea, entirely our decision. We played cards for you, Katie, my girl," he told her, half joking, half serious. "And I won you, fair and square, so Jocelyn gets *my* name. What's the big obligation? You can file for divorce a reasonable time after the baby is born. I'll even let you pay the legal fees."

"Nothing will change, Katie," Greg explained to her more quietly. "We'll live on here the same way we do now. No one on the outside has to know what our arrangements are. It's no one's business but ours."

"Say yes, Katie," Tony urged her.

"Greg?" she asked uncertainly.

He gave her the smile that showed an acre of teeth. "Say yes, Katie," he echoed.

"Yes," Kate told them, and joined hilariously in the singing when Greg started to play again.

During a long sleepless night, however, she developed qualms of guilt and came downstairs in the morning to say she had changed her mind. She was glad to find Greg in the kitchen, warming last night's coffee.

"Call Tony at the studio," said Greg before she could open her mouth. "He wants to make an appointment for your blood tests. You should get them done before you get married."

As he pushed the phone toward her, Katie shook her head. "Greg, I don't think this is the right thing to do . . . oh, not for me," she added quickly, "but for Tony."

"Tony is a grown man. He knows what the score is, and he's doing it gladly."

"And you, Greg? Are you glad, too?"

He gave her a quick, shrewd look. "I won't pretend to misunderstand you. So, from my heart, the answer is—yes, I wanna be a godpapa." He picked up the receiver and handed it to her. "Dial," he said.

Katie dialed.

* * *

They were married, she and Tony, five days later, with Greg as best man and Nobby and Celestine as witnesses. After a celebration lunch, life at the Morgue went on as before.

Katie went to her job every day and took an advanced typing course two evenings a week. She attended WOMAN meetings and off-Broadway shows with Celestine. Over the weekends she went for long walks by herself, getting to know the city. She attended Lincoln Center concerts and art exhibitions with Tony and Greg.

She looked plump rather than pregnant till well past her fourth month. On the day she switched into maternity clothes, Art Driscoll, head of research, handed her an article the magazine had commissioned on quaint courting customs and asked her to check it for accuracy.

Katie's report was handed in toward the end of the day.

"Minor mistakes, as indicated on page 2 and page 6. See correct information below. The section about bundling is completely inaccurate. Bundling didn't end in this country in the 18th century; it was still going strong among the Pennsylvania Dutch well into the 20th, when the outside pressure of publicity caused it to be frowned upon by both preachers and parents. There were Amish sects that split apart and new churches formed due to this one issue. Though largely suppressed today, it still exists—patchily— among some Amish groups."

Mr. Driscoll buzzed her just as she was getting ready to leave for the day.

"Katie, would you come to my office, please."

Katie put down her coat and walked through a network of smaller offices till she reached Art Driscoll's large, un- tidy one.

"Where did you get the information for your report?" he wanted to know.

"From my own background. I'm Pennsylvania-Dutch, brought up Amish."

He looked at her in astonishment. "You!"

Katie laughed. "I'm what you might call lapsed," she explained.

Mr. Driscoll looked her over. "Might you by any chance be pregnant, as well as lapsed?"

"Yes." Katie braced herself. She didn't want to lose this job.

"Does that mean you'll be quitting soon?"

"Just taking a short leave of absence, I hope. I'm going to be a working mother."

"Good." Mr. Driscoll gave her a brief, approving nod. "I don't want to lose an able assistant just when I've got her broken in."

As Katie let out her breath in a deep sigh of relief, he inquired carelessly, "What did you think of the Sykes article otherwise?"

"I didn't much like it," Katie said forthrightly. "I thought the writing was weak and the humor was forced. If you must know," she added, warming to her subject, "when I was just a schoolgirl I wrote a paper on some of the more peculiar colonial customs . . . it won an American Legion essay contest. I think," she mentioned without modesty, "I had a better grasp of the subject at fourteen than Sykes does now."

He answered only with a grunted, "Mmmm," but the next morning, there was a note on Katie's desk: *See A. Driscoll on the double.*

"I've been talking to the Big Cheese about your comments on the courting customs article," he greeted her. "She wants to see you."

"The Big Cheese?" Katie parroted.

He gave his characteristic grunt, this one denoting impatience. "Eleanor Howell, my boss and yours, desires to conduct an interview so that she may pick your brains. Two floors down, Suite sixteen-eleven; her Majesty does not like to be kept waiting."

When Katie, looking young, pretty, and pregnant in an Indian muslin maternity dress with a navy scarf knotted around her neck, walked into the inner office of Suite 1611, Eleanor Howell stood up. She was an inch short of six feet, her hair color was closer to orange than red, and she had a narrow, bony face with disproportionate features, a long nose, small mouth, and incredibly large beautiful green-blue eyes with eyebrows plucked almost to nonexistence.

Within ten minutes of a bone-bruising handshake, Katie realized that Art Driscoll had been correct—she was here for the purpose of getting her brains picked. She began to be more cautious in her answers. Especially now, she agreed with Amos' oft-repeated dictum that the laborer was worthy of his hire.

"Well, what I think we'll do is beef this up a bit. You were right—" The editor's wide-knuckled fingers flicked her copy of "Quaint Courting Customs" with casual contempt—"the humor is a bit labored."

Katie nodded courteously.

"I've decided," Mrs. Howell pursued, "to make this into a general article, the first of several in a series. In each future shorter article, we could perhaps deal more fully with a specific custom, say, bundling. How," she queried Katie directly, "would you like to tackle the piece on bundling? On spec, of course."

"On spec," Katie repeated thoughtfully. "I see. Then if I do it on my own time, Mrs. Howell, and you like the article, I would be paid at the same rates and on the same terms as any other free-lance writer who contributes to the magazine, is that right?"

Mrs. Howell widened her green eyes in haughty surprise. After a moment she gave a brief nod, then asked less grudgingly, "Do you want to tackle it?"

"I've already started," Katie said sunnily. "I was re-reading my old essay on odd colonial customs last night, and I started taking notes." Her smile was pure mischief as she assured Eleanor Howell, "I was planning to give *Love And Marriage* first refusal, I promise you."

Mrs. Howell's thin lips spread into something between a grin and a grimace. "You're not the bucolic country cousin you seem," she observed sourly. "Art tells me you plan to work after your baby is born, is that true?"

"Absolutely."

"Good. Glad your head's screwed on right."

Katie, reporting her first big opportunity to the occupants of the Morgue that night over the Chinese dinner they'd sent out for, could not help laughing. "For a magazine that preaches the joys and virtues of love and marriage," she said, "I'm amazed at so much rejoicing that I don't plan to stay home full time with my baby."

All her spare time for the next few weeks was taken up with her article. She took copious notes, calling first on her memory and then on Brian's old set of *Collier's Encyclopedia,* which he'd left behind when he went to Toronto. On her extended lunch hour, she was a regular visitor to the public library guarded by the great stone lions at Forty-second Street and Fifth Avenue. A diligent search of second-hand bookstores during her weekend prowls turned up a few old volumes containing helpful information.

Katy Stoltzfus had once told her an old family story of an aunt who fell into deep disgrace when she and the boy she was *rumspringa* with were caught bundling in an old trundle bed in the spare room when they should have been courting in the parlor. From this incident, Katie took her title, "Bundle In The Trundle."

Celestine was the first to read the finished article when

Katie triumphantly pulled the last typed page out of her new typewriter.

Sitting on the couch in the living room, while Katie watched from the armchair in an agony of impatience, Celestine read slowly. Several times she smiled, several more she even laughed out loud; but most of the time her face was carefully blank, and Katie—forgetting her friend was an actress—had the sinking feeling she had failed.

"Well?" she queried doubtfully when Celestine was done.

"If," said the cotton candy angel, "those effing Total-Womaners at *Love And Marriage* don't grab onto this, bring it to me. I know someone who will."

"You like it?" asked Katie joyfully.

"I love it. It's fast and smooth and informative and fun all at the same time. Don't worry about your future, kid. You're gonna make it."

Katie's face glowed. She got up and whirled around exuberantly, then had to sit down in haste, she became so dizzy.

"Sorry, baby," she apologized, patting her stomach lovingly. "Very inconsiderate of me."

Celestine grinned.

"Listen. Run off a couple of copies, and we'll send one to Francesca Janis. Remember you met her at WOMAN?"

"Yes, I think so . . . that grandmotherly-looking grey-haired woman with the razor-sharp mind, right? Is she an editor?"

"That's Francesca all right. No, she's a literary agent, a damn good one. I think it could do you a lot of good for her to see this."

"Fine," said Katie. "I'll make some copies at the office tomorrow before I give the original to Eleanor Howell."

* * *

With flattering promptness, Eleanor Howell agreed to buy "Bundle In The Trundle" for five hundred dollars, and Francesca Janis sent word that it had excellent possibilities for expansion into a book.

But it was a long time afterward before Katie could concern herself with either achievement.

The day after she received the good news from *Love And Marriage,* while working at her desk just after lunch, she started staining. When she phoned Dr. Kazanjian, he ordered her straight home and to bed.

A full week of bed rest did not help. Scared . . . impatient . . . Katie called Dr. Kazanjian again and took a cab to his office. When he had completed his examination, she looked anxiously from the doctor to his poker-faced nurse. "Something is seriously wrong, isn't it?" she asked, her clenched fists bunching the short white gown above her knees.

"Well, the pains combined with the spotting are certainly not normal, but you can take that tragic look off your face." He patted her shoulder kindly. "With proper precautions, there's no reason why you can't go to full term and deliver a healthy baby."

Some of the color came back to Katie's stricken face. "What precautions?"

"Well, to start with, I think we had better admit you into the hospital for a few days . . . perhaps a week."

Katie paled again.

"Come now, I don't want you reading undue significance into this, Mrs. Burney," Dr. Kazanjian told her with false heartiness. "Complete bed rest is mandatory, and I want to be able to monitor you constantly. Neither can be done at home."

"I'll do whatever you say, if it will help my baby."

"That's a good girl." He patted her again as though she were two years old. "I'll call and reserve a bed for you while Miss Pitkin telephones for a cab. You go right over and take the elevator straight up to maternity on the fourth floor . . . I don't want you delayed in Admitting for two hours. The processing can be done later. Ask for Mrs. De Carlo; she'll be expecting you."

"Come with me, Mrs. Burney." Miss Pitkin helped her down from the table. "I'll write it all down for you," she said soothingly.

"But I have to go home first," said Katie, still numb with shock. "I'll need—things," she added vaguely.

"You can call your husband from your hospital room. He'll pack a bag with whatever you need. I'll just go and phone for your cab while you get dressed. Try not to worry," she said as Katie shrugged away from any more pats on the shoulder. "Doctor knows what he's doing, and we want to keep that baby right where he is for another three months, don't we?"

"Yes," said Katie with a dry sob after the door closed behind Miss Pitkin, "we do."

In her hospital room an hour later she called Celestine at the off-Broadway theatre where the actress was rehearsing. Celestine agreed to break the news to Tony—"Gently, so he won't get too upset, please"—and pack a bag with whatever would be needed.

"We'll see you tonight," Celestine promised. "Keep your effing chin up, kid," she urged with remarkable restraint. "Everything will turn out fine."

But when she and Tony and Greg and Brian came visiting that night, Celestine turned almost as pale as the men at her first glimpse of Katie, who seemed to be tied in a traction-like position that reversed the laws of gravity. The top half of her was lying back on pillows, and her legs, modestly concealed beneath a wire cage covered by pristine white sheeting, were extended toward the ceiling. The curtains were drawn to give her privacy from her roommate's bed.

"Why didn't you get a private room?" Tony looked about him with disfavor.

"Because it would be silly. Hospitalization covers this—but not a private room.

"Is there a vase for my flowers? Put them on my bed tray, Greg. I'll ask one of the aides when they come by. They're beautiful, thank you."

For the next ten wearying moments, she found herself reassuring her worried friends till a nurse came marching around the curtain, took one look at the patient's strained white face, and felt her pulse. "Out, out, all of you." Like a broody hen, she bustled about, shooing them away. "This girl needs rest and quiet."

The three men shuffled out sheepishly; Celestine insisted on unpacking Katie's bag. "You want me to stay, kid?" she asked Katie belligerently. "If you do, I'll tell that effing white cap to shove it where the moon don't shine."

"Thanks, Celestine, but I really am tired," said Katie with genuine gratitude, knowing her friend undoubtedly had her usual hot date waiting in the wings for her. "Take the guys home, especially Tony. I'm too worn out to try to reassure *them*."

Celestine squeezed her hand. "Is it gonna be all right with the kid, Katie?" she asked bluntly.

"The doctor says probably, the nurses say sure, but I don't know. They seem to think being in this bed makes me automatically deaf and blind. I heard them saying something behind the curtain about imperfect implantation . . . I didn't like the sound of it."

"Effing jackasses," muttered Celestine, squeezing Katie's hand again. "Want anything when I come by tomorrow?"

"Yes, please, Chinese or Italian. The food here is awful. Take some money from my purse in the top drawer."

"Don't *you* be a jackass," said Celestine, walking out.

Katie slept soundly for some time, then suddenly woke

in the middle of the night with horrible pains that she knew with panicked certainty were the onset of labor.

"It's too soon!" she cried wildly to the nurse and orderly who wheeled her rapidly through the dimly lit corridor on her way to the delivery room. "Don't let my baby be born too soon."

Under the blinding lights in the delivery room, she swiveled her head frantically from side to side. "Don't let my baby die!" she wept to the masked faces. She was still whimpering those words over and over when she heard a shrill voice say, "Doctor, the baby is breathing."

"A daughter?" asked a much weaker voice that Katie vaguely realized was her own.

"A perfect little girl," someone whispered close to her ear, and Katie sighed and slipped into blessed unconsciousness.

When she woke she was in a different room—a large single room that was painted a cheerful peach color. There were flowers everywhere . . . on the dresser, the nightstand, the window sill.

Her eyes began to focus and made out the image of Tony, sprawled out in the big armchair near to her bed, his bushy beard resting on his chest.

"Tony," she said.

He jumped up. "Hi, sweetie."

"The baby?"

"She's beautiful, Katie."

"Will she live?"

"She's putting up a fight you wouldn't believe, Katie. The staff says that if sheer guts can do it, she'll make it."

"Can I see her?"

"I'll go get a wheelchair and take you down to her. She's in the neonatal intensive care unit at the end of the floor."

When they got to the unit, he helped Katie out of the

chair so she could stand with her face pressed against the window for the closest possible look at her baby.

"Oh, my God!" She turned to Tony in panic. "I could hold her in the palm of my hand."

"Easy, Katie, easy, she's a scrapper." They both glued their faces to the window again. "Fight, little Jocelyn, fight hard," she heard him mutter, and immediately she straightened up, pulling him away from the window.

"Not Jocelyn," she told him in a sure, steady voice. "That's Antonia Burney lying in there, fighting for her life."

"But—but K-Katie," he stammered, "you said . . . you said . . ."

"I know what I said, but that was only in the beginning. It's months since I meant her to be anything but Antonia."

"You owe me nothing . . ."

"Nothing? I owe you everything. What seems like a long, long time ago now, J.D. planted the seed. Ever since, you've done all the nurturing—you've provided home, friends, comfort, security. You've been my strength and support, a dear good friend always there when I needed you. That's my daughter and *yours* lying in there struggling to live, Tony. Let no one—not even you—ever try to tell me different."

"I won't," said Tony, taking her shaking hands. "That's our daughter lying there," he repeated proudly.

Six days later, when Katie was discharged from the hospital, Antonia was still holding on.

Except for sleeping at the Morgue, Katie haunted the hospital day and night. She spent hours staring through the nursery window, watching for the least sign or change in the tiny perfect little body, cheered by a curling of Antonia's fingers, a twitch of her legs.

She rested in the waiting room at the end of the corridor, trying to read sometimes, and ate meal after tasteless meal in the lobby coffee shop. Tony joined her in the evenings and whenever he could snatch a few hours during the day.

After another week they were allowed to put on hospital gowns and masks and go into the intensive care nursery. They were finally allowed to hold her.

Katie gripped the lightly wrapped little bundle that was her daughter, held it close to her breast, close to her fast-beating heart. This was a different kind of love from any she had ever felt before.

She looked at Tony, her eyes brimming over with tears. "I know, Katie," he said softly. "Me, too."

When the nurse said that she must, Katie returned the baby to her crib. Then she leaned over and put her hands over Antonia, gently and soothingly the way she had when the baby was snug and safe inside her.

"Heal, little girl," she whispered. "Grow big and strong."

"Heal, little girl," she whispered against the nursery window. "Come home and be my daughter."

The call came a few hours before dawn. While Celestine telephoned for a taxi, so as not to waste precious minutes, Katie and Tony scrambled into their clothes.

When they got to the hospital, doctors and nurses were waiting for them in the neonatal ICU.

Katie was given her tiny, beautiful, perfectly formed twelve-day-old girl child to hold so the baby could die in her mother's arms.

Tony would permit no one to disturb her for half an hour after Dr. Kazanjian signaled to him that the little bundle being rocked and crooned over was no longer alive.

Then he took hold of her shoulders, bringing her back to reality. "It's time to go, Katie."

Her lips trembled. "Can we take Antonia with us?"

"No, Katie, not now."

Katie put the still baby back in the crib and stretched

out her empty arms, staring with hatred at her hands. "My healing hands," she sobbed. "My damned healing hands, what good were they when my baby needed them?"

Interlude

Late May, 1996

"Can I come in, Kati—Katryn?"

Katryn Kauffman Coffee released the chain and opened the door wide. "Why not? You're already here. How did you get past the downstairs security, J.D.?" she inquired with genuine interest as she closed the door behind him.

"Good luck and ingenuity. Just at the doorway I met a little old lady in mink carrying a grocery bag. I gallantly seized it from her, chatting sociably as we passed the doorman and crossed the lobby, and everyone thought I was with her."

"You always did seize the main chance," Katryn observed dispassionately.

"You, of all people," he answered, equally dispassionate, "should know that's untrue. I passed up every chance you ever gave me."

Katryn changed color but chose to ignore the challenge.

"Why so devious?" she asked with studied nonchalance. "You could have been announced in the usual way."

"And I could have been refused in the usual way, too. I didn't want to chance it."

"When did I ever refuse you, J.D.?" she asked him mockingly. "And I certainly wouldn't have tonight. I've got my share of human curiosity, you know."

He had made some effort to comb his hair back; as he

tugged at it in his agitation, the dark curls, that now had the slightest touch of gray, sprang to life again. "Is there, by any chance, a spare cup of coffee in the kitchen? I skipped dinner tonight, nerving myself to come see you."

"There's always fresh-brewed coffee in my kitchen, as well as one of my famous pies; didn't you know they were my trademarks? Come on, it's cozier in the kitchen."

"Did it take so much nerve, J.D.?" she flung back over her shoulder, as he followed her.

"You damn well know it did. I've started to come here and turned back a dozen times since that program and—"

She slid a cup of coffee across the counter. "Sit down at the table. I'll cut the pie."

He sat down at the table and put the cup to his lips.

"Be careful, it's very hot," said Katie, but a second too late. He had already burnt his tongue and was swearing softly.

Katie came around the counter with his pie and a full cup for herself and slid into the seat opposite him.

"Just like the last time we were alone in a kitchen together," she said with smiling affability, then bent her head, a little ashamed at the look of dumb misery in the eyes he had suddenly lifted to hers.

He mumbled with his lips against the cup, "How soon did you marry—after California?"

"A couple of months."

"A couple of months?" J.D.'s brows lifted ironically. "I guess I could have saved myself some pangs of conscience. You don't seem to have grieved overlong about your lost love."

Katie laughed out loud "Man's ego . . . what a marvelous thing to behold. I had bigger and better things to worry about than *you*, J.D. I wanted a name and a father for my baby."

All the color fled his face. She had never seen J.D.

other than bronzed and healthy-looking; he was suddenly a sickly paper-white.

"You were pregnant then? My God! When . . . how . . . who?"

His last word took them back full circle. Nothing had changed, after all, most especially J.D.

"The baby," Katryn told him crudely, "was born the proper amount of time after I got back from my trip to Europe. I forgot virgins can get pregnant the first time."

She watched with an almost savage amusement as the color returned to his face.

"Did you marry the Frenchman?" he asked with a brutal politeness that more than matched her own.

"My grand adventure in Europe that sullied me so in your eyes consisted of one rather tedious hour of instruction in a Paris hotel room. I think the Frenchman was as relieved as I when it was over. We never met or spoke again. I doubt that the gentleman would have remembered either my name or my face a few months afterwards."

"How did you manage, then?" asked J.D., the cup actually trembling in his hands.

"How kind of you to care!" said Katryn, then told herself, *Stop it, Katie. You don't have to try to hurt him anymore. Why should you feel the need?*

"Sorry," she added briefly, "that was unnecessary. You must have heard of Tony Burney's place, the Morgue?"

He nodded.

"Well, I went to live there when I landed in New York. Tony and I had become good friends in Europe; Gregorio Grieg and I, too. When I confided in them, they decided to help me out. They played cards for which one would marry me, and Tony—he was nice enough to say—won. Greg elected to be godfather."

"The child? No one ever talks about you and a child, Katryn."

"My private life is my own. I prefer to keep it that

way. My daughter Antonia lived only twelve days. Not very long to be a mother . . . twelve days . . . so perhaps you're right in maintaining that I don't have the proper qualifications to speak on the subject. God and apple pie, maybe, but not motherhood."

"Katie, I'm sorry, I'm so sorry."

"Thank you, J.D.," she said softly, "but don't start grieving for me now. I had Tony to share my pain with at the time. He really felt Antonia was his daughter. He—"

"He was there for you to turn to when you should have had me."

"Yes," Katryn admitted gently, no longer even wanting to hurt him.

"Eight years . . . a little too late to convey my gratitude to him," said J.D. with the bitterness of self-hate.

"I conveyed all there was to give at the time, and he never really wanted it, not then, nor later! He honestly felt repaid having Antonia be his for those twelve days. Later I gave him the best thanks I could—I divorced him."

"You div—it was *Tony* you divorced?"

"Of course. You were the one who originally told me about him, J.D. You must know that, even if I became a good friend, he didn't have the least desire for a wife?"

Twenty-eight

A wonderfully fulfilling relationship may be life's best and most rewarding gift. To live happily alone and free has to be second . . . unless you belong to the gregarious majority that prefers compromise and boredom to your own occasionally lonely company.

from *Maid To Laid*
by Katryn Kauffman Coffee

"I just don't understand you," Tony said for perhaps the tenth time in one hour. "Even if we *are* divorced, why do you have to move out?"

"Because it's the right thing to do."

"Convince me."

"Tony, you're my dear friend. I love you."

"I'm your dear friend and you love me, so you're moving out, leaving me with the best room in the house unrented."

"Tony, you fraud! You've got a waiting list on those rooms more than a mile long. When Celestine went with that road company, you had her replacement before the front door closed behind her. I bet you can get twice the money for *my* room that you've been charging me. Look at the way I fixed it up for you," she tried to joke.

He attempted the plaintive approach. "We'll miss you."

"Tony, I'm going to an apartment on Third Avenue and

Sixty-second Street, not to the Antipodes. The *Love And Marriage* office is ten blocks from your studio."

"I don't understand," Tony said for the eleventh time, "why—"

"Yes, you *do* understand, Tony," she interrupted firmly, "but you're worried about me, you think it's your mission in life to take care of me. That's why I'm going. It's got to stop. Friendship, yes. Friendship, always, but we have Greg to consider now. It isn't fair to him. I don't want him feeling threatened by me."

"Greg doesn't feel threatened by you. Next to me, he cares for you more than—"

"Yes, I know, and I want him to go on caring, because I feel the same way about him. But if he's human, he's got to be resentful."

"That's ridiculous. Greg is busy all day; he's out half the nights in the week. Ever since he got his Foundation scholarship and his citizenship in the same week and gave that interview about the red, white, and blue piano—which you and he thought was so ridiculous when I first proposed it, I might remind you—he's a flaming success. He's away more than he's home."

"And when he's home," Katie said softly, "he's got a right to expect the two of you not to share all your time with me. Everywhere you go, everything you do, *you* try to drag me along. It's Greg who's got more sense than to try and more sensitivity than you're giving him credit for . . . Tony dear, don't be hurt by this, but the truth is—I think you want us both. Greg, because he's the one you really care for, and me, because—well, because, aside from friendship, I provide normalcy and briefly, I was . . . I was Antonia's mother."

She put her hand on his arm. "You've got to face it, Tony. It's not possible for you to have the two of us."

As the color returned to Tony's face, which had turned white above the great hairy shock of his beard, she added coaxingly, "Don't let's argue about it anymore. I've already signed the lease, and at least three people that I know at *Love And Marriage* have begged me to get my room here for them. If you want my opinion and don't have anyone else in mind, take Shirl Cregar. She travels a lot for her cross-the-country features, so she'd be the least trouble. Whatever you do, if Bill Hartley calls, turn him down. He's got a drug problem."

Tony shrugged and said moodily, "I don't know what Greg is going to say."

"He will say," Katie answered cheerily, making her grand exit, "that I am one smart girl. Which he already did—when I told him."

Whatever Tony or Greg might or might not feel, on the night they brought the last box of her personal possessions to the Third Avenue apartment and went home to the Morgue, leaving her alone, Katie knew she had done the right thing.

Four small rooms . . . but all her own. She wandered happily back and forth between them. The privacy seemed suddenly precious and beautiful. Oh, sure, at the Morgue it had been an unwritten rule that everyone respect a closed door bearing a DO NOT DISTURB, Genius At Work sign . . . but to be able to have one's very own space . . .

The smallest room of all would be her study and double as a guest room. Now she could urge Johnny to come down from Boston to see her, without his having to stay at an hotel. He had broken up with Suzy—his last short scrawl had said so without further elaboration—so they might possibly see each other more than two or three times a year.

And certainly—Katie sat down on her new couch and gave careful consideration to this prospect—now that she had her own place and privacy, as well as her divorce, she might decide to take a lover. It was annoying and inconvenient that she still lusted so tiresomely after J.D., but plenty of other women she knew took lovers they weren't mad about.

They took them—and she had overcome the nasty habit of blushing while she listened to such discussions—because they were good friends, good company, or—best of all, they boasted openly—good sexual athletes.

It was a long time since that one night and one day in the Beverly Hills apartment. She might not be able to marry again, feeling the way she did about J.D., but less than twenty-four hours of love just wasn't enough to last her for a lifetime.

It hadn't mattered when she first came to New York because she'd had too many other concerns. There had been her pregnancy, and then the grief over Antonia. Later, as long as she was still married to Tony—even though a marriage in name only—she would have thought it wrong to look elsewhere.

But now she was as free as she would ever be. If some decent, intelligent, virile man came along . . . Oh, please God, she prayed, *let* one come along . . .

She had a rare evening free and chose to spend it alone, celebrating all by herself—with a bottle of champagne and a bowl of strawberries—her first anniversary in the Sixty-second Street apartment.

"Face it, Katie Coffee, you're a phoney," she said, staring into the nineteenth-century beveled mirror with its gold frame that hung over the eighteenth century Pennsylvania Dutch bride's chest in the living room. She had bought the mirror the previous week on a Connecticut antique prowl and the dower chest last year at an auction in Bucks County.

"You may dress New York and talk New York and pretend to be New York," she addressed the mirror accusingly, "but in the heart of you . . . somewhere in the core of your being . . . you're just a damned prudish Pennsylvania-Dutch puritan!"

Plenty of decent, intelligent, virile men had come along, and she had dined with them, danced with them, walked with them, talked with them, gone for car rides, picnics, museum trips, to the theatre, to concerts. She had flirted, fooled around, played the field, and pretended countless times that she was seriously thinking, *maybe this one* . . . And never had she taken a single one of those eligible, available, willing, and eager men to her cold, lonely bed.

Each man she dated for any length of time thought Katryn Coffee was his own private failure. Half of masculine New York was secretly convinced that she had bedded the other half. After all, she was a liberated woman of the eighties, a staff writer now for *Love And Marriage,* and the increasingly famous author of *Bundle In The Trundle,* the best-selling book created from her magazine article of the same name. Her friends were the elite of New York's artier circles; she had just been elected an officer of WOMAN, one of the more active feminist groups; she wrote about men and sex with verve.

Recently she had adopted the suggestion of her agent, Francesca Janis, that she use her full name at all times. "Katie Coffee sounds like kid stuff," she had told her bluntly. "We're trying to sell you as the svelte, sophisticated, sexually aware author who knows whereof she writes. *That's* Katryn Kauffman Coffee."

It all helped the image she had worked so hard to create, but none of it was of any help to the Coffee Katie of Strawberry Schrank who wanted love.

"Fraud," repeated Katie to her mirrored image. "Fake," she said aloud fervently as she poured another glass of champagne. "How the hell many times do you think you can be a virgin? Once? Twice? Forever?"

And even as she said it, big tears rolled down Katie's cheeks . . . while the part of her that was already inextricably woven into the creation of Katryn Kauffman Coffee was reaching for a pad and her gold Cross pen.

Half an hour later when she phoned her agent at home, there was no longer a trace of the tears of self-pity on her face, and the slur of champagne was entirely gone from her speech.

"Francesca? Katryn Kauffman Coffee here," she said with businesslike precision. "Sorry to disturb you at home, but I thought you might be pleased to hear an idea I have for the new book you've been nagging me about. I'll skip the details till I come to your office . . . mmm, mm, yes, tomorrow, if you'd like . . . How does this title grab you: *Once A Virgin, Twice A Virgin?* Good, I gather you like it. When you stop choking, I'll tell you what the subtitle is going to be . . . Okay, *Once A Virgin, Twice A Virgin,* subtitled *A Maidenhead Does Not A Maiden Make.* You like?"

"I like very much. If the book can live up to the title, both titles, it sounds sensational. What's the main premise?"

"Oh, it will be more or less a societal history of virginity, ancient times till the present. Humor—anecdotes—examples—but the underlying theme I expect to hammer home is that it's men who have the virginity hang-up and have used it to control the lives of women and keep them firmly in their place. What do you think?"

"I think that Katryn Kauffman Coffee has conceived a sensational best seller."

"Now all I have to do is give birth," said Katryn. Hearing her own words, she hung up abruptly and dissolved the stirring of pain in more champagne.

Twenty-nine

Whenever possible, get your pasta fresh-cut from sheets of dough in a pasta shop instead of supermarket-packaged. Remember that variety is the spice of pasta, too. Don't limit yourself to egg pasta; buy spinach, tomato, and beet as well as whole wheat. Try linguine, fettucini, manicotti, lasagne, and cannelloni strips; experiment with shells, spirals, ziti, and angel's hair.

Now for a delicious variation on the Pasta Cream Sauce, page 42, toss in snow peas, pimientos, cauliflower and broccoli florets for Pasta Primavera Sauce, which . . .

from *Mama Mia's Kitchen*
by Cable Canatelli

Katie limped into the cubbyhole labeled her office and gave a moan of pleasure as she kicked off high-heeled shoes and pressed her forehead against the coolness of the thermal pitcher of ice water on her desk.

Alice Blakely, an associate editor who shared her space, looked up from her keyboard with a sympathetic grin.

"Bad?"

"Awful." Katie shuddered. "The woman is unbelievably boorish, as well as side-splittingly funny. She agreed—in between the caviar and the Mouton Lafitte—to do the article."

Alice gave a low whistle.

"Exactly," said Katie gloomily, sifting through a sheaf of messages. "Accounting's going to throw a fit when they see the price of this little lunch for two. Do you think they'll believe all *I* had was blintzes and one glass of the wine?" She frowned down at her pink message slips. "Francesca Janis four times. Any problem?"

"No problem. Message one"—Alice ticked it off on her fingers—"was to say the galleys of your book *Once A Virgin, Twice A Virgin*—boy! I can't wait to read *that!*—will be sent over by messenger this afternoon, and your editor would be obliged if you could get them back by Monday."

Katie sank gratefully into her comfortable desk chair and frowned at her calendar. "I'd better take them home to work on tonight; I wanted a quiet evening, anyway. What else did Francesca have on her mind?"

"Call number two was to remind you she's taken a table for eight at the Writers' Awards Ball"—Alice grinned again as Katie groaned—"and did you remember that you promised faithfully to attend, with escort?"

Katie tilted precariously back in her chair. "Number three?" she asked resignedly.

"Would you please—I'm quoting exactly—'would you please break down and buy yourself a new evening gown? Your escorts may not mind, since you change *them* as often as your underwear, but your friends are getting tired of seeing you in that same brown and white number with the Puritan collar.' "

"I *like* my brown and white," Katie grumbled. "Anyway, I hate awards dinners. Writers should write, not talk."

"As my dear old Aunt Emily used to say, you've got high-class problems," Alice told her without compassion.

"I would *love* to go to a formal affair at the Waldorf Astoria."

"Believe me, the boredom outweighs the glamor; there'll be more dinner speeches than dancing."

"So, suffer."

"I expect to. I guess I'd better call Pete Morrison. He mentioned something about a show Saturday night. Maybe I can con him into this instead."

"Oh, better not call him." Alice looked a little sheepish. "Telephone call number four was to say, forget about the escort; she has one for you."

"Oh, she does, does she?"

"You'll like him; he's a *great* date," Alice assured her impulsively, then put her hand over her mouth. "Oops."

"Do tell me about this date that I seem to be the last one to know of," Katie suggested sweetly.

"It's Cable Canatelli, who used to play football for San Francisco. What are you looking like that for? He's divine. Half the women in this country are wild over him. *I'd* give my eye teeth for a date with him."

"I just may take them. What kind of a name is 'Cable'?"

"Oh, his real name is Jack or Joe, something like that; he was nicknamed because he used to ride the San Francisco cable cars for hours at a time."

Katie picked up the telephone and a moment later was inquiring of her agent, "Pray, why a football player?"

"He wrote an Italian cookbook," Francesca answered cheerfully.

"A *cook*book!"

"A damned good one."

"And why doesn't this paragon, whom Alice assures me is divine, have a date of his own to escort?"

"He just breezed into town about an hour ago and came straight to my office. When I invited him, he stated that he'd never in his life gone to a dance without a lady and he wasn't about to start."

"Which charming speech," Katie said politely, "convinced you that he and I were undoubtedly soulmates?"

"As a matter of fact, you'll enjoy him. The English, or lack of it, is put on. He's bright, fun, and refreshing."

"In which case, perhaps he's looking for someone a little more exciting than a 'Plain' girl from Pennsylvania?"

"Not after he heard the title of your book!" returned Francesca provocatively.

"If you weren't such a good agent—" said Katie, and hung up, laughing ruefully.

She couldn't take the time before Saturday to shop for a new gown, but on looking over the brown and white with the broad ruffled organdy collar, she had to admit it was a little too sweetly simple and demure for some of the bashes it had graced recently.

She stood at the open door of her closet for a long time before reaching into the back. Inside a zipped plastic garment bag, splendidly alone, was a dress never worn since California. She walked slowly to the mirror, holding it against her. A moment later she was scrambling into what was still the loveliest gown she had ever seen, her own silk chiffon in muted colors of the rainbow with its watered taffeta petticoat.

On Saturday night, Francesca and her husband Bill picked up Katie in a cab on their way to the Waldorf Astoria. They were to meet Cable Canatelli at the ball.

When Bill helped Katie off with her coat in the plush hotel lobby, Francesca's eyes bulged out. "My God!" she said reverently. "What a gorgeous gown. When you decide to do something, you really do it in style."

"Just a little something I picked up in Beverly Hills."

While Bill checked their coats, Francesca walked around Katie on a tour of inspection.

"Good evening, Mrs. Janis."

"Ms. Janis," Francesca said automatically, "if you insist on being formal."

"I'm just an old-fashioned country boy, Francesca. The Misses and the Mizzes are too much for me."

"Country boy, my foot. Katie, this hulk of a man is the great Cable Canatelli."

Katie looked up, up, up at the "hulk of a man," who carried his startling height and weight with surprising ease and grace. His grey eyes twinkled down at her from a face every bit as "divine" as Alice had said. From the masses of his thick dark hair to the exactly even cleft of his chin, the man was almost indecently good-looking.

"And this is Katryn Kauffman Coffee."

"Hello, there," said Katie, feeling slightly overpowered.

"Hello yourself," he returned, casting an appreciative glance at the rainbow chiffon and its contents.

They were barely seated at their table, greeting Francesca's other guests, before Cable had Katie up again and on the dance floor. He was surprisingly light on his feet; he was a surprising man altogether. Katie realized very quickly that, as Francesca had said, his grammatical lapses and country-boy air were put on and off at will. This was one very bright and conversible man.

She also approved the tremendous appetite with which he sustained his magnificent frame. In turn, she drew groans of delight from him when she described some Pennsylvania-Dutch dishes.

After eavesdropping on their conversation for some time, Francesca leaned across her husband to suggest, "Why not an ethnic cookbook for your next, Cable, with groups of recipes from lots of different cultures? Katryn could help you with the Pennsylvania-Dutch section."

"Not a bad idea. I've been collecting odd recipes for years. *Would* you help, Katryn?"

"I'd consider it," she said cautiously, just as a burst of applause heralded the beginning of the speeches and they all became courteously quiet.

For the next forty minutes, Katie was as thoroughly

bored as she had expected to be. She and Cable exchanged glances of shared commiseration now and then but were otherwise silent until the final and outstanding award was given to Everett Lloyd Langford for his best-selling novel, *Bread, Not a Stone.*

Katie perked up when this award was announced and began to clap so vigorously that Cable, as he joined in her applause, leaned over to inquire, "Does your enthusiasm mean he's good?"

"I've read three of his books. He's a superb writer, powerful, original, and incredibly sensitive in his portrayals of women."

Everett Langford's speech of acceptance was mercifully short and witty. Katie watched him descend from the platform and rejoin his own table not so far from theirs. Instead of slipping into his empty seat, he bent over the lovely brunette sitting next to it. He kissed the back of her neck and made a charming little gesture with the statuette that seemed to say, *This is for you.*

Katie smiled as the music began and Langford drew the brunette up for a dance. She turned to Cable.

"Aren't they a lovely couple?"

"He's a poseur," Cable said shortly.

"I beg your pardon?"

"The man's acting."

"You can tell that from just a single glance?" she asked scornfully.

"Body language, Katie, watch the body language, not just the gestures. That little scene was enacted for his audience. I'll accept your opinion of his writing skills, but I'll stick to my own judgment of his body movements . . . muscles . . . bones . . . cartilage. . . . Shall we dance?"

Blinking at the abruptness of this invitation, Katie agreed, but soon realized why they were on the dance floor.

"I don't blame you . . . she's very beautiful . . . but

aren't you being a bit tactless?" she asked with pretended reproach.

He looked down at her, surprised, then grinned. "Sorry, Katie . . . no . . ." He gave the other dancing couple a quick appraisal. "She *is* beautiful, but not my type. I prefer my women fair—more like you—with some flesh to get hold of, rather than those tall dark skinny model types. I was just wondering why she's wound up tighter than a drum."

"I never knew football players were so perceptive," Katie needled gently.

"Possibly because you're a female chauvinist," he came back at her even more gently. And as Katie burst out laughing, he added, "Also, because I'm a nosy son of a bitch. Look . . . do you mind if I try something?"

"What's the something?"

"You'll see." He steered her determinedly across the dance floor, where he managed to bump artistically into Everett Langford and the brunette.

Both couples stopped for apologies, and Cable managed introductions of themselves as fellow writers, ". . . if you count a cookbook written by a football player. Katryn here, of course, is the genuine thing."

"Oh, you're *that* Cable Canatelli. I shall buy your book for my wife. She's a marvelous cook. This lady"—he eyed his partner fondly—"is my wife Christine."

"How do you do, Mrs. Langford?"

"My congratulations to you, too, ma'am."

She acknowledged both platitudes in a high breathless voice, then fell silent. Cable immediately adopted his country-boy role. "Now that we're all friends, how about we change partners for the rest of this dance, Mr. Langford, so Katie here can tell you how she loves your books—my, your ears would have burned to hear her praise—and I'll just chat a bit with your lovely wife."

Before anyone could answer, he had somehow detached

Mrs. Langford from her husband and was dancing off with her. Everett Langford—given no other choice—was politely putting an arm around the scarlet-cheeked Katie.

Fortunately, the music ended within two minutes and she was returned to Cable courteously but with speed.

"Why on earth did you do that?" she said in an angry whisper as they left the floor. "You really embarrassed me."

"Not so much as her. She's scared to death of him."

"Of *him!* Don't be crazy."

"Don't *you* be. Look at it this way, Katie honey . . . wouldn't any girl who met me alone in a dark alley run screaming just because of the size of me? Except on the football field, I'm one of the gentlest creatures you're ever going to meet. So don't go judging the guy by his appearance and his words. Langford may write with the pen of an angel and look like a real unassuming guy, but there has to be a reason why his wife is so scared stiff of him she begged me to get her back to him before there was any trouble."

He looked over at the other table, where Everett Lloyd Langford was pulling out his wife's chair for her. "Damn! I'm worried that I did the wrong thing. I may well have made bad trouble for that little lady."

Thirty

*There are men who think their marriage license is
no different than one for hunting or fishing—except
that it only permits them to hurt or to maim, not kill,
their prey.*

from *Mucho Macho*
by Katryn Kauffman Coffee

About half an hour later, Katie saw Christine Langford
get up from the table, her gold mesh evening bag tucked
under her arm as she walked out of the ballroom. Katie
jumped up quickly, excusing herself.

Cable gave her a look of quick approval. "Go to it,
girl," he whispered.

Maintaining a discreet distance, Katie followed the tall
slim figure in the metallic gold evening sheath. When she
pushed through the door of the ladies' room, Mrs. Langford was sitting on a pink hassock in the lounge section.
One sleeve of her dress was pulled up, and she was massaging her bare wrist. Her fingers moved in an automatic
circular motion over and over and over as she stared off
into space.

She turned away without looking up when Katie walked
in and sat down next to her on a stuffed brocade armchair.

Katie touched Christine's shoulder gently, and she
whirled around, face white and eyes wild, her two arms

flung up before her face in an unconscious gesture of self-protection that sent a chill through Katie's body.

"I'm sorry, Mrs. Langford," she said in a voice she would have used to soothe a frightened child. "I didn't mean to startle you."

"Oh, no . . . I wasn't . . . you didn't . . . it's all right." She took her trembling lower lip between her teeth, biting down, struggling for control.

"Mr. Canatelli was worried; he thought perhaps he had made trouble for you." Katie's eyes strayed down to the bare wrist, where the marks of four fingertips were imprinted in the flesh. Her husband would have had to press very hard under the table to leave such deep marks. "I see that he was right."

Mrs. Langford pulled the sleeve back over her wrist. "If Mr. Canatelli hadn't given him the excuse, he would have found another," she said dully. "Either he'd say that I talked too much and made myself conspicuous . . . or that I talked too little and let everyone think he had married an idiot. Anything would do. I knew he'd want a reason tonight . . . because of the award."

"Because of the award," Katie parroted stupidly.

"He's excited over the award. When he's excited, he wants me in bed." She might have been repeating a mathematical formula. "He enjoys making love more if he gets to—to hit me first."

"Oh, my God!" said Katie sickly. "Why do you stand it?"

"Why? Because he's bigger and stronger than I am, and if I fight him, he hurts me more."

"But why don't you leave him?"

"I have two children; my boy is seven and my girl is six."

"Does he—does he—?"

"Yes, he beats them, too. Not as badly as me, but he's working up to it."

"For God's sakes, why don't you take the children and get away?"

"How?"

"What do you mean, how? Pick yourself up—and them—and just *go*. How can you let anyone do that to you? To say nothing of helpless kids?"

"And who would put a roof over the heads of my helpless kids? Who would put food in their mouths? I only have enough—dimes and quarters scrimped out of housekeeping money—to keep the three of us for about a week."

She saw Katie's incredulous look at her expensive metallic sheath gown, the pearls around her neck, the diamond and pearl earrings in her lobes.

"Oh, yes," Christine smiled grimly, "I have lots of clothes and jewels and furs. I live in a gorgeous house in Westchester County and drive a Mercedes registered to my husband. I have charge accounts for anything I want to buy, but I have to show him where every penny goes. He even checks my grocery receipts. I—I bought a winter wardrobe once, and I took one of my dresses back and got the money in cash—two hundred dollars—to add to my runaway fund."

She looked off into space again, and Katie said encouragingly, even while she cringed that a woman must so degrade herself, "That wasn't a bad idea."

"Oh, yes, it was," said Mrs. Langford softly. "He found out." She looked directly at Katie for the first time. "Would you like to see the scars? They run from here," she touched her thigh, "all the way up my back. He said I had stolen his money; he said I was a thief. He said thieves had to be properly punished so they wouldn't be tempted to steal again."

Katie's stomach heaved. "Oh, my God!"

"That time he used a wooden lath with bits of metal attached," said Mrs. Langford in the same chilling, robot-like way. "That's why I have the scars."

"Don't you have any family who would help?"

"No, just my mother—my Dad is dead—and she's kind of fire-and-brimstone religious. I was a little wild in high school, so she was glad when I married someone like Everett. He's a lot older . . . he taught a writing class that I took in my freshman year of college. My mother thinks I need a strong man to rule me. She thinks it's disloyal to criticize your husband."

She went on in the same dreary monotone. "My kid sister is married and lives in Germany. Her husband is in the army; he's stationed there. Everett's folks think their son is much too good for me; they would never hear a word said against him."

"There has to be something we can do," said Katie desperately.

"We?"

"I'll help you. Let me talk to people, figure out something. You *do* want to leave him, don't you?"

"I'd give my life to get my kids away from him," vowed Christine, a little expression creeping into her voice for the first time. "I'm not only scared of what he'll do to them—I'm terrified of what they'll become."

"Then, here . . ." Katie dug feverishly into her own small evening bag and came up with an address book. She took a couple of cards out of it. "Here's my business card." She scribbled on the back of it. "And this is my home." She gave the card to Mrs. Langford, who folded it very carefully in a lace handkerchief and concealed it at the bottom of her gold mesh purse.

Katie handed over the pen and the second card. "Write down your address and phone number."

Mrs. Langford's hands shook as she wrote obediently.

"Call between ten and twelve in the morning; he's usually in his study then. If he should answer the phone, don't tell him who you are. Don't—"

"Don't worry," soothed Katie. "I can always say wrong number or pretend to be selling something."

"Yes." Christine stood up. She looked down at Katie, her mouth suddenly quivering. "I'm afraid to hope."

"Hope all you want. I swear I'll help you . . . it may take a little time, but don't lose heart."

"I haven't had any to lose for a long, long time now. Goodbye, Miss Coffee."

"I'm going, too."

"Would you mind"—the words were a frightened whisper—"letting me go a little ahead . . . just in case?"

"Of course," said Katie, sinking back into her chair. She timed two minutes on her watch after the wretched woman left before pushing at the swinging door. As she was about to go through it, she heard a whimpering voice that made her retreat instantly, though she stayed at the door, listening shamelessly.

"I swear, Ev, I never saw him before in my life. How in the world would I have met a football player from San Francisco?"

"Why else would he try to change partners the way he did? You think I don't know how you manage when you want something, you slut, you whore! I saw the way you looked at him when you were dancing."

"I didn't flirt with him; I swear I didn't."

"Don't lie to me; you know how I feel about liars. You know what I do."

The small animal-like sound of pain that followed scraped Katie's nerves raw.

"You know, don't you, I'll have the truth out of you when we get home?"

"Oh, please, Ev, please—"

"Shut up, you bitch!"

There was silence, then Katie felt someone pushing at the other side of the door. She stepped back quickly as a grey-haired woman in a black satin gown walked in. The woman and Katie exchanged civil nods as she walked through to the lavatory section.

Katie pushed cautiously at the swinging door again. . . . Silence. . . . Finally she ventured a peek outside. The Langfords were gone.

A gloriously rich dessert was waiting when she got back to the table. It seemed to contain equal parts of cake, fruit, and a syrupy sauce, topped by a generous scoop of whipped cream. She took one look at her large portion and turned pale.

"It's fairly tasty," said Cable, pointing to his empty plate.

"Have mine if you want." Katie pushed her dish toward him. "I don't think . . . I couldn't keep it down."

He turned in his seat, the better to see her.

"You spoke to Mrs. Langford?" he asked softly.

"We spoke to each other."

"Your body language tells me it was bad."

"Cable, please get me out of here. If you don't, I'm liable to faint, or throw up, or something."

"No, you won't. Hang in there, kid." He stood up, six-foot-six of bruising country-boy. "Ladies and gentlemen, it's been a real memorable evening, but if you'll be so kind as to excuse us now, Katie-girl here and I are off to see more of New York and get better acquainted. I'm surely glad"—he was reaching over, shaking hands all across the table—"to have met you all. Francesca, I can't tell you how much I appreciate your invitin' me. I'll be on the horn with you first thing Monday."

In the taxi going from the Waldorf to her apartment, with Cable's huge calloused hand wrapped comfortingly about hers, Katie—speaking in almost the same low, expressionless voice that Christine Langford had used—told him about the starkly awful session in the ladies' room and the ugly little scene outside it.

"Do you want to keep the cab?" Katie asked him when

it stopped in front of her house. "The doorman will take me up."

"I'd like to come up, too, if I may."

She looked him straight in the eye. "I am not feeling amorous," she said directly.

"Neither am I, love," he said, "not since the last dance. But I'd like to come up and talk."

Katie managed a weak smile. "I'd like that, too. Truth to tell, I'm not very anxious to be alone."

She stepped out of the cab and Cable paid the driver, who winked at him as he handed over his change. "That's a great technique you've got there, mister. Reverse psychology . . . it gets them every time."

Repeating this exchange in the elevator, Cable wrung another, more genuine, smile out of Katie.

"I hope he's wrong," she said, ushering Cable into her apartment. "I'm not in the mood for a struggle."

"Nor am I," said Cable as she opened the closet door and reached for two hangers. He took them from her and hung up both their coats. "I don't pretend to be a gentleman, or anything like that," he told her with an endearing awkwardness, "and I admit that most of this evening I had all kinds of plans in mind about you—provided, of course, that you were willing. But when I think of what that poor woman may be going through . . ."

"I know." Katie shivered. "It's the way I feel . . . how about some coffee?"

"Would you by any chance have some herbal tea?"

"Yes. Orange, lemon, or peppermint?" Katie offered promptly.

"Lemon." He followed her into the kitchen and while she put the kettle on, he found the cups and saucers and set them out, then looked for the silver drawer and the napkins.

"How about some homemade Pennsylvania-Dutch-style

apple pie to make up for my dessert that you didn't get to eat?"

"By all means."

"You do know," said Katie, watching him turn on the oven as she cut the pie, "you aren't exactly the common conception of a football player?"

"That," he said, "is because most people deal in stereotypes."

"Too true, and I'm afraid I've been guilty myself. Cable, would you mind if I switched to a robe while you watch the kettle?"

He nodded amiable agreement, and she returned as he was brewing the tea. She was wearing a loose sapphire-blue velour robe with white piping and a frogged front. Her feet were bare.

"You've got cute toes," Cable said, inspecting them gravely. "Someday I hope to see your legs."

"Sturdy but shapely, like a farm girl's," Katie retorted sweetly. "Fairly longish. They are considered better than average."

"I'll bet they are." His grey eyes twinkled appreciatively. He downed half his cup of tea and disposed in more leisurely fashion of the pie. Then he looked across at Katie. "How the hell," he asked, "do we rescue Christine Langford?"

"I'm not sure of the ways and means," Katie answered fiercely, "just that we've got to do it before it's too late." Her voice faltered a little. "I used to work in the children's ward of a hospital where the abused kids were brought . . . the things that were done to them . . ." She shook her head as though getting rid of the memories. "You wouldn't believe," she whispered. "The scars—they last."

"Who else?" asked Cable.

"I beg your pardon?"

"Who else besides the children?"

"You really *do* study body language, don't you?"

Then she looked away from him, drawing circles on her table mat with one finger, over and over and over, just as Christine Langford had done to her wrist. "There was a man I—I loved once . . . haven't thought of it in a long time . . . he was so damned arrogant and assured, it was hard to think of him as an abused kid."

She turned back to Cable, swallowing hard. "But he must have been. He had . . . the scars . . . on his back. I can't help . . . it's too late . . . but I don't want any more scars on the Langford kids."

"There won't be," pledged Cable. "Between us, we'll damn well make sure there won't be."

Thirty-one

The plight of the individual woman in distress must not be overlooked in the greater struggle to achieve more far-reaching goals.

from "The Battered Wife,"
article in *Love And Marriage*
by Katryn Kauffman Coffee

Three members of the Steering Committee of WOMAN met for lunch at Katie's apartment the next afternoon. Katie suspected that the prospect of antipasto, lasagna, and salad prepared by Cable Canatelli, to say nothing of his overpowering presence, had as much to do with their being there as the urgency of her phone calls.

"I can't believe," she said, setting down a pitcher of iced tea as she joined them at the table, "that an organization like ours isn't prepared to do more about the plight of battered women—to say nothing of the children."

The argument went on. . . .

We haven't the money, Katie . . .

Or the facilities . . .

There are legal points involved . . .

Most of our time and energy now is devoted to the fight for Choice . . .

"Damn it!" said Katie, pounding her fist on the table in frustration. "Does fighting for the larger principles mean that we can give no effort at all to helping individual women? If it does, then the price is too high. Do you think that poor woman in her Westchester mansion being used by her husband as a punching bag gives a damn about anything else? Why should she?"

We're trying to devote some time to the spousal abuse issue, Katie . . .

We can't change the world over night, Katryn . . .

We can spread ourselves just so thin . . .

Seeing Katie about to explode again, Cable kicked her gently under the table.

"Ma'am . . . Ladies . . . I've been a male chauvinist too long"—he coughed apologetically—"to know how to address you, but it seems to me"—he coughed again and offered the platter of lasagna to Marianne O'Conner— "listening to you all, it does seem to me that Ms. Coffee has gotten to the heart of the matter. We've got to convince *all* women that we're concerned with their greater good. You ladies—I mean, women—have got to help your sisters, not just with legislation, but by showing them in practical ways that you care. I'm with Katie here. I don't think there's anything more important than helping battered women and kids and, incidentally, breaking the cycle so those kids won't become batterers in turn."

"Money is still a problem," said Grace Alsop.

"The problem being," added Susan Rubin, "that we don't have enough."

"I understand that," said Cable gently, "and to begin this new effort, I'll pledge ten percent of the profits of my cookbook, *Mama Mia's Kitchen.*"

While the other women broke out in applause, Katie jumped up and, since she couldn't get both arms all around him, compromised by enthusiastically kissing both his cheeks.

"Ten percent of *Once A Virgin, Twice A Virgin,* too," she promised, eyes shining, "but mind, not for the general organization. It is to be used exclusively for aiding battered women and children."

"I'm also willing to aid you in fund-raising and to have my name used in press releases," added Cable.

"Great! It will pack them in."

"God! The publicity value."

"And fund-raising value!"

"We'll have to get lawyers onto it first thing."

"We'll need a shelter for the women . . ."

"Temporary safe houses, too. Some women can't run away openly. Their husbands would intimidate them back, or even blackmail them by taking the kids away."

"That," Katie hurled into the joyful clamor, "would be the case with Christine Langford, I think. Her husband has the money and the clout to get the kids. Once he got *them,* he'd have her back in the palm of his hand. We have to manage things so he can't get at them."

"Now there," said Cable, "is where your lawyer is needed. Who do you use?"

They looked at one another.

"Not Mr. Lerner for this one. He's good, but . . ."

They all nodded agreement.

"How about Tom and Liz Pomeroy?" suggested Marianne.

"Yeah . . ."

"Mmm . . ."

"Katie?"

"I've heard they're good, Cable. I think they might be just right."

Susan jumped up. "No time like the present."

"Use the phone in my bedroom," said Katie. "Out the door and to your left."

Susan was back in less than ten minutes. "They'll be here in half an hour," she announced. "Liz said to please save some lasagna."

Amid the general laughter, Cable scooped a generous

portion into a small roasting pan and set it in the oven to warm.

"The rest of us can go. They only need Katryn and Cable right now; we'll set up special meetings for next week."

They lingered, however, making plans till just before the Pomeroys turned up. Liz and Tom proved to be a vital pair in their late thirties who seemed to read each other's minds and finish each other's sentences. Over lasagna and a fresh salad, which they ate with as hearty an appetite as the last batch of guests, they fired a relentless barrage of questions at Katie and Cable, both of them taking notes.

Liz frowned thoughtfully when the inquisition was over. "Katryn, could you talk to Mrs. Langford and get a phone number for the sister in Germany? It seems to me—this is only off the top of my head, mind; it will have to be thought out carefully—but it might be best if we could get them out of the country until a divorce is finalized and she's rid of him."

"That would be the most wonderful solution," Katie declared fervently, "but I don't want to call today because Langford's probably around. I'll try tomorrow from my office."

"If there is any noticeable evidence of a beating from Saturday night, the sooner we get her photographed, the better," Tom reminded.

"Yeah," Cable drawled, "I don't want that poor lady sticking around longer to provide further proof."

There was a moment's silence as they all absorbed the ugly implications of that possibility. Then Liz said briskly, "Well, back to work. Thanks for lunch, Katryn. Cable, if your book has a section for quickie meals, I'll surely buy it."

"Good Italian meals aren't quick-cooking, but they're highly freezable. You can make a long-lasting supply in advance. I'll tell you what—if you find a way out for

Mrs. Langford, you'll not only get a free autographed copy, the next time I'm in town I'll cook and serve a dinner party for you."

"You're on," said Liz.

"Cable, what a fantastic scheme!" crowed Katie.

They all looked a bit startled. '

"For fund-raising, I mean . . . publicity . . . Wouldn't it be marvelous? Biggest contributor or biggest matching funds . . . biggest something or other, maybe even raffle winner, would get to have a dinner party, supplies courtesy of WOMAN, or its new branch, BATTERED WOMAN . . . maybe even just B-WOMAN . . . and the chef would be Cable Canatelli. Even if we had to fly you out of town, it would pay. We'd have to work out the time element with *you,* of course . . ."

"Thanks a heap."

". . . but those are just details."

"As a matter of fact, I think she's got something," said Tom, directing two fingers toward Katie in a victory signal.

"You ain't seen nothing yet," said Katie buoyantly. "Tomorrow I'm going to try to crack a really hard nut . . . the Supreme Editor of my magazine."

Eleanor Howell graciously granted Katie fifteen minutes the next morning but ran a distracted hand through her orange hair, her great green-blue eyes rounding in astonishment at Katie's proposal.

"An article on battered women in *Love And Marriage!* My dear, we deal with the *romance* of love and marriage, not the more sordid aspects."

"Well, don't you think it's time we dealt with some of the realities? The unpleasant truth happens to be that there are a lot of men out there who think their marriage license is also a boxing license—it gives them the right to beat up on their wives. Some of *those* wives might like to see their problems in print, too."

"Katryn, we are not a crusading magazine."

"No, but we are a magazine that likes, as much as any other, to boost its circulation; and the right series . . . with real hard-hitting articles . . . could boost us sky-high."

The almost non-existent eyebrows arched. "How so?"

"First you send out an investigative team to get the facts and figures. Interviews with victims . . . they're in the hundreds of thousands on any given day . . . Interviews with batterers or ex-beaters willing to come forward—blue-collar workers, ministers and miners, teachers and doctors, attorneys and editors and writers. One-page interviews with the lawyers, social workers, police, emergency-room personnel, people who deal with the victims . . . And then a big spread on what to do and where to go if you already are a victim or are in danger of becoming one."

She threw out a final tempting tidbit. "Also, an exclusive first interview with Cable Canatelli, the great ex-football star turned cookbook writer, who is giving his time and energy and part of the profits of his book, *Mama Mia's Kitchen*, for this cause. Another exclusive can be the dinner he cooks and serves to the prize-winner in a fund-raising effort for battered women. Believe me, all the newspapers will pick that one up—lots of publicity for the magazine," she finished cunningly.

Having made her pitch, she folded her hands quietly in her lap and waited. Eleanor Howell chewed on the rubber end of a pencil for a minute, then ran the lead point through her orange waves for another thirty seconds.

She stood up. "I'll call a staff meeting," she said. "Notify my secretary when you have a written proposal for me to present."

Accepting this dismissal, Katie stood up, uttered a quiet "Thank you," and went rushing back to her office to call Christine Langford.

The high, almost childish voice uttered a breathless "Hello" on the second ring.

"Christine, this is Katryn Coffee from the Waldorf," Katie said rapidly. "Can you talk?"

"Oh yes, he's upstairs in his study typing. He almost never comes down then"—the voice became a breathy whisper—"but if I should start talking about something else . . ."

"I'll understand. This will be quick. I just wanted you to know that we've already put our lawyers to work on your problem. We'll get you out of there as soon as we can. In the meantime, have you any objection to our letting your sister and her husband—what's his rank, by the way?"

"He's an Army captain."

"Captain . . . that's good. Do you mind if we contact them? Do they know anything about this?"

"No—I mean I don't mind, and they don't know . . . they were so far away and we weren't much in touch . . ." Her voice was getting fainter and fainter; Katie had to strain to catch the final words. "There didn't seem to be much point."

"Can you give me the address and phone number?"

"I have it in my book right here. Just a minute . . . here it is, Wheeler, James." She started reeling off numbers.

"Wait. Start again, please, and speak a little slower and louder. Calm down, Christine."

Christine slowed down and managed to supply all the needed information.

"I'll be in touch," said Katie as she scribbled the last two digits of the phone number.

"Wait!" cried a panicked voice at the other end.

"What is it, Christine?"

"You mean it? You'll get us out of here? I—I—"

"Tell me, Christine."

"I can't hold on much longer."

"You won't have to," pledged Katryn Kauffman Coffee. "I swear it."

Thirty-two

. . . I have long been thinking
What a good world this would be,
If the men were all transported
On this side the Northern Sea.

Unknown

"Don't be nervous, Christine. Susan has your complete shopping list . . . she'll go to all the places you wrote down; there'll be the receipts and sales slips to prove it. The photographic session won't take any longer than the shopping."

"But suppose he finds out about our taking Tommy out of school?"

"Is Tommy likely to tell him?" Katie asked her softly but firmly, looking down at the bright-faced boy who clutched his mother's hand.

"No, but—"

"He *won't* find out. You'll sign Tommy back in, then go home with the groceries. Here, this is the suite. We rented it for a half day. A woman photographer for you"— she beat a double signal on the door—"and a man for Tommy, so there's no need to be nervous, you—"

"Oh, no!" Christine grabbed Katie's arm as the door was opened. "Not a man for Tommy," she said close to Katie's ear. "Don't you see . . . a man telling him to undress . . . what he would expect? Even at the pediatrician he's gone to for years, we have trouble."

"Oh, dear God! I didn't think. We—none of us did." Katie got hold of herself. "Let's go inside. You take charge. You tell us what to do."

Christine went into the bedroom first while Cable stayed in the living room entertaining Tommy with coloring books and conversation. A milkshake and his favorite cookies had been provided beforehand.

Christine undressed in the bathroom and came out in the Japanese kimono the photographer, Elissa, had given her. The camera was already set up.

Christine's panicked eyes flew to Katie, who was preparing to depart. "Stay with me."

"As long as you want me to," Katie promised, and was promptly sorry when the robe came off.

Christine lay stomach down on the bed. Her bare back looked like a latticed gate; an almost symmetrical pattern of broad welts decorated her flesh all the way down to her thighs.

It was even worse than with J.D., because these were fresh stripes, still red, still puffy, not faded and set into the skin as his had been.

Retaining her breakfast with difficulty, Katie stood by the bed, smiling encouragement while Elissa gave brisk, seemingly impervious instructions, though her eyes exchanged a far different message with Katie's.

"Now for this one I want you to lift your head and turn it toward me . . . we don't want any misunderstanding about its being *your* face that goes with the body . . . Good . . . very good . . . that's fine . . . just one more. Now Katie, hand her that towel, put it between your legs, hon, and turn and face me . . . Oh, just stick a pillow over your breasts . . . bend your knee, get that leg forward . . . it's the thigh I want . . . good . . . good . . . that's just right. Okay, now if you'll just sit. Gather up your hair and bend forward; it's the shoulders I need this time . . . Turn your face around again. Great. Now one more and this is the last. You did fine, hon. You can get dressed now, and then I'll take a passport shot."

Katie helped the trembling woman on with her robe. She was amazed to hear an entirely different Christine, cool and confident, talking to Tommy less than ten minutes later.

"Mommy had her picture taken, Tommy, and now it's your turn. It won't hurt at all, I promise you. I'll be with you every minute. It's so we can go on that vacation, just you and Giselle and Mommy."

"Not Daddy?"

"Daddy won't go as long as you remember that it's our secret."

The little boy took a deep breath. "I'll remember, Mommy."

She took his hand and they went into the bedroom together. In less than fifteen minutes they were back, and in answer to Katie's questioning look, Christine nodded almost happily.

The photographers packed up and left, and a few minutes later the desk phoned up to say that Miss Rubin was waiting in the parking lot in front of the hotel.

They all trooped downstairs. The five bags of groceries and the smaller parcels from the pharmacy and the bookstore were transferred from the rented station wagon to Christine's Mercedes.

"Remember," Katie warned her just before the Langfords drove off, "you've got to be ready to leave any day, any time—at thirty seconds' notice, if need be."

"Don't worry." It was the first spontaneous smile Katie had ever seen on Christine's face. "I've got two packed suitcases in plastic bags behind some thick bushes in the back yard. But if I have to, I'll leave without them. I've got everything I really need in the tote bag I carry every day"—she indicated it on the back seat—"including my total fortune of three hundred and thirteen dollars and three new toothbrushes."

She waved almost gaily and drove off. Cable and Susan and Katie got into the rented station wagon and drove in complete silence back to the city.

Cable took Katie out for an Italian dinner the next night. He was due to leave for Atlanta the morning after, to audition for a job as a TV sports commentator.

"God, I'm sorry I can't see this through to the end," he told Katie for at least the tenth time as they walked back along Fifth Avenue to her apartment shortly after nine.

"I'll call you," she promised, "if you'll tell me where; or you can call me. No matter what happens, I hope we won't lose touch." She squeezed his arm. "You've become very dear to me as a friend."

"Dear enough?" he asked bluntly.

"I—you—what d'you mean?" she hedged.

"Come on, Katie, coyness isn't your style. You damn well know what I mean."

"It wouldn't be a good idea," she said weakly.

"Says who?"

"Why should we spoil a perfect friendship with sex?"

"I can think of six minor reasons—to say nothing of one very major one—and I don't think we *would* spoil it."

"Affairs inevitably end. Friendship needn't."

"Is it the guy with the scarred back?"

Katie thought for a moment and realized that this time it really wasn't.

"No guy at all, unless you count Tommy Langford. It's him and his little sister and Christine. Even at the office, when my mind should be on other things, all I can think of is the battered women and the kids."

"It's a wonderful cause, Katie, but it's not an entire life."

"I know that, but right now it's all I can seem to concentrate on. You see . . ." She swallowed hard. "I had a baby girl once, Cable—she never got to be a grown one. It sort of helps me . . . about her . . . to give other kids a new life."

"And is it for *him,* too?"

"Him?"

"The guy who seemed too arrogant and assured to have been an abused kid?"

"Maybe. I don't know. I guess, yes, but mostly for me, I think."

"Okay, Katie Coffee, I picked the wrong time if not the wrong girl. Let me know if you change your mind."

"When I do," said Katie, relieved at his easy acceptance, *"you* probably won't be available."

"A very strong possibility," Cable said severely. "During my football days I played the field in other respects as well; but now that I'm turning solid citizen, writing and hopefully reporting, I aim to settle down and start a family. You're missing out on a good prospect, kid."

"I know I am," said Katie sincerely as they reached her apartment building. "I'll probably hate myself in the morning."

"Still time to change your mind," he said, all six-foot-six of him managing to look winsome and wistful.

"Will you settle for a kiss instead?"

For an answer he swept her literally off her feet and into his arms, holding her up in the air as though she weighed no more than a kitten. First he kissed her lightly and leisurely; then his lips claimed hers with all the bruising strength and power of a football player clutching a pigskin. When he finally set her down on the ground, Katie's buckling knees knocked, and her hands curled around his biceps to help her stay upright.

"It ill becomes me to boast," said Cable somewhat smugly as he helped support her, "but that was just a small sample of what you will be missing."

"Good night, Cable," Katie gasped, letting go and bolting through the door, which for some minutes had been patiently held open for her by the carefully poker-faced doorman.

"Who, undoubtedly," she told Francesca at lunch the next day, "was watching the entire episode."

Francesca laughed. "Just as a matter of curiosity, *were* you sorry in the morning?"

"Yes."

"Why the hell didn't you let him stay?"

Katie looked off into the distance, seeing not the crowded restaurant but a scarred back . . . a raised hand . . . a small headstone . . .

"I don't know," she said huskily.

Francesca shrugged. "If *you* don't," she said skeptically, "who am I to tell you? Now, about *Virgin* . . ."

"Christine Langford called," said Alice when Katie got back to the office. "She says to phone her, it's urgent."

Katie looked at the pink message slip; it was an unfamiliar number. She dialed quickly.

Christine answered on the first ring. "Katie?"

"Yes."

"Oh, thank God, I had to go outside to a public telephone, but I just wanted to tell you that a week from Wednesday he's taking the shuttle to Boston and he'll be gone for the *whole* day. It's a God-sent chance for me to leave. Without him around, I could take all the luggage I want and not worry when I go for copies of the kids' school records . . . We'd have a full day's head start."

"I don't think the passports will be ready by then, but you're right. It seems too good a chance to miss. Listen, let me speak to Liz Pomeroy and get back to you. Tomorrow morning okay?"

"Yes. After ten."

The passports weren't likely to have arrived, but Liz agreed that it was much too good an opportunity to pass up.

"What time will your husband be out of the house?" Katie asked Christine when she phoned back the next morning.

"He's taking the nine A.M. shuttle from LaGuardia, so he'll leave for the airport before eight. Then he's got a one P.M. lunch, so there's no way that he could get home before four or five, and probably much later."

"That's perfect. You don't have to bother sending the kids to school. After you're picked up, you can stop off at the school to say you're moving and need copies of their records. Oh, and Liz says, don't take any *inherited* family jewels of his, but make sure to bring along all the ones that he bought you. Jewelry can be turned into cold hard cash to support you till the Pomeroys wring some money out of him while you set about supporting yourself."

"I just want to be rid of him, I don't want his money."

"The hell with that; you're entitled. You've been married to the monster for ten years, including the lean ones before he became a best-seller. You've borne him two children. You've . . . it's none of my business, but take my advice and listen to your lawyers. You have Tommy and Giselle to think of."

"You're right. I know you're right. Will *you* pick us up?"

"I don't drive, Christine, but I'll come along for the ride. Figure we'll be there about nineish, but we'll phone first in case he gets held up, or is home sick, or—"

"I'm sorry," said a suddenly remote voice at the other end of the line, "but I don't contribute to organizations that solicit over the telephone."

"He's there, I gather. See you." Katie hung up.

On the planned day, the pick-up went smoothly. The two suitcases wrapped in plastic were rescued from the bushes and Christine was able to fill two more even larger ones.

"Did you bring your jewelry?" asked Tom Pomeroy, who was driving.

Christine nodded solemnly. "What I didn't have on hand, I picked up from our safety deposit box at the bank yesterday, and I took the children's bonds from it as well. All we need now is their school records."

Not until after they had procured the records and were driving along the New England Throughway did she ask where they were going.

"To my sister's in Trenton," said Tom. "We'll stash you out with her till the passports come, then it's off to Germany. Your sister's got an apartment for you already and a possible job at the P.X. WOMAN has already bought your tickets . . . all we need is a reservation date."

"Will there be any trouble about the divorce?"

"I doubt it."

"How can you be so sure?" she asked wistfully.

"My dear, if your husband was caught in a love nest with another woman or in a fraudulent land scheme, his readers might only shrug; but for a best-selling male writer, who has built his reputation on his sensitive portrayals of women and family relationships, to be known as an abuser of his wife and children! He'd be laughed right off the best-seller lists. We've got photographic evidence, remember . . . and you'll be out of the country . . . though he doesn't have to know that yet."

"Did you leave a letter for him?" Katie inquired curiously.

"I left one on the kitchen table. I just said not to worry, my lawyer would be in touch with him." Christine actually giggled. "And P.S., there was a chicken casserole in the refrigerator he could warm if he was hungry." She hugged her children to her exuberantly. "He *hates* chicken casseroles."

Thirty-three

*. . . which leads to the obvious conclusion that the
pleasure of puncturing his bride's maidenhead—regarded right into the twentieth century as a husband's
immutable right and privilege—smacked strongly of
medieval droit du seigneur.*

> from *Once A Virgin, Twice A Virgin*
> by Katryn Kauffman Coffee

"Katryn, I just spoke to Enid Salisbury, the new publicity honcho at World-Wilder. She wants you to do a promotional tour of six European capitals—six in six days is
what they're figuring—just as the foreign editions of *Once
A Virgin* hit the bookstores."

"Europe, yes. Six capitals in six days, no," said Katryn
firmly. "Remind them that the idea is to promote, not kill,
the goose that writes the golden books. Say I'm willing
if they can come up with a less suicidal schedule."

"I'll try her again, but she's a tough one."

"So am I," snapped Katryn. "Tell her that unless I can
get a layover in each city—even flight attendants get
that—I won't go."

"She's already talking contractual obligations."

"Good. Remind her contractual obligations allow for ill
health. Mine can get very ill indeed if I so desire."

Francesca laughed. "You're right, m'dear. I'll match you against La Salisbury any day of the week.

"A decent schedule, not flattery, will get you—rather, me—everywhere."

Which is how, feeling more than just a slight touch of déjà vu, Katryn Kauffman Coffee found herself, five years after the first trip, once more in Paris, Amsterdam, and Copenhagen, with Rome instead of Venice this time. It was the reverse order of her previous visit, and she was grateful that she could get this not-altogether pleasing taste of the past entirely out of her system by winding up in London, where after the two days of bookstore autographings, interviews, and personal appearances, she proposed to take two weeks' vacation at her own expense.

First, she would do the London scene and the theatres. Then she would take a series of bus tours to all the other places on her itinerary: Brighton. Bath. Winchester. Oxford. Cambridge. Canterbury. Stratford-upon-Avon. Stonehenge.

She had come later in life than most to her love of English literature and history, and as much as possible now, she would eat and drink her fill of both.

It would be business as usual, too, of course, for *Love And Marriage*. Much of her note-taking would later be used in pieces for the magazine, with which she was now associated as a free-lance writer and part-time editor.

And, of course, the national leadership of WOMAN wanted her to interview some of the leading English feminists. She had also promised to give a speech to an organization for battered women.

A trail of telegrams and letters of inquiry and instruction followed Katryn from city to seaside to country and from hotels to remote inns. There was nothing about the familiar wire envelope that arrived at the Hampshire inn to fill her with alarm. Not the slightest twinge of premonition troubled her mind.

She looked at the signature first, as she always did, and smiled happily: *Gregorio G.* She read the message over three times before she could comprehend the starkly simple message. And then she kept reading it over and over, stupidly disbelieving, the silly, empty smile still plastered onto her face.

Tony died instantly in car crash yesterday.
Memorial service on Friday evening at the Morgue.

She had plenty of time to arrange the return journey home, and, in fact, arrived early Friday morning. The elevator man at her apartment building helped her with her luggage. As soon as he dumped it into her hallway, accepted his tip, and left, she kicked off her shoes and fell face down across her bed. She slept half the day away.

She awoke rested but unrefreshed and, with her suitcases still unpacked, chose a dress from her closet that Tony had been particularly fond of, a soft red wool with a geometric pattern and a broad patent leather belt. And to go with it, the almost-matching red shoes . . . her Dorothy-of-Oz shoes, he used to call them.

It was raining lightly when she left the apartment in late afternoon; the doorman went outside with an umbrella to get her a cab.

The Morgue had already begun to fill up with old friends, old faces, but she didn't see Greg. Suddenly, unable to face even the old friends, Katie made her way to the kitchen, where two uniformed maids were setting out plates of cold cuts.

"Can I help you, miss?" asked one.

"I'd like . . . can I have a cup of coffee, please?"

When it was silently handed over, she sat down at the familiar old table, prolonging the drinking. Greg found her there, and they just stood, gripping hands and looking at each other's drawn faces.

"Don't worry, I won't weep all over you," she finally said shakily. "I'm all wept out. I cried from Hampshire to London and from London all the way across the ocean. Greg, what happened? How could it be?"

"He was in a car with that new model, Vanessa. They were headed uptown on the East River Drive on their way to a shoot. A guy in the downtown lane had a heart attack and went right across the barrier, straight at them. Neither he nor Tony ever knew what hit them."

"The girl?"

"Minor cuts, bruises, and shock. She'll be fine."

"I'm glad, but . . . but *Tony!*" It was a cry of pain, wrung from her heart.

"I know, Katie. I know." He added softly, "He was cremated as soon as the police released the body . . . it's what he preferred. Tonight is just for a few good friends to—to talk about him a little."

Some time later in the evening, when the brief service was over and the friends still lingered, eating and drinking, somehow reluctant to let go, Greg came up behind Katryn. She was talking to Brian Scully, who had flown in from Toronto, and another photographer.

"Could you come with me for a moment, Katie?"

She excused herself and followed him to the study, where another man stood waiting for them. Greg introduced him as Tony's lawyer, Phil Halpern, and they all sat down.

"This only concerns the three of us, Katie. Phil has Tony's will, and I'm the executor."

"Of course," Katryn murmured.

"Mr. Grieg inherits the Morgue, quite a valuable property, but he did help pre-pay the mortgage."

"Well, of course," Katryn said again rather bewilderedly. "I wouldn't expect anything else."

"He also gets the complete contents, including some

valuable antiques, the stocks and bonds—just a few thousand dollars' worth—and a few thousand in cash."

"It isn't necessary for me to be told this, Mr. Halpern," Katryn told him very decidedly. "It only concerns you and Gregorio. I suppose you think that just because Tony and I were once married . . . but I assure you I have no claim at all on his property. Tony and I were *divorced!*"

"His will specifically mentions a life insurance policy, with you as beneficiary, which he took out during the time of the marriage."

"But surely it's an old will . . . he must have dropped the policy later on . . . or perhaps changed the beneficiary to Greg," Katryn suggested eagerly.

"I never met anyone so ready to disclaim an inheritance. No, you remained the beneficiary and, as a matter of fact, he upped the amount several times, from twenty-five to forty thousand, the last increase a year after your divorce. And it was double indemnity in the case of accidental death."

Katryn stood quite still for a moment. "Are you trying to tell me," she asked presently in a crisp, cool voice, "that I get eighty thousand dollars?"

"Yes, Ms. Coffee. Greg seemed to think it was news that would have to be broken to you gently."

"Well, Greg was wrong!" stormed Katryn, raging up and down the small room. "Because I don't want his damned eighty thousand dollars. I won't take it. Damn it, even dead he's still trying to take care of me. Why did he have to go and get himself killed? I don't want Tony's money. I want Tony . . . Tony . . ."

At a silent signal from Gregorio, the lawyer left the room.

When they were alone, Greg said quietly, "Katie, sit down and stop carrying on; I've had about as much as I can take myself. There's too much to do . . . I start an

Australian concert tour in two weeks, and I just can't cope with hysterics."

As he had known she would, Katryn responded at once to this bracing appeal. She sat down, nervously smoothing out the skirt of her red dress. "I'm sorry," she said huskily.

"Now, about the money." His tone was purposely prosaic. "Let's face it, Katie. Tony was young and healthy. No one thought it less likely than he that you would collect it any time in the forseeable future. But I *do* know that he always wished he could give you the security of a home of your own, the kind of security owning the Morgue gave him—me, as well—particularly in the days before the money started rolling in.

"Tony always said"—for the first time in days, a real smile crossed his face—"that you were too much a Pennsylvania farm girl under the city veneer—just as he was a prairie boy—not to want to own a chunk of property that was your own, even if the property happened to be twenty stories up in the grimy air of New York City.

"I know you earn good money yourself now, Katie," he went on persuasively, "but a fair portion of it is siphoned away by the government and you live pretty high, wide and handsome on what's left after what you give away to your battered women's causes. To say nothing of royalties not being that dependable an income. But with a chunk of money like eighty thousand in one lump sum—he had you as owner of the policy, so it's tax-free— you can get yourself a piece of New York real estate. It would be a little security for you, and it would make Tony—wherever the bastard is—very happy."

Six weeks later, Katryn Kauffman Coffee moved into the Fifth Avenue condominium on which, with her inheritance as well as by denuding her bank account, she was able to make a one hundred thousand dollar down payment.

The apartment was on the twentieth floor of a block-long building a short walk from the Metropolitan Museum of Art, where she and Tony and Greg had spent so many happy hours together.

She walked out onto her living room balcony and looked north toward the Museum while the movers unloaded her furniture.

"Are you satisfied, Tony?" she asked out loud. "I'm here, twenty stories up. I've got my own piece of your city, but where are you? Oh God, how I wish I could believe that you and Antonia are together!"

Thirty-four

Men and women make love for reasons other than overwhelming desire. They are cold, they need comfort; they want reassurance or reaffirmation of life; there is nothing good on TV or their town suffers a two-hour blackout.

from *In Bed Unwed*
by Katryn Kauffman Coffee

"Are we by any chance boring you, Katryn?" Eleanor Howell asked her new associate editor in the sudden silence of the *Love And Marriage* conference room.

Katryn came out of her reverie to see the rest of the assembled staff gazing at her expectantly.

She started to laugh, then gasped, "Oh, dear, I'm sorry; I was wool-gathering."

"We had already deduced that."

"Did I miss something important?"

"We were waiting for your report on the new project—you recall, the minor matter of whether the entire Christmas issue should be dedicated to marriage as the in-trend."

Katryn poked among the papers in her file folder. "Oh, dear," she said again. "I think I left it on my desk. I'll just—"

"Never mind." Mrs. Howell, her hair even more improbably orange than on the day Katryn had first met her, nodded to her secretary, who jumped up and went into an inner office to phone downstairs.

"What the hell's wrong with you, Katryn?" asked Art Driscoll energetically.

"I was thinking of home," said Katryn nostalgically. "When I lived there, a good little Amish girl, I couldn't wait to get away, and all I could think of today, would you believe it, was

> *O, to be in Strawberry Schrank*
> *Now that April's here.*

I can just see the green, green grass on the rolling hills and smell the spring. It's so fragrant in the air, it even clings to your clothes; they smell of springtime instead of stale smoke and soot and smog."

"Well, for God's sakes," said Eleanor Howell, "it's Thursday. After we go over your report, why don't you take off for the weekend for your godforsaken Pennsylvania Shangri-La? Maybe you can cover a wedding there on Sunday. Take Monday off, too, if you can. Would you like a photographer?"

"Amish weddings usually take place in November after harvest, not April. And being photographed violates Amish religious beliefs."

Art Driscoll was not to be discouraged. "That would make a *great* piece for the November issue if you could hurry it. There must be old photographs in the public domain, and it could be fleshed out with pen-and-ink sketches."

Mrs. Howell's secretary came back with Katryn's report.

"It's up to you, Katryn, whether you want to do an Amish wedding story," the editor told her as she looked over the report, "but take the weekend home and come back on Monday alert and alive, please. Art is right; if we're going to do it for November, we haven't much time."

It was not their business to know she could not go home. Instead, Katryn decided to fly up to Boston to be with Johnny. She hadn't been there since Thanksgiving, when they had driven up to Cape Cod—in his new Lincoln Continental—and stayed at a nearly deserted motel along the rough Atlantic coast.

It had been splendidly desolate, and she and Johnny had taken long, wonderful beach walks during the day and found marvelous seafood places to eat in at night. But after they went back to their separate rooms, Katryn suspected, Johnny sometimes kept company with a bottle from his suitcase.

At Christmas he had come to New York and stayed with her. At first it had been wonderful.

The Broadway shows had been wonderful. And the off-Broadway shows. And Chinatown. And the Macedonian Tea Room. Also, the Japanese, Italian, and delicatessen meals. The ice skating rink and the towering Christmas tree at Rockefeller Center had been sparklingly alive, even at midnight.

But the parties hadn't been so wonderful. Too many parties she had mistakenly taken him to. Too many parties and too much holiday drinking.

They hadn't been together since.

On Friday, without informing him that she was coming, she took an evening shuttle plane to Boston, registered at her usual hotel, and took Johnny by surprise at his Newbury Street apartment.

Johnny was home, surrounded by his *Wall Street Journal*s, *Barron's,* and *Richland Report*s, as well as an empty bottle of Scotch. Johnny was sullenly, sickeningly, overwhelmingly, odoriferously drunk.

Five minutes after she had arrived, she was kneeling behind him in the bathroom, holding his head over the toilet bowl while he retched and groaned and coughed up his guts. Coffee Katie, with grim unsisterly lack of compassion, wiped his brow with a cloth dampened in cold water, supplied sips of water, flushed the toilet each time he threw up, and occasionally uttered unwelcome platitudes like, "Serves you right . . . You reap what you sow . . . If you burn the candle at both ends, you have to expect to pay the piper."

"Katie, I appreciate the womanly help, but for God's sakes, put a sock in the conversation, pul-lease," he moaned once between bouts. "I need womanly symp"—he gulped and lowered his head quickly—"sympathy," he finished a minute or two later as Katie flushed again.

"You want sympathy? Go look it up in the dictionary; that's the only place you'll find it. I have no sympathy for a man who deliberately does this to himself."

"Not deliberately. Not anymore."

"What do you mean? Who else does it to you, if not you?"

Johnny stumbled to his feet, using her bowed shoulders for leverage. He leaned against the bathroom wall while Katie, too, scrambled up. She supported him into the bedroom, where the minute she let go of him, he toppled over onto the bed. He lay so still that she was scared for a moment, and then she heard the snorting sounds of his breath.

He looked so awful; he *smelled* so awful. Her eyes filled up and overflowed with stinging tears of grief and pain and regret for what had happened to this beloved friend and foster brother.

She pulled off his shoes, unbuckled his belt and stripped down his trousers, then rolled him under the blankets. Johnny slept on, undisturbed by all the pushing, pulling, and prodding.

He slept all night and most of the next day, rising only to make several somnambulistic trips to the bathroom. He was unaware that Katie had called a cleaning service to scrub his apartment from top to bottom.

In the middle of the afternoon Johnny appeared in the doorway, dressed just in his shirt and underwear, the way she'd tucked him into bed.

"Have you been cleaning this place all day like a nut?"

"Like hell I have. A cleaning service straightened up this pigsty. The bill's on your desk. I expect you to pay me back. And speaking of nuts, just how do you define that word, Johnny? It wasn't me stinking drunk and throwing up in the toilet and sleeping the whole day away," she reminded him sweetly.

Johnny's shoulders shook. His laugh sounded surprisingly clear and natural. "I stand corrected, and I'll write you a check."

"To continue our conversation where we broke it off," Katryn asked him, "what is this bull about your not doing this deliberately? Who else makes you drink?"

"*I* make me drink . . . but not deliberately anymore. Why don't you face it, Katie, the way that I have? For more than a year I've seen you trying to hide the truth from yourself. I'm an alcoholic, Coffee Katie."

They went at it hammer and tongs for what was left of the day, both getting more and more Pennsylvania-Dutch in the process.

"So I'm finally facing what you faced nearly a year ago. You're a damn drunk! What else is that supposed to make you? Some kind of a hero because you admit the unpleasant truth? Like hell it does. You're a *coward*, Johnny Stoltzfus. That's right, glare at me all you want. I stick by the word. What else but coward can I call a man who goes right on with such willful self-destruction, never thinking to turn to those who love him?"

"Sure. I should have burdened you. For what? Was telling you going to give me the will to stop?"

"We both know the answer to that one, Johnny. Only you can do it—if you want to."

"Oh Christ, Katie, of course, I *want* to . . . but not as much yet as I want that . . . I don't know what it is . . . *oblivion* . . . the pretending I can do . . . the way out that seems to come at the bottom of the bottle."

"Has your life been so bad then, Johnny? If it has, a poor kind of friend and sister I've been to fail you and not even know."

"Katie, that's just it. My life hasn't been bad at all. I can't offer that excuse."

"You've fulfilled most of your ambitions. You work for a good brokerage house. You have money and the life you said you wanted. Is it because of Suzy? Is the drinking why you broke up?"

"Partly she left because I drank, though for a long time I kidded myself it was the other way around, I drank because she left me."

"I'm trying to figure it out, Johnny, and it baffles me. You had a wonderful girl who loved you; you were happy, first at school, then in your work. You were making money, enjoying yourself. What more could a man ask?"

"I wanted the farm and the family and Strawberry Schrank to be part of my life in Boston, just as back in Pennsylvania I wanted to have *there* all the things I have *here.*"

"Johnny, you can't have it all. No one can. We all have to make choices. You made yours years and years before you left home. So did I."

"But you had been out in that non-Amish world before, and I hadn't. Maybe that was it. Maybe you're just naturally a stronger person. You fit, and I don't. It's as simple as that."

"Bullshit!" Katryn told him robustly. "To me that sounds like a typical alcoholic's excuse!"

"You're probably right," Johnny returned amiably, and

the next moment was in receipt of a ringing slap on the side of his face.

"Coffee Katie," he groaned, "how can you be so cruel? Is that a way to treat a man with a sick headache?"

"Sick or not, if you try to be smart with me, you'll get what you deserve. So you lost your love; you're not the only one. It's rough for a while, but it's not the end of life. Try looking around among your other girls."

"There's been no girl since Suzy."

"You mean—?"

"Yes."

"No one since . . . that's a long time, Johnny."

"Tell me something I don't know." He shrugged expressively. "Not that you have to hand out too much sympathy. The alcohol dries up the natural juices, I guess. Maybe that's another way Suzy found me lacking. It was happening even before she left. Drunks don't make good lovers, you know."

"Oh, Johnny!"

"Don't tell me you're sad that I'm no longer such a good lover." There was not much gaiety in his laughter. "Why should it matter? How long has it been since you cared about me—like that?"

It suddenly seemed to Katryn that he had not just uttered a tired old joke but posed a question fraught with significance.

"When?" she repeated. "That night in the spare room at home when we said goodbye, that's when. You gave me my first lover's kiss, Johnny . . . have you forgotten it? I never could. It was special in my life. And then you told me you loved me, and I confessed to loving you."

"And then you sent me away."

"I had to, Johnny. If I had said the words I wanted to say to you . . . *stay with me on the spare bed, Johnny, I want you to make love to me*—what would have happened?"

"I would have made love to you, Coffee Katie, and—"

"And never gone away. And some day hated me for it."

"Or perhaps been happier?"

"You think so now, Johnny, but then . . . Ah, Johnny, don't try to fool yourself. You think you'd be drinking less as a farmer than as a stockbroker?"

"A farmer, no, but maybe a husband and father."

"Our heredity wasn't so good for making you a father. There were three stillbirths before Mem had you, remember?"

"Your parents had four healthy children."

"Their genes may have passed me by." A small, sad smile quivered along her mouth. "This is a day for confessions, I guess. I had a baby not long after I went to New York. She was born when I had carried her less than six months and lived for only twelve days."

"And you never said a word . . . you never turned to me, either."

"Johnny, believe me, I thought of it in my first panicked moments. But it was not long after I had met Suzy. I couldn't expect her to put her life on hold for a year or so just to accommodate me. Tony was willing to help me, and he didn't have any entanglements that would get in the way."

Johnny laughed so hard that tears spurted out of his eyes and he had to hold his aching head between his hands to keep it steady.

"Katie, Coffee Katie, did you ever get things ass-backwards!"

Katryn stared at him, bewildered.

"Do you know what Suzy's parting words to me were?" asked Johnny, wiping his eyes with tender care so as not to make his head wobble.

"How could I?"

"She was standing right in that same spot where you're standing now, but not looking nearly so belligerent." He grinned. "She had a sweeter nature than you, Coffee Katie, and God knows a sweeter tongue. 'Johnny,' she said, 'I could fight the alcohol and the Amish guilt and the damn Pennsylvania-Dutch culture difference, but I can't fight Coffee Katie.' "

"Me!"

"She felt she was constantly compared to you and competing with you," Johnny said thoughtfully. "She said that in the lovemaking—when we had any—she often felt as though there were three in our bed."

Katryn Kauffman Coffee put her hands on her hips. "Bullshit!" she said again with all the belligerence that Johnny had accused her of. "You think you're smart, don't you, Johnny Stoltzfus, but I'm pretty familiar with the technique of indirection. So don't expect me to be led down the garden path and away from the main topic. Never mind your love life, or mine—or the lack thereof. Never mind the past. Perhaps we're both emotionally crippled; perhaps we're not. It's not important to this discussion. What we're talking about here is that you are a drunk, and that's the one problem that won't go away. Where's your phone book?"

"On the shelf under the desk. Are you calling in reinforcements?"

"No, *you* are. Here's the number." She pointed with her finger. "Alcoholics Anonymous. It's your business whether you call or not; I'm going back to New York, and I won't even know. I work at the magazine almost every day when I'm not on promotional tours; I write most nights. My weekends are for fun and relaxation. In short, I have a life of my own, and I'm not interested in being your full-time crutch or your part-time shoulder to weep on."

She got her coat from the closet, gathered up her scarf, gloves, and purse, then faced Johnny aggressively as before.

"My last word on the subject is this: You claim you

drink because you're unhappy. You claim I'm the missing link in your life that would give it meaning. Well, I'm calling your bluff, Johnny. Just let me know when you've been dry for six months—absolutely dry. That doesn't mean just the hard stuff—I'm talking about not so much as a drop of wine or a glass of beer . . ."

"And if I am . . . if I do . . . ?"

"Then there'll be the two in your bed you claim to want there."

"You and me?"

"Yes, you and me . . . but only for as long as you stay sober. I'm no martyr."

"Six months?" Johnny repeated.

"Six months."

"You'll marry me?"

"If that's what you want."

"I want," said Johnny, eyes gleaming. "You're on, Coffee Katie Kauffman. It's a deal."

"I shan't hold my breath," retorted Katryn Kauffman Coffee, slamming out of the Newbury Street apartment.

Thirty-five

Every bout of lovemaking doesn't achieve the heights of passionate ecstasy beloved of the novelist, whose glamorously misleading descriptions never allow for the mattress that slips, a head knocking against the bedpost, two hearts beating as one but two bodies not quite in sync, or a piece of necessary equipment out of reach at a vital moment.

from *Bawdy Bedroom Laughter*
by Katryn Kauffman Coffee

Ms. Katryn Kauffman Coffee, Assoc. Editor
Love And Marriage *Magazine*
150 East 39th Street
New York, New York 10016

Dear Ms. Coffee:
I have been asked to contact you, as party of the second part, regarding an April contract entered into between you and my client, John Stoltzfus of Boston.
Mr. Stoltzfus has directed me to inform you that the terms of your six-month agreement, as outlined by you and binding on both parties, will be fulfilled on the twentieth of this month at 9 P.M. The ceremony heretofore agreed upon has been scheduled to take place at 11 A.M. on the twenty-first of this month in

the Municipal Building, 20 Court Street, Boston, Massachusetts, officiated over in his private chambers by Judge Samuel Erskine.

The party of the first part desires written notification as to whether you intend to honor your contractual obligations. He also wishes to know if you still prefer garden flowers to orchids.

Very truly yours,
Mark Loyall Hampton III

Dear Mr. Hampton:

Please notify your client, Mr. John Stoltzfus, that the party of the second part always honors her contracts.

She wishes you to inform Mr. Stoltzfus that she will be registered at her usual Boston hotel as of the evening of the nineteenth if he cares to re-negotiate any minor details.

Please further notify Mr. Stoltzfus that Ms. Coffee has two weeks' combined vacation and sick leave, starting the twentieth, if he wishes to consider so trivial a matter as a journey following the ceremony.

In conclusion: The party of the second part utterly detests orchids!

Sincerely,
K.K. Coffee, Assoc. Ed.

Johnny raised first one eyebrow, then the other. "Bunny slippers?" he said in pained surprise. "Cotton *flannel?*"

"I've got a sexy apricot number, bridal as all get-out, sitting right there in that suitcase," Katryn informed him, teeth chattering, "but if you think I'm going to put it on in this sub-zero room, you're out of your mind."

"Very traditional, I'm sure," Johnny murmured. "Our

mutual great-grandmother probably received great-grand-
pappy in a gown quite like it."

"Consider yourself lucky I'm not wearing long johns,"
Katryn retorted. "Maybe our conception of geography is
different, but when you said driving south, I—foolish
me!—pictured Florida sunshine, not an isolated refriger-
ated inn in Connecticut."

"I said south*ward,* not south . . . and the stop here was
a bit unpremeditated. Remember that it was *you* who
looked out that restaurant window and mentioned that it
was beginning to snow. Nor do I remember," he reminded
her, smiling benignly, "your expressing any regret that we
stopped, while you were packing away that staggeringly
un-bridelike quantity of food."

"Okay, okay, while you're scoring points, I'm turning
to a pillar of ice. Do you mind if I get into bed?"

"I've been wishing for the last ten minutes that you
would," Johnny told her politely.

Katryn kicked off her slippers, dived under the covers,
and let out a shriek.

"The sheets are absolutely frozen!" she said, jumping
out again.

"I can't believe—" Johnny addressed the ceiling as he
lifted the phone—"that this is the night I've waited seven—
or is it eight?—years for . . . Yes, desk please . . . this is
Mr. Stoltzfus in Suite . . . what the hell suite is it, Katie?
Suite Three D . . . we don't seem to have any heat in
here . . . uh huh . . . mm mm . . . I see . . . yes . . .
yes . . . please do."

He turned to Katryn, now squatting on top of the bed,
Indian style, with a blanket wrapped around her flannel
granny gown.

"What were all those cryptic utterances about?" she demanded.

"It seems the boiler is on the blink."

"You could have fooled me."

"And the repair truck is having trouble getting here because of the snow."

Katryn moaned.

"But the lady of the inn, Mrs. Burns, is sending us a thermal jug of hot mulled cider spiced with cinnamon."

Katryn looked faintly cheered.

"And a gentleman, improbably named Heskith, Senior, is coming up with a supply of logs for the fireplace in our living room. Shall we cavort together on top of the bed until he arrives? According to you, in *Bundle In The Trundle,* there's no heat like body heat."

"I," said Katie, fitting shiveringly into the curves of the offered body, "will accept any damned source of heat available."

A few pleasurable moments followed before there was a pounding on the door.

"Better stay here," said Johnny, reluctantly freeing his lips. "Even in cotton flannel, unless he's over eighty, you might send Heskith Senior's blood pressure soaring."

He covered her tenderly with all the blankets around and went to answer the door.

In less than ten minutes Johnny was back. "Almost all set," he reported cheerfully. "Katie, would you mind going into the bathroom for a minute? Heskith wants to check the thermostat in here."

Grumblingly, Katie slid out from under the layers of wool and, wearing only one blanket, trailed off into the bathroom. When Johnny signaled the all-clear, she came scurrying back, only to find the blankets, as well as the mattress, gone.

"In here," Johnny called, and she ran barefooted into the living room, where a blazing fire roared satisfyingly up the chimney and the mattress was spread in front of the fireplace, neatly re-made with the sheets and blankets tucked underneath and the pillows heaped in place.

"Heskith Senior," said Johnny, smiling as he poured out

two mugs of cider, "was a very understanding fellow." He pointed. "He brought enough logs to last the night."

"May his name forever be inscribed among the blessed!" said Katie fervently.

"His name was inscribed among the well-and-truly tipped," grinned Johnny, clinking mugs with her. "To you, my wife."

"To us," said Katryn, lowering her eyes and sipping.

"That can't possibly be a blush I detected! Katryn Kauffman Coffee, author of *Once A Virgin, Twice A Virgin, Bawdy Bedroom Laughter . . .*"

"Oh, shove it!"

". . . and other similar books would not blush," Johnny finished imperturbably, "at the mention of being someone's wife. No doubt it was the reflection of the fire on your otherwise snow-white cheeks."

Katryn ignored him.

"Warm yet?" Johnny asked.

"Mmmm."

"Then would you mind getting into that bed? If I don't make love to you soon, and I do mean *soon,* I'm going to embarrass the hell out of both of us."

Katryn scrambled so far under the covers, not even the top of her head was visible. The next minute a bare arm emerged, and a balled-up bundle that proved to be the flannel granny gown went sailing halfway across the room.

Johnny stood with his back toasting at the fire and hastily stripped off his own clothes. Before sliding in beside Katryn, he loaded an extra thick log onto the fire.

Katryn lay curled on her side, her toes twined backwards to tuck against his feet, twisting and turning to accommodate his roving hands while she groaned deeply and pleasurably.

"You make me feel no end of a red-hot lover carrying on that way," Johnny whispered.

"I cannot tell a lie, sir, I was brought up Amish. It's the

heat from the fireplace I'm in ecstasy about right now, not you."

Johnny gave a shout of laughter, then seized her around the waist and pulled her down on top of him. "I never could resist a challenge where you were concerned, Coffee Katie. Want to bet I can make that lie come true? Now I didn't get to *see* the package," he went on consideringly, while his hands became more explicit in their exploration, "but everything feels right to me. Mm mm, yes, two of these . . . lovely . . . lovely . . . and just *one* of those . . . lovelier still . . . Never mind, Katie, my wife, there aren't many people at the inn tonight. Scream a little if you want. What the hell? Scream a lot."

They finally fell asleep, wrapped in each other's arms, but not before Katie, his wife, had satisfied him with more than a few ladylike shrieks of ecstasy.

The snow had stopped by morning and the day was clear and cold . . . but they were in no hurry, Johnny mentioned lazily . . . and the inn cuisine was great, Katie agreed. That the heat was now back on had become a matter of indifference, since there were still plenty of logs.

They accepted fresh towels when the maid came around, but declined her other services. Heskith Senior knocked, offering to return the mattress to its proper place, but was told they liked it just where it was and went off instead to give the kitchen an order for two of what the Room Service menu called the Farmer's Breakfast. The Farmer's Breakfast, Katie discovered happily a short while later, consisted of "practically everything."

They ate at a small table, decorously dressed in robes; and as soon as they were finished eating and had put the trays outside, they shucked off these extraneous garments and returned to their mattress.

They spent most of the day pleasurably in bed, sometimes even sleeping.

On the second morning Johnny rolled her ruthlessly

from under the blankets. "Come on, lazy one, we're traveling today."

"Tired," Katie mumbled, trying to get back under.

"You can sleep in the car."

"Wanna sleep now."

Johnny stripped all the covers off her. Their fire had finally gone out. She sat up naked and shivering. "Sadist!" she complained.

"We'll have breakfast before we leave," Johnny promised, tossing over her robe. "Now start packing."

After her shower Katie took an ashtray and a bath towel, both embossed with the inn name, and stuffed them into her overnight bag. "I want something to remember this place by," she answered Johnny's raised eyebrows defiantly.

"I had hoped," he said with a wickedly significant smile, "that *I* would provide that."

Katryn, who had put on panties and bra but was otherwise still undressed, actually blushed all over from her waist up to her hairline.

"You know what I mean," she muttered.

He pulled her into his arms and kissed her from her hairline down to her waist. "I know," he said between kisses. "Only, teasing, Coffee Katie; you're so wonderfully teasable, my *leeblich* wife."

When they checked out, he was unsurprised to hear his *leeblich* wife tell Mrs. Burns at the desk to please put one of the large bath towels and an ashtray on the bill. "I took them as souvenirs," she explained casually.

The astonished Mrs. Burns handed a hefty bill across to Johnny. "In my thirteen years as an innkeeper," she confided, "hundreds of towels and ashtrays have vanished with our guests each year, but this is the first time any of the takers has ever offered me payment. Please accept what you took from the inn as a gift, Mrs. Stoltzfus, in honor of a rare occasion."

A while later in the car, after maneuvering them from

behind an oversized van, Johnny cast a quick look at his silent companion.

"I'm offering whatever amount of money you want in exchange for your no-doubt profound thoughts."

Katryn smiled faintly. "They're yours for free." After a moment, she continued hesitatingly, "Johnny, it was all so sudden . . ."

"Sudden?" he scoffed. "Us?"

"You know what I mean. I'm talking about the marrying and our arrangements from the time I got your Mark Loyall Hampton the third's letter. It *was* sudden; we never had any time to talk about . . . well, day-to-day things like, well, like Mrs. Burns at the inn calling me Mrs. Stoltzfus. I'm not a fanatic, Johnny; and I'm not going to start correcting every chance-met person about something like that, but I'm *not* Mrs. Stoltzfus. I'm your wife, but I'm also my own person, Katie Kauffman in our home, and outside of it, *Ms.* Katryn Kauffman Coffee."

"You're *my* Katie and *my* Katryn and *my* wife?"

"As long as we both shall live; I thought I'd made that clear."

"Then that's good enough for me, Katie. It's you I've wanted for long hungry years. Now that I have my heart's desire, I'm not going to feel castrated because I can't brand you with my name."

Katryn laughed aloud in relief and delight, and Johnny took one hand off the wheel to stroke her nearest thigh possessively. "Any other pressing problems?" he wanted to know.

"Yes, where the hell are we going?"

"Could you let that be my surprise . . . for just a few hours longer?"

"If you want." Katie yawned, then stretched her arms lazily over her head.

"Put the seat back," suggested Johnny, and she did, as

far as it would go, turning on her side, facing him, with her legs curled under her coat.

Johnny pulled the car over to the shoulder of the road, got out, and came back with a plaid car blanket from the trunk. He tucked it in all around her, and Katie murmured sleepy appreciation. "I'm damned if I know why you're so tired," he whispered in her ear, kissing her cheek. Provocatively, he added, *"I* did most of the work."

"I'll get you for that," promised Katie as he started the car again, but the threat lacked her usual vigor. She yawned twice more, looking so like a sleek, contented, well-fed cat that Johnny smothered a smile.

"Music?"

"Mm."

He turned on the stereo, Katryn closed her eyes, and Johnny managed to keep his hands and eyes away from her—except occasionally—and concentrate on his driving.

Though Katryn lay with her eyes closed for a long time, she was thinking, not sleeping. Her heart was singing a hymn of thanks and praise for the gift that she had been given. After so many years, she had almost given up hope that he would come along—that man she had prayed for. A man she didn't necessarily have to be madly, wildly in love with as she had been with J.D., but one she could love and respect, laugh with, have fun with, share common interests and common goals . . . a decent, intelligent, virile man who would satisfy her as well as himself both in and out of bed.

And to think he had been within easy reach all that time, that he would turn out to be Johnny, her foster brother . . . No, no, not her brother . . . She curved her face into the crook of her arm, smiling smugly to herself in remembrance . . . never, never her brother again! Johnny Stoltzfus, stockbroker, her husband.

Katie slept.

* * *

"Lancaster?" she said aloud quite a few hours later. "We're in *Lancaster?*"

Since they had already parked and were walking two blocks from the town's main street, Johnny didn't feel the need to answer a question so rhetorical.

"I just wanted to show you something," he said, tucking her arm in his. "That."

He pointed to a shabby storefront. On the window in modest gold lettering was the name *Pierce, Diamond, Hanna, & Stoltzfus. Investment Counsellors.*

Pierce, Diamond, & Hanna was the name of Johnny's Boston firm.

"You've been made a partner?"

Johnny chuckled. "Not really. Just been given a small percentage of the action plus my usual salary and commissions. That, of course, was after I convinced the top echelon that down here in Amish and Mennonite territory, the name Stoltzfus would carry more weight than all the Pierces, Diamonds, and Hannas put together."

He laughed, seeing Katie's troubled look. "Don't worry, Katie. I know what I'm doing. I've been studying it for years. Stock-broking is big business in any major town, and there is a lot of non-Plain-people business to be had in Lancaster. But I found out something pretty damned interesting in my investigations. Plenty of the brethren happen to be hot on investment, too."

He laughed again at Katie's skeptical look.

"Katie, say a man lives in New York or Boston and he has a great year in business, what does he do?"

"He buys a car," said Katie promptly. "Even," she sniffed pointedly, "if his old one is practically new."

"Right," returned Johnny amiably. "Or his wife—extravagant creature—re-furnishes the living room, which was just re-furnished last year."

"Or maybe they buy a bigger and better house instead."

"Now you've got it," Johnny encouraged her. "And there's always a mink coat for her . . ."

"And a Rolex watch for him . . ."

"A diamond ring for milady . . ."

"A new set of clubs for milord . . ."

"They join the country club, the snobs . . ."

"Or go on a Mediterranean cruise . . ."

"That's the whole bankroll," said Johnny, running out of ideas. "But how about Eli Mast, hard-working thrifty Amish farmer, when his tobacco crop is the finest in ten years and his harvest is the best he's ever had? No cars, no trips, no re-furnishings, no fur coats, no jewelry for his wife Rebecca and him . . . maybe just some livestock, or more acres of farmland—if he can get it. What else can he do with all those lovely profits?"

"Invest?" Katie asked doubtfully.

"You're damned right. Quite a few of our people mightily like to take a little flyer—not so little either, if the truth be known. They're not about to go to New York or Boston, so what could be more convenient than a little storefront operation with the entrance, if you noticed, out of the way on a side street. And in that office they find not a businessman in a fancy suit, but Johnny Stoltzfus, who grew up one of them. Johnny Stoltzfus in a work shirt and dungarees, with a little farm dirt on his boots, doing his work on an old wooden carpenter's table. I have a Mennonite secretary who dresses Plain and just one old dial phone on the table. All the files, the computer, the fax machine, the ticker tape, and all the rest of the inner workings are in the back."

"I can't believe it. How long has this been going on?"

"We set up two months ago, part-time. I have a direct line to Boston. I doubt I'll have to fly up there more than once or twice a month."

"But Johnny—" Katie hesitated. "It's a wonderful concept, and I can see it makes you happy, but it would mean living here for you, wouldn't it? I thought of us commuting back and forth between New York and Boston . . . this would be a bit harder."

Johnny seized her hands. "Harder, but not impossible. I won't have to be here full time, so I can spend time in New York with you. And you once told me you were thinking of cutting down on your magazine time. If you did that, you could be here half the week. Why not start a Lancaster chapter for your battered women? We'd manage, Katie; believe me, we will. Just understand that I don't want or expect you to give up a single part of your life that is important to you."

Katryn looked up into his eager face and seemed to be reassured by what she saw there.

"We'll have to find a place to live . . . maybe even rent a house. I wouldn't mind a home with a garden," she said nostalgically, "providing someone else does the gardening."

"You have only to wave your magic wand," said Johnny mysteriously. "That, too, has been taken care of. Come on back to the car; you can see the office some other time."

They drove the old remembered way . . . along old remembered roads . . . then they were in Strawberry Schrank, driving right past the hilly turn that would have taken them to the farm where they had both been raised.

Johnny answered her unspoken question. "No, I haven't. I was waiting so we could go together. But not today. Today is just for us."

"Oh, Johnny," she cried out a moment later, "we're going to pass the Levi Luke Fisher School."

"We're not going to pass it," said Johnny in a strange, gruff voice. "We're going to stop there."

Katie twisted around in her seat as they flashed by the farmhouse where Levi Luke had lived. "It's all painted and spruced up. I wonder if it's the same tenant or if he sold it."

"He sold it," said Johnny, slowing down. Katie looked out the window wonderingly as he pulled into a graveled driveway. The old sagging wire fence was gone, replaced by a stout wood fence and sturdy wrought-iron gates.

Katie got out of the car. "Oh, my God!" she said.

The crumbling stone ruins of the Levi Luke School House had been restored to the colonial home it was two centuries before, stark and upright in front, but made graceful and modern by the new brick wing added on either side. Neat rows of ornamental plants in front led down to the gates, and box hedges on either side formed a path to the door of the house.

"All this space between the plants and hedges will have the garden flowers in the spring," said Johnny in that same gruff voice. "The old flowers, Katie; you know, hens and chicks, marigolds, dusty miller, petunia, cockscomb, asters . . ."

"Scarlet sage and snapdragons?"

"Yes."

"Larkspur, hollyhock, zinnias," Katie finished rapturously. "Oh, Johnny, it will be beautiful. Have you really rented it for us?"

"I didn't rent it. I bought it. For you. Look at the mailbox."

Katie ran to the gate and looked at the white-painted mailbox on its wooden post. It was lettered in black: *Katryn Kauffman Coffee* and underneath, *John Stoltzfus.*

"So you see," he teased, "I wasn't fooling about not minding whether you were Ms. or Mrs."

Coffee Katie threw her arms around his neck and burst into tears; a moment later, Katryn Kauffman Coffee kissed him passionately.

"You're very welcome," Johnny whispered against her

tear-damp neck. "Would you like to walk into your parlor, *Ms.* Coffee?"

What Johnny called her parlor was the original Levi Luke Schoolroom turned into a huge family room, with its whitewashed stone walls sparkling clean, its plank and nail floors polished and looking like new, and a small, cheerful fire burning in the vast stone fireplace of a later generation.

Johnny's prize trophy of a geometric figure on top of an atlas stood once again on the old brick mantel, now restored; and over it hung a framed sampler, embroidered *The Levi Luke Fisher School.*

"We used the original foundation and rooms and added the master suite with a bathroom and office for you on one side and the guest suite with a bathroom on the other. My architect," Johnny explained eagerly, "was able to find lots of the period hardware, like hand-wrought iron door hinges. All those in the original part of the house are eighteenth century. Of course, we took liberties with things like picture windows. I furnished the guest bedroom so we could sleep here now, but I left most of the furnishings for you to choose except a couple of pieces I picked up at auctions . . . a big black walnut *Kas* and a smaller cupboard . . . some wood candlesticks . . . and just take a look at this . . . it's the best find of all . . ."

He led her over to a dictionary stand in a corner of the room. On it lay a big old leather Bible covered by a glass dome. Carefully, Johnny lifted off the dome and set it on the floor. Reverently, he turned the pages.

"Look," he said again.

Katie looked at the fine faint script. "You know, my German was never very good," she apologized.

"This Bible belonged to Hans Luthy, an eighteenth-century Anabaptist. A worker found it in one of the beams during the renovation. This page of births and deaths is almost a capsule history of his life. He and his wife Lizbet must have been driven out of Switzerland because of their faith. They set sail from Rotterdam, Holland on the *Charming Nancy,* which arrived in Philadelphia in 1737. It must have been a hell shop and a hellish journey because this—right here—is a list of their four children who died on the way across the ocean. A fifth child, born after they arrived, died in Philadelphia. Their son Daniel was born here in this house and then three daughters . . . Right here there's a poignant entry in which Daniel was written out of the family . . ."

"He died, too?"

"No, he went to join Washington's army in the Revolution; so he was dead to his family." Johnny's mouth twisted wryly. "Nothing much changes in Strawberry Schrank, does it, Katie?"

"Oh, yes, it does," said Katie confidently. "We're going to visit the family tomorrow and break through Pap's stubborn pride. Now show me the rest of *my* house and tell me how you got to buy it."

"I always wanted to . . . and I kept in touch with Levi Luke through the years. When he set up his carpentry business in Canada, he left the Faith completely; but he held onto this property as long as his mother lived. Years ago I had asked him for first refusal, so when he decided to sell he got in touch with me. I bought it, but except for hiring a man to farm, I more or less let it lie fallow until you made your deal with me. Then I really moved fast. Tom Hartz of the Fellowship lives in the farmhouse now; he caretakes and works the place for me. His wife will cook and housekeep, and there's a sister who wants to help out, too. You don't have to worry that your work here will be interrupted with household chores."

He lifted her up and kissed her breathless. "Your only interruption will be me."

"I'll manage to withstand it!" Katie returned his kisses with equal fervor.

"There's one other thing," Johnny said rather hesitantly.

"Yes?"

"The old cemetery. It has just a few graves from the Luthy family, and then the Roeblings who lived here after them. But I discovered from my attorney at the closing of the house and farm that there's a very, very old grandfather clause that permits anyone who owns and farms the property to make use of the cemetery—even now. So if you want . . . it would be up to you, of course . . . I had it tidied up, so it's not so overgrown . . ."

"Yes, Johnny?"

"I thought you might like to—to bring your baby here."

Katryn looked out the picture window. It didn't give a view of the cemetery, but she could see it in her mind's eye . . . that hilly triangle of land with its small, scattered, crumbling stones and lots of trees, especially the big oak where they used to tie Johnny's horse, Einstein. It was a small, homely place surrounded by the rolling green hills of Pennsylvania.

How she hated the endless concrete city cemetery where her tiny daughter had been laid to rest.

"I would like very much to bring Antonia here close to us," she said in a voice she tried to keep steady. Then she took Johnny's hand, bending her lips to his palm.

"I love you, Johnny Stoltzfus," she told him.

Thirty-six

Bawdy bedroom laughter—mutually shared—can be as powerful an aphrodisiac as naked flesh.

from *Bawdy Bedroom Laughter*
by Katryn Kauffman Coffee

After all the tears and grief and anguish and the many unanswered letters, the years of separation ended with an Amishly quiet absence of drama.

It was lunch hour, and Amos, Gideon, and Paul John were just sitting down to the table. Mem was about to ladle out the chicken corn soup.

Her ladle dropped to the floor when Katie and Johnny walked in, and Johnny bent to pick it up and wash it at the sink. When he returned it to his mother, he took her by the shoulders and kissed her first on one cheek, then the other.

"My *soohn*," Katy Stoltzfus whispered joyfully.

"We're married," Katie announced brightly, hugging Mem but looking at Amos.

"When I heard *he* bought the Fisher farm but put it in *your* name, I thought you might be," Pap told them calmly. "So sit. Don't let the food grow cold."

And there was Johnny's place, vacant after all the years, and Katie's place, next to Mem, as though they had been expected to walk in at any time.

Gideon and Paul John, both almost full grown, were shy at first. Though Johnny wore Levi's and a dark work shirt and Katie had dressed conservatively in a grey wool skirt and an unornamented black sweater, they still seemed like dashingly different outsiders to the two Amish brothers in their barnyard britches. They didn't even talk the same.

But soon Johnny and Amos were deeply absorbed in the subject of how the Fisher place was being farmed . . . Katy and Katie were making plans to go to an auction . . . And Gideon and John Paul grew excited at the prospect of being hired in their spare time to work for Johnny and maybe being allowed to have a drive in his car.

"If Pap says it's okay," Johnny told them.

"So long as it's for a useful reason; somewhere you need to get to—the feed store, the market—not just for idle pleasure driving," Amos specified.

"Okay, Pap," Johnny promised gravely, with a quick wink at his foster brothers.

"So tell me, Johnny—" Amos lingered even after his coffee and the silent blessing "—what's this business of yours in Lancaster?"

Johnny told his father about Pierce, Diamond, Hanna, & Stoltzfus; and after a while it was Katie that Johnny winked at. It was obvious that Amos, too, had an interest in investment.

"Happy?" Katie asked her husband as they lay together that night in one of the twin beds in the guest room.

"So happy it scares me," Johnny confessed seriously. "The old fears are gone. Both worlds and both lives all meshed together—my family, my business, and . . ."

"And?" she prompted.

A sudden smile broke through. "And a lusciously naked Coffee Katie beside me to share it with."

"If I'm so lusciously naked, why are you lying there like a log?" asked Katie, joining him.

"*That's* my only worry," said Johnny, not moving a muscle.

"What?"

"That I won't have the strength to keep up with you. Did anyone ever tell you that you're insatiable, Katie Kauffman?"

"How could they when I've been sex-starved all these years? That's why I'm insatiable, I have a lot of celibacy to make up for." Her fingers traveled ticklingly across his chest and stomach. "So you don't think you're man enough to take care of me, poor thing," she cooed.

Johnny tried to pull her under him, and she made such a strong show of resisting, in the ensuing tussle she landed on her backside on the round hooked rug between the two beds. Johnny followed her, voluntarily.

"Ouch, Johnny, don't, it's too hard."

"A little while ago you were complaining that it wasn't."

"You fiend, you *know* I meant the floor."

Johnny reached up for a pillow and managed to get it under her head.

"It's women's lot to endure," he said piously, and returned to kissing her.

Katie tried to pull his hair, and he caught hold of her wrists and held her arms wide and pinned her legs while his lips tickled her body.

When he had her writhing and laughing helplessly, she managed to gasp, "Please, I'll be good."

"Promise?"

"Yes, pul-lease, yes."

Released, she wrapped her arms around him and brought him back to her. Presently Johnny lay beside her, sharing the pillow. "Maybe we should get back in bed," he suggested after a while. "It might be more comfortable than the floor."

"Maybe *I* should get into one bed and *you* should get

into the other. That way we might manage a full night's sleep."

"Good idea," said Johnny, struggling upright. He reached a hand down to Katie, and she got staggeringly to her feet. They kissed chastely and snuggled down in separate beds.

"We forgot to turn out the light," Katie said after a while.

"I'm not getting up again."

"So you've already mentioned."

"You've got some mouth for a bride of three days!"

Not deigning to answer, Katie got out of bed and switched off the light. Before she returned to her own bed, she stopped by Johnny's. Her hand crept under his blankets and was touching him before he even realized she was there.

"If I wanted to," she whispered, "I could have you on your knees."

Then she whisked her hand away and got back in her own bed, but she could hear Johnny's soft laughter in the darkness.

Later she would remember with great gladness that the one wonderful year they had together was full of laughter. Not just the bawdy laughter of their bed antics but the laughter of friendship and fondness and fun. She had never even known in the dark days of their shared past that there was so much laughter in Johnny, just waiting to be released.

About a month after their first anniversary, Johnny had gone for his once-a-month trip to Boston. He cut his hand with a bread knife at the Newbury Street apartment and went to a hospital emergency room to get it attended to.

There had been a gang rumble that night, and the hospital was full to overflowing with victims. Afterward there was no way of proving Katie's theory that in the press of administering stitches and tetanus shots, a non-sterile needle or procedure might have been used on Johnny, exposing him to contamination.

Six weeks later he had developed dread remembered symptoms. His skin was sallow, his appetite gone; there was pressure in his chest, and he had grown weak and tired . . .

It was Katie who detected the yellowing of his eyeballs and insisted they go straight to the hospital for blood tests. Neither of them was surprised at the results. Johnny had hepatitis again.

Hepatitis was bad the first time, serious the second. Hepatitis working on a liver already weakened by too many years of too much drinking was frightening.

Johnny had been superstitiously scared of so much happiness, and Katie had scoffed. Now she was scared, too, and with reason.

There was little that could be done for him except to nourish him intravenously and to try to make him comfortable during a devastatingly uncomfortable illness.

Johnny lay in his hospital bed, always tired, never complaining, growing weaker and weaker, quieter and quieter. There was no laughter anymore, though he always tried to smile for Katie.

She came to the hospital as early in the morning as they would admit her and stayed till they threw her out at night. As he grew progressively worse, she badgered the local doctor left in charge until he agreed that a cot could be installed in Johnny's room for her. Then she stayed with him all through the night.

She sat on his bed one day quietly stroking his hands, while Johnny lay, eyes closed, saving all his strength for each labored breath.

Looking at him lying there, Katie finally forced herself to admit what the doctor had only seemed to hint: *He's going to die.* Her mouth quivered, her face contorted; it was all she could do not to scream and cry out loud.

When Johnny's eyes opened, the radar that had sparked between them since their teenage days was still very much alive.

"Katie, let's go home," he said quietly.

She opened her mouth to protest, and there was the merest shake of his head. He spoke so softly she had trouble hearing him. "Come closer, dear heart."

She wriggled a few inches nearer, lifted his blanket, and draped it over both of them. When her thigh was lodged firmly against Johnny's, she felt the slight quiver of his flesh. Not arousal now. Not desire. Only warmth. Comfort. Kinship. All the other ties that bound them.

"Katie, I love you. I love you so much."

Katie blinked back her tears.

"Likewise, I'm sure, sir," she said teasingly, and was rewarded with another faint smile.

"No, I mean—from the very beginning. You were my first fresh breath of the outside world. Someone who felt as hungry as I did to explore new ideas, someone as starved as I was for books."

He paused for a minute, gathering strength. "We both wanted a different life than the one I was born to and you were ordered to accept. The two of us—"

He had to interrupt himself as a fit of coughing convulsed him. His once-strong body, now almost skeletal, was racked by each spasm. His shoulders shook and his eyes teared. After two long minutes he lay back against his pillows, exhausted.

Katie offered him a glass of water, shoving the bent hospital straw into his mouth. Johnny took a few sips and then signaled with his eyes that he was through.

She set the glass on the bedstand and put one hand on each side of his face. "Johnny, you don't have to tire yourself so. What you're trying to tell me—it's wonderful—but truly, I know. We have shared so much in our lives. It's hard to remember a time when you were not my dearest friend. This last year has been the best of all. To be lovers, husband and wife as well as friends . . . that was icing on the cake. You are one wonderful lover, Johnny Stoltzfus."

He managed to grin. "Praise from the customer is always appreciated." The grin faded. "But you just said it yourself, Coffee Katie. *This last year has been best of all.* Think of it, Katie. One full year of Heaven. It would be tempting the fates to expect anything more."

"Oh, Johnny, no, *no!*"

"Oh, Katie, yes, *yes!*" he mocked her gently. "Listen to me, sweetheart. Listen well." He reversed their handhold and tried to squeeze her fingers. "As long as I can remember, you have filled my heart with all the love and laughter it ever knew. After our marriage, we reached the heights. I think this is the way it was meant to be . . . to go out like a candle on the upswing of a glorious, golden year."

He touched two fingers to her lips. "Hush, Katie, let me finish. And look at me."

She blew her nose hard on a tissue before obeying. He watched lovingly as she bit her lips against denial.

"There are dark parts of me, dark thoughts I've never been able to keep at bay. Who knows that better than you? I've lived all my life in the shadow of those bars on the window and my all-pervasive Amish guilt. How much better to leave with joy, filled with gratitude for the bountiful gift of *you.*"

"How about *me?* Do you think *I* will feel fulfilled?"

"You may grieve awhile, girl of mine; but mind you, not to excess. Then, after a while, get yourself into the fray again. Grab with both hands at whatever life experiences come your way. You know how, Katie. You've done it any number of times before."

Her tears splashed down on his hands.

"We should go home, Katie. We would be happier in our own home, looking out at our own land."

"Yes, Johnny, we'll go home."

The doctor objected, exhorted, and threatened, but Katie was adamant. A hospital bed was rented for the Levi Luke Fisher Schoolroom so that Johnny could look out the window without any effort and see his green hills. Katy Stoltzfus moved into the guest room and they had nurses in shifts around the clock.

Sometimes Johnny spoke to Katie briefly of how happy they had been. Sometimes, before he became too disoriented to know what was going on, he uttered random thoughts that wrenched at her heart.

No Amish funeral, please, Katie.

"I promise, Johnny."

See my lawyer about the grandfather clause. I want to be part of my land.

"You will be, Johnny. Next to my baby."

So much happiness. You were up there, Lord, after all.

"I guess You were, forgive me for doubting."

Light and laughter. From Katie to me . . .

"And from you to me."

No more fear. Joy . . . joy and peace.

"Joy and peace? No, that I can't accept."

I love you so much, Katie Kauffman.

Saying it, he fell asleep one day and from sleep slipped into a coma. Two days later, he died.

Interlude

In scuffed leather loafers, white duck pants, and a loose navy sports shirt, Gregorio Grieg might have been unrecognizable to TV and concert audiences accustomed to his tailored trousers and startling spangled jackets.

As he came through the new low gate into the small cemetery, he saw Katryn sitting casually between the only two headstones that bore dates in the twentieth century. She was scattering wild flowers on either side of her.

The small pillow headstones were identical except for the names and dates: *John Stoltzfus. Antonia Burney.*

"I am always touched by the simplicity," Gregorio told her quietly.

"Well, I never did go for all those 'beloveds' carved in granite," Katie said, accepting his hand to get up. "It's too public a declaration of one's feelings."

She brushed herself off front and back before she hugged him. "I'm so glad you could come, Greg." She linked her arm through his as they walked back through the gate.

"Yes, you always were a private person . . . that's why the interview you allowed Elizabeth St. Clair seemed quite extraordinary."

Katryn turned away from him with an almost petulant

shrug. "I don't see why. After all, I had a right to defend myself from all those things J.D. said to me on 'Celebrity Brunch.' "

"Is that what you were doing?" Greg asked her with studied interest. "I thought perhaps you were reaching out to him."

"I don't understand."

"Oh, I think you do, Katie. I know you far too well to believe that you can possibly have deceived yourself. You wanted to say something to Mr. Shale, wanted it so very badly that you chose a rather public forum to get his attention."

Katie closed the gate carefully and stood leaning against the new fence, her back to him. "I had to get this put up to keep the cows out," she said inconsequentially. "Damn you, Greg, why do you always have to be so annoyingly right?"

"Did he get in touch with you?"

"Yes."

"Ah."

Katryn turned back to Gregorio. "That was a very profound-sounding *ah,*" she told him crossly. "What did it mean?"

"It meant that I was glad my plan worked."

"Your plan?"

"When I heard that Shale was being transferred to the New York office to head Continental Films East, it was I who suggested him as a guest to Dodie and Chuck Mitchell."

"But you—"

"And then," he finished complacently, "I bribed Hansi Fuller with a guest appearance on my next concert tour to bow out sick at the last moment and offer *you* in her place."

"But why, Greg, *why?"*

"It appeared to me . . . it always appeared to me—and

to Tony as well—that there was much unfinished business between J.D. Shale and you."

Katryn's eyes were wide with shock; deep hurt quivered in her voice. "I can't believe that you set me up for that—that awful travesty."

"Katie, please don't sound as though I betrayed our friendship. No one who was at 'Celebrity Brunch' that day and no one who watched the program can possibly doubt that a tremendously strong current of feeling runs between that man and you. Whether it is primarily love or hate—perhaps both—it exists. You know it, and so do I."

"So it's there," Katryn said nonchalantly, "and a fat lot of good it did either of us. I went on St. Clair's program and he came to see me, and it was all an exercise in futility."

"Tell me about it."

"I would hate to see whatever I tell you in your next magazine interview."

"I don't think I deserved that, Katryn."

She looked at him suspiciously, unsure whether he was just pretending that she had hurt him. Then he gave her a private smile, followed by the flashy public one, and Katie melted. This was Greg, who cared. As they walked toward the house, she began to talk about her abortive and unsatisfactory visit from J.D.

There was a wooden swing seat that Johnny had installed under the weeping willow to the side of the house so she could swing and look at her garden. Katryn sat in it, talking and swinging lightly, while Gregorio stood with his back to the trunk of the tree, listening.

When she had finished there was a long silence, broken only by the hum of insects and the cries of birds.

"Well," she asked finally, "haven't you anything to say?"

"I don't believe, Katryn, that you want to hear what I have to say."

She gave a light, artificial laugh. "We've never minced words with each other before, Gregorio."

"In that case, Katie, my friend," he told her gently, "I have to say that I am rather disappointed in you and more than a little ashamed."

Katie's hands shook in her lap.

"Whatever Shale did or did not do in the past, *you* carried a nine-year grudge into that visit. You seem to have spent most of it trying to stab him in the same wounds that may never have healed for him."

Katie gave a sudden small cry as his words pierced her unexpectedly. All at once, as though it were yesterday that she first saw it, she was remembering something that she had managed to gloss over through the years under the impact of her own less obvious wounds . . . J.D.'s back, with its ugly network of scars, each the symbol of a past agony.

Gregorio was looking at her strangely. "Katie?"

"Please finish what you started, Greg," she said through stiffened lips.

"You had the opportunity to tell him what he always had a right to know . . . that Antonia was his daughter."

"He was *so* sure my pregnancy was the result of my whoring around in Europe," she said with something of the old bitterness.

"And that's what you can't forgive him . . . even while you did your best to convince him your pregnancy was exactly what he believed. You laid your heart at his feet like the natural, naive girl you were in those days, and he turned you down. You're still punishing him for that rejection."

"Was I supposed to love him for it?"

"Did you ever stop to ask yourself *why* he rejected you? He was a sophisticated man of the Hollywood-Europe scene who wasn't going to fall down into fits because the girl he loved had had a brief fling before they came to-gether."

"That's what you think; you should have been there. He almost hit me."

"So he was angry. We told you that he would be. But he *didn't* hit you, did he?"

"No, but . . ." She shivered, remembering. "He looked at me as though I were loathsome . . . he told me to get the hell out . . ."

"And you didn't argue it. You didn't have it out with him. You just wrapped yourself in injured pride and made your getaway, which is exactly what you accused *him* of doing. Later you chose not to tell him about the baby. That was the way you punished him, hugging your grievance to you and keeping her to yourself, letting Tony father her—or me, if the cards had come out that way—anyone but the obvious candidate, J.D. I think you punished him with the same passionate intensity with which you once loved him."

She was shivering so visibly, it might have been January instead of June.

"Katie, I'm sorry," he said. "The lecture's all over." He put out his right hand. "Friends still?"

Katie gave him both of hers. "Friends always."

But that night, when he had gone to sleep in the guest room, she threw a wool stole around her nightgown and walked around the garden again. She sat in the wooden seat, swinging gently, while the memories—pushed away for so long—crowded in on her thick and fast.

Her early infatuation for J.D. . . . the mindless lust . . . and then the night she had sensed his vulnerability, the hurt boy beneath the cock-a-hoop man.

She had fallen in love with him all over again. Differently in love, deeply and truly in love, wanting to give as well as to get from him. No longer thinking him—or even wanting him to be—a macho superman.

Except briefly, when she and Cable rescued Christine

Langford, she had forced herself to forget that J.D. had ever been a small hurt child. She had wanted to remember him only as the insensitive man who could take her lovingly and tenderly to his bed one night and turn on her brutally the next day. She had needed to forget so she could go on hating him.

And in spite of all her efforts—and his—it was still there, more like a roaring ocean wave than just the current Greg had described, love and hate both flaming furiously between them. It had been obvious to everyone from coast to coast who watched national TV. It had been obvious to everyone except that stubborn, prideful fool, Ms. Katryn Kauffman Coffee.

Thirty-seven

Without minimizing the importance of verbal communication (essential in any good relationship), there are those occasional moments (especially after a quarrel) when an affectionate pat on the bare backside is worth several hundred words.

from *Maid To Laid*
by Katryn Kauffman Coffee

On the Saturday Greg's visit ended, Katie, too, drove back to New York in the sleek hired black limousine that picked him up. All week long she had thought about what she would say to J.D., and she'd reached only one conclusion: Whatever it was could not be said over the phone. In spite of their last two disastrous encounters, she must meet him face to face.

Greg's driver dropped her off at her apartment towards evening. Knowing she would not be able to call the offices of Continental East to contact J.D. until Monday, she felt a fever of impatience. On the off-chance that he had recently rented an apartment, she asked telephone information for a new listing for him, but drew a blank.

They had no mutual friends she knew of to help her track him down. Why did he have to be so damned elusive; and why, oh why, hadn't she asked where he was staying when he stopped by?

A voice inside her that wouldn't be suppressed any longer supplied the answers just as Greg had done . . . tormented her through a long, lonely evening with unpleasant truths . . .

. . . *you wrapped yourself in injured pride* . . .
. . . *you're still punishing him* . . .
. . . *hugging your grievance to you* . . .
. . . *trying to stab him in the same wounds that may never have healed for him.* . . .

Some unforwarded mail contained the notice of a guitar concert with tea to be held the next day at Cable House, WOMAN's shelter for battered families on Twelfth Street.

Katie decided that it would take care of her Sunday afternoon. She felt restless, anxious, wanting to be going somewhere or doing something, yet was curiously reluctant to notify any friends that she was back in town.

She washed her hair and went to bed early. On Sunday morning after breakfast she wandered for some time in Central Park and sat on a grassy knoll for an hour to watch a neighborhood softball game. Then she went home to change her denim skirt and sleeveless jersey for a black-and-white striped shirtwaist dress.

She took a taxi to Cable House, named—a neat little plaque in the front hallway informed the interested—for Joseph "Cable" Canatelli, who had raised the funds to buy this home.

The sliding doors between the dining room and living room had been opened to make one large room for the concert. Three teenagers were setting out rows of folded wooden chairs. A toddler kept getting under their feet until Katie, on her way to the backroom study in search of tea, scooped him up.

He burst into noisy howls and one of the teenagers bore him off. Katie turned, smiling ruefully, and absolutely froze. J.D. stood watching her from the doorway.

She closed her eyes for several seconds. She must be

seeing things; she had the man on her brain. When she opened her eyes, he was still there.

One of the teenagers, trying to circle around Katie with two chairs under each arm, misjudged the space he needed and careened into her.

Chairs fell, Katie let out a yelp, and the boy uttered a short but stringent curse. Women came running as he massaged his cut chin and she nursed one raised foot.

As he mumbled apologies, the boy blushed furiously, probably more for what he had said than what he had done. Katie insisted it was her fault for stopping so suddenly. Confusion reigned until J.D. waded in.

"Better go put some iodine on that cut, son," he told the boy. "I'll take care of Ms. Coffee. Come along, Katie," he said with the kind authority of an elderly uncle. Meekly she took his proffered arm and hobbled along with him.

He sat her down on the back stairs and bent to remove her ankle-strap sandal. "Wriggle your toes."

Katie wriggled them.

"Where does it hurt? Here?"

"No, the one next to it and the big one." She winced as he handled her toes gently.

"Bruised . . . they'll hurt awhile . . . but nothing broken." He slipped her sandal on again, then his fingers fumbled awkwardly at the straps.

"I'll do that, thank you." Katie bent forward, glad of an excuse to hide her face for a moment. She must have imagined the light touch of his hand on her hair because when she sat up straight again, he was perfectly upright, too, with both arms at his sides.

"How did you know I would be here?" Katie blurted out.

"I didn't."

"You mean, you weren't looking for me?"

Hot color stained her cheeks at the sudden amused look

that came over his face. His air of tension seemed all at once to be transferred to her.

"Battered children," he told her, smiling pleasantly, "are *my* particular cause, Katie. I've spoken and fund-raised on their behalf for years in California . . . in fact, long before it was fashionable. I even organized several of the groups in the L.A. area. When it became known I had moved east, my name was transferred to all the groups here. Not that I mind," he added gently but pointedly. "You may remember, perhaps, that for me it holds a special interest."

Katie had lowered her head again, pretending her sandal straps still needed attention. She was embarrassed about her egotistical assumption that he had come to Cable House in search of her.

Most of all, though, she was mortified to have been so wrong. She wanted to believe that he was there in search of her, even as she recognized her complete lack of the right to nourish any such hope. After "Celebrity Brunch," he had taken the first step with his abortive visit to her apartment. She was the one who had rebuffed him.

"J.D.?"

"Katie?"

She filled her lungs to capacity and said all in one breath, "I'm sorry for the way I behaved when you came to my apartment. Someone told me—well, it was Greg as a matter of fact; he visited me in Strawberry Schrank last week—he said I was still trying to punish you for not loving me back . . . long ago . . . the way I loved you . . . then," she finished in haste.

"And just how," J.D. asked almost mockingly, "did you love me long ago? *Then,* but, of course, not now."

Bright red color stained Katie's cheeks again. "You know," she mumbled.

"I know you experienced a brief childish infatuation," said J.D. carelessly. He sounded almost bored.

Katie jumped up, forgetting her hurt foot. With a grimace of pain, she grabbed onto the banister. "Oh God, if you aren't still the same smug, know-it-all bastard!" she accused him furiously. "How dare you deal with *my* emotions in that light manner? Who are you to dismiss so cavalierly what *I* felt?"

"What did you feel, K-K-Katie?"

"Damn it!" Two tears streaked crookedly down her cheeks. "I may have been a kid, but it was no childish infatuation. I loved you. I loved you with all my heart. That's why . . ." She stood one-legged on the steps above him, staring off into the distance. "I guess it's mostly why I—I was convinced that you had behaved quite b-badly to me. It's only recently that Greg—well, it occurred to me that perhaps—maybe, I had treated you badly, too."

"It only occurred to you *now* . . . after all these years?"

"Don't you see," said Katie hardly above a whisper, "that with the love as one-sided as mine was for you, it was difficult to accept that I c-could hurt you the w-way you c-could hurt me?" She finally looked into his face. "You hurt me terribly, J.D."

"One-sided, you little donkey! I was head over heels in love with you."

"And never thought it important enough to mention?"

"Anyone—everyone could tell."

"Anyone—everyone! What good was that? *I* couldn't tell."

It was J.D.'s turn to look away. "I didn't—dare."

"Dare! You're not going to tell me you were shy, J.D., not *you.*"

"Not shy," J.D. told her in a low, unsteady voice, "but I didn't think I had the right to love anyone . . . let alone the right to be loved."

Katie put her hand on one of the bare tanned forearms

stretched across the banister. "Why ever not, J.D.?" she asked in astonishment.

He shied away as though her touch were burning hot, and she drew her hand back quickly.

"That's the way you acted that last day in your kitchen," she reminded him painfully, "as though there was something contaminating in my touch. Because of a stupid mistake—misjudgment—whatever you want to call it—because of one awful idiotic hour in a Paris hotel room, you threw away . . . Do you think I'll ever forget the way you looked at me—with that utter loathing? And then . . ."

"Tea? Sandwiches?" asked a perky voice behind them. A short slim redhead with one very swollen cheek and a purplish shiner stood balancing a heavy round tray. "Last chance," she said. "The concert's about to start."

"No, thank you." Katie smiled mechanically.

J.D. took two mugs from the tray and passed one to Katie as he thanked the redhead. "It will do you good," he said.

Katie sipped the tea and found that he was right; the trembling in the pit of her stomach began to ease.

A teenage girl dashed by and offered to take their cups.

"The concert's beginning," she told them hopefully.

"We're coming." He handed her his mug. "Finished, Katie?"

Katie took another gulp, then gave him her half-full mug. "J.D.?" she said pleadingly.

Nine years. Nine years since that day in his kitchen. But the thought of another hour, listening to amateur musicians . . . a single hour more between them with all the things left unsaid . . . She couldn't bear it!

"There isn't a very full house," J.D. reminded her gently. "They need all the audience they can get. We'll talk, Katie; never fear, afterwards we'll talk."

Thirty-eight

The woman who unconsciously insists that her mate be Superman puts unbearable strain on the marriage and the man. If he doesn't crack under the burden, or gladly embraces the role, they are both dehumanized; he becomes a domestic tyrant and she degradingly infantilized.

from *Mucho Macho*
by Katryn Kauffman Coffee

The concert was mercifully over, though afterward Katie could not remember hearing a single note. Thankful that courtesy demanded no more, as they exited she had stuffed her folded bill and J.D. his prepared check into the canister provided hopefully on a table near the door.

J.D. slipped on the tan blazer he was carrying when they got into their air-conditioned cab.

"The Plaza," he told the driver, and to Katie, with a laughing look at his jogging shoes, "I think I can slip by inspection at the Oak Room. If not, we'll walk down to one of the Japanese restaurants."

"Would . . . would you like to go to my place?" she suggested diffidently.

"I think perhaps this time some neutral ground would be better," J.D. said, faint amusement in his voice, and, remembering the last time at her place, she accepted this decision in dignified if pink-cheeked silence.

J.D. was recognized and, at his request, they were tucked out of sight in a far corner of the Oak Room.

"Just a pot of tea, please, and some finger sandwiches," said Katie, waving away a menu.

"Make that two, with a few more solid sandwiches," J.D. added.

"Now, Katie"—he turned to her with a slight smile when they were alone—"you were saying, I think, that I looked at you with loathing?"

"Well, you did, don't try to deny it. For years I would see that look in my dreams. It haunted me over and over. And you raised your hand as though you wanted to hit me!"

J.D. pounced on those last words . . . the ones he had been waiting for.

"Yes, I raised my hand to you as though I wanted to hit you. I did want to—for a few seconds—and it was the death knell for all the wonderful plans I had made while you were in Europe, the hopes and dreams I'd begun to allow myself. It took me years—and going back to the shrinks—to figure out that what I had felt was plain ordinary jealousy of that Frenchman you'd been with and fury at myself for ever letting you go to him in the first place! The loathing? It wasn't for you, Katie, never for you. It was for myself. What that raised hand said to me *then* was that I was Mike Shale's son, and running true to form. When in doubt, raise your hands, lift your fists."

"Mike Shale. Your father?"

"Yes, my father, a hulking brute of a man who tried to compensate for his own failings by using his fists and any other weapon to hand on his wife as well as his sons."

"Sons?" murmured Katie in surprise. "You never mentioned that you had a brother, J.D."

"I don't." His face contorted briefly. "He's been dead

a long time. I try not to think of him . . . of my mother standing by, just bleating, 'Oh, please,' as he got beaten. To this day I don't know if she was terrorized or simply a masochist, or if she loved the brute so much that she— God, I don't know! There weren't any shelters in those days, it's true, no protection at all for battered families, but Aunt Marion and my Uncle Nate were just a phone call away. She could have reversed the charges, and they would have come running to the rescue. It's been over thirty years, and I still don't understand why she never did." His white-knuckled fists gripped the edges of the table. "We were her kids. How could she let *us* endure that hell, not just herself?"

Katie asked, dry-mouthed, "What finally happened? How did you get away?"

He looked at her for a long moment, then drew out a worn billfold. He opened it, lifted the leather corners, and from the "secret" compartment where most men kept a few stray bills, he took some folded bits of newspaper and spread them out on the table in front of her.

"This clipping is old and crumbling a bit . . . I haven't looked at it in a long time . . . but I think you can make it out."

Katie smoothed out the papers. They were from a New York tabloid no longer in existence and dated April of 1969. *Three Dead in Family Tragedy* screamed the head-line. And underneath, in only slightly smaller type, *Murder and Suicide in Sheepshead Bay.*

Katie lifted incredulous eyes to J.D.'s for a moment, then unable to bear the naked pain in his, looked back at the clippings. It was a minute before her vision cleared and she could resume reading. She scarcely heard J.D.'s huskily murmured excuse as he pushed back his chair and walked away.

She read breathlessly,

This quiet family neighborhood has been rocked by the savage murder of 36-year-old Gloria Shale and her 9-year-old son, Mickey.

Michael Shale, a former construction worker, said to have inflicted savage beatings on his wife and two sons, last night shot his wife and younger boy to death with a .32-caliber handgun before putting a bullet through his own brain.

An extraordinary and bizarre escape from the mass slaughter was made by an older son, Jocelyn, 13, who was obviously intended to share the family's fate. Jocelyn had stolen out of the house to attend a friend's party, leaving by way of the fire escape outside the window of the bedroom he shared with his brother. He had stuffed pillows beneath the bedcovers to simulate his presence. The top pillow—lying where his head would have been—was found to contain three bullets from his father's gun.

Katie moaned slightly and put her fingers to her lips, feeling nauseated. The next moment a small glass of brandy was thrust into her hands. She gulped it down gladly.

"Never mind the rest. It's mostly sensationalized nonsense," said J.D.'s brusque voice as he gathered up the bits of paper, balling them in his fist. He sat down opposite her again. "I'm sorry," he said tiredly. "I should have prepared you."

Their waiter arrived with the tray of tea and sandwiches. J.D. looked at Katie, who shook her head. "We're not hungry, after all. Just the check, please."

Katie took deep breaths of the muggy June air when they got outside, wishing suddenly that she was back—no, that *they* were back—in Pennsylvania. The air there would be honey-sweet with the scent of the flowers Johnny had planted in their garden . . . sweet and clean and pure, not heavy with gasoline and exhaust fumes . . .

She thought of J.D. and herself lying in a corn field . . . and of all the years since, all the pain and tears since. She thought of the awful desolation of his life. Arrogant and assured . . . oh, God!

"Would—do you want to walk in the park?" she asked, and when he only nodded, she took his arm almost timidly, feeling his muscles tight and taut under the tentative touch of her fingers.

They walked for some time, looking for an empty bench.

"Let's sit on the grass," Katie proposed finally.

"You'll stain your dress."

"I don't care."

They sat on the grass under a tree, facing each other, not the passers-by.

"Tell me the rest, J.D., please, if it isn't too hard for you."

"Like I said, it's been twenty-five years. I've grown accustomed."

She reached out impulsively and took both his hands in hers.

"Don't, J.D. Don't pretend."

He swallowed hard. "I came home late that night from Bernie's party, crawling into our room through the fire escape window the same way I crawled out. I whispered Mickey's name and he didn't answer, so I figured he was asleep. I was glad." His short bark of laughter was perilously close to a sob. "I was glad he hadn't stayed awake worrying that Mike Shale might catch me. When I woke up in the morning, he was still asleep. I-I-I went over to his bed and pulled back his covers to shake him."

"Oh, my God!"

"I-I had a glass of water I was going to pretend to throw. I think I dropped it on him. For a long time I used to wake up at night sweating about that . . . I don't know why . . . I used to feel so awful that I'd spilled the water on him, as though it mattered when he was already cold and dead with that great bloody hole in his chest."

"Oh, my God!" said Katie again, appalled.

"God wasn't around that night, Katie," he told her.

She squeezed his hands convulsively. "Did they ever find out why?"

"Not really. My mother was supposedly offered a managerial job at the supermarket where she worked part-time. Someone else at the market mentioned that she had talked of leaving her husband if he laid a hand on her again. Perhaps she got up the gumption to tell him so. Who knows? Maybe it was nothing special. For years he'd been a dangerous explosive, needing only a tiny spark to set him off."

"What about you, J.D.?"

"You mean, what happened next?"

"Yes."

"I'm not sure. I remember screaming, running to get help for Mickey, and they were both lying on the living room floor . . . tables and lamps overturned . . . the place was a bloody slaughterhouse. After that, the next thing I remember is sitting outside and it was raining, and Mr. Durrell, a nightwatchman who lived in our building, kept asking me, 'What's wrong, son? What have you got there?' It seems what I had, all wrapped in a blanket, was Mickey, and I kept insisting he was asleep. I guess Mr. Durrell called the police. I don't remember much about the next few weeks. I was catatonic. I didn't even get to go to the funeral. Uncle Nate arranged everything, but first they took me to a sanitarium in Connecticut, where I spent the next eight months. Aunt Marion flew in once or twice a month to be with me for a weekend. When I was released, she brought me to California. I had three years of analysis and then—while I was in college—four years of therapy. On the whole I am considered to have made a remarkable adjustment in spite of survivor's guilt."

"Survivor's guilt? You mean—like soldiers in war?" Katie asked hesitantly.

"Yes, soldiers in war or anyone else who comes out alive from a situation in which someone else dies. The survivor feels guilty about living when his friend—or brother—is dead. He feels guilty even about being *glad* that he's alive. I kept thinking—in my worst moments— that if I hadn't sneaked out that night, I could have prevented Mickey's death. Ridiculous, of course. I know that Mike Shale would simply have blasted me to bits, too."

Katie pulled her hands away and covered her face, taking deep breaths.

J.D.'s voice was a harsh ragged monotone she scarcely recognized. "Katie, I never loathed you. I loved you. But I felt such a desperate terror of being my father's son."

She lifted her head. "But that's ridiculous!" she said hotly.

"Not really. Abused children do become abusers. I'm sure you know that statistically, it's a grimly repeated cycle. I was so afraid. Never mind what the psychiatrists said . . . *I* knew Mike Shale's son had no right to a relationship with any woman that could end in marriage. I couldn't offer permanency to a woman or dare bring children into the world who might become *my* victims. Then you came along, and I fell in love and found myself weakening . . . bit by bit . . . wondering if maybe I hadn't been too hard on myself. I suppose it all changed that day you told me about your . . . episode."

"Episode," Katie repeated, her lips twisting wryly. "I really blew it, didn't I? I knew I had at the time. I just never dreamed how much."

"You couldn't possibly have known, Katie, any more than I could make a rational estimate of my own reaction—then. A moment's quite human jealousy, a moment's quite human anger . . . that's all it was. The anger might have continued. I might have ranted and raved a bit, but I've never struck a woman in my life. Only, *that* day all I could see was another Mike Shale raising his hand to a woman, *his* woman, and I started hating myself again. My aim was not to be rid of you, my dear love, but for you to be rid of me. So I told you to get the hell out. It didn't matter how you felt—just so you got safely away."

Katie put her arms around his neck and her head onto his shoulder. She began to cry. She cried very hard, very loud, and very long.

"Shh, Katie, don't," he soothed her. "People are looking."

"Wh-who the h-hell c-cares?"

She felt him shaken by sudden laughter, and then his arms were around her, too, and his tears were dripping into her ears. "Who the hell does?" he agreed unsteadily.

After a while they broke apart, both hunting in their pockets for handkerchiefs. Presently, their faces dry, J.D. looked at his watch and groaned, "Katie, ah Christ, I have to meet the Italian representatives of Continental in half an hour. I'd call it off, but—"

"No, that's all right; I need a bath and a change of clothes and—"

"I'll call you first thing tomorrow."

"Yes, please do. But first, would you write down where you're staying? I was planning to call you when I got to town yesterday, but I didn't know where. I don't—"

"Were you really?" He looked up, his face aglow, from the small notepad he was scribbling in.

"I said so," Katie told him with dignity. "I don't ever *not* want to know where you are again."

He tore off the page and handed it to her. "I'm at Continental's apartment just across the park until I buy a condo. Now you know."

"Now I know," said Katie, not referring to the address.

Thirty-nine

Journeys end in lovers meeting . . .
from *Twelfth Night*
by William Shakespeare

"Now I know," said Katie later that night, soaking in bubble bath up to her chin.

Cool and clean, she couldn't eat, she couldn't sleep; she tried music, TV, and a book, all in vain.

At about nine o'clock she gave up her restless prowling around the apartment and went into the bedroom. The small piece of paper with J.D.'s address and telephone number lay on her dressing table, held down by a perfume bottle.

She shed her pajamas and started dressing swiftly. Her yellow linen dress with its matching bouclé sweater. Flat ballerina slippers and her big cream leather tote bag, into which she threw a packaged toothbrush, her make-up kit, a change of underthings, her wallet, and a copy of *Bawdy Bedroom Laughter* with her photograph on the dust jacket.

"Ms. Coffee for Mr. Shale," she told the downstairs doorman who admitted her to the lobby twenty minutes later.

"I'm sorry, miss, but Mr. Shale hasn't returned yet this evening."

"I know. He said he might be late but that he would leave his keys for me."

"He must have forgotten."

Katie smiled winningly. "But you can let me in, can't you?"

"Sorry, miss, but it's strictly against the rules without permission from the tenant."

"Come on now, do I look like a housebreaker?" Katie delved into the tote bag and came up with her book, showing him the photograph. "See, that's me. I'd be easy to track down if I were here to commit robbery. I *promise* you, Mr. Shale will be sorry *not* to see me when he comes home."

The book, the smiles, and a ten-dollar bill combined to convince him. He used his pass key to let Katie into the Continental apartment, # 17 B.

There was a light on in the hallway, which led her to a big living room and from there to the bedroom. She felt for the switch and saw an inviting sight as the bedroom light flooded on, a queen-sized bed with the covers neatly turned back. Suddenly she was desperately tired.

After kicking off her shoes, she undressed, scattering her clothes every which way. She flipped off the light and fell onto the bed, where she crawled between the sheets and was instantly asleep.

The light coming on an hour later didn't wake her, only the sudden shouted, "What the hell are you doing in my bed?"

Katie turned over and sat up groggily, pushing her hair back from her face.

"You sound like the three bears," she greeted him.

"For God's sakes, cover yourself."

"Oh." Katryn looked down at her bared breasts and obediently raised the sheets to a modest level. "Were you thinking about ravishing me? If you were, be my guest.

I'm pretty exhausted, but if it will make you happy, just ravish away."

"Katie, for God's sakes!"

"You're getting redundant. Listen, J.D., we've had our wires crossed most of the time we've known each other. Could we please this one time get things straightened out between us? Now, *I* happen to be in love with you still . . . not calf love, not schoolgirl crush, not just lust anymore. It's genuine fourteen-karat, wake-up-together-every-day, let's-have-children and fights and holiday dinners with Aunt Marion and Uncle Nate and visits to Mem and Pap because we're neither of us getting any younger, kind of love. What I want to know is, do you love me, too?"

"Katie, I—"

"Oh, yes, and before I forget, no more nonsense, please, about protecting me from big bad old you. I'm a lot more likely to take a poke at you than you are ever liable to sock me. And suppose you *did* try; do you by any chance think I'd be standing there sweetly, taking it? Buster, you'd get a kick in the *bolla* you wouldn't ever recover from. And about our kids . . . let's say you do turn into some kind of Jekyll and Hyde character. What do you think I'd be doing while you were beating up on them, huh? Sitting in a corner, wringing my hands? Not likely. I, Mr. Shale, would be bus-ily engaged sticking a knife"—she held her hands wide—"*that* deep right into your unsuspecting back."

J.D. had gone from dazed to overwhelmed to slightly amused in a few short minutes.

He dropped casually down on the bed beside her. "It sounds as though *I* should be the one to be apprehensive."

"Exactly," said Katie smugly. "That's what *I* was trying to tell you."

He rubbed her stomach absently through the blankets. "About kids . . . I've always been so scared, Katie."

"It comes easier the second time."

"But there has to be a first."

"You've already had your first. My baby Antonia was yours, J.D. She was three months premature."

"Mine!" J.D. said, stunned. "Mine, and you never told me." He looked at her, his eyes narrowing. "You let me . . . you married Tony. You . . . you little bitch, I ought to beat the bloody hell out of you!"

"Yeah," Katie agreed blandly. "You probably should."

He gathered her to him instead, held her so tightly she found it pleasurably hard to breathe. "Oh God, Katie, oh God! I never thought I could joke about it . . . You should have told me . . . you should have . . . Oh Katie, K-K-Katie, I adore you."

"Adore? Is that better than love?"

"I love you, too, you irritating wench!"

"Fourteen-karat, wake-up-together, let's-have-children love?"

"Fourteen-karat, wake-up-together, I'm close to forty and you're on the shady side of thirty so what the hell are we waiting for, let's-have-children love."

"In that case"—Katie folded back the sheets—"step into my parlor, Mr. Shale."

Epilogue

J.D. Shale stood in the lounge of the Macedonian Tea Room waiting patiently for Katryn. While he waited, he looked, smiling ruefully, at half a dozen framed newspaper accounts of the Macedonian's famed "Celebrity Brunch," featuring his encounter with Katryn Kauffman Coffee.

As he turned from the wall, he collided with a pretty brown-haired girl in beige and a serious-looking young man in a pin-striped business suit.

"Sorry," they all three apologized together.

The young man's jaw sagged in instant recognition, the girl squealed, "Oh, my goodness!" and J.D.'s brow wrinkled in puzzlement. Though he couldn't put a name to them, he was sure he knew them from somewhere.

Then he heard the girl's clear voice as he walked away . . . "Marty, did you realize? That was J.D. Shale again."

He remembered at once. She was the same girl he had encountered at the celebrity brunch, the one who had said, *I can't believe any man in his right mind would want to walk out on Katryn Kauffman Coffee.*

He beckoned to Dimitri, the maitre d'. "Dimitri, do you know that pair?"

"Ah, yes, the young couple, very shy, very much in love. I think this is for them on special occasions, the way you Americans say it, 'their place.' "

Katie came from the ladies' room just then, and Dimitri

showed them to an isolated booth in the smaller, more intimate Poseidon Room.

After they ordered, J.D. told Katie about the young couple.

More than an hour later, in the crowded, noisy Aegean Room where Julie and the young stockbroker sat, holding hands across their dessert dishes, Dimitri himself came in answer to a request for their bill.

"There is no check tonight, sir. Your dinner was paid for by a friend, who also asked"—he snapped his fingers at their waiter—"that you be so kind as to drink a toast to him."

"I—I think there must be some mistake," stammered the young stockbroker.

"Oh, no, sir," smiled Dimitri as their waiter set down two brimming flutes of champagne. "He requested I give you this, too."

The two dark heads eagerly bent forward together to read the words scribbled across the front of the menu over the sprawled signature, *J.D. Shale:*

No man in his right mind could walk out for good on Katryn Kauffman Coffee.

Dear Reader:

Once upon a time (in my teens) when I was gobbling down all the novels, poetry and fairy tales in the New York Public Library, I became fascinated by the books of a *"lapsed"* Mennonite woman, whose stories all dealt with the customs and faith in which she was born and bred and from which she eventually fled.

The life was so different . . . almost like stepping back in time. It was intriguing that so few people could successfully shut out so many.

Years later, motivated by personal curiosity, I tried to discover more about the Amish and the Mennonites. Later still came another yearning. Could a *"foreigner"* (me), an *"Englisher"* (almost all of us) find the right words to present these people authentically . . . their faults and failings as well as their virtues and values?

It was a challenge from me to me I could not refuse!

So here they are . . . Coffee Katie and Johnny . . . Levi Luke and blind Sarah . . . Mem and Pap . . . Annie and Crist . . . Flat Joseph . . . and most unpredictable *"Englisher"* of all—J.D. from Beverly Hills by way of Brooklyn.

Happy reading.

Jacqueline Marten

P.S. I have always had a love of books. Even as a child, to be given a book was one of life's greatest gifts. Nothing has changed over the years, only the quantity that are mine, *all mine!* My sixteen bookcases are bulging with new and second-hand books, first editions, limited editions, all my *"keeper"* paperbacks—beautiful literature found in dusty, dank places! I am trying to figure out where I can squeeze a seventeenth bookshelf . . . and when a newscaster announces cheerily that a hurricane is headed straight for Virginia Beach, guess what I worry about?

One of the enjoyments of being a writer is to hear from fellow readers. Sometimes a special letter makes my day. You can write to me at:

> Jacqueline Marten
> c/o Ethan Marten
> Atlantic Studios
> 1000 Filmway
> Suite 1776
> Suffolk, VA 23434

Please include a self-addressed, stamped envelope for your reply.

*If you liked this book, be sure to look for the September releases in the **Denise Little Presents** line:*

The Bawdy Bride by Amanda Scott   (ISBN 0182-8, $4.99)

"A master of her craft!" —*Romantic Times*

When Anne Davies married Lord Michael St. Ledgers on a bright British morning in 1800, the longest conversation they'd had before the fateful day was shorter than the ceremony that bound them together for life. Now Anne is embarking on a journey with a man she's barely acquainted with, and she's going to know him a *LOT* better, very soon. Awaiting her—thrills, chills, aeronauts, an adolescent Duke and his too-quiet sister, adventure, danger, and laughter. Who is responsible for the mysterious events at Michael's ancestral home—and the recent death of his brother, the Duke? Is there something sinister going on at her new home, the Priory? Is Anne in danger of losing her life, or is it her heart she should worry about? And is the man she married the perfect gentleman she's tempted to love, or something darker, more dangerous, and more tempting than she could ever imagine? Read *The Bawdy Bride,* and find out.

The Dream by Kasey Mars   (ISBN 0203-4, $4.99)

"An enthralling tale of love, trust and ghostly vengeance guaranteed to give you hours of reading pleasure!"

—*Romantic Times* on *The Silent Rose*

Librarian Genny Austin is a haunted woman. Since her husband's murder, she's been tormented by dreams—terrible, unforgettable, and highly prophetic dreams of the past. Jack Brennan is being haunted, too, but his problems are entirely real and his future is being threatened. When Jack and Genny meet one night in an adrenaline-packed rescue on a Santa Barbara beach, they don't realize that their problems are intertwined, their enemies are shared, and their survival is linked. In a world where every night is torn by dreams of torment, where each new dawn could be their last, Jack and Genny find that love can be an anchor, an answer, and the fulfillment of *The Dream.*

AVAILABLE IN SEPTEMBER

Available in September wherever paperback books are sold, or order direct from the publisher. Send cover price plus $.50 per copy for mailing and handling costs to Penguin USA, P.O. Box 999, c/o Dept. 17109, Bergenfield, NJ 07621. Residents of New York and Tennessee must include sales tax. DO NOT SEND CASH.

**If you liked this book, be sure to look for others
in the _Denise Little Presents_ line:**

MOONSHINE AND GLORY by Jacqueline Marten   (0079-1, $4.99)

COMING HOME by Ginna Gray   (0058-9, $4.99)

THE SILENT ROSE by Kasey Mars   (0081-3, $4.99)

DRAGON OF THE ISLAND by Mary Gillgannon   (0067-8, $4.99)

BOUNDLESS by Alexandra Thorne   (0059-7, $4.99)

MASQUERADE by Alexa Smart   (0080-5, $4.99)

THE PROMISE by Mandalyn Kaye   (0087-2, $4.99)

FIELDS OF FIRE by Carol Caldwell   (0088-0, $4.99)

HIGHLAND FLING by Amanda Scott   (0098-8, $4.99)

TRADEWINDS by Annee Cartier   (0099-6, $4.99)

A MARGIN IN TIME by Laura Hayden   (0109-7, $4.99)

REBEL WIND by Stobie Piel   (0110-0, $4.99)

SOMEDAY by Anna Hudson   (0119-4, $4.99)

THE IRISHMAN by Wynema McGowan   (0120-8, $4.99)

DREAM OF ME by Jan Hudson   (0130-5, $4.99)

ROAD TO THE ISLE by Megan Davidson   (0131-3, $4.99)

_Available wherever paperbacks are sold, or order direct from the
Publisher. Send cover price plus 50¢ per copy for mailing and
handling to Penguin USA, P.O. Box 999, c/o Dept. 17109,
Bergenfield, NJ 07621. Residents of New York and Tennessee
must include sales tax. DO NOT SEND CASH._

HISTORICAL ROMANCE FROM PINNACLE BOOKS

LOVE'S RAGING TIDE   (381, $4.50)
by Patricia Matthews

Melissa stood on the veranda and looked over the sweeping acres of Great Oaks that had been her family's home for two generations, and her eyes burned with anger and humiliation. Today her home would go beneath the auctioneer's hammer and be lost to her forever. Two men eagerly awaited the auction: Simon Crouse and Luke Devereaux. Both would try to have her, but they would have to contend with the anger and pride of girl turned woman . . .

CASTLE OF DREAMS   (334, $4.50)
by Flora M. Speer

Meredith would never forget the moment she first saw the baron of Afoncaer, with his armor glistening and blue eyes shining honest and true. Though she knew she should hate this Norman intruder, she could only admire the lean strength of his body, the golden hue of his face. And the innocent Welsh maiden realized that she had lost her heart to one she could only call enemy.

LOVE'S DARING DREAM   (372, $4.50)
by Patricia Matthews

Maggie's escape from the poverty of her family's bleak existence gives fire to her dream of happiness in the arms of a true, loving man. But the men she encounters on her tempestuous journey are men of wealth, greed, and lust. To survive in their world she must control her newly awakened desires, as her beautiful body threatens to betray her at every turn.

Available wherever paperbacks are sold, or order direct from the Publisher. Send cover price plus 50¢ per copy for mailing and handling to Penguin USA, P.O. Box 999, c/o Dept. 17109, Bergenfield, NJ 07621. Residents of New York and Tennessee must include sales tax. DO NOT SEND CASH.